# sing
### me a
# secret

# sing
# me a
# secret

## Julie
## Houston

HEAD
*of* ZEUS

An Aria Book

First published in the United Kingdom in 2020 by Aria,
an imprint of Head of Zeus Ltd

This paperback edition published in 2021 by Aria

9 7 5 3 1 2 4 6 8

A CIP catalogue record for this book is available from
the British Library.

ISBN (PB): 9781800246485
ISBN (E): 9781789546644

Typeset by Siliconchips Services Ltd UK

Printed and bound by CPI Group (UK) Ltd, Croydon, CR0 4YY

Aria
c/o Head of Zeus
First Floor East
5–8 Hardwick Street
London EC1R 4RG

www.ariafiction.com

*For my sister, Valerie*

# Prologue

### *London, 2004*

The atmosphere in the overheated TV studio was thick enough to cut with a knife. She had a sudden vision of just that: a knife chop-chopping its way determinedly and erratically through the heavy coagulating air as it clotted and curdled around her. She turned slightly, remembering she wasn't entirely alone, but the demeanour of the one other girl standing next to her, awaiting the final, irrevocable decision, was inscrutable.

She felt another single bead of sweat descend between her breasts to join the dampness that was in danger of turning the scanty light-blue dress Aunt Georgina insisted she wear, navy, but her smile never wavered. She wanted this. Wanted it so much it hurt. She wouldn't think about the alternative. There wasn't one.

Gemma Joseph, the charismatic compere who'd orchestrated and held the whole thing together since the very start of this round of *TheBest*, held up one slim, tanned hand and that was enough. The studio audience, made up of crucial members of the music industry together with the press and those who'd schmoozed their way in for whatever reason, as well as the near hysterical families who'd accompanied their girl through all the stages, was spontaneously and instantly silenced.

'We are now left with two *exceptionally* talented girls standing here with me this evening. These two have *battled* their way through all the odds over the past ten weeks to end up here while you, the audience, and you at home, make your final decision. The girl that you decide is the best, the *absolute best*, will work with Steve Silverton either as a solo singer or be the lead vocalist in his next girl band. One of you…' She turned to the two girls now holding hands. '*One* of you will be going home.'

She closed her eyes, willing, praying that all she'd ever wanted, all she'd worked so hard for the past two years or so, would be hers. She couldn't go home now; she couldn't go back north after all she'd been through. It had to be hers… It just had to.

'You, the audience have chosen.' Gemma Joseph slowly and deliberately opened the gold envelope. 'And the winner of *TheBest* 2004 is…

'…Lexia!'

Lexia Sutherland stood rooted to the spot on the stage unable, it seemed, to open her eyes as the audience erupted and some sort of gold tickertape started to fall, landing on her blonde hair, her face, her shoulders.

She'd done it. She'd done it. She'd won, and there would be absolutely no stopping her now.

# 1

*January 2019*

Marian Potter, office manager at Westenbury village surgery, peered over her spectacles and glanced meaningfully at the clock behind her as Juno knocked on the glass door of reception.

'ID?' Marian mouthed, one eyebrow raised. 'Do I know you?'

'Forgot it,' Juno mouthed back, smiling with what she hoped was an air of contrite apology.

'Again?'

'Again. Come on, Marian, let me in.' A small patch of mist appeared on the cold glass as Juno peered through the door which led directly into reception and absentmindedly wrote *I Love Boyzone* before obliterating the sentiment into a wet puddle with her gloved hand. God, it was freezing out here. 'Do we have to go through this pantomime every morning?' she asked irritably once Marian acquiesced and pressed the button behind the counter, opening the doors and letting her through into the warmth.

'*I* can't be sure who you are if *you* constantly forget your identity card,' Marian sniffed. 'For all *I* know you could be a terrorist or... or a stalker.' Kyra, one of the junior receptionists had had trouble with an ex-boyfriend who wouldn't accept he *was* an ex, constantly sending flowers he couldn't afford to the surgery and waiting in the carpark for her shift to finish. Hardly a stalker, but Marian, enjoying the whole drama of it all, had revved it up as such and threatened to call the police. In the end Juno had gone out to his battered old Corsa, opened the door and sat with him while he sobbed. Ten minutes later he was gone, his stalking career finished before it had even started.

'Haven't got the time or energy to stalk anyone, Marian. I wish I had – Morning, Declan – it might liven up my somewhat mundane existence.'

'Dr Armstrong, I hardly think trivialising stalking—'

'Juno, staff meeting at one. Don't forget.' Declan patted her absentmindedly on her shoulder as he walked towards his room. 'And I think Izzy wants a word.'

Juno glanced at the clock. Ten minutes before her first patient. On this miserable Monday morning in the second week of January, the punters were already forming a queue outside the surgery, coughing their weekend-acquired bugs into man-sized tissues and alternating between wiping viscous green snot from offspring's noses and admonishing owners of said noses as to the dire consequence of continuing to run out into the rapidly filling-up carpark. Ten minutes to grab a coffee, fire up the computer and warm up her hands before placing them on a pregnant abdomen, a swollen neck or – please God, no, it was a Monday morning and she'd not had time for breakfast – a problematic penis.

Juno had been working three days a week as a GP at Westenbury surgery for the past two years, ever since Fraser, her husband, had landed his dream job at PLK Chemicals just outside Leeds, moving them down from Aberdeen to head up the research team there. While Fraser was a Scot, born and bred in Glasgow, Juno was back on home territory in Westenbury, her parents having moved to this rather beautiful part of Yorkshire from Oxford when she was just six. She'd not particularly wanted to come back to Midhope, the large town bang in the middle of Leeds and Manchester – she'd been away since she was eighteen, first at Aberdeen University studying medicine and then, once they'd married, settling with Fraser and the kids on the outskirts of Aberdeen itself – but they'd not wanted to live in Leeds and, with Juno's mother and two of her sisters still here in Westenbury, they'd just sort of drifted back this way.

Izzy, Declan's wife and partner at the surgery, popped her head round the door as Juno started to divest herself of coat, scarf, gloves and fleece. 'God, Juno, how many layers have you got on? I'd have thought coming down from Scotland you'd find Yorkshire positively tropical.'

'I need something hot now I no longer have a man to keep me warm at night.' Juno pulled a pitiful, poor little me face.

'How's it going?' Izzy smiled sympathetically. 'You know, first weekend on your own and all that?'

'Bloody marvellous.' Juno grinned. 'Nobody snoring in bed, the TV control to myself, no having to make a big Sunday lunch, no being reminded I shouldn't be eating all the chocolates left from Christmas, no having to put the loo seat down in the bathroom; the list is endless. Do you know, I went to bed on Saturday night in my old winceyette pyjamas and bed socks and watched *Pretty Woman* while I worked my way down a whole pack of M&S Millionaire Shortbread and a big mug of hot chocolate.'

'I'm so jealous. That sounds like utter heaven.' Izzy pulled a face. 'Mind you, I hope you cleaned your teeth after that lot?'

'Nope. I just snuggled down and had randy thoughts about Richard Gere.'

'Are the kids not missing Fraser?'

'No, not at all. It's only been five days, and Tilda is so in love with both Mr Donnington and Harry Trotter, neither Fraser nor I ever really got much of a look in anyway.'

'Mr Donnington and Harry Trotter?' Izzy frowned.

'Mr Donnington's her year six teacher – he's the new deputy at Little Acorns – and Harry Trotter is that damned pony of hers. It's a vicious little sod. I keep well away from it, but Tilda has the upper hand – she'd have been totally at home in the Gestapo, jack booting about in her riding boots and wielding her crop at anyone daring to cross her.'

Izzy laughed. 'She is a bit formidable, that daughter of yours. What about Gabriel?'

'No idea. I don't think he's spoken more than twenty words since his twelfth birthday. He grunted a bit when we told him Fraser would be spending the year in Boston but he just re-plugged himself into whatever device was to hand at the time and said, "Cool man, I can go with that" and that was it. As long as I keep the fridge stocked and take him down to football practice twice a week, he's happy.'

Izzy laughed again. 'Tell me about it. Robbie's no different. These adolescent boys just seem to change overnight, don't they? One minute they're your gorgeous little boy wanting good night kisses and making you laugh with terrible jokes and the next they're all arms and legs, big noses that don't fit their face anymore and stinking of sweat and hormones. Right, Juno, important meeting at lunchtime.'

'Oh?'

'We need to ask you something. Bring your sandwich.'

'On a diet after the sugar orgy in bed.'

'Well, bring your carrots and whatever. Right, eyes down, look in. Marian's letting in the hordes.'


'Morning, love, it's me foot.'

Juno looked up from trying to get the computer to actually log on and made two new year's resolutions to: a) get herself to work at least half an hour before kick-off and b) be ready with a big smile on her face rather than the usual panicked, hell-I-can't-even-log-on face.

'Ah, Mr Kendal.' She looked up at the octogenarian sitting in front of her and slipped into caring, enquiring GP speak. 'How are we? You've a problem with your foot?'

'Been hurting to buggery since yesterday.' He winced as he spoke and proffered one shod foot in Juno's direction.

'In your left foot? And where did the pain start?' She'd finally managed to log on and brought up Mr Kendal's notes which she scrutinised. Hmm, diabetic. Not good to have a pain in your foot if you were diabetic.

'In Aldi.'

'Sorry?'

'It started when I was in the tinned-food aisle in Aldi. I just fancied some beans. I know they make you fart – excuse me French, love – but you know, when you get the taste for beans on toast, you just have to go with it.'

Juno stared. 'Right, OK, Mr Kendal. But the pain actually started in your foot. Nowhere else?'

He stared back. 'Why would it start anywhere else, Doctor? The bloody tack's stuck in me left shoe. Gone right through it. I've come in because me back's so bad I can't bend down to get it out meself.'

'Right. Fine.' Juno took a deep breath. 'So, are you sure that's what's causing the pain?'

'Am I sure? Aye, course I'm sure. I might be eighty-nine but I can still tell when a tack's stuck in me shoe.' He gave her an offended look.

'But, Mr Kendal, didn't it occur to you to pull it out once the shoe was off your foot? You know, before you put it back on this morning? Then you wouldn't have had to bother that bad back of yours?' (*And you wouldn't have to be fart arsing around bothering me – excuse* my *French*.)

He looked even more offended. 'And not turn up for my appointment? Oh no, I wouldn't do that to you. I know what these people are like who just don't turn up. Now, if you could just bend down, pull off me shoe and use one of your metal scalpel things to get it out, I'd be right grateful, love.'

By lunchtime Juno was starving. She'd processed numerous January sore throats, coughs and colds which could have been sorted with a trip to the village chemist and an early night, and turned away with a flea in his ear the forty-year-old rep demanding a medical sick note to cover his three-day jamboree with his mistress. She'd hidden a snort of laughter at a note from the hospital which said the ninety-year-old former vicar in front of her was suffering from an abnormal *lover* function, listened to one of the local farmers worried he was developing 'titinuss' and sympathetically patted the arm of the totally embarrassed village scout cub Akela who, when asked if she was OK while undergoing a rectal examination, had murmured 'that's nice' instead of the expected 'that's fine.'

It was well after 1 p.m. by the time Juno had finished her morning list. The sky through her surgery window was grey with unfallen snow but she longed for fresh air and a quick walk to stretch her legs before the afternoon post-natal clinic. Crying new babies, together with their crying new mothers sporting every real and imagined postpartum problems weren't her favourite thing even when she'd been – *especially* when she'd been – a new mother herself.

Declan, Izzy and Marian were already underway with their working lunch and Juno looked enviously at the pile of sandwiches they were tucking into.

'... So we need to be empowering ourselves organically...' Declan was saying through a mouthful of cheese and Branston. He was just back from some course or other and was insistent on cascading good practice to the rest of them. Give it a couple of weeks and he'd have forgotten all his good intentions in educating and sharpening up his staff and once more be out the back having a crafty fag with Juno come lunchtime. Izzy pulled a face in Juno's direction, crossing her eyes in despair, but Marian was making copious notes and nodding her head towards Declan. Izzy and Juno reckoned she was half in love with Declan – actually probably more like seven-eighths the way she sucked up to him, made him constant cups of coffee and re-applied her *Marshmallow Skies* lippy whenever he was in her vicinity.

'KYC?' she was saying as Juno pulled out her carrots and cottage cheese.

'Oh God, yes please,' Juno said, looking round hopefully for her favourite takeaway. 'Have you brought some in?'

Marian tutted and Izzy laughed at both Juno's and their office manager's expressions. '*Know Your Client,* Juno. That's what your aim should be.'

'I do.' Juno smiled sweetly. 'Intimately. You can't have a gloved finger up someone's backside or investigate their fanny without knowing them *intimately*.'

'Is there any need for vulgarity?' Marian winced theatrically, glancing at Declan for backup. 'This is a surgery, you know, not a bawdy house.'

'A bawdy house? What the hell's a bawdy house?' Juno started to laugh and Izzy joined in. It was often Izzy and herself pitted against Marian and Declan unless Declan was on for a promise from Izzy when he got home, and then poor old Marian was on her own.

'Right, come on you two, we've things to discuss.' Declan obviously wasn't being persuaded over to the dark side this lunchtime and Marian preened, giving Juno one of her looks.

Juno crunched a carrot or two, devoured the cottage cheese which, because it was the one from the local Longley Farm and contained cream, was really not half as bad as cottage cheese can be and sat back. 'I'm all ears, Declan.'

'OK. Now, as you know, Juno, our patient footfall is increasing massively, particularly since the new housing development at the edge of the village has got underway. We're being stretched—'

'Tell me about it.'

'—stretched beyond what is good practice for a village surgery.' Declan and Izzy had moved from the surgery where they'd worked together in the less salubrious area of Midhope, buying into the Westenbury practice on the outskirts of the village just a few years previously. Declan now glanced towards Izzy; it was obvious they'd discussed the matter beforehand. 'The thing is, Juno, we need you to work full-time – to up your three days to five.'

'I don't *think* so.' Juno was adamant. Five days of general practice was enough to try the patience of a saint and knacker said saint to an early grave. 'I'm sorry, no, Declan. It's not what I signed up for when I came to work here.'

'We thought you'd say that.' Izzy was placating.

'You really should put the needs of your patients and this surgery first, you know, Juno.' Marian spoke as if she were a naughty child hauled in front of the headteacher. 'We all have to pull our weight.'

'There is another solution,' Declan said hastily as he sensed Marian and Juno coming to blows as they often did. 'We can take on another doctor. A locum maybe until we see how our numbers pan out.'

'We've only three rooms.' Juno frowned. 'Where are you going to fit a fourth doctor?'

'Well…' Declan hesitated looking across at Izzy for confirmation. 'We can very easily turn the storeroom into another practice room.'

Juno frowned again. 'I can't see any potential new doctor

wanting to spend his days in there. There's no window for a start and it's absolutely tiny.'

'Sorry, Juno,' Izzy cut to the quick, 'It'll become *your* room.'

'Oh, great stuff. I've got to spend my days in a... in a cardboard box?'

'You do exaggerate, Juno.' Marian sniffed, glancing at the clock. 'It will make a perfectly serviceable practice room... for *you*.'

'So where do you think you're going to suddenly find this temporary doctor?'

'Well,' Izzy said excitedly, 'you know Declan was two years above me at med school?'

Juno nodded vaguely.

'So, I can't say I remember him...'

'Remember who?'

'Scott Butler.'

'Sounds like he should be in some epic American Civil War film,' Juno said crossly. She *was* cross. 'And you know I'm claustrophobic,' she lied. 'Put me in that coffin of a storeroom and I'll end up hyperventilating just as I'm ordering some innocent man out of his undercrackers. I'll be breathing heavily like some dirty old man in a raincoat and then the whole surgery will be on the front page of the *News of the World*...'

'Shut up, Juno.' Izzy was laughing. 'The *News of the World* folded years ago.'

'As will I if you banish me to that room.'

'Scott Butler was in my year,' Declan said somewhat impatiently. 'He's a New Zealander – from Auckland – and went back there a couple of years after we'd qualified.

He's back in the UK, wants to stretch his legs a bit, see the world—'

'Westenbury's hardly *the world* by any stretch of the imagination.'

'—and he rang me the other night asking if I knew of any surgeries needing a locum for six months or so.'

'So why ask me if I wanted to up *my* hours if you'd already approached this… this *Kiwi*?'

'Racist undertones there, Juno,' Marian snapped. 'Not part of our mission statement, you know.'

'We knew you'd say no.' Izzy grinned. 'And once you had, we'd be well within our rights to move you to the storeroom.'

'Well, I might just say I'll go full-time now then in order to keep my room. I do have a certain affection for it, you know.'

'No, you won't,' Izzy said cheerfully.

'Whose side are you on?'

'The surgery's, Juno. At the end of the day I'm partner with Declan and it pays our bills. So, come on, stop sulking.' Izzy patted her arm. 'You can choose the colour scheme for the storeroom. Your new practice room,' she amended quickly, once she saw her face.

As they walked back through reception to their respective practice rooms, Izzy picked up a copy of the *Midhope Examiner* left by one of the morning's patients. 'Ooh look.' She stopped suddenly and, trailing sulkily behind her, Juno bumped into her.

'What?'

'Look at this.' She began to read. 'Golden couple, ace footballer Theo Ryan and his wife, Lexia Sutherland, former member of top girl band "Gals", are moving to Midhope after Ryan signed yesterday with Midhope Town. Chelsenal's record goal scorer, Theo Ryan, has joined Midhope for an undisclosed fee, raising hopes that Town's second season in the Premier League will go from strength to strength...'

Juno grabbed the paper from Izzy who looked at her in some surprise. 'I didn't know you were a football fan.' She frowned.

'I'm not. I can't stand the game.' Juno continued to read: 'Ryan, who has signed a two-year deal, said he was "ecstatic" and would be doing everything in his power to continue Town's success in the top league...'

Izzy peered over Juno's shoulder, reading along silently with her. 'Ooh that'd be good if they decide to settle round here: some famous bits and pieces to check out at last.'

'I can assure you,' Juno snapped, 'bits and pieces are the same the world over, regardless of how famous their owner is.'

'Yes, but fancy having Theo Ryan in front of you with his shirt off. He's pretty damned hot. Robbie'll be impressed as well; I'm sure he used to have his poster on his bedroom wall.'

'I can't imagine Lexia Sutherland wanting to come back here.'

'Come back?' Izzy looked at Juno, ignoring the first patient of the afternoon who was making her way towards the practice room. 'Is she from round here then?'

'Yep.' Juno folded the paper and instead of replacing it on the table put it into her bag.

'Do you know her?'

'I should do,' she said shortly. 'She's my sister.'

# 2

Once surgery was over for the day, Juno went straight round to her eldest sister, Ariadne's, place. She didn't think she'd be at home but, by taking the long way round, skirting the village of Westenbury itself rather than passing through it, she knew she could lean out of the car window – somewhat precariously, it was true – to look up the end of her road and see if her car was parked outside her house. Unusually, it was. Juno skidded on the wet slushy stuff that had accumulated at the end of Ariadne's cul-de-sac and, reversing, manoeuvred her Mini down towards her sister's trusty old Fiesta.

'How come you're home?' Juno called as she pushed open Ariadne's front door before heading through to the sitting room.

Ariadne was, as she expected, sitting in the corner of the room at her desk, marking books.

'Got a cold,' she sniffed, expending any remaining surplus energy onto myriad huge purple ticks on the exercise book in front of her. 'Feel bloody awful; I had a free period at the end of the afternoon so came home early.'

'I'll keep my distance then.' Juno frowned, backing away from her and shifting a pile of books from the large winged armchair onto the floor before sitting down heavily and closing her eyes for a few seconds.

'I assume you don't say that to your patients?' Ariadne asked rhetorically before sneezing and blowing her nose loudly. 'What's up? Had a hard day?' She closed the book in which she'd written crossly: *See me, Chloe. Listerine is a mouthwash designed to combat bad breath. It was not the name of the woman whose mission it was to end the Peloponnesian War by denying men their sexual favours. That, Chloe, was Lysistrata*!

'Jesus,' Ariadne went on, not at all interested in whether Juno had had a good, bad or totally indifferent day, 'I don't know why I bother. Do I teach these feckless sixth-formers anything?' She threw the book towards the pile of marked books, missing its target – Ariadne was always more scholarly than athletic – and got up from her chair, reaching for another tissue and wrapping her cardigan more closely around her waist. 'I long for sunshine and places to explore, not day after day with arrogant girls who've only opted for Classics because they think it must be easier than Maths or Physics. All they're interested in is *Love Island*, getting pissed and how many boys they can fellate while still hanging on to their virginity.'

'Blimey, if I wasn't depressed before, I am now,' Juno tutted. 'Shall I go out and come back in again and we can start over?'

'Start *over*?' Ariadne frowned. 'You're obviously watching too much American TV, Juno. The phrase, here in good old Yorkshire, is "start *again*".'

'Oh, for God's sake, Ariadne, you are in a sodding mood,

aren't you? I came here to tell you something. Something good. Well, I think it is...' She trailed off.

'About Lexia, you mean?'

'Oh, you know?' Juno stared at Ariadne.

'Saw the front page of the *Midhope Examiner* when I stopped for petrol on my way home,' she said shortly. 'First time I've ever bought it, I think.' Ariadne indicated, with a nod of her head, the local paper folded neatly next to the morning's edition of *The Guardian* on the top of her piano at the back of the room. 'Bit of an amazing coincidence that footballer husband of hers suddenly ends up here in Midhope, don't you think? You know, back to Lexia's hometown?'

'Well, I suppose with Midhope Town now in the Premier League, you're going to start getting the big names here.'

'I don't know much – anything, really – about football, but Theo Ryan was always football's *biggest* name,' Ariadne snapped. 'He'd have been playing for England – probably captain of England – if he hadn't been Irish. He must be coming down in the world if he's ending up in a backwater like Midhope.'

'No, honestly, Ariadne, you speak to Gabriel. Midhope Town are really flying.'

'I thought fading football stars – and you have to admit, Juno, Theo Ryan must be past his sell-by date now – all end up playing for some American football club. You know, like Beckham or Rooney?'

'Maybe that's the *final* step and this is just an *interim* transfer. Gabriel will know.' Juno glanced at her watch and gathered her gloves and scarf. 'I'm going to have to get off or Doreen will sulk.'

'Doreen?'

'You know, my mother's help.'

'Mother's help?' Ariadne raised an eyebrow. 'Aren't your two big enough and bolshy enough to help themselves by now?'

'Tilda's only ten.'

'Nearly eleven surely? Isn't it her birthday soon?' Not having children of her own, Ariadne was often irritated by what she perceived as the over-mollycoddling of middle-class kids. 'I had my own door key and had to round up both you and Pandora after school when *I* was eleven. Get you both home and feed you beans on toast if Mum had spent the day in bed once again.'

'Well, that was in the good old days,' Juno said, smiling and ignoring Ariadne's bad temper. The last thing she wanted right now was a trip down memory lane to hear about how poor old Ariadne, being the eldest of the four sisters, had landed the lion's share of helping to bring them up. 'Things are different now.' Juno rattled her car keys and headed for the door before turning back to Ariadne, who'd picked up the local paper and was reading it once more. 'She won't want to come back, you know. I'm amazed she's even agreed to it.'

'The diva hasn't landed yet,' Ariadne said, not looking up from the paper. 'I'll believe it when I see it.'

'Good day?' Doreen was already waiting with her coat on, buttoned up almost to her chin, and on the starter block to make a quick exit. 'The kids have eaten what was left of that fish pie you had for your tea last night but there wasn't a great deal—' Doreen looked pointedly towards the empty dish '—so Gabriel will be starving again in half an hour. I microwaved some frozen peas and they said you'd be OK with them having a Magnum for their afters.'

'Who said?' Juno asked vaguely, scanning the post left neatly on the dresser for anything interesting. 'The frozen peas?' With her mind still on the possible return of her little sister back to Yorkshire, she wasn't concentrating.

'Sorry?' Doreen frowned. 'Matilda says she's done her spelling homework but I don't believe her. She was wanting to go out and see Harry Trotter but I said she'd have to ask you: it's dark out there, and anyroad, Brian'll have seen to him.'

Doreen and Brian came as a pair. When Juno and Fraser had finally capitulated – worn down to the ground by Tilda's constant nagging and worrying at them, like the little terrier she was, for a pony of her own once they'd moved down from Scotland – they'd been given the name of Brian Goodall who 'knows all about horses and sorting gardens'. Neither Fraser nor she knew the first thing about either, and pretty quickly came the realisation they'd just bought a house with two acres of vegetable garden, fruit trees and a paddock, and the dream Juno had of spending weekends in harmonious togetherness, lovingly tending serried rows of peas and runner beans was absolute bollocks. They therefore pursued the said Mr Goodall and lured him into working for them by offering ridiculous amounts of money for doing two days in the garden and basically being at the beck and call of both Tilda and Harry Trotter. All three – man, girl and pony – were as curmudgeonly as one another and got along famously, but part of the deal was that Doreen – Juno was never sure if she was married or living in sin with The Constant Gardener – would spend a couple of mornings cleaning for them as well as being at the house to welcome Tilda home from the local village school, Little Acorns, on the three days Juno worked at the surgery.

The problem was that, while Brian might be a superb gardener and stood no nonsense from either Harry Trotter or his mistress (Harry's, not Brian's; Doreen definitely wore the trousers in the Goodall household) Doreen was a pretty crap cleaner and nosy into the bargain.

'So,' she now said as she pulled on pink woollen gloves and covered her permed hair with a rather snazzy purple rain hood, 'I see your sister and brother-in-law are coming back to Westenbury.' She gave Juno a sidelong glance from underneath the purple plastic, gauging her reaction to what she'd just said.

'How on earth do you know that, Doreen? Did Tilda tell you she was my sister?' Juno did wish Doreen and her daughter wouldn't get so chummy over the packets of custard creams and Yorkshire tea Doreen always had to hand in her bag.

'She certainly did. Ooh, I remember your Lexia winning *TheBest* all them years ago.' She paused, cocking her purple-covered head to one side like some inquisitive tropical bird, as she tried to remember the date. '2004, wasn't it?'

'I believe so, somewhere around then.'

'You believe so?' Doreen frowned. 'Weren't you there with her then? You know, behind the curtains, offstage, like? Smiling and cheering her on and crying like the families do?'

'No, Doreen, I wasn't.'

'Oh, right. Bit of a funny do that then?' Doreen wasn't going to let it go.

'So, Brian's sorted Harry Trotter this evening, has he?' Juno asked, trying to change the subject. 'Lovely. I'll leave a note for you tomorrow, Doreen; I reckon the downstairs loo needs a real good seeing to.' She ushered her towards the door, thinking, not for the first time, she could do with a real good seeing to herself. Fraser had only been gone a week but there had been no 'real good seeing tos' for many a good month before that. Juno reached for the bottle of red on the dresser – sod the diet, this was medicinal – and poured a healthy glassful, trying to recall the last time Fraser and she had even contemplated sex, never mind actually done anything about it. She'd bet any money it was over a year. Even on the night before his departure they'd not indulged in any goodbye nuptials; the spark had gone, the fire well and truly out, and neither of them seemed to have any desire or inclination to rekindle it.

It wasn't as if they didn't like each other – although to be honest Juno found his constant throat-clearing highly irritating – but she no longer had any desire to run her fingers over or through any part of him. He obviously felt the same. Juno knew they should have talked about it, but far easier to kiss cheeks chastely and, with some relief, turn over to one's own side of the bed than start a conversation that could open a whole can of worms. A year apart might rev up their relationship.

Or not.

'I'm starving.' Gabe's appearance at the kitchen door stopped in their tracks any guilty thoughts Juno was having about her relationship with her husband. Fraser and she were both equally to blame for the lack of care and cosseting they should have given their marriage but hadn't.

Juno had read all the books and articles about how to spice up your marriage but, knackered after a day's doctoring, she'd pulled on her old comfy tracky bottoms once again and reached inside the cake tin for another slice of Victoria Sponge instead of out to *her man*, as they suggested in the Sunday supplements.

'Hello, Mother dearest, how are you? How was your day?' Juno smiled theatrically at Gabe, who ignored her and headed for the fridge instead.

'What can I eat?'

'I thought you'd just had supper?'

Gabe grunted his reply and surveyed the contents of the fridge before pulling out a box of eggs.

'You'll be clucking soon, the amount of eggs you get through in a week.' It was a good job Brian regularly brought eggs from his *girls* or the shelves from the little Tesco down in the village would constantly be laid bare by Gabe's daily compulsion for an omelette. Tilda and Brian were both working on her to have some hens of their own but, so far, Juno had put her foot down. She knew who'd be the one to end up rounding them up at night as well as disposing of any mangled bodies once the fox that was always hanging around the bins down the end of the garden had finished his orgy of killing.

'Do you want me to do that for you? I'll have an omelette myself seeing as you two haven't left me anything for supper.' Juno reached down in the cupboard for the pan. 'Pass me the eggs and that butter.'

'Thought you were on a diet?' Gabe frowned as he hacked off a wedge of Cheddar from the huge economy pack she regularly bought to satisfy her son's apparently insatiable appetite, and chewed thoughtfully. 'So, is it true then?'

'Is what true?'

'Theo Ryan has signed with Midhope Town?'

'I'm sure you know as much as me.'

'I don't get it, Mum. How can Lexia be your sister – my aunt – and Theo Ryan be your brother-in-law – my uncle – and yet we've never even met them?'

Progress here. This must be the longest sentence Gabe had uttered in months. But of course, anything to do with football was, in Gabe's world, noteworthy enough to elicit some sort of conversation, however brief.

'Nobody believed me at school,' he went on, 'when I said they were my aunt and uncle. Even Mr Thompson laughed when Jacko told him, in games, what I'd told him, and said I was some bloke called Walter Mitty.' Gabe shook his head. 'Don't know who the hell *he* is...'

'I don't get it myself, Gabe. Lexia was just seventeen when she became really famous after winning *TheBest*. It all seemed to go to her head and she didn't want anything to do with us after that. She met Theo Ryan at some party apparently, and by the time she was twenty-one she'd married him and become a WAG and was all over *OK!* and *Hello!* magazines every week.'

'A WAG?' Gabe frowned as he hacked off more cheese from the block. 'What's a WAG?'

'And you a footballer?' Juno laughed. 'Mind you, I'm not sure footballers' wives feature as much as they did.' She stopped beating the eggs to think. 'Probably gone the same way as Furbies and The Proclaimers...'

'I don't know what you're on about, Mum. Can you get a move on with that omelette? I'm—'

'Starving,' she finished for him. 'Yes, you said.'

'So, I know me and Tilda have never met Lexia and Theo Ryan, but *you* must have been in touch with them. Didn't you go to their wedding? Weren't you in the magazines?'

'Nope,' she said shortly. 'Your Aunt Lexia cut herself off from us once she left home to go to London. She went to live with Granny's sister – my Aunt Georgina – in Wimbledon while she was going through all the heats of the competition and never came back. Didn't want to have anything to do with us.'

Gabe frowned. 'Not even with Granny? Or Grandpa?'

'Particularly with your grandfather. She never forgave him for leaving Granny and going off with Anichka. Lexia wasn't much older than you when he upped and left. Aunt Ariadne and Aunt Pandora and I had all left home by then; Ariadne was living in California, I was up in Aberdeen at university and Pandora was married to Uncle Richard and living back here in Westenbury.'

Gabe was quiet for a few seconds, obviously doing sums in his head. 'So, she'd only have been a few years older than me when she left home? And never came back? Don't you think that's weird?'

'What is? What's weird?' Tilda thumped down the stairs and into the kitchen, Lady Gaga, peeping an inquisitive nose from the sleeve of her red school jumper.

'Our auntie – the one we've never even met – is coming back to live in Westenbury.'

'Well, I don't know about Westenbury itself, Gabe,' Juno interrupted. 'Somewhere in Midhope maybe, seeing as how

Theo Ryan has signed with Midhope Town... Tilda, could you put that creature away before it disappears again?' The bloody gerbil was always going AWOL, reappearing when she least expected it. She'd been lying half-asleep in the bath the other day when the damned thing had run along its edge, stopped and eyeballed her and she'd had to grab the flannel to cover herself, feeling strangely embarrassed and at a disadvantage under Lady Gaga's haughty, critical stare.

'The wee thing likes it up my sleeve, doesn't she?' Tilda purred. Despite being almost two years in Yorkshire, Tilda had managed to hang on to her Scottish burr. 'So, is this the mythical aunt we've never met? The one who was once in some girl band we've never heard of?' Tilda continued to stroke Lady Gaga who was obviously getting restless and about to make another bid for freedom.

Juno stared at her daughter. Mythical? Where did a ten-year-old girl learn such vocabulary? She was obviously doing Myths and Legends in preparation for her SATs or she was some sort of child prodigy. Juno had a feeling it might be the latter and that she was following in the steps of Patrick, her grandfather, and her Aunt Ariadne, both of whom were arrogant in their supposed superior intellect. 'Just because Theo Ryan has apparently signed with Midhope Town doesn't mean he's going to live round here, you know. I really can't see Lexia coming back here at all – she might decide to stay in London. She has a four-year-old son; he's probably just started at school and she won't want to move him.'

'You sound like you don't want her to come back?' Gabe and Tilda both looked at Juno as Gabe handed her the two plates she'd put to warm in the oven. She slid the omelette onto one before dividing it unevenly into two, giving Gabe the bigger portion.

'Oh gosh no, you're wrong,' Juno protested, taking her plate to the kitchen table where Gabe was already in the process of squirting tomato ketchup. 'I do wish you wouldn't ruin good food with that stuff, Gabriel. No, you're wrong,' she went on, shaking her head, 'I'd love it if my little sister came back to Yorkshire – I just don't want to get my hopes up in case she doesn't…'

'It's only me,' Pandora sang as she pushed open the kitchen door. 'You're as bad as Ariadne, Juno; you really should keep your door locked, especially now you've no man to protect you. Do you have that cake tin I asked to borrow?'

'Oh, Auntie Pandora says she's coming round.' Gabe had the grace to look slightly guilty for not passing on the message. 'She wants to borrow some cake tin or other.'

'Isn't it exciting, Auntie Pandora?'

'What? The cake I'm going to make for Hugo?' Pandora trilled. 'It will be, Tilda, once I've really gone to town on it. I'm thinking green sugar paste and little golfers on the top. Hugo achieved a bogey when he was home over the Christmas holiday; golf-mad just like his father. He's back for the weekend – an exeat from school – and I want to have a cake ready and waiting for him after we've been up to pick him up.'

Gabe sniggered, the way only an adolescent can snigger over the word *bogey*, while Tilda was scornful. 'I wouldn't have thought a fifteen-year-old would want *golfers* on a cake. I don't think *that* would be very *exciting*.' Juno glared at Tilda but she carried on regardless. 'No, I mean the news about Auntie Lexia…'

Pandora stood stock-still, the jollity over her planning of Hugo's celebratory golf cake evaporating like a puddle in a heatwave. 'What about your Aunt Lexia?' she snapped, staring at Tilda with such intensity that even the usually sanguine Tilda began to wilt.

'You know…' Tilda, wavering slightly, turned to Juno for help. 'She's coming back, Mum, isn't she? She's coming back to live in Midhope.' Tilda thrust the front page of the local paper towards Pandora.

Pandora snatched the paper from Tilda, scrutinised the headlines and then, glaring at all three of them at their apparent complicity in welcoming back the prodigal sister, stalked back towards the door with the local rag still in her hand. 'Not if *I* have anything to do with it, she isn't,' she snarled, all thoughts of Hugo's green icing and golfers clearly history as she slammed the door behind her.

# 3

*January 2019*

*Lexia*

'I'm not. I'm not going. I'm not going back.'

'Well stay here in London then.' Theo Ryan shook his head in exasperation. 'What the fuck is wrong with you?' He drained his glass and, pulling up the sleeve of his Emmett of London navy chambray shirt, glanced at his Rolex. 'I really can't be doing with this, Lexia. I'm off, having a final drink with Darren and the lads. You make your mind up what you're going to do – whether you're moving north with me and Cillian or staying here in London by yourself.' Theo glared at his wife, looking her up and down with what was tantamount to disdain – dislike even.

'I'm staying *here* and Cillian is staying *here*. With *me*.' Lexia Ryan reiterated what she'd been telling him for months. Ever since he'd dropped the bombshell that he'd signed with Midhope Town. Midhope Town, for heaven's sake? OK, they were up there in the Premier League once again and flying high but what were the chances of his being

28

taken on by the town where she'd been born and grown up? It was unbelievable that it had actually happened. Lexia rubbed away the tears that seemed to be ever-present and tried to control her breathing.

Theo turned and came back towards her, grabbing his wife's shoulders with both hands. She could smell alcohol on his breath and see contempt in his small, shrewd eyes as his fingers dug into her flesh. 'And you think you'd be able to look after a four-year-old by yourself? Look at you, you mad bitch. Just take a look at yourself.' He moved her, none too carefully, towards the huge mirror hanging above the neo-classical marble fireplace. 'You can't even look after yourself.'

'I'll get help...'

'Well, you certainly need it.' Theo frowned down at her, wiping away the remains of yesterday's mascara from underneath her eyes with the ball of his thumb. He bent slightly and sniffed. 'You smell, Lexia. When was the last time you had a shower? And what the fuck are you wearing?' He grimaced as he saw the stain on her sweatshirt. 'You're *welcome* to stay here in London, Lexia. I don't *want* you to come with me. But don't think for one minute my son is staying here with you. You're not capable of looking after yourself or him. And come on...' He paused and laughed dryly. 'There's absolutely no way Cillian would ever be parted from me; he has football in his blood...' He looked her up and down once more, taking in the grubby maroon tracksuit bottoms and pink top, the mousy hair with the last hint of blonde highlights. '... While you, my darling girl, have enough Valium in yours to sedate the Pope finding himself in a mosque.' His beautiful Irish burr belied the contempt in which he held her. Laughing at his own wit and without another backward glance, he snatched up the keys to his car from the now empty cut-glass fruit bowl and headed for the door.

She'd met Theo Ryan at a party in Knightsbridge in 2007, one of those parties she'd always dreamed of attending when she was a girl practising with a hairbrush for a microphone up in the attic at home, and where now she suddenly seemed to be the main event with everyone lining up to speak to her, to be seen talking to her.

Jaz Burnley, her new American PR, had taken her over completely since her split from the girl band Gals, reinventing her as Lexi and making sure she was not only at the top of every music chart going, both in the UK and in America, but insisting she attend all the parties and social events that would further her already burgeoning career. She was on the point of becoming the most successful UK female artist of all time, and it seemed everyone wanted a slice of the Lexi pie being offered.

Theo had approached her at the party, introducing himself simply as Theo and, not having any interest in or knowledge of football, Lexia had had no idea that he was an internationally famous premier-division player. She'd simply fallen for his lovely persuasive Irish accent, and was soon caught up in the whole idea of 'Theo and Lexi' as portrayed in the media and the press and particularly in the huge, colourful magazines that couldn't get enough of the pair.

Theo had told her, on that very first evening, that he'd fallen in love with her after watching her on some TV programme where her singing had almost moved him to tears. He'd smooth-talked her, pursuing her with flowers, with presents and with the love she so desperately sought for herself now that she didn't see her family anymore, and was quite open about his determination to have her for himself. One evening over dinner and rather a lot of wine, she'd told him she was estranged from her family up north.

'You poor little darling,' he'd crooned, kissed her fingers, one after the other. 'Is it the singing and your being famous they don't approve of?'

When she'd nodded, not knowing what other explanation to offer, Theo had smiled and said, 'Don't you be sad, my darlin'. I'm here to look after you now. It means I don't have to share you with anybody else. You can be all mine.'

They'd married a year later in the Caribbean and, although Theo had wanted a huge, showy wedding in Ireland, Lexia told him she'd only marry him if they did it quietly without any fuss. He'd cajoled, sulked and argued but, on this, Lexia wouldn't move. Such was his determination to have Lexia for himself, Theo had had to go along with the rules she'd stipulated but, on their honeymoon, after drinking too much rum, Lexia had seen a different side to him when he'd had a major strop over her refusal to allow the paparazzi access to the occasion.

As the wheels of Theo's black Porsche now crunched and skittered up the pebbled drive, Lexia looked out of the window to where the gardeners had spent the afternoon clipping and tidying the already sterile garden, taking in the outlines of the bare winter trees, stark in the cold January evening air and then onto the crimson Sold sign triumphantly pasted across the burgundy and gold For Sale sign. She wasn't a bit bothered about the house – it was just that: a house. An overheated interior-designed modern box with far too many rooms and not enough love. But although she actively disliked living in London, the very thought of making the move back to Midhope made her pulse race.

Lexia felt the beads of sweat on her top lip and between her breasts that always heralded the start of a panic attack. Moving away from the window, she walked up and down the ridiculously long sitting room, concentrating on the breathing exercises she'd been shown by her CBT therapist. Slowly, slowly, putting all her sustained effort into not allowing her body to hurtle her in the direction of, and down, Panic Alley where too often it had taken her, she felt her breathing ease itself down and the slight buzzing in her ears cease before it could take a hold.

Lexia caught sight of herself in the mirror once more. Jesus, she was a mess. She pulled a face, lifting up her long hair and pouting at her reflection as she had so often done for the paparazzi when they all wanted a piece of her. Were they still called *paparazzi*? She didn't know. All she knew were the tabloid hacks, obviously with nothing better to report on, who would lie in wait beyond the hedge of the gated complex she'd called home for the last seven years or so, in order to snap her as she now was – too thin, too scruffy, without a bit of makeup – and convince their editors they were worthy of their salary as they compared her to Theo's latest bit on the side. There was always one. There always had been – football groupies ready to drop their knickers for the superstar Theo Ryan had once been.

'I make coffee. You want one?' Nika, the present Croatian au-pair in a long line of au-pairs they'd employed to help with the running of the household and Cillian, appeared in Lexia's line of vision as she struggled to bring her breathing under control. 'You OK?' she continued as she saw how drawn and pale Lexia had become. 'You not look too hot, Lexia.'

'I'm fine. Really. Is Cillian waiting for me upstairs?'

'Well, I don't know about that.' Nika grinned and went on, 'He's had bath and is shooting goals into wastepaper basket at the end of landing. I tell him you cross but, hey, he never take notice of what I say.'

'Tell him his daddy won't take him to football practice next week. That'll soon have him in bed. Actually, don't, I'll go up and tell him myself. Make me a coffee – decaf – would you, Nika? I'll be down in a while.' Both Lexia and Nika knew that the coffee wouldn't be drunk, that once on her own Lexia would pour herself a large glass of wine in its stead, but they both acted out the little charade as they did most evenings. It was only ever one glass – she certainly wasn't a big drinker – but it had the capacity to numb the edges, to blur the reality of her life and to make what she'd done in the past – the thing that always came back to haunt her – that little less dreadful.

Relieved that the potential panic attack had receded, at least for the moment, Lexia made her way up the huge central staircase, turning left at the top and along the cream-coloured carpet until she came to the sixth door along. How ridiculous, she thought as her bare feet trod the soft thickness – seven bedrooms and just for the four of them. Nika had said she wouldn't be leaving London to go to Yorkshire with them; she'd heard it was cold and wild up in the north. She wanted to be near Jo Malone and Harvey Nicks. When Lexia had protested that even Harvey Nicks was now in Leeds and Manchester, Nika had shaken her head and laughed and said she wasn't venturing into the unknown. Anyway, she said, she was fed up of looking after kids – no disrespect to Cillian – and had already had a couple of interviews for work as a croupier which was much more up her street than wiping snotty noses and trying to force sprouts and broccoli down unwilling throats.

'Goal!' Cillian kicked the ball with force and the wastepaper bin flew in the air with a clatter. 'See, Mum? See how good I am?'

'Come on, darling, bed.'

'No.'

'What do you mean, *no*?' Lexia heard her voice rise. She mustn't get into a confrontation with Cillian again. She must be fair but firm – show him she was in charge, but that she loved him at the same time. She'd read the books; she knew the theory.

'No, means no. That's what it means,' Cillian said in a sing-song voice. 'I'm going to be better even than Dad and I have to practise.'

'Not when it's bedtime. Right, have you cleaned your teeth?'

'Yes.'

'No, he hasn't. Don't you believe him.' Nika, on the way up to her room, was listening. 'Cillian, you know what happen to little boys that lie? They have their tongue cut out. And then because you no clean your teeth your teeth drop out too...'

'Thanks, Nika, we'll sort it,' Lexia said hastily. It was perhaps a good job the au pair was going off to do her own thing; she suspected Cillian was already swearing like a Croat. What was it he was always muttering under his breath: *Govno jedno*? Theo thought it hilarious. But then, more than likely, her husband was shagging the au pair. God, she needed to get a grip and become a proper mother. She was so tired though. So tired of it all.

Lexia took a deep breath. 'OK, Cillian, I'm going to count to five and then you're off to your bathroom, clean those teeth in double quick time, and then it's bed. One... two...'

'No, no it's not.' Cillian stuck out his bottom lip mutinously. 'Where's Dad? I want Dad to put me to bed.'

'Daddy's gone out. He'll come up and see you when he gets back. Now, I'm not going to tell you again.'

'You always say that.' Cillian turned his big brown eyes – her mother's eyes, Lexia thought – and smiled sweetly.

'OK, enough, *govno dedno*, I have enough of this. Don't you talk to your mama like this. In my country you'd be having your backside slapped.' Nika, towel wrapped round her well-endowed chest, exited her room and descended like a Valkyrie. She picked Cillian up in one swift movement, threw him over her shoulder and headed for his bedroom where she put him down not too gently and marched him to his en-suite bathroom. 'Teeth, you clean them now. Properly. You hear? And don't you paddy with me. You big boy? How you expect Jose Mourinho choose you for Man U if you not big boy? And no teeth? You ever see top footballer with no teeth?'

Cillian's extended lip began to tremble. 'It's not Jose Mourinho... you don't know anything... and I don't want to have no teeth...' Big fat tears began to fall down his face. 'Mummy, I don't want to not have no teeth.' He flung himself into Lexia's arms.

Lexia breathed in every bit of her son as she stroked

his hair. She could feel Nika palpably bristling at her capitulation over Cillian, but she didn't care. 'Come on, Cilly, let's clean those beautiful strong teeth together and then bed.'

'Will you sing?'

'Of course. What do you want?'

'Hush, Little Baby.' Cillian frowned. 'But *I'm* not a little baby: *I'm* a big boy – I just like the words *Mama's gonna buy me a dog named Rover*. Dad says when we get to Midhope, I can have a dog. I'm going to have a big dog and we're going to call him Rover.'

Oh Jesus, was this Theo's latest tack in getting Cillian to move with him up north? A bloody dog?

Behind her, Nika tutted and muttered to herself. '*Krvavi pas sadu. Jebeš me...*'

'I know you're being rude, Nika, so cut it out.' This was more like the old Lexia, she thought to herself. More like the feisty kid who'd bunked off lessons, left school before she was sixteen and become the youngest singer ever to win *TheBest*. She could do this, stand up for herself. Become the proper mother she desperately wanted to be.

'*Hush, little baby, don't say a word...*' Lexia sang the first few words as Cillian climbed into bed and snuggled down under the crisp cotton sheets with Ronaldo, his stuffed penguin. Ron was desperately in need of a good bath – a bit like herself Lexia conceded as the ripe whiff of stale sweat drifted upwards from her armpit – but, the good intention she'd had that morning of putting Ronaldo in the washing machine had, as so often happened with most of her intentions, good or otherwise, gone by the wayside in a fog of Valium, wrapping its comforting arms around her anxieties until they receded back into the dark cave from which they habitually crawled.

'Mummy?' Cillian opened one sleepy eye.

'Hmm?'

'Why aren't you on television anymore?'

'That was a long, long time ago, darling. Before you were born.'

'Mrs Sanderson said you were the best singer in the world.' Cillian yawned and closed both eyes once more.

'Mrs Sanderson?'

'You know, the lady who helps in my class. She hears us read and puts pictures up on the wall?'

'Oh, right.' Lexia felt a pain so intense it threatened to floor her. She *had* been good. The best.

'Mrs Sanderson says she'd like your augi...'

'My augi?'

'Your augi traff...' Cillian trailed off, his mouth open, little fingers slipping from around Ron's arm. Did penguins have arms? Wings that was it. But they couldn't fly, could they? Just like her. They couldn't fly away.

She loved Cillian so much. He was her total world. Without him she was... Well, what was she? Nothing. Could she keep him here in London with her? Buy a small house around here and have some continuity by keeping him at the school he'd only just started? Surely that was better for him than taking him up to a new school, a new town? Even as she put forward the arguments, the reasons that had been in her head for months now, Lexia knew it wasn't possible. She couldn't do it by herself. And even if she could, if she was as strong and, let's face it, as *sane* as the next single mother wanting to bring up her child alone, Theo wouldn't allow it. He'd drag her through the family court, bring in the most expensive legal advocates and put forward and expose every little thing that made her the crap mother she really was: the anxiety, the depression, the phobias... the list was endless. And Cillian adored his father. His behaviour was not the best now; what would it be like just her and him with no Nika to pass him over to and Cillian resentful of her, knowing it was her that was keeping him from his daddy?

Lexia bent and kissed her son's sleeping face. She couldn't be parted from him. Far better, surely, to go with Theo and Cillian back up to Yorkshire. She'd have her big sisters, Ariadne and Juno there. Juno was a doctor, for heaven's sake. They'd both help her to get better. And her mum. She missed her mum so much. A big tear tolled down Lexia's cheek, falling onto the stain on her sweatshirt where it glistened for a couple of seconds before sinking into the absorbent fabric.

She wanted her mum.

# 4

Bloody car. Juno jumped out, kicked the Mini a couple of times before shifting herself back into the vehicle once more, sent up a prayer to that great mechanic in the sky and turned the ignition again. Yes! Success. The engine throbbed into life and she pulled out of the drive and onto the road that took her towards the village. She was having real problems with the car; the engine kept cutting out for no reason that she could see. Not having a clue what was under the bonnet of cars, she'd always relied on Fraser to sort pistons and oil, brake lights and hoses etc. (Weren't hoses the fancy tights Elizabethan men wore? That showed off their stalwart bits and pieces?) Without Fraser, who to be honest she didn't think was any more mechanically minded than she was herself – he just pretended to be – Juno had had to turn to Brian Goodall for help the last couple of days when the Mini was being particularly moody. Brian had sorted a couple of things – he'd actually found the dipstick which had gone AWOL and done something manly with the electrical wiring – but the sodding thing still kept cutting out when she least expected it.

Towards the middle of February, a Friday morning, she was on her way into work and, as she pulled up at temporary traffic lights in the middle of the village, glanced across at the notice board outside the village hall. This area was Pandora's domain. Not needing, or wanting, to go back to her career as a defence lawyer once she'd had Hugo – *I'm a mummy now and need to be at home for my little boy* – Pandora had thrown herself wholeheartedly into the role of Yummy Mummy and hadn't done a stroke of paid work in the fifteen years since his birth.

To be fair to Pandora, being called out yet again at two in the morning by another petty burglar or drunk driver in the police cells didn't quite fit in with her aspiration to be both a stay-at-home mum and Westenbury's Lady of the Manor and, even when Hugo had trod the traditional path of all little Boothroyds and gone off to boarding school, Pandora had never shown any inclination to go back to her career.

Instead, she was a school governor at Little Acorns; she was in charge of the church flower rota; she pressganged, assembled and took charge of the group of volunteers to keep the village library afloat when it was in danger of closing and encouraged tepid, rubbery cottage pie down the aged throats of the recipients of Meals on Wheels when, Juno was convinced, they'd prefer a KFC or McDonald's and a glass of Merlot. She was also a member of the WI, Brown Owl to the village brownies and President in situ – no one dared knock her off the top spot – of a ghastly village group calling themselves Young Wives. Ariadne dubbed this scary band of women Old Hags and also reckoned that, if

Westenbury were on the coast – 'you know, like Scarborough or Filey' – Pandora would have a yellow sou'wester and hat behind her front door and, at the first sounding of her pager would be off down to man the lifeboat – singlehanded if necessary – and, with a shout of *chocks away*, would launch said lifeboat and save those in peril on the sea in the manner of Grace Darling.

Pandora's main raison d'être, however, was her choir in the village hall.

All four of the girls, Juno included, could hold a note and sing. Well, more than hold a note, if she was honest. If there'd been a couple more of them when they were growing up, and Helen could have been persuaded to cut out and sew them all little lederhosen-type outfits from the sitting room curtains, they'd have been dead ringers for the Von Trapp family. Or, she mused, as she adjusted the rear mirror and deftly applied the lipstick she'd not had time for at home, if they'd been boys, and there'd been one more of them, they could have rivalled the Jackson Five. As it was, Helen, often in some world of her own, floating – and sometimes struggling – through her days, had absolutely no thoughts of putting any one of them on the stage. And Patrick, the flamboyant, adored, but often absent father of their childhood was – here, Juno frowned at the memory – too busy shagging his students and being made to leave his lecturing positions – *lechering positions*, Ariadne had renamed them – to be remotely interested in his daughters' musical ambitions.

While Ariadne didn't, as far as Juno was aware, sing at all these days, Pandora was the driving force behind the Westenbury Warblers, a large group of local singers who met weekly in the village hall to practise and who were – according to their website – available for weddings, christenings and Bar Mitzvahs as well as their annual Carol Concert and Summer Evening Concert in the Park which, to be fair to Pandora, were becoming ever more ambitious and well attended, with tickets changing hand on the black market for ridiculous amounts of money. OK, she'd just made that last bit up because, to listen to Pandora going on about it, one could be forgiven for thinking the Westenbury Warblers were on a par with Take That or One Direction.

And it amused Ariadne and herself to take the piss out of Pandora in an attempt to bring her back down to earth when she went off on one.

Juno was so intent on wondering whether Pandora would be able to persuade Lexia – now that they knew she and Theo and Cillian were definitely coming back to Midhope – to join the Westenbury Warblers, she didn't notice the lights had changed until somewhat rudely made aware of the fact by a loud blasting on the horn from the car behind her. She re-adjusted the mirror back to driving mode, giving an apologetic little wave to the driver of the silver sports job behind her and was quite startled when the driver appeared to raise his middle finger in her direction. Had she imagined it? Surely no one would be so rude? Juno continued taking little surreptitious glances through her mirror at the driver but no more hand signals appeared to be forthcoming and, accepting she'd imagined his dextrous manoeuvres, she soon forgot about him and let her thoughts slip back once more to Lexia.

Lexia had rung her, quite out of the blue, a few days after the piece had appeared in the local paper. She hadn't said much, apart from confirming their plans to move to Midhope, albeit more than likely temporarily, but was sounding Juno out about local schools for her four-year-old. Juno was excited that she, Theo Ryan and their little boy were not only moving back to Midhope but were actually going to be renting one of the brand-new upmarket houses at Heath Green on the outskirts of Westenbury itself, a matter of a couple of miles from where Juno and Fraser had bought two years previously.

She'd be able to get to know her little sister all over again and, while she wasn't overly keen on four-year-olds, she'd have a new nephew. Despite her having three sisters, Pandora had, up until Cillian's appearance, been the only one to produce a single cousin for Juno's two, and, being up in Scotland when he was born, Juno couldn't really say they were close to Hugo or knew him well at all...

Jesus, what the hell was that? The sodding engine of the Mini had, without warning, cut out once more while myriad red lights on the dashboard were intent on making sure she was aware of the fact. They were surplus to requirements; the Mini was reverberating from the impact of the car behind her slamming into it.

'You shouldn't be on the fucking road...' Mr He of the Middle Finger was out and banging on the Mini's window.

'Neither should this fucking *car*,' Juno retorted crossly as she opened the door. 'It needs a damned good seeing to but, I would remind you, *you've* banged into *me*. You were obviously driving far too close.'

'You've been meandering down this road as if you were out for a stroll and a picnic. It's forty down here and you've been creeping along at twenty like some old bloke on a Sunday afternoon spin. No one can get past you. Your mind obviously wasn't on the road. Just look at my car.'

'Tough. You knocked into me. Your fault, buster.' Juno attempted to get out of the car but he stood in the way, towering over her. He must have been around her age, longish dark hair curling onto his – rather lovely – dark blue suit collar and quite vivid green eyes looking down at her in anger. What a cross patch. 'Let me out and I can see for myself what damage *you've* done to *my* car.' Juno scrabbled around for her heels underneath the pedals – she always drove bare foot ever since developing a hallux rigidus (stiff big toe to the man in the street) from too much wearing of said heels – and eventually stepped out onto the road. 'Where? What? What's your problem? I can't see any damage at all.'

'There, look…' Mr Pointy Middle Finger pointed – his index finger this time – towards the direction of his front bumper that was resting gently against the Mini's back one.

Juno actually laughed out loud. 'Oh, for heaven's sake, get a life. There's a tiny scratch. A drop of T-Cut, some spit and polish and it'll be right as rain. What a fuss about nothing. Now, if you don't mind, I'm already late for work: I'm a *doctor*—' she put much emphasis on the handle '— and I have patients who are *waiting* for me.' She gave him a withering look and marched – hobbled on her too-high heels – back to the Mini, turned the ignition and roared off leaving him standing in the road.

What a pillock.

Two minutes later he was back on her tail and Juno was starting to get a bit tense. One heard so many stories of road rage these days and, to be fair, she had been a bit flippant with him. Arrogant even. She turned off down the lane towards the surgery and he indicated and did the same. As she approached the surgery entrance, she made the quick decision not to indicate and then did a quick shifty turn into the car park hoping Middle Finger Man would shoot past and be on his way. He didn't. *Of course, you daft bint,* Juno chastised herself, *you boasted of being a responsible member of the community – a GP; it was obvious where you were headed.*

She pulled up and parked in her slot and the silver car pulled up next to her, its owner glaring in through the Mini window as it did so. She was actually a bit frightened by this stage. *Oh, for heaven's sake, Juno. What can he do?*

Apart from thump her? Stab her? Shoot her?

He got out from the silver car. No, he didn't – he *strode* from it and towards Juno. A rather gorgeous F-type Jag, she now realised (only because Gabe was as much into cars as he was football and had asked for the self-same model – a model of the model of course – for his tenth birthday and she'd admired the same many a time as she'd lifted and dusted it on Gabe's windowsill where he kept it). Juno accepted she was a pretty crap driver at the best of times and she *hadn't* been concentrating on the road and she *had* been pretty cheeky telling him to rub out the scratch on his F-type, for heaven's sake, with a bit of spit and polish.

He stood by her car, arms folded, and Juno considered leaping across to the passenger door and making a dash for it into the surgery. Their eyes met and he raised a sardonic eyebrow. Did road-ragers raise eyebrows? Surely, they just lunged without foreplay? Juno raised one back at him and then almost jumped out of her skin as Izzy knocked on the passenger window.

'Oh, good, I see you've met,' she mouthed, as she signalled, with a complicated winding gesture that Juno should open the car window. Juno pressed the Mini's window button – did Izzy think they lived in the last century? – and nothing happened. Damned electrics again.

Feeling braver now that she had Izzy to protect her, Juno pushed open her door and, with a somewhat drawn out *'Ex…c…use me'* at Middle Finger Man, jumped out and looked across at Izzy. 'Met? Met whom?'

'Oh, you seemed to know each other.' Izzy frowned. She shrugged. 'Juno, this is Scott Butler, our new locum. He's come in today to find his feet before he actually starts with us after the weekend.'

Bad enough that Scott Butler had pinched her consulting room and was an arrogant tosser, but then Declan suggested Scott accompany Juno – shadow her – on her rounds that afternoon. She spent the morning in a bad mood, breathing in the not-quite-dry paint of her new practice room and warning patients to avoid leaning on the walls and to not touch the door as they went out. While the new paintwork – ghostly white (*ghastly white* would, in Juno's piqued mood, have been a more appropriate name) – did lighten the cell-like box where she'd been sentenced to spend her working hours, she hated the new room. Izzy tried to placate her by suggesting she pop down to the Monday Market to find some new jolly curtains with which to brighten the place – on her and Declan, of course – and then got the giggles when Juno reminded her there was no sodding window. One can rapidly go off people, Juno told her, adding that she was already contemplating searching for a new part time job in a surgery where *all* members of the staff were valued and loved, and not just the full-time and old-best-friend members.

'But *I* love you,' Izzy continued to laugh. 'We *all* love you.'

'Marian doesn't...' Juno sulked.

Izzy pulled a face. 'Yes, OK, you're right there,' she conceded.

'... And the Speedy Gonzales Kiwi doesn't. That, if you do the maths, is only 50 per cent who do.' Juno began to feel a bit sorry for herself. Was she so unlovable? Even her husband had gone off for a year without her.

She should have *insisted* Declan and Izzy shove Rhett – sorry Scott – Butler down here in the storeroom; she should have stood up for herself when the idea of taking on a locum was mooted. By the time she'd got her computer up and running – Declan, apparently, had been in since sparrow fart unplugging and rebooting and doing whatever IT was necessary to have it ready for her for 9 a.m. – Juno was still muttering to herself about jobs for the boys and old uni mates and even Marian, who usually had the upper hand, had looked a bit nervous and disappeared before reappearing with a coffee for her.

Once the patients on her morning list began to appear, Juno was so wound up she wasn't overly sympathetic to their problems. She assured the ridiculously thin woman who thought she had a lump in her breast that it was actually her breastbone and that if perhaps she put on a bit of weight she wouldn't be conscious of it. She continued to be in a bad mood, prodding and poking and issuing prescriptions all morning and, it was only when eighty-year-old Mr Gardener broke down in front of her, telling her he was trying so hard to get over the death of his wife six months previously but seemed unable to find any joy in life without her, that Juno remembered why she'd become a doctor, held his hand and, ignoring the six-minutes-per-patient rule, let him simply talk.

After a quick walk around the village during her lunch break in the fresh but chilly air, Juno decided to take the initial plunge about the new bathroom she and Fraser (well, probably not Fraser, Juno wasn't convinced he ever noticed his surroundings) had been promising themselves, and popped into the trendy new bathroom shop for a most entertaining chat with the incredibly camp, but obviously very talented, designer.

Then, after devouring the best ham and cheese sandwich she'd ever tasted from the deli next door, Juno was feeling much better – in fact almost perky – until she remembered Scott Butler was on a promise to accompany her on her rounds that afternoon. Well, she'd show him what a competent, caring professional he'd helped throw out of her practice room.

'OK, are you ready?' Juno put her head round the staffroom door where Izzy and Declan were in the process of sharing sandwiches – M&S, by the look of it: the posh party ones, instead of the usual homemade variety – with the new recruit.

'You've ten minutes yet.' Declan frowned. 'Come and have a sandwich.'

'Already eaten,' she snapped.

'Oh, have you been out?' Izzy asked. 'If I'd known, I'd have asked you to bring me back a loaf from the bakery.'

So, the three of them hadn't even noticed she'd left the surgery over the lunch break? That's how much they cared. 'I'll be in the car,' Juno said, looking pointedly at her watch. 'I do have rather a large caseload this afternoon.'

'Flipping heck, Juno, you sound like that chap off Dr Finlay's Casebook. Was it Dr Finlay, or the other one, who was always going on about his caseload?' Izzy took another mouthful, her question obviously rhetorical.

'Dr Cameron.' Scott Butler affected a Scottish accent over his New Zealand burr. He smiled and stood up, knocking crumbs onto his paper napkin before screwing it into a tight ball and lobbing it successfully into the waste bin. 'Shall we go?'

Juno walked off in the direction of her car and Scott hurried after her, pulling on his suit jacket and straightening his tie as he did so. 'Shall I come with you in your car?'

'That might be a good idea,' she said shortly. She unlocked the passenger door for him, fastened her seatbelt and started the car. Except it didn't. Start, that is.

Scott Butler sat at her side, without saying a word – no manly advice as to how she should have one foot on the clutch and one on the brake and not to flood the carburettor etc etc. Which was good seeing as how the Mini was automatic and didn't possess a clutch in the first place.

After a good long silence, when Juno felt herself growing hotter and crosser with every passing second, Scott said, 'So, do you think we should perhaps go in mine?'

'I would have thought that *huge* dent on your car's front

bumper would have prevented you going anywhere,' Juno snapped crossly.

'Look,' he smiled. 'We seem to have got off to a bad start and I apologise.'

'For what? Giving me the finger?'

'Oh heavens, did you see?' He laughed, not in the least embarrassed. 'Look, I was wanting to create a good impression on my first day in a new job. I was incredibly late, I was already lost, and you were driving like an absolute pillock. You were even putting on your lipstick at one point.'

'I don't think there's any law against that, is there?' Juno said angrily, stung at being called a pillock. Who *did* he think he was?

'I'm sure there is, actually. Anyway, I apologise unreservedly for my boorish behaviour. You were right, I was wrong. Now, shall we transfer over to my car and you can take me round the area and introduce me to some of the patients?' He held out his hand and she realised it would be perhaps churlish not to respond in kind. His skin was tanned and felt warm and for some reason Juno really couldn't explain, when she glanced up at him, taking in his green eyes fringed with the longest black lashes no man should ever be allowed to own and at the full mouth smiling lazily down at her, her heart did a little flip. Now, what on earth was all that about?

# 5

'So, what's the surgery's criteria for offering a home visit?' Scott Butler was manfully endeavouring to keep up with Juno as, now in her flatties, she strode resolutely up the path of 15 Tivydale Ave, determined to show this interloper her efficient, caring and totally professional qualities as the village GP of choice. She'd show him how her patients loved and respected her sensitive, concerned and non-judgemental attitude to each and every one on her list.

With the good doctor hot on her heels, Juno quickly scanned the notes she'd hurriedly made on her return from the bathroom shop and checked the door number. Yes, Number 15, for Mr Samuels with – she quickly checked the reason for the call-out – acute back pain. 'Mr Samuels,' she said with assumed authority, advising the shadowing medic over her shoulder as to the potential problem with the old man, before whisking, purposefully as a spring tide, up the three steps to the back door and knocking once. 'Over eighty years old… possible cauda equina syndrome… might need an ambulance…' There, that would fox him; Juno had actually had to Google Declan's possible diagnosis herself before she left the surgery. She pushed open the door leading directly into the kitchen. 'Mr Samuels…' she sang, in her best Mother Theresa voice, 'Bloody hell...' She stopped abruptly and Scott, hot on her heels, bumped into her, carrying them both into the neat, immaculately clean kitchen.

No dirty dishes on the work tops, no lunchtime plates ready for washing up in the sink. Nothing at all out of place on the immaculate pine kitchen table except, somewhat unusually, Beryl Foggerty, the village librarian – obviously taking a break from issuing overdue fines – being shafted, doggy style, by an extremely fit looking young man.

'Oh yes, that's it, that's it, Justin, that's *it*.' Beryl's substantial bosom quivered momentarily in the black balcony-cupped corset as, with closed eyes and total oblivion to any audience, she gave herself up to the final conclusion of her extra-curricular lunchtime activity.

Scott Butler grabbed Juno's arm, backing her out of the kitchen door and reversing with her down the steps the way they'd just come. 'Bloody hell indeed,' he breathed. '*Not*, I assume, Mr Samuels with the bad back?'

'Not unless he's changed his name to Justin, regressed fifty years and discovered a new way to cure back pain.' Juno made a huge effort to speak calmly, professionally, but all she wanted to do was giggle hysterically. She made a big show of looking at her notes. 'Right, well, anyone can make a mistake: it's 15 Tivydale *Dve* we need, not *Ave*. Next turning on the right, I believe. Shall we go?'

Dr Scott Butler knew his stuff, she'd give him that. Once Juno and he had walked round to where they *should* actually have been to begin with, he quickly confirmed Declan's initial diagnosis and suggested to Mr Samuels' daughter, who was waiting for them with her father, that they ring for an ambulance and get the old man into hospital.

He took his time with each patient on the round, introducing himself but allowing Juno to do what she had to do first while he stood back, taking an onlooker's position. As the afternoon went on, however, she began to include him in any initial diagnosis and was glad of his thoughts and expertise on more than a couple of occasions.

By late afternoon, Juno was exhausted and wanting only to get home to curl up on the sofa with a glass of wine, the lovely new bathroom catalogues she'd picked up at lunchtime and her latest good read. She'd only recently got into reading novels, having spent the last twenty years stuck into Biology and Chemistry textbooks, and just discovered Thomas Hardy. She'd adored *Far From the Madding Crowd* so much she'd looked for and found an old DVD of the Julie Christie and Alan Bennett film on Amazon and couldn't wait to get stuck in to it. She'd been really looking forward to an evening to herself knowing that Tilda was being picked up straight from school for a sleepover. And, while Gabe would usually need very little attention apart from stuffing full of pizza and plugging into some electronic device for the evening before reminding him to clean his teeth and, at some point, to go to bed, she wouldn't even have to do *that* as he was off that afternoon, on a three-day Geography field trip to somewhere near Morecambe. God, rather him than her, Juno thought, stretching her stiff shoulders.

So, when her phone sprang into action and she quickly scanned the text message, she closed her eyes and said, 'bugger.' Not only was she unsure whether the Mini would get her back home, but she'd totally and utterly forgotten she'd promised – much against her better judgement – to make up numbers at some supper party Pandora had invited her to weeks back, and who was now texting her asking what pudding she was bringing.

'Pudding?' Juno snarled at the newly painted walls. 'Pudding, my backside.' Back in her dungeon, she almost stamped her foot. In fact, realising she was either going to have to throw some pudding together when she got home or stop off at M&S – which would be mighty difficult without a car – or plead some dreadfully infectious but highly mythical virus she'd picked up on the rounds that afternoon, she did actually stamp it and, when her hallux rigidus responded painfully to this little outburst of temper, threw in another muttered 'fuck' for good measure.

Jesus, the last thing she needed was an evening with Pandora's mates. There'd be the usual crowd: a selection made up from Tricky Dicky's golfing set and their braying wives; a couple of 'Old Hags' and their husbands and, always, Dr Jennifer Danton-Brown, Westenbury's answer to Lady Baden-Powell, Pandora's best mate and all-round ally. Singly, the two of them were pretty formidable but, as a pair, with a glass of prosecco and a mushroom vol-au-vent or two inside of them, Jennifer DB and Pandora were untouchable.

'How are you going to get home?' Izzy knocked and popped her head round the door of the cell. 'This paint's still wet. Did you know?' She tutted, wiping a sticky patch from her knuckles with the last of the tissues plucked from the box on Juno's desk, but didn't wait for an answer. 'Right, I'm off now. Done my stint for the day.'

'You're not going my way, are you?' Juno looked down

at the clock leaning against the skirting board which still needed fixing to the newly painted wall above the computer. 'I'm out for supper at my sister's in, oh gosh, less than ninety minutes.'

''Fraid not,' Izzy said. 'Got a concert at Sid's school this evening.' Sid was Izzy's eight-year-old. 'Taxi?'

'I'll see if the Mini will start and, if not...'

'Oh, I bet Scott's going your way. Scott? Are you going home? Could you give Juno a lift?'

Scott Butler was pulling on his pin-striped jacket and loosening his tie before heading to reception where Declan's evening patients were already muttering among themselves about the senior partner's inability to keep to time. 'Sure. If she's ready to leave now.'

'Hang on,' Juno said, gathering her things and rifling through her bag for car keys. 'You never know, the Mini might be behaving itself now.'

It wasn't.


'What will you do for a car over the weekend?' Scott glanced across at her as he drove. 'Do you have a mechanic that can sort it for you?'

Juno nodded. 'Joe Watson in the village is pretty good. I'll give him a ring in the morning and ask him to pick the Mini up and look at it for me.'

'Won't you need transport? You know, to meet this Joe Watson back at the surgery?'

'I can use my husband's car. It's a Volvo – a bit of an old man's car really, and I hate driving it – but there if I need it.'

Scott drove quickly, hands that had gently assessed

Mrs Dixon's swollen legs an hour earlier now confidently guiding the F-type through the country roads on the outskirts of the village. 'So,' he said after five minutes' silence, 'your husband won't need it then? The car that is?'

'I doubt it. He's in Boston.'

'Lincolnshire?'

Juno frowned. How the hell did someone from New Zealand know about Lincolnshire? She knew nothing about *his* country apart from it consisting of two islands. Or was it three? 'No, Massachusetts.'

'On holiday?'

'No, he's working there for a year. He's only been gone a couple of weeks.' Why did she feel the need to tell him this?

'Oh?' At the lights, Scott turned once more, scrutinising her until she felt herself redden slightly. Goodness, he was rather gorgeous when he smiled.

'Yes.' She wasn't quite sure what else to say. 'Right, if you just turn left here… and pull in over there… This is me. Many thanks.' Juno quickly gathered her things as Scott drew up outside the gate. 'So, are you staying far from here then?' she asked, concerned he might not know how to return home. 'Do you know where you're going?'

'Rushdale Avenue. I'm renting for six months while the owners are off somewhere. It's at the other end of the village. You know, beyond the woods?'

'Molly Carr Woods? Gosh, are you living out there?' Juno looked at him in some surprise. 'I *should* know it. My sister Pandora and her husband live on Rushdale Avenue.'

'Ah, the inimitable Pandora? She's your sister?' It was Scott's turn to look slightly taken aback. 'You don't look alike, do you?'

'Actually, I think we all have a slight look of each other; it's the nose,' Juno added, prodding her own in his direction. 'Rather on the big side.'

He didn't take the expected gentlemanly stance, contradicting any opinion she might harbour on the size of her nose but, instead, just said, 'All?'

'I have three sisters and we all have a certain resemblance in a certain light. So, you've met Pandora?' Blimey, she did hope Pandora had been gentle with him, and then inwardly smiled. She hadn't been overly gentle with him herself until they'd come together – possible wrong turn of phrase there – on the same side, joint spectators of Beryl Foggerty's pine table gymnastics.

'Met her, had a cup of sugar and a welcome cake from her, plus an invitation to supper actually. You know, a "get to know the neighbours" sort of thing…?' Scott trailed off as Juno stared. Westenbury wasn't a small village; what were the chances of him meeting two sisters at two totally different times within the first couple of days of his moving here?

'Right, OK, so this supper? When's this invitation for?'

Scott lifted his hand from the steering wheel, shifting his jacket sleeve and staring at the watch face with the same narrow-eyed look of intensity he'd applied to Juno's medical notes on the rounds earlier that afternoon. 'In exactly an hour,' he said. He looked at her directly, his quite sensational green eyes never leaving her face. 'I don't suppose you'll be there, will you?'

The coming evening's anticipated perusal of a catalogue of sinks, showers, bidets and stopcocks interspersed with rampant thoughts on Sergeant Troy in his red jacket had, for some reason, suddenly lost its thrall. Even pudding-less, the alternative seemed far, far superior. Juno smiled up at the good doctor. 'I will actually,' she said, opening the car door and stepping out.

Scott smiled back. 'That's good,' he said, his eyes crinkling rather deliciously in his Antipodean-tanned face. 'That's really good.'


'So, what have you brought?' Pandora looked beyond Juno to the plastic carrier bag she'd just landed onto the kitchen granite with a thump. 'What pudding?'

'One of Mum's banana loaves from the freezer,' Juno said, bravely. Helen Sutherland's latest, almost frantic, obsession with baking after a lifetime of doing little, if any, cooking at all, was marked only by the notoriously bad cakes she almost daily produced. 'And a tub of Dixon's ice cream I've just picked up on the way here to go with it,' she added in order to soften the blow. Dixon's ice cream, unbeknown to the rest of the foody world, was a Midhope secret.

'Really, Juno, I do think you could have made more of an effort.' Pandora sniffed and took the carrier, handling it with some disdain. 'It'll either be a solid brick we can't get through or will have the appearance, consistency and smell of monkey vomit.'

'Lovely,' she said cheerfully, trying to see past Richard, her brother-in-law who appeared to have put on even more weight since she'd last seen him only a couple of weeks previously. He came over, his double chin wobbling alarmingly as he bent to kiss her. Potential heart attack case if ever she saw one. 'Richard, you're looking... well,' Juno lied as he put a meaty paw on the small of her back and ushered her into the sitting room.

'A couple of inches off my waistline—' Richard patted his huge ursine stomach straining manfully against the sky-blue wool of his Pringle sweater '—and I'll literally be zipping round the golf course.'

Or not. Juno smiled dutifully in the direction of Tricky Dicky's middle as he led her to a group of three women standing by the mantelpiece. The room was crying out for a real log fire but Pandora would, Juno knew, have no truck with such a thing. She wouldn't have the patience to light a fire every evening, and most certainly harboured no appreciation for the heady scent of apple tree logs that she herself burned in her own grate at home. Pandora needed the same instant, automatic control over any heat in her sitting room as she had over Tricky Dicky and her fifteen-year-old son, Hugo.

'Ah, Juno, just the person. How fortuitous is that? Now, we're just discussing Raymond's bowel movements – or lack of them, I should say. Your wide expertise as a GP will, I'm sure *trump*—' Juno wanted to giggle at that '—any knowledge I, as a simple consultant, may hold.' Jennifer Danton-Brown, who did love everyone to know that she was a consultant obstetrician, proffered a plate of several pieces of Cumberland sausage in Juno's direction while ushering her into the little group. 'When he *does* manage to go, the result isn't totally satisfactory.' She popped the glistening brown sausage into her mouth and chewed enthusiastically, eyebrows raised in Juno's direction, awaiting her professional verdict.

'Er...' The three women – two of whom could have been no more than five-foot-tall – leaned towards Juno expectantly for her opinion. 'Prune juice. A big glass before bed. Best thing for, er, that sort of problem.'

'Right, I'll remember that.' Josie Gledhill, a Young Wife and always desperate to prostrate herself at the feet of Pandora and Jennifer and thus ingratiate herself into a trio, nibbled at her sausage as though it were a lollipop and beamed dutifully. The third woman in the group, a tall willowy blonde in black skin-tight leather trousers gave a hastily covered up bark of laughter, grinned at Juno and held out her hand.

'Hi, you must be Pandora's sister? I'm Tara. I'm actually registered as a patient of yours but, so far, touch wood, I've not needed you.'

'Juno Armstrong.' Juno held out a hand and was going to add: 'Who do you have to shag round here to get alcohol?' when she thought better of it. This Tara woman could be in Pandora's inner circle and sprag her up over the church flower-arranging rota. And, as Dr Scott Butler was heading their way with a bottle of Merlot and a couple of glasses in his hand, it didn't seem overly appropriate or necessary. He'd changed out of his formal navy work suit and, in faded jeans and a pink shirt, was looking suitably underdressed next to the chinos-and-jacket-attired golfers who appeared to be out in force.

'Ah, you've met Tara?' Scott topped up her drink and offered Juno an empty glass. It had been a long day and she accepted gratefully, wondering why on earth her heart had done a little dance as he approached and then plummeted with the realisation that Tara must belong to the new doctor. She didn't appear to have a New Zealand accent – he was obviously a quick worker if he'd only been in the country a couple of weeks and had already found himself a particularly gorgeous girlfriend – but maybe she was the reason he'd left Auckland.

'Scott's just arrived from New Zealand,' Tara informed Juno. 'He's living across the road from us.' Juno's heart did the same little dance as before, but this time appeared to have wings.

'We have met.' Juno beamed. What the hell was the matter with her? 'We're working together at Westenbury surgery.'

'I'm not sure taking me into the village den of iniquity on a Friday afternoon straight after a cheese and pickle sandwich could be classed as working.' Scott grinned down at Juno and she began to giggle. Beryl Foggerty's heaving bosom was obviously still imprinted on both their mind's eye.

Tara gave a little smile but obviously had no idea to what they were alluding. 'Tara's husband plays for Midhope Town,' Scott went on. 'Footballer.'

'Oh,' Juno said delightedly, 'my sister is married to Theo Ryan…'

'*The* Theo Ryan?' Scott stared and then whistled.

'She is moving back up north with him any day now.'

It was Tara's turn to stare. 'Your sister…? Pandora's sister as well then…?' Here Tara glanced over at Pandora who was giggling somewhat coquettishly at something the small, sandy-haired man in front of her was saying. 'Your sister is *Lexia Sutherland*? Mikey, d'y'hear this?' Tara pulled the man towards them by his jeans' belt loop. '*Lexia Sutherland* is Pandora and Juno's *sister*…'

'No! Haddaway, man…' Mikey Fairbairn stared in turn.

'Lexia? Got all her albums. I reckon she was the love of my life. Before you, of course, Tara, pet.' He spoke in a wonderful Geordie accent and grinned widely while Tara patted his head somewhat condescendingly. Brought to heel like the family dog at Tara's high-heeled side, Mikey came up just below her shoulder while Pandora, cross that attention was now on Lexia rather than herself, had a face like thunder.

'OK, everyone, I think we can eat,' Pandora sang, pasting a rictus of a smile on her face. She snapped her fingers like a Spanish dancer and her cleaner, Sheila, resurrected from cleaning Pandora's latrines and reinvented as trendy café-culture waiter for the evening, appeared in black leggings, T-shirt and upmarket black cook's apron to take the guests' drinks into the kitchen. 'Just simple kitchen sups tonight, I'm afraid, peeps,' Pandora trilled and then, glaring at Tricky Dicky, who was eyeing Tara's rather glorious chest, suggested he led them to their places.

'We're not standing on ceremony this evening,' Pandora continued, 'so do sit where you want.' She nevertheless ushered her guests meaningfully to where she really wanted them to sit and, placing her hand firmly on Scott Butler's arm, leading him away from any younger, more attractive females, allocated him a seat so that she had him to her left and the trusty Jennifer DB to her right.

'Now,' Pandora exclaimed, simultaneously ringing a little bell and shaking her head vehemently at poor old Sheila who thought it was the signal to bring in the starter, 'I bring great news, everyone.' She gazed benevolently round at her audience and, in the manner of a suburban Angel Gabriel, proclaimed, 'Joyous news. Wonderful, exciting news.'

# 6

'Lexia Sutherland is moving back north?' Tara Fairbairn offered. 'We know *that*, Pandora, we do read the local paper. And we're all really excited—'

'No, no, that isn't what I was about to tell you all. Much, *much* more exciting news...'

'Who's Lexia Sutherland when she's at home?' Janet Sykes, Westenbury Golf Club's Ladies Captain frowned across the table at Tara.

'A WAG... You *know*...' Tara's eyes were bright with excitement.

'I didn't know Lexia Sutherland was a girl guide now,' Jennifer interrupted. 'You never told me *that*, Pandora.'

'A guide?' Pandora snapped, her reddening neck and tone of voice betraying the cool and collected air she'd assumed as the harbinger of good news, now that all attention round the table was being directed towards Lexia. 'What *are* you talking about, Jennifer?'

'Tara just said she was a WAGG, didn't she? You know, the World Association of Girl Guides...' Jennifer DB, as the county's Chief Guider, was persistent in her determination to acknowledge Lexia Sutherland as a member of the guiding fold.

'No, I *didn't*,' Tara frowned. 'The gorgeous Lexia Sutherland is not only the most superb singer and performer of this century, but she's married to Theo Ryan—'

'And who is Theo Ryan when *he's* at home?' Janet Sykes frowned at Tara.

'Well, I'm assuming, seeing he's married to Lexia Sutherland, that he'll be at home with *her*, Janet.' Tara pointed her glass towards the Ladies Captain and continued excitedly, 'He's one of Ireland's greatest footballers and, because Lexia is married to him, she's therefore classed as a WAG – Wives and Girlfriends, they were dubbed in the Nineties. *I've* never been called a WAG,' Tara went on somewhat sadly. 'We're not encouraged to accompany our footballing partners to World Cups anymore.'

'Right, can we get on?' Pandora, desperate to bring her guests under control, rang her little bell once more and, again, shook her head at Sheila who'd put one step forward before retreating back where she'd started, and who was now dithering between the huge kitchen's island, where plates of smoked salmon were ready to be picked up, and the waiting guests at the kitchen table.

Juno smiled sympathetically in Sheila's direction, but Sheila, who appeared to be in the middle of doing her own kitchen version of the Hokey Cokey, had eyes only for Pandora and the signal to serve her starter, and was biting her lip with the concentrated effort of waiting for the go-ahead.

'*Can* we get on?' Pandora smiled through gritted teeth as those who'd not been aware of Pandora's and Juno's relationship with the iconic Lexia Sutherland were brought up to speed by those who were. 'Now...' She paused for effect. 'I've invited you lovely people here tonight for a reason...' She paused again and frowned, before adding, 'not *you*, Scott – with your being so *new* to our little community, I really didn't know whether you *swing* or not...' Scott's, Tara's and Juno's eyes met over the Emma Bridgewater crockery and glassware. (Please, Juno pleaded silently, let it not be true that her sister was in the process of introducing Scott Butler to some neighbourhood swingers' club.) Pandora gave a little squeal of laughter. 'Sorry, I'm *so* excited, I can't get my words out properly. *Sing*. I don't know whether you *sing*, Scott.' Pandora paused for breath and smiled fondly at her potential new protégé who, still in shock at the thought of his having to throw his keys into a bowl at the end of the evening, nervously cleared his throat. 'Now, the rest of you here tonight are all in my... all in *the* Westenbury Warblers...'

Dr Jennifer DB, the sycophantic Josie Gledhill and the Ladies Captain nodded with a slight smirk at one another and then at their leader who went on. 'We, the Westenbury Warblers, have been invited to put forward to Sir – I beg your pardon – *Lord* Andrew Lloyd Webber himself, plans to put on the musical of our choice...' Pandora broke off to smile beatifically at the table as 'ooh' 'aah' 'really?' and 'goodness' floated back towards her and then held up a hand – rather in the manner of Donald Trump – to get attention back towards herself once more. 'Now, there's a long way to go. As your choir mistress, I received a letter from Andrew's *Really Useful Group* giving details of a competition to perform a musical of our choice in the summer. I didn't say anything to anyone at the time for fear of disappointing the choir if we were turned down. At this stage, I just had to give details of the size of our choir, our past productions and performances and some idea – although not binding – of which musical we might be interested in undertaking...'

'But, Pandora,' Janet Sykes interrupted, 'surely that was a choir committee decision and not one for you to make by yourself?'

'Well yes, Janet, absolutely. I totally agree with you, but...' Pandora broke off and had the grace to look slightly shamefaced. 'I thought the letter was some unsolicited mail, you know, some circular, and didn't bother opening it. In fact, to be honest, it nearly went in the *bin*. Can you imagine?' She gave a theatrical little shudder and then went on. 'And, again to be quite honest, I thought we were too small a choir to even be considered. So, with just a day to go before the deadline, I filled in the form and sent it off. This was ages ago – last summer in fact – and I'd totally forgotten all about it until I received this at the beginning of the week.' Pandora held the letter aloft.

'Read it out, Pandora. Go on.' While Juno adored singing, and Pandora was forever trying to get her to join the Westenbury Warblers, the couple of rehearsals she'd gone along to hadn't really been her thing, especially with Pandora in charge, and she'd not made any commitment to the group. She *had* made up her mind, with Fraser disappearing for the year, to join one of the local Rock Choir groups that were springing up everywhere, but this was something different. She really quite fancied getting involved with putting on a musical; she loved musical theatre – had probably sat through just about every production going – but adored *South Pacific* and *The Wizard of Oz*. Juno could really see herself as Dorothy.

It was a good job the starter was a cold one. As Pandora proceeded to read the contents of the letter, Sheila sighed deeply and adjusted her black leggings whose elastic appeared to be cutting into her waistline.

'*Dear Pandora.*' Here Pandora paused for effect at the writer's chummy use of her first name.

'Thank you so much for your interest in the Really Useful Group's current competition for groups and choirs to perform the musical of their choice. I'm delighted to inform you that your application has been accepted... blah, blah... and, subject to your choice of musical from the list below... blah, blah... of which I must be advised by the 28th February at the latest, as well as confirmation of the number of those taking part...'

'But Pandora, do we have enough members to put on a whole musical?' Jennifer DB looked doubtful. 'How many singers did you specify would be taking part?'

Pandora looked decidedly shifty. 'Oh, I said we had around a hundred and fifty.'

'A hundred and fifty?' Both Jennifer and Janet spoke at the same time.

'We're lucky if we manage *half* that at any rehearsal,' Jennifer went on. 'And *that's* when we're putting on the concert which leads up to all the little choirs joining up for the huge concert at the Albert Hall. People do *love* the pull of the Albert Hall, you know,' she added for the benefit of Scott Butler who was looking perplexed, as well as at his empty wine glass.

'Well,' Tricky Dicky came to Pandora's rescue, 'if you were to put on *The Sound of Music*, for example, you'd only need Captain Von Trapp, Julie Andrews, a few Nazis, a couple of nuns and... was it seven... children?'

'But the choir doesn't *have* children,' Jennifer argued. 'You have to be at least twenty-one to join the Westenbury Warblers although, if you recall, Pandora, I *did* suggest lowering the age to sixteen to up numbers...'

'Pandora, do you think we should eat?' Juno was starving, it was going up to nine and, she noticed, Sheila was beginning to look mutinous. 'We can eat and discuss at the same time, can't we?'

Pandora frowned but glanced at Sheila and nodded as, immediately, both Tara and Juno jumped up and went over to help with plates and the bread basket. Food, Juno thought. Halleluiah!

While Pandora's singing mates argued among themselves as to the feasibility of putting on the production of a full length musical, Juno accepted Mikey Fairburn's topping up of her wine and, once she'd eaten the smoked salmon starter and devoured enough bread to sink a duck, sat back slightly, the better to observe Scott Butler. He'd not made any attempt over the last hour that they'd been sitting at the table to catch her eye, and she began to wonder if she'd imagined the slight frisson between the pair of them when he'd dropped her off at home earlier that evening, seemingly pleased that she was also actually going to be a guest at Pandora's little do.

Juno realised she was obviously out of practice with the little nuances that went with flirting with an attractive man. Of course she was; she knew she'd never really been the overly flirty type of girl, although had totally envied the girls at school and then at university to whom flirting and getting off with a particular love object was seemingly second nature. Her first couple of years at university had really been spent keeping her head above water. While Ariadne and Pandora had always been the clever ones at school, segueing seamlessly from constantly top of the class at primary school to straight As at GCSE and A level and then both onto Cambridge, racing through exams with little effort, Juno had to really study hard in order to keep up the standard the pair of them had set with such ease. Lexia, as far as she could see, just hadn't bothered with academia, her only aim in life to be the star in a number one girl band. So, while there'd been a couple of boyfriends up in Aberdeen, by the time Juno was in her fifth year, Fraser was on the scene and that was it really, she supposed. At a time when she was away from home, feeling not only vulnerable, but awful guilt that fifteen-year-old Lexia was having to bear the brunt of their mum's despair and mental instability when Dad left home, Fraser was a nice solid rock on whom she felt she could depend. A pregnant Juno and Fraser were married on her twenty-fifth birthday (ridiculously young, she felt now) and, despite being taken on as an extremely junior house officer in a small cottage hospital in Aberdeen, Juno was a mother not very long afterwards.

So, let's face it, she mused as she sat at her sister's table, heels kicked off and at that lovely stage of drinking when the world and all that was in it seemed full of promise, she was up for it. Up for what, Juno wasn't overly sure, but something was stirring in her toes (and it wasn't her hallux rigidus) and working its way north as she took surreptitious glances across at Scott Butler. He was engrossed in conversation with both Tara who, flirting shamelessly with the good doctor, obviously had the hots for him, and the very pretty redhead who, Juno later found out, had been asked not only to balance Pandora's table as the single woman to match Scott's status as single man, but whom Pandora had headhunted, and was in the process of poaching, from Midhope's largest choir with the nausea-inducing handle of 'The Midhope Melodymakers'.

Juno decided, after the main course of an admirably delicious lamb tagine which accompanied her fourth very large glass of wine, that not only was Scott Butler really rather gorgeous, but if she *was* to be up for whatever it was she was thinking of being up for, then she'd like to be up for it with the good doctor. Unfortunately, she realised, he hadn't looked her way all evening. He was entertaining Tara and the redhead with tales of his travels and, while Tricky Dicky to her left was apprising her for the third time that evening of his first ever hole in one as well as boring the pants off her with how Brexit was going to be affecting Boothroyd, Boothroyd and Dyson, she was becoming beautifully relaxed with an excess of Merlot and, at the same time, having the loveliest visions of what she might get up to with the good doctor were she to ever have her way with him. It was lovely, really. It was Friday night with the prospect of no work for the next four days, she was pleasantly tipsy and, best of all, having sexual fantasies about her new work colleague which she knew, practically, would never materialise into reality.

Juno had just, oh so very slowly, unbuttoned her white work shirt to reveal her best, laciest Janet Reger bra (that was a fantasy for a start; there was nothing in her underwear drawer fancier than a greying M&S balcony) and her head was thrown back against the (windowless) wall of her new cell at the surgery as Scott Butler reached forwards, when Jennifer Danton-Brown barked, 'Your mother's banana cake, Juno, or one of my special meringue Mont Blancs?'

Juno jumped slightly as Jennifer interrupted her shamelessly salacious conduct with Scott Butler over the surgery desk, the peaks of her own Mont Blancs, erect with alcohol-fuelled fantasies, melting to nothing at Jennifer's demand for her choice of pudding.

'Now, Juno,' Jennifer said as she allocated the last of her meringues round the table and Juno's mum's brick sat to one side of the table, as unsullied as the Virgin Mary, 'with your Fraser away for the duration, you're going to have lots of time on your hands.'

Was she? Juno stole one more glance at Scott Butler who was involved in a seemingly meaningful conversation with the pretty redhead, and sadly nodded her agreement. It didn't look as if she'd be spending any time acting out her fantasies with the good doctor opposite. Juno sighed and concentrated on what Jennifer was saying. 'I don't know about that, Jennifer. With Fraser away, I'm going to have double the parenting roles – just me to take Tilda to horse events and Gabe to football practice and matches. Just me to...'

'So, I'm sure we can put you down for the Westenbury Warblers and this new Andrew Lloyd Webber venture.' It was a statement rather than a question and Juno quailed somewhat under Jennifer's steely eye. 'Pandora is going to need all the support she can get, particularly with the re-appearance of your sister—' Support? Why was Pandora going to need *support*? '—and with singing ability obviously *rife* in your family, you too must be able to hold a tune as well? Hmm? Hmm?'

Juno was about to counter Jennifer's argument by saying it wasn't a known medical fact that the singing gene necessarily ran in families, but then had second thoughts. What the hell. She would – depending on what musical was decided upon – get involved with this Village Singing lark *if* it managed to get off the ground. If it was going to be *The Sound of Music*, forget it. No way was she going to be a nun or one of the kids dressed in lederhosen made out of someone's bedroom curtains. Pandora, as choir mistress, would drive her mad she knew, but Juno was sure she could get Izzy – who was always singing something, usually Abba, round the surgery – to have a part and even though Ariadne, who was a fabulous singer, would initially scoff at the very idea of getting involved, she bet she could, with a little persuasion, bring her along for a laugh, too.

'I think this singing competition sounds great,' Juno suddenly announced to the table when there was a lull in the conversation. Pandora stopped in the middle of pouring ridiculously dainty cups of coffee and looked across at her with some surprise. As well she might, Juno thought; she didn't think the pair of them had agreed on *anything* as kids, and there'd been little let up to their differences of opinion and disagreements over the years.

'Really?' Pandora was pleased. 'You know, I think we have what's needed to put on a great performance – it's never easy to obtain the rights to Sir Andrew Llyod Webber's musical scores when you want them, and here we are being handed them on a plate just about. It would be churlish to not make the most of this wonderful opportunity – and who knows, if we all pull together, we could actually win. Goodness, wouldn't that be something?'

Juno knew the wine was making her mellow and much more open to Pandora's musical ambitions than had she been stone cold sober and, more than likely, by the morning, with a hangover, the house to clean and the pile of ironing that Doreen had pretended she'd not seen, she'd be having second thoughts and eschewing any absurd notion of getting herself involved with the whole daft idea of Climbing Every Mountain or Following The Yellow Brick Road. But, just for the moment, she felt relaxed and amiable and willing to go along with any absurd idea of Pandora's that, not only would she be able to garner enough support for this little venture but could, as was her dream, possibly win into the bargain.

# 7

*November 2002*

*Lexia*

'Lexia, come on, for heaven's sake, get up.' Pandora stood at the bedroom door, Lexia's maroon school sweater and tie in one hand. 'It's nine o'clock. Come on, I have to get to work.'

Lexia yawned, opened one eye and then turned over, dragging the duvet with her and over her head. 'It's a teachers-only day, I don't have to go in.'

'Don't give me that. It was teachers-only day last week, according to you. I fell for that then. You have to go to school, Lexia, you know you do.' Pandora attempted to pull the duvet from Lexia but her sister was hanging on to the cover, just as determined she wasn't going anywhere.

'What's the point?' Lexia muttered from the depths of her pit.

'What's the point? What's the point?' Pandora was getting cross. 'Your GCSEs are the point. And then A levels and university...'

'Oh, come off it, Pan,' Lexia yawned, placing one tentative foot out of her warm bed before quickly pulling it back under the duvet. 'You know as well as I do I haven't got the Sutherland brains. It's alright for you, standing there in your little black suit, off to do whatever it is you solicitors do all day. To be honest, I can't think of anything more *boring*. So, even if I *was* clever like the rest of you, I wouldn't be interested in being a solicitor like you or a doctor like Juno...' Lexia yawned once more, pulled her pillow into a more comfortable position while muttering, almost to herself, 'Or a bloody teacher like Ariadne. That was a waste of her grand Cambridge education, wasn't it? Ending up teaching, even if it is somewhere wonderful like California!'

'Look, Lexia, I've got a meeting at ten and I need to see that Mum's OK before I go. She's not up either.'

'There you go then,' Lexia said, almost in triumph. 'What do you expect, with me living with a mad mother? One of us had to end up like her.' Lexia rubbed sleep from her eyes and yawned once more.

'Mum isn't mad,' Pandora protested.

''Course she is. You're not here when she's wandering round the house at three in the morning either crying or singing. I don't know which is worse, to be honest.'

'Singing? Mum's singing again?' Pandora stared.

'Yep, all the oldies. You know, the Joan Baez stuff. If I hear, "*My daddy was a handsome devil*" just one more time, I'm going to end up as loopy as her. It's all a bit spooky, waking up with Mum standing at the bottom of my bed crying and singing either lullabies or songs about deserted wives...' Lexia broke off, unable to carry on and dashed an angry hand across her face. 'Anyway, I can't go to school and leave her all by herself. I'm frightened to leave her. I don't know what she's going to do. What I'll find when I come home.'

'Oh, Lexia, I'm so sorry.' Pandora tutted, sitting down heavily at the end of the bed. 'I don't know what to do....' She hesitated. 'Look, I'm just wondering...'

'What?' Lexia opened one eye suspiciously.

'I'm just thinking whether you and Mum shouldn't come down to stay with Richard and me. You know, maybe just for a while until Mum feels a bit better?'

Lexia gave an incomprehensible snort. 'You're joking, aren't you? For a start, Mum won't leave this house; you know that, Pan. And *I* certainly don't want to come and live with you two either. The dreadful Boothroyds are always there...'

'The dreadful Boothroyds? You are *rude*, Lexia, that's my in-laws you're talking about.'

'God, don't I know it. Lady Barbara is always round at your place, poking about, trying to see what's going on.'

Pandora didn't reply, knowing Lexia was right but not able to admit to her little sister that, after two years of marriage, she hadn't yet been able to come up with a way to stand up to Richard's parents, William and Barbara Boothroyd. Barbara Boothroyd – Bee-Bee to her golfing chums – was a notorious snob, convinced that Pandora should be giving up work and joining her for ladies' luncheons, as well as constantly eyeing her up to see if she was yet pregnant with the heir to Boothroyd, Boothroyd and Dyson.

'She always looks me up and down as if she can't believe I could possibly be your sister,' Lexia complained, 'and she brought that golfing friend of hers round the other day

– Monica somebody – to look at your new kitchen and she didn't realise I was in the dining room and could hear everything she was saying. You should have heard what the old cow was saying about Mum.'

'About Mum?'

'Hmm. She said she was a scruffy bohe… bohay…?'

'Bohemian?'

'Yes, that's it, a scruffy Bohemian who needed to get her hair cut and her grubby clothes washed and was it any wonder that *Professor* Sutherland had finally upped and left. The bitch. So, no, thank you, Pandora, Mum and I are staying right here.'

Pandora sighed heavily and tutted once more. 'I just don't have time for all this. Dad should be here, sorting you both out.'

'If Dad was here, Mum wouldn't *be* in this state. You know that.' Lexia swung her legs out of the pink duvet cover and sat up, running her fingers with their bitten nails through her long blonde hair and rubbing at eyes puffy with the previous day's cheap makeup.

Pandora glanced at her watch once more. 'Lexia, I *have* to go. Promise me you'll get in the shower – get rid of all that makeup – and get yourself to school. Have you got a clean shirt? Money for the bus and for your lunch?' She reached into her briefcase and, pulling out her purse, found a ten-pound note and laid it on the dressing table. 'Do *not* go spending that on cigarettes. Right, I'm going to check on Mum again, try and get her in the shower too. Mrs Delaney's coming in this morning so you don't have to worry about her being by herself too much. I'll leave Mrs Delaney a note to say I'll ring her this evening and ask her to up her hours and come in every single day to be with Mum. And, I'm going to ring the surgery today when I get chance and have a word with Doctor Ali. We can't carry on like this. I'll be back this evening with a casserole or something so at least the pair of you will have something decent to eat.'

'Mrs Delaney never does much apart from sit with Mum and drink tea and talk about Dad. I'm not sure how much cleaning she ends up doing, you know. Anyway, doesn't it worry you?' Lexia rubbed again at her eyes, picking off flakes of mascara, not looking at Pandora as she spoke.

'Doesn't what worry me?' Pandora turned, desperate to be off but not wanting to leave without the reassurance that Lexia was actually going to set off and make it in to school.

'You know,' Lexia hesitated. 'That you might end up like Mum? She's never really been right, has she? I'm frightened...'

'Of what?' Pandora frowned, knowing full well where Lexia was heading.

'That I might have inherited what Mum's got? That I might end up like her.'

'Lexia, the only thing Mum's got is an adulterous husband. Look, I'm sorry to be brutal, but Dad's been an absolute sod to Mum all their married life. Why do you think we ended up here in the north? Why Dad had to leave his lecturing jobs in Oxford and then the LSE? There probably wasn't a university left in the south of England that wasn't aware of Patrick Sutherland's habit of having it off with his students. If Dad hadn't led Mum a merry dance all these years she would have been as right as rain.' Even in her twenties, Pandora favoured the clichéd phrases of a less literate, older woman.

'Do you think?' Lexia, eager to have Pandora's affirmation that Helen Sutherland's problems were caused solely by their father's behaviour rather than some ingrained mental illness that might easily be passed down to her, was, for a moment, reassured. 'It's just, Pan, you know, you three are all like Dad, clever and *focused...*' Lexia paused for a second, surprising herself at using such a big adjective, 'While I *look* like Mum, sing like Mum too and to be honest, have obviously *inherited* her lack of brains.'

'Oh, don't be ridiculous, Lexia. Mum's bright, she just never had a career apart from singing and looking after us four girls whereas you, well, you're as academic as the rest of us. Your problem is you won't *go to school*. Come on, or I really will ring your headteacher.'

Lexia looked mutinous. 'You're not my mother, Pandora.'

'For the moment, while Mum's not herself, think of me as just that, Lexia. Ariadne and Juno don't appear to be coming home to help. It looks like it's up to me to sort the pair of you as well as do my own job and look after the house and Richard.'

'Lucky you haven't any kids of your own at the moment then,' Lexia said, looking slyly in the direction of Pandora's middle and then, when Pandora's usually pale face flushed a deep pink, crowed, 'Ah ha, are you *pregnant,* Pandora? Whoa, I'm going to be an auntie! Auntie Lexia!'

'Lexia, will you be quiet and get off to school. I'm going now. And don't you *dare* tell Mum you think I might be pregnant.'

'Well, are you?'

Pandora relented and smiled, putting a hand to her stomach. 'I hope so, Lexia. I really hope so.'

\*

'Did you watch *TheBest* on TV on Saturday night? Who did you vote for?' Abbie Broughton drew heavily on the remains of her cigarette before tossing it carelessly to the ground, grinding it almost into oblivion under her non-regulation school shoe. 'God, I wish this was Mrs Hogan's sodding head.' She stamped once more on the tab end for good measure and added, 'Cheeky cow gave me a demerit for not handing in my project on time. I told her I'd done it but she didn't believe me when I said I'd left it on the bus.'

'Hell, I was going to use that excuse myself.' For a moment Lexia looked worried and then shrugged. 'Oh, sod it, I'm off. I'm not going back in this afternoon. There's no point. I don't understand a word of that Chaucer stuff. There was that really funny bit about some random old husband farting out of a window at somebody – that was cool – but the rest is totally beyond me.'

'The Miller's Tale,' Abbie said knowledgably, breaking a piece of chewing gum in half and offering it to Lexia.

'Well,' Lexia sniffed, chewing contemplatively, 'why they couldn't speak English like us, that Canterbury lot, I'll never know. Right, I'm off. Are you coming with me?'

Abbie gathered up her school bag. 'Nah, it's not worth it. My dad'd have a fit if he found out I was bunking off. Jesus, they don't half nag, my two: get your grades, get your A levels, go to a good uni... I have it shoved down my throat every second of the day. Anyway, Mum's making her fabulous roast pork for tea – crackling and *everything*. And then sticky toffee pudding. And *then* we're off to see the new James Bond film, *Die Another Day*. If I bunk off and they found out, I'd be in real trouble, and they'd pull all that and we'd not be going anywhere and I *really* want to see it. What do *your* mum and dad promise *you* if you get all As?'

'Oh.' For a moment Lexia hesitated. 'They're going to take me to London to see Holly Vallance. We're going to stay at some posh hotel and Dad's promised to buy me something from Topshop on Oxford Street.'

'Wow, you lucky thing.' Abbie stared, impressed. 'They really spoil you, don't they? You must be mad to mess that up by missing lessons. Right, bell's gone. See you later.'

Lexia continued to sit on the wall at the bottom of the playing fields chewing on her already gnawed fingernails, picturing her mum at home. Mrs Delaney would have left by now, gathering up the tins of furniture polish and bottle of Toilet Duck she had to provide herself because no one at home ever remembered to buy such things, placing them in her plastic Morrison's bag and reappearing with them every Tuesday morning. Lexia wasn't sure how she was paid, but assumed Pandora had it all under control, along with other grown-up things such as the electricity bill and council tax which she, Lexia, didn't have a clue about.

She should go home really, make sure her mum was alright. For a minute, Lexia dithered, trying to make up her mind between Chaucer and her mum. In the end, she jumped down from the wall, took off her school tie and shoved it in her pocket and, buttoning her black coat right up to the neck, set off in the direction of Midhope town centre.

\*

'Shouldn't you be in school?' The barman, a tall skinny man of indeterminate race and age glanced up from the racing pages of the *Daily Express* and frowned as Lexia ordered a coke.

'I've left. I'm sixteen.' Lexia shoved her hands deep into the pockets of her winter coat to hide Westenbury Comprehensive's tell-tale pink-striped shirt cuffs.

'What're you doing down here on a Tuesday afternoon in a place like this? There's no one around.' The barman frowned again. 'If you're a hooker, clear off.'

Lexia went scarlet to the roots of her very blonde hair. 'Do I look like a hooker?'

'No, you look like a little schoolgirl who's swinging a leg. What do you want?'

'I want to sing.'

'Sing? Oh, Jesus, not another one. Look, love, since Mr Scascetti got Avril Black on the road to success, the place has been overrun with kids like you – as well as their daft parents – thinking he's God and has the answer to fame and fortune. Most of 'em can't hold a note, never mind what it takes to make it big. Go on, down that coke and get yourself back to school before they notice you've gone.'

'Is he here?'

'Is who here?'

'You know, Mr Scascetti.'

'No, he's not. It's the middle of the day; things don't get started down here until at least ten o'clock. Anyroad, he's on holiday – he always spends November in the Caribbean. You know, before things start to rev up around Christmas?'

Lexia wanted to cry. It had taken a lot of courage to walk into the Club by herself on a Tuesday afternoon when she should have been in school, studying Chaucer, in the hope of being able to talk to Joe Scascetti. Everyone in Midhope – Yorkshire and beyond even – knew of the little Sicilian's success in establishing the Ambassador Club on one of the town's back streets, building his empire over the years by extending what had, at first, been a bit of a sleazy drinking hole, into a club with several bars, a restaurant and a venue for both established and fresh new talent. The cabaret in the gay bar at the Ambassador was legendary, with coachloads of both straight and gay punters descending on the place every weekend but, as well, Scascetti appeared to have the knack, like Pete Waterman with Rick Astley and Kylie Minogue, of discovering new talent. Everyone in Yorkshire was ridiculously proud that Avril Black, the singing mega star from Sheffield, discovered by Scascetti when she was just seventeen, was one of their own.

'He's not here, I tell you.' The barman shook his head and went back to his paper.

Lexia stood up, fighting the tears. She couldn't go back to school at this time in the afternoon and she really didn't want to go home. The responsibility of looking after her mum was just too much. A single tear ran down her cheek and she pushed back her chair, defeated. She *would* go home. Sit with her mum, hold her hand and listen once more to how she'd first set eyes on her dad and it was love at first sight. Lexia shook her head slightly. She didn't *want* to sit there and see the naked pleading in her mother's eyes. It frightened her. And her mum would keep on asking Lexia to ring Patrick for her; to beg him to come home. And Pandora had said she mustn't. She mustn't do that for her mum.

Lexia sighed, sat back down at the bar as another tear rolled down her cheek. Actually, maybe she'd go and *see* her dad. He was only in Manchester, for heaven's sake. She could get the train over – she had enough money with the £10 Pandora had given her – and find his office in the university and just wait for him. She missed her dad, but Pandora refused to have anything to do with him, and Lexia had taken her cue from her big sister and not seen him for what must be six months. Not since he'd moved out and gone to live with Anichka. Not that her dad had made much of an effort to try and see *her*, his youngest daughter. He'd rung her a couple of times, said he needed to explain, but he hadn't been able to tell her anything that she didn't already know. Patrick, according to Pandora, would never be able to justify his behaviour. He'd never be able to justify that, after more than thirty years of being married to her mum, and constantly leading her a merry dance with a whole load of affairs, he'd finally upped and left for a younger model. A much younger model. Anichka – the Russian Pole Dancer, as Pandora had dubbed her – was younger than Pandora herself.

'You OK?'

'Sorry?' Lexia turned on her stool. A man stood at her side, smiling down at her. For a split-second she had the mad idea it was Duncan James from her favourite band, *Blue* who was looking at her with such concern. He had the same longish blonde-streaked hair, the same Brad Pitt good looks. Even Pandora, eyeing Duncan James's picture pulled out from *Smash Hits* and stuck up on her bedroom wall, had stopped and stared and actually said, 'Goodness, he's rather lovely,' which, when comparing him to tubby

Richard Boothroyd whom Pandora had married a couple of years previously (Lexia had, as a thirteen-year-old, been forced into a quite horrible raw silk dress as bridesmaid) had made Lexia want to laugh out loud.

'I'm fine, thank you.' Lexia stood up and started to wind her scarf around her neck.

'But you're obviously not fine. What's up?'

'I just want to *sing*. I *can* sing. I'm a really *good* singer.' Lexia was suddenly defiant. One day, she'd show this lot. Joe Scascetti would be pleading, begging for her to sign – sign what, Lexia wasn't sure – but he would be begging for her to sign with him.

The man grinned. 'Go on then.'

'I'm going, I'm *going*. I'm going to *Manchester* now,' Lexia snapped crossly.

'No, I mean, go on, go and sing. Look, the stage is there. There's a mike set up. Go and show us what you can do.'

Lexia stared. 'What, now?'

'Yep. Off you go.'

Lexia froze for a second and then, glancing at the barman who was still totally engrossed in the 1.45 at Aintree, walked over to the stage. She walked up the steps, put both hands into her school coat pocket and, ignoring the microphone, launched.

*'Mwah... When you look at me, tell me what you see...'*

And kept going, word perfect, every note sublimely in tune, until the end. She was Holly Valance. She was *better* than Holly Valance. She kept her eyes closed throughout, as much to concentrate on the song as in an effort to eliminate her audience of two. As she brought the song to its conclusion, she kept her eyes closed not wanting to face the reality of being a fifteen-year-old schoolgirl in a club in the backstreets of Midhope rather than Holly Vallance, superstar. So she didn't see the couple of office workers, three kitchen staff and the two cleaners who'd all abandoned their tasks around the club to gather, spellbound, in the bar to listen and watch as she sang.

'Bloody hell.' The bartender who she'd sat and talked to and who'd told her to leave started to clap and the others joined in. And clapped and clapped and clapped.

# 8

'Mum, do you know what time it is?' Tilda stood, arms folded and face like thunder, a small bundle of self-righteous indignation at the bottom of Juno's bed.

'No, I don't know. And, to be honest—' Juno stuck her head under her pillow and stretched her legs sideways into what had previously been Fraser's personal space '—I really don't *want* to know.' Jesus her head was pounding. She'd certainly drunk more wine at Pandora's supper do than was probably wise, and she had a sneaking suspicion she'd probably been overly flirty with the new locum who, let's face it, was rather gorgeous. Except he'd spent all evening entertaining Tara, the would-be WAG, and the little redhead who'd hung on to his every word throughout dinner.

'Mum, *you* might not want to know, but *I* have a pony that needs schooling. We have to get him used to traffic, Brian says. You *promised* you'd walk him down to the village with me this morning.'

Visions of falling – literally – into a taxi and singing 'Climb Every Mountain' in her best Julie Andrews voice were beginning to creep, and then crowd, into Juno's brain. Hell, she really had been pissed. She shook her head slightly. She felt a bit nauseous; actually, downright sick.

She sat up and the room spun. 'Hang on, Tilda, what are you *doing* here?'

Tilda tutted. 'Doing here? As in? I do live here, you may recall.'

Juno peered over the duvet at this daughter of hers. She was, Juno was beginning to realise, her mother-in-law's granddaughter. Tilda had much more in common with Fraser's mother, Jean Armstrong, than Juno herself. A feisty, opiniated Scot, originally from somewhere in the Highlands, determined that, one day, Scotland would be independent from 'tha wee chancer' in government in London, Jean had sniffed with some disdain when Fraser had taken Juno up to Aberdeen and announced he was about to marry her. Jean, a large raw-boned, red-faced matron, had been even more disparaging when she saw her future daughter-in-law's obvious unease over the three Scottish Deerhounds that freely roamed the freezing cold, high-ceilinged, rooms of the large Victorian house. Jean had seen Fraser's father off at the tender age of just fifty-five and now spent her days out in the wind-swept paddock, rearing the grey, hardy Eriskay stallion ponies she bred and reared solely for the purpose of putting out to stud.

With a good few of both her Aunt Pandora's and Aunt Ariadne's genes thrown into the mix for good measure, Tilda had, Juno finally accepted, very little in common with her own mother.

'What do you mean, what am I *doing* here?' Tilda repeated, frowning, as Juno endeavoured not only to sit up without wincing at the pain over her right eye, but to try to bring Tilda into some sort of focus.

'You're supposed to be having a sleepover at Bea's house.'

Juno rubbed the remains of last night's mascara from her eyes and attempted, but failed, to do the same from the white pillowcase on which she now tried to once more lay her pounding head.

'I *did* have a sleepover at Bea's.' Tilda tutted again. 'That was last night. Now it's morning. In fact—' she squinted at her Fitbit '—it's now well after eleven and you *promised* you'd come with me down to the village. Although, why you won't let me take Harry Trotter down by myself, I don't know. I mean, *you're* not going to be a bit of help when he bolts if a car backfires or something.'

'It's after eleven?' Juno was horrified. 'But how did you get in?'

'Bea's mum dropped me off and I walked through the door. How else would I get in?'

'But the door was locked. And the alarm was on.'

'No, they weren't.' Tilda raised an eyebrow, and sniffed, a parody of Jean Armstrong if ever Juno saw one. Blimey, Juno needed to put a spoke in that little wheel before she ended up living with a clone of her mother-in-law, perish the thought.

'You've been drinking, haven't you?' Tilda went on, still sniffing the air. 'I think we need a window open in here.'

Jesus, had she fallen into bed without locking the door? And not put the alarm on? She could have been robbed of all her possessions, murdered in her own bed and not known a thing about it. 'Of course I locked the door,' Juno said, not quite meeting Tilda's eyes. 'I got up and made some tea and brought it back to bed. I unlocked the door for you, knowing I might be in the shower.'

Tilda, looking round for the non-existent mug of tea,

folded her arms once more. 'You do know that telling habitual fibs can desensitize the brain and encourage bigger lies in the future? Mr Donnington says—'

'Fine. Put a sock in it now, Matilda.' Juno attempted to get out of bed. 'If you want to make yourself useful put the kettle on and a couple of slices of bread in the toaster. I'll be ready to walk down with you in half an hour.'

Harry Trotter behaved beautifully, carrying Tilda down the lane that led to the main road of the village and through Westenbury itself as Juno walked beside the pair of them, only letting himself down – literally – when, for some reason, he decided to stick his cock out and, at a bit of a trot round by the church, managing to knock sideways the wing mirror of Ben Carey, the vicar's, ancient Morris Minor with his swinging appendage. Quite a feat – Juno was most impressed. She actually started to laugh but Tilda's raised eyebrow soon put a stop to that. 'Don't be juvenile, Mum,' Tilda tutted.

Juno stopped at the newsagent to buy *The Guardian* and a birthday card for the eleven-year-old whose party was being celebrated by all the girls in Tilda's class at some disco, followed by pizza and a sleepover at the host's house, later that afternoon. Harry Trotter continued to do as he was told and only shied once when a police car, siren screeching like a banshee, came hell for leather past them.

'Because he's been so good, do you think we can go and look at some friends for him?' Tilda's tone was unusually wheedling.

'Friends?' Juno frowned. 'I'm not having any *more* horses, Tilda... or a dog...'

When Tilda didn't say anything but set off at another trot, Juno puffing along at her side in an attempt to keep up with pony and girl, she managed to gasp, 'or a cat...'

Tilda stuck her hand out expertly – Juno was beginning to think she must have snuck down to the village and done all this before without her, so confident was she at manoeuvring the pony through parked cars – and they turned left towards the little hamlet where Brian and Doreen lived in a somewhat ramshackle smallholding at the edge of the village. 'Just come with me to look, Mum...'

'Could you just slow down a bit?'

'You really shouldn't drink so much, Mum. Especially as you said you were doing dry January to make up for all the gin you knocked back over Christmas.'

'If you don't button it, Matilda, and begin to show a little respect for your elders...' Juno came to a standstill, bent double on the wet pavement outside the Post Office as Peter Thompson, the local postman, began to divest the red Victorian pillar box of its contents.

'You alright, love?'

'You're not going to throw up, Mum, are you?' Tilda brought Harry Trotter to a standstill with a curt command and a single pull of the reins, peering down at her mother with a pained expression. 'That would be, like, *so* gross.'

'Yes, thank you, Peter, I'm fine.' Juno attempted a smile at the postman who'd laid a damp pale hand on her bent back. She'd been at junior school with Peter – *Pervy Pete*, Juno and her mates had dubbed him once they were in Y6 and starting to understand about such things, as well as Peter's predilection for staring at their budding bosoms through their tight, outgrown yellow aertex shirts in PE.

'And no, Tilda, I'm not going to throw up. Just got stitch that's all.' Juno made a not very successful attempt to touch her toes. While she wasn't convinced there was any medical pedagogy behind the action, it had always appeared to work in the past and, she realised too late, was having some sort of effect on Pete, clutching Westenbury's residents' mail in an increasingly clammy hand.

'You need to go to the gym with Aunty Pandora.' Tilda frowned, turning around to evaluate any traffic behind her, impatient to be off once more. '*She'd* have no problem keeping up.' And then, seeing Juno's face and mindful of wanting her to accompany her to Brian's place, she relented and, with one swift move, dismounted. 'Come on, it's only another five minutes. I'll walk Harry the rest of the way; let you get your breath back.'

Whenever she'd been down to Brian and Doreen's place, Juno always marvelled anew that her woman that *did,* so very obviously *didn't* around her own place. Too busy cleaning other people's toilets, she mused as Doreen beckoned her inside. Doreen was in the middle of making Brian's favourite steak and kidney pudding, pummelling the suet pastry into submission before deftly measuring it against the circumference of a white basin full of strong-smelling meat and, with one practised move, trimming the edges of excess pastry before throwing it haphazardly through the kitchen stable-door and out into the yard, presumably for the birds. With her hands still covered in flour, Doreen lit a Benson and Hedges and inhaled deeply. The cigarette smoke which drifted towards Juno, together with the pungent odour of fried, ripe pig's kidney, made her want to heave; she prayed she wasn't going to disgrace herself in front of Harry Trotter's friends whoever – or whatever – they might be. A white, impressively stalwart, Billy Bunter of a cat gazed malevolently at Juno out of narrowed yellow eyes from its resting place on the kitchen worktop, just a couple of inches from the floured surface on which Brian's Saturday dinner had originated. Juno hid an involuntary shudder as the cat stretched, arching its substantial back and sending a flurry of white hair towards the detritus of congealed flour and meat scraps before settling down and closing its eyes once more.

'Tea, love?' Doreen gave the cat an absentminded pat before going to fill the kettle.

'Coffee, if you have it, please.'

Doreen frowned. 'I think there's some here somewhere.' She opened a cupboard, moving a variety of sticky jam and marmalade jars to one side before pulling a dusty, ancient looking jar of Mellow Bird's instant coffee towards her with some triumph. 'Knew we had some, somewhere. Me and Brian only drink tea. Our Douglas's wife brought this with her a while back—' a hell of a while back, Juno surmised, squinting at the faded label '—because she said me and Brian were – what was it she called us? – *heathens* for not drinking coffee.'

'Right.' Juno smiled. 'Actually, Doreen, I'll just have a glass of water if you don't mind. Tilda's had me running after her and Harry and I've worked up quite a thirst.'

'So, she's persuaded you to have a couple then, has she?' Doreen squinted at Juno through a cloud of cigarette smoke. 'She's a bugger, that one, for wrapping you round her little finger and getting her own way.'

'A couple of what?' Juno's heart sank as the white cat suddenly launched from the work surface, making her way to a corner of the kitchen where a number of tiny white furry faces were stretching and mewling in anticipation of dinner.

'Sorry, love, you can't have one of Snowball's kittens. They're all taken.'

'Snowball? How original! And what a shame they're all gone.' Relief at being denied one of the colossal cat's offspring had Juno quite giddy with praise.

'Here's Myrtle, she's ready…' Doreen broke off to light up once more.

'For the pot?'

'For her new home,' Doreen finished as a particularly ugly brown chicken stepped tentatively over the doorstep, her head cocked inquisitively to one side.

'She's not very attractive, is she?'

Doreen stared at Juno. 'What do you want? Miss World?' Snowball gave a warning low-throated growl as Myrtle tiptoed forwards, lifting one graceful foot after the other.

'What do you think, Mum?' Tilda came through the open kitchen door, eyes bright with anticipation, Brian hot on her heels. 'Just think of the fresh eggs. You won't have to go out at ten o'clock at night to buy more eggs for Gabe's omelettes.'

'Oh, I don't know, Tilda. You know I'm not keen on the idea.' Snowball's mewling kittens were actually looking a better bet as Doreen, Brian, Tilda and Myrtle all squared up to Juno.

'Brian'll sort you out a coop and hen run for that paddock of yours. They'll need quite a bit of space if they're going to run around.'

'They?' Juno interrupted. 'How many is "they"?'

'Brian says we should have four to begin with,' Tilda said excitedly. 'We can have Myrtle, Miranda, Mrs Thatcher and Theresa May.'

'I'm assuming Myrtle and Miranda are Corbynites,' Juno said faintly. 'You know, to even up the political balance as it were?' She rubbed at her forehead and was surprised to find her hangover headache receding. 'To be honest, I quite like the idea of keeping hens. But,' she added as Tilda gave a whoop of triumph and high-fived Brian's outstretched hand, 'I want *nothing* to do with them, apart from collecting the eggs and throwing them a bit of grain and seed.' Juno suddenly had a romantic vision of herself as Bathsheba Everdene, Myrtle and her mates rushing to greet her whenever she came back from the surgery and was headed for the paddock. Maybe it would encourage some Gabriel Oak character into the bargain? Or, even better, a soldier in a red jacket...

'Mum...?'

'Sorry, darling?'

'Where were you? Are you still feeling poorly?' Tilda, now she'd got her own way, was obviously prepared to be solicitous, gracious even, in victory.

Being gloriously tumbled into a haystack by a rampantly red-coated Sergeant Troy was obviously not the correct response to her ten-year-old daughter. Instead, Juno smiled bravely and, gathering her woollen hat and gloves said, 'Not 100 per cent darling. Come on, lead on. Introduce me to my other girls.'

# 9

By the time Juno and Tilda arrived back home after calling at the fabulous artisan bakery and deli in the village for one of their wonderful – but ridiculously expensive – sourdough cobs, it was well after one and both of them were starving and already pulling off chunks and sharing the bread as they walked.

'You've twenty minutes before we need to go,' Juno warned as Tilda led Harry Trotter through the gate at the bottom of the paddock. 'You'll stink of horse so, once you've done what you have to do with him, jump in the shower and get your party dress on.'

'Party dress?' Tilda scoffed over her shoulder. 'I'm nearly eleven, not five.'

Juno quickly cut the remaining hunk of bread into pieces, found pate and cheese as well as marmite for Tilda and, sat with a huge mug of tea at the kitchen table, contemplated what she might do with the free Saturday afternoon ahead of her. She certainly had some medical notes to write up, there was still the ironing to attack and, really, she should go up and check on Helen and maybe take her to Sainsbury's.

Helen didn't drive much anymore; a fear of crowds, and medication that had interfered with her ability to

concentrate while in the car meant that, although her old
Fiat still sat on the drive, she very rarely had the confidence
or felt the need to wander far from home. Pandora had
taken it upon herself to be in charge of their mother and,
while both Juno and Ariadne considered Pandora bossy in
the extreme, they were most grateful that the responsibility
for Helen had been taken on by their sister. At the end of the
day, Pandora wasn't in paid employment like Ariadne and
Juno and, in the same way that Pandora had assumed total
responsibility for the sixteen-year-old Lexia, taking her to
live with them when Patrick, their father abandoned them
for Anichka, and Helen finally gave herself up to mental
illness and was sectioned, she'd taken on the mantle of care
for their mother.

'What are you up to this afternoon?' Tilda, wearing the
eleven-year-old's party uniform of black tights, faded denim
shorts, her new DM boots and hoody, spread butter and
marmite thickly on a huge chunk of bread.

'I'm just considering,' Juno said, cutting a wedge of
cheese to go with the remaining heel of the cob. 'I might
actually just lie here and read all afternoon.'

'I thought you were wanting a new bathroom?'

Juno looked suspiciously at Tilda. 'Are you wearing
makeup?'

'Of course,' Tilda retorted. 'There's no way I'm going to
Lulu's party without it.'

'But your skin is so beautiful and unmarked at your age.
I was fourteen before I wore so much as a dash of lipstick.'

'Ah, the good old days.' Tilda reached for the biscuit tin.
'This is *nothing* compared with what Emily, Martha and
Poppy will have on their faces. So, your bathroom?'

'What about it?' Juno eyed the M&S flapjacks, reached out a hand and then thought better of it.

'Don't you have to start pulling all the old stuff out? You know, ready for the new?'

'Me? No, the workmen will do that.'

'Save yourself a fortune if you did it yourself. Good exercise too.'

And so it was, once she'd dropped Tilda off at her party, Juno drove back through Westenbury calling in at the village hardware store for a wallpaper scraper, sandpaper and the bottle of yellow sugar soap the assistant advised would be needed to prepare surfaces prior to painting. While she had no intention of pulling out showers and demolishing tiles, and she accepted it was downright daft to even think about the paintwork when the old stuff hadn't been pulled out or she'd even sat down with the catalogues and chosen the new bathroom, she had a sudden urge to be a bit proactive. The old, peeling wallpaper definitely needed to come off. That's where she'd make a start.

Juno remembered helping Patrick to rub down paintwork when she was just a little girl. She must have been seven or eight and Helen hugely pregnant with Lexia. Patrick, adoring Helen's fecund, fruitful body full of promise, was happy to be at his wife's side and with his three daughters rather than straying, as was his wont with his twenty-year-old students once the reality of giving birth and crying babies replaced the tableau he created for himself as father and husband while Helen was pregnant. Juno recalled Patrick reaching out a hand to his wife's rounded belly and Helen clasping it to herself before covering it with kisses.

Ariadne, almost seventeen and already deeply suspicious of her father as well as totally embarrassed that there was yet another baby on its way, kept herself out of the way in her bedroom poring over her Classics, English and French A level studies and counting the days until she could leave for university and distance herself from what she perceived to be her father's hypocrisy and her mother's ridiculously blatant need and desire for Patrick.

All Juno could remember was how much she'd enjoyed the rubbing down of the old pink cot brought down from storage in the loft and loving being with Patrick and helping prepare the nursery for the new baby. Despite her medical training, Juno was not of the nature to wonder why, recalling her seven-year-old self, she might feel the need to rediscover that lovely feeling she'd had, working together with Patrick, having her daddy to herself for once, her father at home and so in love with her mother.

As she grew older, she eventually began to understand, and ultimately had to accept, that the wonderful father who had shown her how to rub down paintwork was actually not so admirable after all. That snapshot, of preparing for her new baby brother or sister – Juno secretly longed for a brother – was probably the most favoured she carried in her subconscious, bringing it out for a good airing in order to persuade her younger self that, really, Patrick had been a good and loving, as well as present, father. The reality that he was often absent from their lives or, when he was at home, selfishly into his own world, distant, even irritable with his offspring, Juno had never been prepared to admit even to herself and certainly not to others.

By moving to Scotland to study medicine, rather than choosing an English, more readily accessible university, she knew she was guilty of deliberately distancing herself not only from her parents' fracturing marriage but also the fallout the three older girls dreaded if Patrick ever finally made his temporary absences permanent. Juno knew she would carry the guilt that she'd abandoned her mother for the rest of her days.

Wanting to in some way assuage that guilt, Juno also knew she didn't want her own children to be at odds with their father. While she was beginning to realise she probably no longer loved Fraser as she should, she didn't want Gabriel and Tilda to suffer because of it.

Putting all thoughts of her mother's marriage, as well as the state of her own, from her mind – she was actually getting quite good at doing just this – Juno knew she was in the mood for action, to set the ball rolling towards a new bathroom. If she didn't start stripping off the old Eighties' wallpaper – did anyone have wallpaper in bathrooms anymore? – she might go off the whole idea of a new bathroom and nothing would have changed by the time Fraser was home.

After Googling how to go about stripping wallpaper, Juno searched out her oldest jeans and sweatshirt, assembled a bucket of water and her long-handled broom, a spray bottle with hot water and vinegar and, tuning her old ghetto-blaster radio to Radio 4 and the afternoon play, set to. She soaked the walls above the banana-coloured tiles thoroughly and was amazed when the decades-old rose-strewn yellow wallpaper scraped off easily. There was something incredibly gratifying about the long strips of paper that lifted, curled and fell to the bathroom floor in one piece, rather like peeling the skin from an apple in one continuous strand.

If she'd known it was going to be this easy, Juno assured her red-faced reflection in the bathroom mirror, she'd have done it immediately they'd moved in. Within an hour there was a satisfying mound of wet, yellow paper on the cork-tiled floor and Juno opened the heavy sash window slightly to let out the smell of damp paper and vinegar and went downstairs to the kitchen to put the kettle on and find the roll of black bin-bags. She glanced out of the kitchen window and watched Harry Trotter grazing peacefully at the bottom end of the paddock. Although she knew he could be an absolute ruffian, getting his kicks from terrorising walkers who took their lives into their own hands walking down the public footpath through his paddock, he appeared, this afternoon, such a well-behaved pony. She continued to stand, gazing out at the garden where, at the edges of the lawn, the daffodil bulbs had pushed out the first green shoots with their promise of the spring to come. Although cold, the afternoon was still fine and sunny, but there was quite a wind getting up and Juno watched as the cedar trees swayed and bent to the left as the breeze caught the naked boughs. Where would be the best spot for the hen coop? She'd never let on to Tilda, but she was actually beginning to feel rather excited about Myrtle and her mates being part of their family.

Juno frowned and tried to picture Fraser. It'd not been six weeks since he'd left and already it seemed like he'd been gone for ever. Did she miss him? Hand on heart, she didn't think she did. Both of them had known their marriage was just plodding along, but then, weren't all marriages like that? Juno sighed. She'd married too young, that was it. She really should have made more of an effort, suggested weekends away perhaps; date nights – wasn't that what they were called? A surprise bottle of champagne on a Friday night after work instead of a cup of tea and a catch up of Coronation Street. She wasn't yet forty for heaven's sake. Would she fancy Fraser if she met him, as he was now, today? She had a horrid feeling she wouldn't, and the thought of the next forty years spent with someone she merely rubbed along with, rather than adored, suddenly filled her with panic. She breathed deeply, took a good slurp of strong coffee and reached for those damned flapjacks in order to calm herself and make herself feel better. She really mustn't think like this; she had a lovely husband, fabulous kids and a great home – well, it would be once she'd done some of the renovations. And, really exciting, Lexia was back. She'd get to know her all over again. She made the decision to clear up the mess upstairs, have a long hot shower and then ring Fraser and tell him she loved him and was missing him. Juno made sure they spoke at least once a week without fail, but she didn't like to admit, even to herself, that she didn't look forward to the chats. She needed to make more of an effort. One did need to work at marriage after all. And tomorrow she'd find Lexia and go and visit her. Maybe take Helen.

It didn't take long to shove the piles of old soggy wallpaper – as well as rather a lot of the actual plaster that had also come down – into two binbags and then sweep the bathroom floor. Because, after discussion with the man in the bathroom shop yesterday, the new bathroom was more than likely going to be almost completely tiled, so the only real paintwork that would need doing was the actual bathroom door. Juno stood and looked at it. She remembered Patrick telling her, as he set to with a screwdriver in the nursery, that to rub down, prepare and paint a door properly, one should always remove the door handle. Only sloppy decorators painted round it. Juno knew there was, for some reason, a screwdriver in her knicker drawer – she'd no idea why – and she went through to retrieve it and soon had the handles off and a pile of screws which she took back into the bedroom with the screwdriver for safekeeping. She then spent ten minutes washing down the paintwork with the sugar soap and another twenty with the sandpaper before realising she wasn't really making much progress on that score and she'd either have to hire one of those sanding machine things or, even better, leave it to a professional decorator.

Juno sat back on her heels and surveyed her handiwork, feeling satisfied that she'd at least started the ball rolling and there was now no going back. Sweating and dirty, she cleared up as best she could and went into her bedroom and stripped off. She kicked her dirty clothes into a corner and went back to run the shower planning how she'd spend the evening. She had some episodes of *Luther* to catch up and watch but, she reminded herself, she'd been quite frightened when that mad murderer in the clown mask had crawled along the floor of the top deck of the bus to his victim in the episode she'd watched during the week. Feeling a bit spooked, her mind now wandering to the shower scene from *Psycho*, Juno hurriedly washed her hair as she tried to recall if she'd locked the back door. She had a horrid feeling she hadn't. The wind was beginning to blow a bit of a gale, the old blind she should really have taken down before stripping the wallpaper, lifting and rattling in the draft through the open window. She stopped the shower and stepped out, reaching for the towel on the wooden towel rail. Bugger. She'd taken rail and towels into the bedroom before she'd started wallpaper stripping.

A particularly strong gust of wind set the blind dancing once more and, as Juno went to close the window, the bathroom door slammed behind her at the same time as the first notes of Vivaldi's 'Spring' sounded from her mobile where she'd left it in the next room.

'I'm coming, I'm coming,' she shouted, heading, dripping and naked, for the bedroom.

Except she wasn't. Going anywhere, that is. The bathroom door, without its handles, had slammed shut imprisoning her, without a stitch on, in the now quite chilly bathroom.

Juno slid the tips of her fingers under the door and pulled. Nothing. Bugger. She rattled the metal steel cylinder through the exposed hole in the bathroom door but, without anything to grip and bite into, it simply rotated freely mocking her, it seemed, with its refusal to open the latch.

Whoever was phoning persevered once more and then there was silence. Nothing. Just the sound of Juno's breathing and the increasing stream of profanities that met the quiet of a cold, locked bathroom.

She was a prisoner. A prisoner in her own damned bathroom without a stitch of clothing, dripping hair and, because she'd thrown everything, including the towels, into the bedroom, not even a flannel or loofah to cover herself.

She glanced at her wrist and swore again at the futility of doing so; her watch was also in the bedroom and only the darkening sky, when she moved the blind to look down into the front garden, told her it must be around 5 p.m. 'I can't stay here all night.' She spoke the words out loud for the reassurance of hearing her own voice and, as she felt in vain for heat from the bathroom's one antiquated radiator, began to shiver from the cold. 'Damn, damn, damn, the sodding central heating system's playing up again. I'm bloody frozen. Perished.' Juno heard the little tremor in her voice and, crossly admonished herself. 'Get a grip, Juno. You're a grown woman, a doctor.'

She turned and stamped – as much to get her circulation going, as to frighten the lock into submission – back to the door and tried once more, patiently at first, pleading, teasing, speaking softly as she gently turned the metal thingy through the door. And then, when it refused to play ball, rattling the door and kicking its half-rubbed down paintwork with fury until the cylinder slid smoothly out and onto the bedroom floor beyond. Great stuff. Now she'd lost the effing pole thing.

Juno was just considering filling the bath and immersing herself in hot water in order to prevent death from hypothermia (she couldn't afford to die just yet; she and Fraser hadn't ever been able to agree on where the kids should end up in the event of their own untimely demise and, as such, the wills lay, incomplete, in the kitchen drawer and would more than likely remain there until Fraser's return) when there came the welcome sound of someone knocking on the kitchen door.

Oh, thank goodness. Someone was down there, in the

garden. Juno reached her fingers, numb with cold, to the old Victorian sash window once more and heaved with all her might. An icy blast of wind swept over her naked body and wet hair but, fear that whoever was down in the garden would leave, abandoning her once more to her fate as Prisoner Cell Block Bathroom, lent volume to her lungs and, taking a deep breath she yelled, 'Help, I'm up here.'

More knocking on the back door. 'Help, I'm locked in,' Juno yelled, part of her wanting to titter at the ridiculous vision of herself as Rapunzel, letting down her wet hair to whoever was in the back garden on this bitterly cold late January afternoon. 'Help, help, bloody well help, somebody...'

'Good job you'd left your back door unlocked,' Scott Butler shouted cheerfully from the other side of the bathroom door. 'Hang on, I'll just stick this cylinder back through the door and then attach the handle this side... and it should... yep, there you go... you're free. Oh, you poor little thing, you're blue with cold.' Scott turned his back, scanning Juno's bedroom for something – anything – to cover her and then, finding Fraser's old white bathrobe which she'd thrown out onto the bedroom floor together with the towels and towel rail in her eagerness to get on with stripping the wallpaper, helped ease her frozen body into its depths.

'I can do it,' Juno muttered, embarrassed.

'Don't be ridiculous.' Scott frowned. 'Trust me, I'm a doctor.' He tied the belt of the bathrobe around her waist as Juno continued to shiver and then, reaching for a towel, sat her down on the bedroom armchair wrapping it deftly and expertly turban-like around her wet hair. 'I'm surprised there aren't any icicles on the ends of your hair. There's a really raw wind out there.' He disappeared into the bathroom to close the window. 'Don't you have any heating on in this place?'

'The central heating usually clicks in up here at four.' Juno glanced across at the clock at the side of her bed. 'But for some reason it hasn't come on. The whole system is on its last legs, but I think this wind has probably blown the pilot light out on the boiler.' She looked up at Scott who was standing, arms folded across his warm navy Crombie coat and felt ridiculously underdressed as well as totally embarrassed at this rather gorgeous man finding her in such a state, and standing here now in her bedroom. 'Was that you ringing earlier?'

'Earlier?'

'About fifteen minutes ago?'

Scott frowned. 'No, I'd only just arrived, knocked a couple of times and was about to leave when I heard your shouts for help.' He grinned. 'You *will* see the funny side of this eventually, you know. So, no, I didn't know your phone number, so couldn't let you know… but thought you might be wondering where it was…'

'Where what was?' Juno stared.

'You left your briefcase in the boot of my car when I gave you the lift home after work yesterday. I only saw it myself this afternoon when I'd been to the gym and threw my bag in there.' He smiled. 'You obviously hadn't got round to thinking about work yet.'

Obviously, Juno thought. Too sodding busy trying to escape from Alcatraz. 'Oh,' she said airily, 'Monday is my day for catching up with work. That's the beauty of being part-time.'

Scott gave an involuntary shiver and looked at the bedroom door. 'Look, it really is cold up here; I'm still not used to your British weather. You're going to get ill if you don't warm up a bit. Why don't you run yourself a hot bath?'

'I'm not going back in *there*. No way.'

Scott began to laugh. 'You do realise you'll have a total phobia about locking the door on a bathroom now? You'll have to pee with the door open wherever you are.'

Juno began to giggle and then found she couldn't stop.

'Look,' Scott said, moving towards the bathroom, 'I'll run you a really hot bath, pour you a whiskey – do you have some somewhere? – and then see if I can fix the boiler and get the central heating going again.'

'Really, there's no need,' Juno half-protested. 'I'm sure you have other plans'

'Nope, not at the moment.'

'Damn.'

'What? What now?' Scott reappeared at Juno's side as she scanned the messages on her phone and the comforting sound of water filling the bath reached her ears.

'My daughter, Tilda, is out on another sleepover. She's left several messages reminding me to make sure Harry is tucked up for the night.'

'Harry?'

'Tilda's pony. I need to get him in his stable.'

'Where is he? In that paddock at the back of your garden?'

Juno nodded.

'OK, have you a torch?'

'There's one by the back door. New batteries in it. Are you sure?'

'Don't mind a bit. I like horses. Right, I'll sort him first and then come back to sort the central heating and then you can direct me towards alcohol. I think I'll need a stiff drink myself after all this drama.'

'This is really good of you.' Juno met Scott's eyes for the first time since he'd arrived. He smiled down at her and stroked her arm through her bathrobe. *Fraser's* bathrobe, she reminded herself as her heart began to quicken for some reason at his touch.

'Won't be long,' he said, before turning and leaving her bedroom.

'Be still my beating heart,' Juno muttered to herself as she braved the cold of the bathroom once more, poured half a bottle of Christmas-present-bath-stuff into the steaming contents of the old Seventies avocado bath and, shrugging off the bathrobe, slid beneath the depths and closed her eyes.

# 10

Lexia Ryan was home. Could she call Midhope, the town where she'd been born, home? Staring round at her new sitting room, devoid of any sense of thrill or expectation, she made a swift calculation: exactly half her life here in the north and then the other half in London. And now she was back. At least this house where they'd ended up wasn't in the large upmarket village of Westenbury where she'd lived as a child and where her mother still lived, and to where, amazingly, all three sisters who'd left for further education and careers had, over the years, returned. Theo had been told it was the village of choice, likening it to the area of Prestbury in Cheshire to which Manchester United footballers aspired. Unable to find anything suitable in Westenbury, on the advice of his new team mates, he'd signed a twelve-month rental on this house in the next village along, Heath Green. And for that Lexia was grateful.

It certainly didn't feel like home, although this house, that the football club had suggested to Theo when he'd told them what he was looking for, was really not that much different from the house in Essex they'd just left: another huge, five-bedroomed modern box with an overwhelming amount of space, seemingly acres of cream carpet and softly blonde wooden floors, but very little character. And not a huge amount of garden, although Theo was already sizing up the lawn for a mini football pitch for Cillian. If she'd had any choice in the matter, Lexia would have gone for something old, something a bit messy and cottagey with a few beams and an attic and maybe a cellar. If her head was in a better place she'd have insisted. Had her own way for once.

Lexia liked attics. She used to spend a lot of time up in the attic at her mum and dad's when she was fifteen and should have been doing her homework. Instead, once her dad had gone, unable to take being with her mum any longer, Lexia would leave Helen Sutherland sitting staring into space in the kitchen, unable to finish the makeshift supper Lexia had made for them both – she seemed to remember beans on toast often featured – and make her way to the top of the house. There, in the musty warmth or the freezing cold of the winter that followed her dad's leaving, she would sing. And sing. Lexia smiled to herself remembering belting out Shakira's 'Whenever, Wherever' and doing a pretty good hip roll into the bargain. But her favourite singer, the one she aspired to, was Holly Valance. With her long straight blonde hair and big brown eyes, Lexia knew she could do a pretty good take of the Australian star and also knew that one day, one day, she would be as big a star, if not bigger, than Holly Valance herself.

Lexia and Juno had always sung and been sung to by their mother but Ariadne, her eldest sister was almost seventeen years older than Lexia and, once Lexia was of an age to appreciate her eldest sister's presence in the family home, Ariadne was already off to Cambridge and Lexia had never been really sure if she'd been able to sing like the others. Pandora, she knew, was a particularly good singer. In the months when Lexia had to go and live with her, after that awful January day she'd come home to find her mum wearing nothing but a pair of lilac knickers and slashing furiously with the huge kitchen knife at the rusty heads of the previous summer's roses, Pandora was in rehearsal for an amateur production of the Mikado. From the minute she woke, Pandora had practised scales, her true-pitched Soprano reaching every corner of the smart, large detached house she and Richard had moved into two years previously, until Lexia had wanted to strangle bloody Yum Yum and her sodding repertoire of songs.

Lexia sighed, pushing the unwelcome memories from her mind, schooling herself back into the present. It was Sunday, they'd already been in the new house three days and, really, she'd done very little to help sort things. Even the removal men had done more than she had, skilfully manoeuvring their furniture and belongings into the rooms specified on the huge tea chests packed, just as expertly, by the company in London. She'd probably over-tipped them hugely of course, but what was money?

This was a new beginning. She was home. Lexia glanced at the kitchen clock and realised, once again, she'd been sitting there for almost an hour. Just staring into space. Thinking. She knew she had to face her mum. She was desperate to see her, to take Cillian over to meet his grandmother for the first time, but her pulse raced at the very thought. She'd left it too long, hadn't she? What if her mum refused to see her?

Lexia had given Cillian his breakfast and then, almost giddy with excitement, he'd set off with Theo down to the Midhope Town football ground in order that Theo could show him where his dad was going to be playing from then on. Although Cillian was an out and out Manchester United fan first, and a Chelsenal fan second – having been spoiled rotten down at Theo's old club – he'd pulled on the rather too big blue and white Midhope Town football shirt Theo had been given for Cillian at his first meeting with the club's boss, manager and trainers, and raced down the drive to the Porsche and off with Theo without a backward glance at Lexia.

Lexia climbed the stairs slowly, stopping at the window on the landing to take in the view over the village of Heath Green and beyond. She could just make out the distant rooftops and trees of Westenbury, the village where'd she'd been born and lived until she was sixteen. The January morning was unusually bright, the duck-egg blue sky interrupted only intermittently by lazily-moving cirrus clouds and the condensation trails of jets on their way to who knew where, as well as several planes already making their descent to both Manchester and, towards the east, Leeds Bradford airport.

The door to one of the spare bedrooms – she'd been insistent, to Theo's surprise, that Cillian shouldn't have what, in effect, was the second biggest bedroom – was firmly closed and Lexia meant to keep it that way. She wouldn't be standing at *that* window, gazing out over the fields at the view beyond, as she was now doing, and happy to do, from the landing window.

There was no way she was going to look across at the view from that spare bedroom. It was beautiful, far superior to that from the master bedroom suite, the rolling fields and farmland morphing seamlessly to the woodland beyond and on to Norman's Meadow, the particularly beautiful wildflower meadow on the edge of the village.

Lexia knew that taking in that view, those verdant fields and beautiful meadows she'd kept away from for the last sixteen years, would, however sublime, send her into a complete and utter state of panic.

'You're not telling me, you *still* haven't spoken to your mum? Or your sisters? For fuck's sake, Lexia, they're your *family*. What *is* your problem?'

'Shh, will you?' Lexia hissed, indicating with a nod of her head Cillian at the other end of the room, eating a roast beef sandwich while engrossed in some cartoon on the cinema-sized TV. It was like, Lexia had thought, once it was installed by a team of three technicians the previous day, something out of a dystopian, futuristic world. Everywhere she moved, it seemed to follow and watch her; maybe this *was* the future.

Theo Ryan glanced up from a text, a slight smile on his face as he read. He did a double take, staring at his wife. For the first time in months, she'd made an effort with herself. Her long blonde hair, admittedly needing a good cut and the roots seeing to, was clean and shiny, hanging in a soft curtain to beyond her shoulders rather than carelessly pulled back in a greasy knot at the back of her head. She was wearing a short skirt that showed off her long slim legs encased in black woollen tights, together with expensive-looking flat leather brogues, and she was wearing makeup for the first time in ages. She was too thin – Theo Ryan liked his women with a bit of meat on them – but he could see the young girl he'd lusted over and chased when she was at the height of her fame, regaling her with flowers and expensive presents until she'd begun to drop her guard and he'd been able to persuade her he was what she needed in her life.

What a pair they'd made: Theo Ryan and Lexia – the golden couple, up there together with David and Victoria Beckham and Ashley and Cheryl Cole. Constantly in the tabloids and able to command huge sums from *Hello!* and *OK!* magazines just for lying round on a sofa in their sitting room or bedroom in designer clothes, and having their photographs taken.

Shame Lexia had blown it all, starting to show a different side to herself after several years together, but totally losing it once she found she was pregnant and had given birth to Cillian, refusing to have anything to do with the pop world any longer, despite eye-watering sums of money being offered to her for come-back tours, or even photo sessions with Cillian. She'd dismissed the lot of them out of hand without even consulting him.

'You know as well as I do,' Lexia snapped, 'I've had nothing to do with any of my family since I left here sixteen years ago. My dad's an adulterous old dog who sent my mum mad with his screwing around. I hardly know Ariadne, and neither she nor Juno were ever around for me when I needed them.'

'They came to see you,' Theo protested. 'In London. They made a big effort to find you and to try to work something out with you.'

'But not when I *needed* them. Not when I was just fifteen… Anyway, I sent my mum flowers.'

'Big deal. A couple of stupidly expensive bunches of flowers in sixteen years? Sure, look at it, Lexia, how could you treat your mammy like that? Especially when she wasn't well? You really are one selfish bitch.' Superior in the knowledge that he rang his widowed mother every week without fail and had taken on the responsibility for the upkeep of the neat little house he'd bought her in County Clare on the west coast of Ireland as well as sending her, with her sister, on her annual fortnightly holiday to Portugal, Theo could afford to be self-righteous in his familial benevolence.

'Do you mind not calling me names like that?' Lexia was angry. 'Cillian already hears things he shouldn't and takes your side. *I* don't stand a chance trying to bring him up as a normal little boy when you're encouraging him to think he's going to be the next football superstar and using foul, locker room language in front of him.'

Theo laughed mirthlessly, taking another look at his mobile before reaching for his leather jacket and car keys. '*You* don't stand a chance with him, Lexia, because *you've* let a whole string of au pairs bring him up while you've wandered around the place cushioned on a fog of tranquilisers.'

'Yes, well,' Lexia snapped back with more conviction than she felt, 'I'm here for him now. We don't need any au pair.'

'Lexia, you've not even sorted out a damned *school* for Cillian. Did you look at the school brochures the club sent me?' Theo frowned, looking at his watch before glancing round the sitting room for the large white envelope which contained the booklets for the various private schools in the area. 'Apparently, Greave House School is the favourite. Quite a few of the team send their kids there, although they tell me they go further afield to Leeds or Wakefield at eleven.'

'He's going to the local school,' Lexia said quietly.

'Sorry?'

'Little Acorns. It's the primary school I went to – we *all* went to. I can walk him down there myself.'

'You're never *up* at school time, so don't give me that, Lexia. Greave House is on the way to the training ground. I can drop him off at school every morning.'

'You're *not* driving him, Theo. I don't want him in the car with you. And don't look at me like that... you know why. No, he's going to the local primary with all the other kids round here.' Lexia was adamant, meeting Theo's glare with one sustained look of her own. 'He's not getting dressed up in the same poncy cap and blazer you insisted on in London.'

'Up to you, Lexia. I'm off, got a meeting with the gaffer...' He headed for the door, intent on making his exit before Cillian realised and clamoured to go with him.

'On a Sunday lunchtime?'

'... But I tell you this for nothing. If Cillian's not in school, *every* day and on time, I'll pull him and make the arrangements myself.'

It hadn't taken Theo long, Lexia sighed, to be off sniffing round other women again now that he had a whole new fan base up here in Midhope. Trouble was, and knowing this she sighed again more heavily, she really didn't care. At all. If it kept him away from *her* with his constant criticising of her, all well and good. Women had always loved Theo's laid-back manner, his easy charm; he was so good at making you feel you were the only one. Hadn't he been that way with her in the early years of their relationship? He'd loved buying clothes for her. He seemed to know just what would make her look good, although – here, she frowned at the recollection – there had been occasions when the outfits he'd wanted her to wear were a bit too revealing, a bit *too* short and scanty.

Lexia glanced across at Cillian who was now opening the bag of Maltesers Theo had bought for him. 'Only two of those, no more, Cillian. They're not good for your teeth.'

Ignoring her completely, Cillian reached into the bag for more chocolate, shoving two into his mouth at once, laughing with a mouth full of sugar at something on the TV.

Lexia sat and just looked at her child. He was stunningly beautiful, she knew that, with the blonde hair and huge brown eyes inherited from her mother's side of the family. And he was everything to her – he was the one good thing in her life. She had to face it, he *was* her life.

But she hadn't wanted him. Hadn't wanted a baby at all. She and Theo had been married almost six years when, worn down by Theo's constant haranguing of her for them to have the footballing son he craved, she finally gave in and came off the pill. Lexia assumed getting pregnant wouldn't happen overnight but, to her dismay and Theo's absolute delight, she – as they say up north – 'caught on' almost immediately. She'd hated being pregnant, hated the pain and ignominy of giving birth and hadn't felt a huge deal once the tiny baby that was Cillian was put, squalling, into her arms.

Now though, she absolutely adored him and she was trying so hard to be a proper mother to him. Lexia knew if Nika were here, the bag of Maltesers would have been taken from him. Standing up, she walked over to Cillian, removed the bag of warm, melting chocolates to her pocket and, ignoring any potential tantrum, said, firmly, 'OK, Buster, let's go.'

Twenty minutes later, Lexia had them both dressed in warm coats, boots and gloves.

'Where are we going?' Cillian whined as she fastened up the top button of his navy duffle coat and sat him down once more to change his boots over to the correct feet.

'We're going to my see my mum.' Lexia kissed her son's head with more conviction than she felt.

'Your *mum*? You've got a *mummy*?' Cillian looked up at her in some wonder from beneath his ridiculously long eyelashes.

'Of course.'

Cillian stared. 'Have I seen her?'

'Well, no, darling. She hasn't been very well and wasn't able to come and see us in London. It's such a long way away. You know that.'

Cillian frowned. 'But Nanna Ryan lives in another *country* and I've seen *her*. *And* she talks to me on the phone. *And* she sends me birthday presents and Christmas presents.'

'Well, we're going to walk over there now. To see her.'

'Is she very poorly? Is she in a hostipal? Does she need an annabalance?'

Lexia smiled despite her racing pulse that was beginning to make her feel sick. Should she take another lorazepam? 'No, darling, she's at home, not in *hospital* and she certainly doesn't need an *ambulance*.' Well, she didn't think she did.

'Mummy, it's a long way. My feets are hurting me and it smells funny.' Cillian was beginning to whine once more, dragging his feet as they walked.

'That's the countryside for you. So much better than the smell of cars and buses.'

'But I *like* cars and buses. I *love* the smell in Dad's car. I don't like this smell. Pooooo.' Cillian dropped his hand from her gloved one and held on to his nose.

Lexia smiled. 'They've been muckspreading.'

'Who has?'

'The farmers. They put cow and pig poo onto the fields to make the crops grow.'

'Yuck, that's horrible.' Momentarily distracted from his feet at this revelation of what country folk got up to, Cillian trotted along in silence beside her.

Sixteen years on and, really, the house didn't look that much different. Smaller maybe, and the red-painted front door Lexia remembered her dad meticulously rubbing down, before becoming bored and disappearing for the weekend, certainly was due for some TLC. Lexia stood a couple of yards from the garden gate, willing herself to go through it, her feet seemingly rooted to the lane she and Cillian had just walked down.

'A cat. Mum, a cat.' Cillian let go of Lexia's hand and bent to stroke the huge arthritic-looking ginger tom that was now weaving its furry limbs through both their legs. Lexia stared down at the creature, unable to believe it could be Hercules, the kitten Patrick Sutherland had brought home just a couple of weeks before he himself had finally left for good. Whether he'd intended the kitten's introduction – into a household that had never, before, had so much as a goldfish as a pet – as compensation for his own, planned departure, it was never clear, but Helen had lavished the stultifying love and attention onto Hercules denied her by Patrick's final and absolute relinquishing of the marriage.

'Hercules?' Lexia bent down, running her fingers through the animal's fur as the cat closed his eyes in ecstasy.

'Curilees? Is that what he's called?'

'Hercules.' Lexia smiled, feeling some of the tension and anxiety begin to leave as she continued to stroke the cat. Maybe this is what she needed – wasn't there some proof that caring for animals could temper mental illness? 'Come on.' She took a deep breath and walked through the gate, up the path and towards the door, Cillian, gazing round at the unkempt garden, at her side. Should she knock?

Lexia tapped lightly on the red paint then, on impulse, turned the handle and went straight in, walking down the hall's threadbare Persian rug of her childhood and through to the kitchen beyond.

'Mum?'

Shy for once, Cillian grabbed Lexia's hand, burrowing his hand into her coat pocket, intent on keeping as close to her as was humanly possible while the old lady standing at the sink turned to stare. Her hair, Lexia saw at once, was quite grey and, although the beautiful blonde tresses that Patrick had loved to run his fingers through were no longer her mother's crowning glory, her hair was still luxurious, hanging in one long plait down her back, jauntily adorned with a pink spotted silk scarf. Helen's eyes, the beautiful brown eyes that had always been such a contrast to the fair hair, were still her mother's, still darkly luminous, but no longer filled with the sadness and tears that Lexia seemed only able to recall when she needed to conjure up her mother's features.

'Lexia?'

Helen Sutherland put out a hand as if to reach out to her youngest daughter but then, with a laugh that was half a sob, rushed over to Lexia, pulling her into thin arms and holding her tightly, their grip belying the insubstantial look of her limbs.

Lexia closed her eyes, breathing in the faint, but oh so familiar smell of the Arpège perfume Patrick had apparently brought Helen on their very first date, and which she continued to use even now, almost fifty years on. It was going to be alright; her mum had forgiven her. She felt safe.

Helen finally released Lexia from her grasp, holding her at arm's length while she studied her face intently. 'Oh, but you are so beautiful, my darling girl. You're just like your pictures...'

'Pictures?' Lexia smiled.

'You know, in the magazines? I've got them all. Cut them out and kept them.' Without another word, she quickly turned, disappearing through the door to the sitting room while Cillian, whom she'd not yet acknowledged, gazed after her in wonder.

'Here. Look.' Helen returned, a huge smile on her face, her arms full of scrap books and photograph albums. 'They're all you. All of you, Lexia...' She placed them carefully on the kitchen table and suddenly sat down heavily in the armchair by the ancient Aga, staring at Cillian. 'And you... you must be Cillian. Oh, but you are such a little man.'

'I'm quite a big man really,' Cillian said seriously. 'And I'm going to be a famous footballer, like my dad.'

'I bet you are.' Helen reached forward, stroking Cillian's face, drinking him in. 'Oh, Lexia, I can't believe you're here. That you've come back... You are back for good, aren't you?'

'Well, Theo has signed a twelve-month contract. We're renting a house in Heath Green.' Lexia hesitated. 'How *are* you, Mum? Are you... you know, are you OK?'

'Oh, darling, I have my good days and my bad, the good more now than the bad. You know?' Helen's face dropped for a few seconds and then she smiled. 'Cake. We must have cake. Would you like cake, Cillian? Oh, but I must ring your sisters and tell them you're here. Have you seen them, darling?'

Lexia shook her head, obviously distressed at the lack of contact with her family, but also feeling a certain resentment knowing, as she did, that she wasn't totally to blame for this. 'Mum, I want Cillian to go to Westenbury C of E – it's called Little Acorns now, isn't it? – like we all did.'

Her mother almost clapped her hands. 'Oh, that's wonderful. You'll like it there,' she added for Cillian's benefit. 'Your cousin, Matilda, goes there.'

'Is she a big girl?' Cillian looked a little fearful, remembering the bigger, noisier boys at his prep school in London.

'Well, yes, I suppose she is. She's a very *clever* girl.' Helen frowned, shaking her head. 'She knows some *stuff,* that girl. She's very much like Ariadne was at her age – nothing like Juno at all, really. Now, I'm going to ring Juno and Ariadne and Pandora, tell them to get over here as quick as they can...'

'Mum, do you mind? Not Pandora.'

'Not Pandora? But why not, darling? Why ever not?'

Lexia hesitated, not knowing how to reply. 'Erm, it's just that I've been in touch with Ariadne and Juno over the years – they came to see me in London, you know – and I've not had any contact at all with Pandora.'

'I know, I know. I insisted they find you. Why *have* you kept away all this time, Lexia? Was it my fault? Was it because of... you know...?'

'No, Mum, no.' Lexia almost shouted the words. 'It's all been *my* fault. You did *nothing* wrong. And then, as time went on, it became harder to get in touch. And then I wasn't very well...' She trailed off, unable to continue as tears started at the back of her nose and she felt her breathing accelerate. She tried to breathe deeply, not wanting Cillian to see her like this. 'Look, Mum, I really want to see Juno and Ariadne. Would you ring them? Now? And tell them I'm here? And then,' she smiled at Helen, 'we'd love some cake, wouldn't we, Cillian?'

# 11

Juno woke early on the Sunday morning following the bathroom lock-in debacle to the extremely pleasant realisation that, not only was she totally alone in the house but that she was loving every single minute of the experience; she was alone but no way was she lonely. There was no Fraser clearing his throat on the way to the bathroom, no having to avert her senses after following him in there – she'd never known another human be so regular, and so, so prolifically *productive* in his toilet habits – and, best of all, there was no conversation to have to make: Did you sleep OK? How's your stiff toe this morning? Leave that shirt out and I'll put it in the wash...

There was no one to tell her what to do, no one to make demands on her time. She had a couple of hours at least until the kids were back from their weekend jaunts, filling the house with their noise and their arguments, issuing demands on her time. For at least two hours, she was free to do exactly as she pleased and, for the first time, perhaps ever, Juno was starting to understand how Ariadne relished her independence and freedom. Her eldest sister, she knew, had never wanted the constraints of just the one man and children in her life, being totally at one with her own company, and with the confidence to set off whenever she wanted, travelling the world, often in her camper van, that the long school holidays from her teaching job afforded.

Juno jumped out of bed and walked over to the window where the February dawn was heralding the promise of a fine, but cold, day ahead. She usually hated winter, hated battling the cold under the layers of warm sweaters, coat and scarves she'd had to don to face the long and often excruciatingly cold Aberdeen winters, but today she felt different. The high winds from last night had dropped leaving, in their stead, a slight covering of frost which, by the time she was up and about would be gone.

Juno caught her reflection in the mirror as she turned from the window. She looked the same: her favourite red spotty pyjamas, her hair the usual blonde, tousled nest that needed a daily taming with a hot brush, the same large brown eyes all four of the girls had inherited from Helen, their mother. Juno smiled, baring her teeth at herself. It wasn't, she knew, the idea of a couple of hours to herself, nor was it the beautifully cold but bright morning, with its promise of a lovely day ahead, that was totally and utterly lifting her senses and having her out of bed while a never-experienced-before sense of utter excitement and terror filled every fibre of her being.

She was in love.

There, she'd admitted it to herself.

'I'm in love.' She said the three little words out loud for effect, the sentence forming easily and unbidden, slipping out, floating above her head and smiling down at her as she continued to stare at her reflection. 'Bloody hell. For the first time in your life, Juno Armstrong, you're in love. In love with a man that's not your husband.'

Did the mere *thought* of such, without any accompanying action, make her guilty of being unfaithful to Fraser? Juno pulled on her dressing gown, turned off the burglar alarm and made her way down to the kitchen and the kettle. Oh Jesus, was she her father's daughter after all? Was this how Patrick had felt each time it had started once again, despite all the recriminations from, and promises to, her mother? That intoxicating, addictive flirtation, the catching of the eye of one of his students, the hand on the arm, the knowing smile, that had him falling in love yet again? Maybe Patrick had been an addict in the same way one became addicted to alcohol? As a doctor, she felt much sympathy for both the men and women who turned up in her surgery, particularly after a bender when their family could take no more, asking, begging, for help. Alcoholism was an illness, often passed on genetically through families. What if she'd caught her father's compulsion to fall in love?

Juno smiled at her thoughts, too happy to care as to *why* she was feeling this way. She just *was*, that was all, and Patrick and his infidelities over the years were really nothing to do with her. Patrick had ruined her mother's life, but only because Helen Sutherland had *allowed* him to, taking her adulterous husband back again and again, believing everything he said when he promised 'never again'. Juno had no doubt Patrick meant it at the time, meant it when he said all he wanted was to be with Helen and his four girls, but he was an addict, a slave to that wonderful feeling of falling head over heels in love.

Juno frowned as she poured milk into her mug and

stirred. Had she ever been *in love* with Fraser? She frowned again, recalling the first sight of her husband in one of the laboratories at university in Aberdeen. He was studying for a PhD in Chemistry and was intent on some research figures, hunched over his notes at the front of the lab and muttering to himself over something that wasn't coming together as it should. An hour earlier, starving and with her mind only on the best means of sating her hunger with cheaply-bought carbohydrates at one of the many cafés around the university, Juno had dashed out to avoid the lunchtime rush and queues, leaving her file with all her precious notes where she'd been sitting. Fraser hadn't even noticed it, pushing it absentmindedly to the end of the bench, and didn't look up as Juno returned, appetite quietened, to find it.

'Oh, thank goodness,' she'd said, 'you've found it.'

Fraser had looked up from his notes, confused. 'Found it? Found what?'

Juno had taken in the pale face, the reddish-blonde hair standing up at ninety degrees from where Fraser had pulled tense fingers through its ends, smiled at his puzzled face and, when he appeared not to really notice her, had picked up the file and left without giving him a second thought or a backward glance.

She and Fraser had got together at some party, several months later. Juno remembered him vaguely, knew she'd seen him somewhere before previously, but it had taken all evening for her to finally put a memory to his face. Fraser himself didn't have a clue, so little impact had she made on him at their first encounter. This was when Juno was in her penultimate year at Aberdeen and worried that she wasn't keeping up, that she wasn't going to make the grade; in a state of indecision about where she wanted to actually end up and not even convinced that being a doctor – a GP possibly – was what she really wanted to be anyway. And always, always at the back of her mind, nagging away, was the knowledge that she might be better off at home in Yorkshire, making sure her mother stayed out of hospital.

She knew she wasn't in love with Fraser. She spent much of her time at Aberdeen only just keeping her head above water with regards the gruelling, almost unsurmountable amount of work she had to get through and was seriously on the verge, near her finals, of jacking it all in and coming back to Yorkshire to be with her mum. Any indecision regarding a long-term future with this quietly serious, sardonic man was neatly taken from her when just after her finals and a bout of food poisoning – she'd not touched mussels since – she'd obviously flushed the required protection of her contraceptive pill down the loo along with the rogue mollusc. Gabriel was the result. Fraser supposed they ought to get married. Juno supposed that they should. And so, they did.

Really, Juno thought, going off at a tangent as she sipped her tea curled up in her favourite kitchen armchair, it was no wonder Tilda was such a bossy little brainbox with a research chemist for a father as well as having a grandfather who, at the end of the day, as well as his reputation as a lothario, was also Professor of Classics. Thank goodness that Tilda appeared, so far, to be keeping fairly well grounded through her love of horses and hens – her paternal grandmother's genes coming to the fore there, Juno supposed.

Recalling the embarrassment of being locked in her own bathroom, Juno laughed aloud into the warmth of the empty kitchen at the memory of the previous evening: her trying to get back some warmth into her frozen extremities in the hot bath, desperate to cover up her spare tyre and floating bosom in the bubbles when Scott had reappeared, somewhat dishevelled and red-faced, after a good fifteen minutes chasing Harry Trotter around the paddock in order to lock him up for the night.

Scott had gone back downstairs in order to give her some privacy and, once Juno had finally got the circulation going in her frozen hands and feet, she'd hastily pulled on a pair of jeans that didn't make her backside appear *too* big. She'd scrabbled through the wardrobe for her favourite navy polo-necked sweater and brushed her blonde hair into submission before feverishly adding blusher, smudged eyeliner around her large brown eyes and painted a pinkish lipstick onto her full mouth.

Downstairs, Scott had found the whiskey, poured a couple of fingers for both of them and was engrossed in reading messages on his phone.

'I don't know what I'd have done if you hadn't come round,' Juno said almost tearfully as the ramifications of being locked in a freezing bathroom all night suddenly crowded into her brain. 'Do you reckon I could have died? You know, frozen to death?'

'Don't be daft. Someone would have heard your shouts in the end. Where are your children? They'd have been home, eventually, wouldn't they?'

Juno shook her head. 'No, that's the thing: Matilda – she's my ten-year-old – isn't due to be picked up from her sleepover birthday party until tomorrow morning. She's got a better social life than me at the moment. And Gabriel – he's almost thirteen – he's gone off on some geography field trip to Morecambe with school for the weekend. He's not back until Monday evening.' Juno laughed, knew she was speaking too fast, twittering almost. She shivered slightly. 'Blimey, I could have died of hypothermia. I mean, I don't know how many hot baths I could have kept drawing – with the flame blown out on the central heating it wouldn't have taken long for the hot water to run out.'

'Good job I came round then.' Scott grinned, eyeing Juno over his glass.

Gosh, he really was quite gorgeous was this man standing in her sitting room, drinking her husband's whiskey and grinning down at her.

'So, Dr Armstrong, are you safe to be left by yourself?'

Juno felt herself go pink. Was Scott Butler flirting with her? Was he asking to stay for the evening? It was such a long time since anyone had flirted with her, looked her up and down, as this man was now doing, she wasn't quite sure if that was his intention. Fraser, she admitted to herself sadly, had never once flirted with her. He just wouldn't have known how.

'Erm, are you hungry?' Juno had finally asked. 'Can I make you something to eat?'

Scott had put his glass down, then turned and walked up to her, taking her own empty glass from her hand. The shock when his hand briefly touched hers was electric.

'I'm starving,' he'd said, his beautiful green eyes holding hers. 'But I'm just on my way out to dinner. Your place was on the way – that's why I called in with your briefcase. If you're sure you're not going to lock yourself in again, I'd best be on my way.' He'd smiled at her, stroked her arm fleetingly and headed for the door. 'See you next week.'

Juno now got up from her chair only to pour more tea

and then, with some difficulty, made herself stop reliving last night's little drama with Scott. Instead, she concentrated her thoughts on Lexia. Did her mother know she was probably coming back to the area? It might cheer her up a bit if she knew her youngest daughter was coming home. Juno was certain her reaction would be totally different to that of Pandora's when she'd called round to borrow the cake tin. She'd never understood the way Pandora constantly bad-mouthed Lexia, refusing to keep in touch with her once she'd left sixteen years previously. Pandora, married just a couple of years, had taken Lexia in and given her a home for more than four months at the age of fifteen when their mother, distraught at Patrick's leaving her for Anichka, had finally given in to the breakdown she'd been threatening most of their childhood and been sectioned.

Mind you, Juno thought to herself, perhaps it was Lexia herself who was to blame for this huge and relentless yawning rift between her and Pandora; she'd never appeared grateful for Pandora and Richard's help at a time when Pandora, pregnant with Hugo, had stepped in and tried to be a mother to their youngest sister. Juno knew she herself wasn't totally without blame either. She'd always felt very guilty that she'd stayed away, up in Aberdeen, during the time their mother was in hospital, but she was twenty-two and in the third year of her medical degree and desperately trying to keep her head above water as she struggled with the workload. She'd made the journey back to Yorkshire to see Helen, their mother, several times, but Helen didn't appear to want to see any of them – they weren't Patrick – and Lexia was a sullen fifteen-year-old who made it abundantly clear she didn't *like* any of her family or want to *be* with any of them either. As far as she knew, Lexia had had no contact with Patrick since then, despite his trying to make amends for his defection from the family; perhaps, as the youngest and still very much in need of her daddy, she'd seen his departure as a personal affront to herself.

Juno's thoughts came back constantly to Lexia and her past. While, as far as she knew, Lexia had not once been back to Yorkshire since she left for London when she was just sixteen, and Helen and Pandora certainly hadn't seen her since, both Ariadne and she had kept some contact – albeit minimal – with their baby sister. Lexia was the only one of them born up here when Patrick's job as Professor of Classics brought him from a stint in London, after Oxford, to Manchester University when Ariadne was fourteen, Pandora ten and herself just five and, while Lexia was now thirty-two, the elder three, nonetheless, still considered her to be the baby.

Several years ago – it must have been quite a while before Cillian, Lexia's four-year-old, was born – Ariadne and Juno, unhappy at the family rift and lack of any contact from Lexia, had set off to London for the weekend to find her. Not *find* her, exactly. They did have an address from their mother's elder sister – Aunt Georgina – with whom Lexia had stayed as a sixteen-year-old when she first left for London and eventual stardom through winning *TheBest*. They knew that Lexia and Theo were living in some horrible gated complex in Essex, some huge modern pile with swimming pool, gym and a ridiculous number of upmarket cars in the drive, and so took the train from Wakefield to Kings Cross and then a taxi to the address given to them and, basically, just turned up.

To be fair, Lexia did seem pleased to see them. At this point she was probably at the height of her fame and had already left Gals for a solo career. Her adoring fans knew her simply as Lexi and you couldn't pass through WHSmith without images of their little sister staring down from the front cover of every conceivable magazine. Which was totally weird.

While she *was* pleased to see them, and Ariadne and Juno met their brother-in-law, ace footballer Theo Ryan, for the very first time and Lexia really did want to know how Helen was, she made little reference to Patrick – apart from scathing remarks as to his new wife, Anichka being 'the Russian Pole Dancer' – and absolutely none to Pandora.

Ariadne and Juno stayed for a couple of hours. They were taken on a tour of the house by Theo – soulless and quite dispiriting without one single book on view in any of the many rooms – while Lexia made coffee in some expensive looking built-in machine, and then had left without achieving their goal: for Lexia to promise she'd come back up to Yorkshire to see Helen, to at least introduce her new husband to the family and to stay in contact. She did continue sending her mother birthday cards and, twice, ridiculously over-the top bouquets of flowers, but that trailed off after a couple of years. They only got to know Lexia was pregnant and had given birth to a little boy, Cillian, when it was splashed all over the media and, at the same time, had become the name behind a new line of baby and toddler clothes – Lexi Baby – brought out by M&S.

Juno glanced at the kitchen clock. She realised, with a start, she'd been sitting thinking, daydreaming about the good doctor and then about Lexia for a solid hour, and if she and Ariadne were going to find Lexia's place and pay her the visit they'd been planning on, she needed to get a move on. A staccato of bangs and knocking coming from the direction of the paddock had her on her feet, pulling her dressing gown around her and heading for the back door.

'Oh, Brian? You're up and at it early for a Sunday morning.' Juno peered round the door, not wanting Brian Goodall to see her still in her night clothes.

'Aye, well, the chucks are ready for their new home.' He indicated, with a nod of his head and a large lethal-looking hammer in his hand, the rusting green Land Rover parked at the bottom end of the paddock near the five-barred wooden gate. 'I've driven them over and they've been in a *foul* mood all morning.' Juno started to laugh but realised Brian's demeanour and words were totally without humour. 'I've got to make the coop secure – you don't want the bloody foxes thinking there's a new takeaway in the village.'

Juno smiled at that. 'Hang on, let me get my wellies on. I want to say hello to my new girls.'

Brian tutted as Juno reappeared in Fraser's ancient black Barbour, her red spotty pyjamas stuffed into the pink wellies she'd inherited from somewhere. 'Car door's not locked, but don't let 'em out yet,' he called after her as she made her way to the bottom of the paddock, one eye on Harry Trotter who gazed, uninterested, in her direction several yards away, and one eye on the fence she'd have to vault if he suddenly changed his mind and headed her way.

'Hello, ladies, how're you doing?' Juno pressed her nose against the window of the Land Rover. Moaning Myrtle – she thought that was her – glared back at her, obviously cross at being incarcerated in the back of the car. 'I do hope you're going to like it here.'

Life, Juno thought to herself, as she breathed in the cold morning air and smiled at her girls, was really quite lovely.

'We have to go to Granny's.' An hour later, Juno was being glared at by the biggest and bolshiest of her girls. Really, Moaning Myrtle wasn't even in the running when it came to Sunday morning cross-patches devoid of sleep and good humour after a birthday party sleepover with friends.

A stream of mothers – and several fathers – was ushering its offspring towards waiting cars. Hungover with a surfeit of sugar, back-to-back movies and lack of sleep, ten bleary-eyed pubescents, yawning and rubbing at their eyes, appeared one by one, passing through their host's front door still in the pyjamas and onesies of the previous night. The procession reminded Juno of that bit in *Far From the Madding Crowd* when Sergeant Troy gives all the farm workers free alcohol to celebrate his wedding to Bathsheba. The next morning the farm hands troop out, a shambolic, hungover line of drunks met by their cross wives. Juno smiled at the analogy. What was it with her and Thomas Hardy at the moment?

'Granny's? Oh Mum, no. I'm sooooo tired. I want to go *home*.'

'Your Aunt Lexia and your cousin Cillian are there,' Juno said.

'Really?'

'Yep. Granny rang just before I set off. We're meeting her there with Aunt Ariadne.'

'I can't go like this, dressed like a badger.' Tilda pulled a face, spitting on a finger and rubbing at a pink patch on her onesie. 'Raspberry sauce,' she added for Juno's benefit.

'I can't go and meet a world-famous icon dressed like a badger with raspberry sauce down my front.'

'*Icon*? Where *do* you learn such words?' Pulling up at a junction, Juno glanced across at her daughter.

'It just comes naturally to me,' Tilda said seriously, still rubbing at the patch. 'I see and read a word somewhere and then it just seems to hang around in my brain until there's an opportunity to use it. I'm very lucky really.' She paused. 'I just hope I'm not peaking too early.' She paused again and then went on, 'Mr Donnington says I'm very probably gifted and talented.'

Juno tutted, accelerating to overtake a party-goer's BMW which was pulled over onto the hard shoulder to allow its ten-year-old to part company with the remains of the chocolate muffins, salt and vinegar crisps and pizza imbibed seemingly nonstop throughout the evening. 'Oh dear,' Juno sympathised, 'better out than in.' She glanced across at Tilda. 'Are *you* OK? How ridiculous, allowing you girls to eat so much before you went to bed. And Mr Donnington has absolutely *no* right to tell you such things. It will just make you big-headed and full of yourself.'

'Well, Mr Donnington says—'

'Enough, Tilda. I'm *not* interested. Look, there's Aunt Ariadne in front of us. Isn't this exciting? Just give your hair a bit of a brush—' Juno peered at her daughter as they pulled up at her former family home '—and rub that black from under your eyes. Best behaviour please: say hello, and how are you? And don't forget to give Granny a kiss.'

Ariadne jumped out of her car in front of them and actually ran into the house so that, by the time Juno and Tilda made their way along the hall way and into the kitchen, Ariadne and Lexia were wrapped round each other, their mother standing smiling at their side but with tears rolling down her face.

'Why?' Ariadne was saying. 'Why on earth have you kept away from us for all these years? Not sent any phone numbers or forwarding addresses or replied to letters once we did know where you were? A few measly Christmas cards, Lexia?'

'I know, I know… I'm sorry… Juno? Oh Juno.' Lexia flung herself into Juno's arms, hugging her until Juno felt the very breath would be squeezed out of her.

'And this is Cillian?' Juno managed to loosen the arms around her, enough to smile down at the blonde-haired little boy who was standing in awe, taking it all in. 'Oh Lexia, he's gorgeous. How could you have kept him from us?'

'I know, I know,' Lexia repeated, laughing through her tears. It's all been such a… such a damned awful mess.'

'Where's Pandora?' Ariadne asked, turning to Helen. 'Pandora should be here…'

'I am, I'm here.'

All eyes turned to Pandora who stood at the entrance to the kitchen, a small orange Le Creuset dish in her hand. 'I brought lunch for you, Mum.' White-faced, she turned to her youngest sister. 'Hello, Lexia, I'm surprised you've come back.' She walked over to Lexia who had moved, equally white-faced towards Cillian, distancing herself from her mother and sisters. So, as Pandora put her arms around her baby sister, no one except Lexia herself heard the whispered hiss directly into her ear, 'You promised, Lexia. You *promised* you'd never come back.'

# 12

The following morning was Monday, which, on this week's roster, meant no work for Juno but, for the first time ever, she wished she worked full-time. She was dying to see Scott Butler, just to see if he was as gorgeous as she remembered. He couldn't be that lovely, could he?

It was his first day as locum at the practice and Juno could have been there to show him the ropes and advise him of the eccentricity of the kettle in the kitchen: one had to turn it on and off twice before switching it back to ON, when it was then more than happy to spring into life to do the intended job of boiling the water. She could, Juno thought, have been there to show him where the staff chocolate biscuits were hidden and the spare loo rolls were kept. On second thoughts, maybe not.

Bloody Marian would be in there first, lipstick good to go, fresh percolated coffee at the ready rather than the instant Tesco stuff that usually sufficed, merrily bubbling away (Marian herself, as well as the fresh coffee) to welcome him to his new post. Since her divorce last year, Marian appeared to have acquired a somewhat voracious appetite for younger men, particularly the gym-toned, or suited and booted, attractive ones. Any over fifty were soon given short thrift and sent on their way after queueing patiently forever for blood tests and flu jabs while Marian conversed with the younger variety through the reception desk, squeezing them into unavailable appointments with a little, 'seeing it's *you*, I think I can just pop you in, in the next half an hour'. The hopes of the now optimistic chap with the greying comb-over, standing patiently in his work overalls, were dashed when, with a dismissive sniff, Marian would bark, 'Two weeks on Thursday, Mr Seddon? Doctors are *very* busy.'

Juno had helped Tilda feed Moaning Myrtle and her pals, unfastening the coop and watching in delight as the four chickens had tentatively stepped out in an orderly queue, feet delicately held high, each gimlet eye alert to its new surroundings. There was, Juno acquiesced, something incredibly soothing about these creatures. She was glad she'd been persuaded to have the four of them in the paddock, particularly when she found two warm eggs nestling in the straw of the coop.

'But no more,' Juno warned, as Tilda began to suggest a cockerel, several more hens, some ducks and even, perhaps, a pair of peacocks. 'Peacocks? You can forget that. Right, school. Now, or you'll be late. I'm actually coming into school in—' Juno looked at her watch '—an hour or so to see Mrs Beresford.'

'Are you? Why?' Tilda looked at Juno with some suspicion.

'Don't worry, it's not about *you*. I'm going to pick up your Aunt Lexia and Cillian and go with them to see the school. She wants him to start in nursery there.'

'I wouldn't be worried if it *was* about me,' Tilda said

with some indignation. 'You can see my algebraic equations on Mr Donnington's new maths display in the hall. Mr Donnington says—'

'Enough already,' Juno said putting up a warning hand. And then, frowning, glanced across at this daughter of hers. 'Algebraic equations? In a primary school?'

'Where's Theo?' Juno looked around the incredibly huge kitchen with something akin to envy; she could have fitted her own three times into this one. The seemingly acres of shiny black cabinets appeared to stretch forever below their sleek black worktops. They wouldn't have been her cup of tea, but she could admire their sheer, sexy beauty. Myriad ovens, coffee makers and magnificently shiny freezers and dishwashers sat haughtily in and among the worktops, as well as appliances she didn't recognise. 'What's this thing?' Juno pulled at the handle of something she couldn't name.

'That *thing* is something called a sous-vide; don't even begin to ask me what it does. And Theo's gone straight down to the club. Apparently, they've not been doing so well since Christmas and all the players are in for a bollocking.' Lexia stood, twirling her hair around her fingers, appearing uncertain as to what job she should be doing next.

Juno frowned, glanced meaningfully across at Cillian who was totally engrossed in playing a football game on an iPad, having made no acknowledgement of her presence.

'Oh, don't worry.' Lexia smiled. 'Once he's on that thing, he doesn't take in anything else going on around him.'

'He probably does, actually; they're little sponges at this

age. Right, are you ready? I told the school secretary we'd be there for ten-thirty.'

'Oh, Cillian's not had breakfast yet…' Lexia looked round vaguely as if hoping a child's breakfast might materialise in front of her. 'Right, come on, Cillian. Put that away. Come and have some cereal.'

Cillian ignored her.

'Cillian, come on.' Lexia frowned, glancing at Juno, embarrassed.

'No.' Cillian didn't look up, his tone adamant.

'Cillian, we're going to look at your new school. Aunty Juno's come to take us there.'

'Not going. Don't want to. Don't want to go to school.'

'Well, come and have your breakfast. Come on, darling. What would you like?' Lexia glanced at the breakfast bar where Theo had obviously broken his fast earlier. A large white pack of protein powder sat next to a six-carton of eggs, their broken shells spilling out onto the granite. 'How about Weetabix? You like Weetabix. I think we have some somewhere?' Lexia pulled anxiously at the handle of one of the cupboards. 'Not done a big shop yet…'

Juno said, 'Lexia, why don't you go and get showered and I'll make Cillian some toast and milk?'

'No, really…'

'Go on.' Juno smiled at her little sister. She really did appear to be such, this morning. 'I've not had *my* breakfast yet, Cillian,' she lied. 'I'm starving.' She could always manage a second breakfast. 'Right, OK, matey. What do you reckon? Scrambled eggs?' Juno had gone to what she assumed was the fridge and found at least twenty-four eggs, a half-full bottle of milk, a full loaf of wholemeal sliced bread, two bottles of Sauvignon Blanc and what looked suspiciously like a jockstrap. A jockstrap in the fridge? Presumably to keep Theo's balls cold. Did that make him a better goal scorer? If that was the case, she'd better do the same for Gabe; she'd stood, the previous Sunday, freezing her tush off, while Gabriel had attempted to score goal after goal without success. And she wouldn't need, she reflected, as she looked for a pan and something to beat eggs, to be offering any of Moaning Myrtle's to this household.

'Don't like brown bread.' Cillian had moved as far as the breakfast bar but was still attached to his iPad.

'Really? Now that's interesting that you don't like it. Gabriel says eating brown bread toast is absolutely *essential* for footballers. And even more so covered in scrambled egg.'

Cillian tutted. 'The Angel Gabriel doesn't play football, you silly. That's just bollocks.'

Oh heavens, Juno thought, automatically tutting back loudly at this four-year-old.

'The Angel Gabriel is Jesus's dad, anyway,' Cillian said authoritatively, beginning to wander away from the breakfast bar once more.

Ah, that's who Mary blamed, was it? Fair play. Juno sat at the breakfast bar and tucked into her plate of eggs, making appreciative noises, not only for her nephew's benefit, but because she was genuinely enjoying this second breakfast. 'Gabriel is my *big* boy. He's your cousin. He *loves* brown bread. Look, shall I cut the toast into footballers? Right, that's Ronaldo, that's Rooney, that's…' Juno paused, her repertoire of Manchester United footballers hazy and obviously wrong if the look of disbelief on Cillian's face was anything to go by. 'Beckham? Erm, George Best…?'

'You silly woman. Pogba, Lukaku...'

'Hang on,' Juno said seriously. 'The rules of this game are that you must *eat* every footballer – with egg – if you're going to name them.'

'Alright.' Every strip of toast was christened and eaten and washed down with a mug of milk. By the time her sister reappeared, looking rather more like the photographs Juno recalled of Lexia when at the height of her fame, Cillian was in his navy duffle coat, woollen pom-pom hat on his blonde head and, holding on to Ronaldo the penguin, ready for the off.

'Keep your head down. Just don't look at them.' Lexia took Cillian's hand, bundling him none too gently into Fraser's Volvo, Juno's car of choice since the Mini had been taken into the garage in the village.

'Is it always like this?' Juno was afraid to accelerate the heavy vehicle out of the huge gated complex, terrified she'd knock down one of the waiting journalists.

'It has been since we moved back last week.' Lexia nodded. 'It was like this for years and I loved it to begin with. Theo still does. So does Cillian.' She turned to her son who was waving and blowing kisses from the back seat to the two men and one woman who were aiming cameras into the car. 'Then I just found it tiresome and intrusive. Claustrophobic even.'

'Maybe if you just got out, talked to them and gave them the pictures they want, they'd move on,' Juno said. 'I mean, if you act as if you've something to hide, they'll think you have, and keep hounding you until they find out.'

Lexia looked across at Juno, now on the road out of Heath Green village and intent on driving the three miles or so into Westenbury and the village school, Little Acorns. They were already over half an hour late for their appointment. 'What do you mean, something to *hide*?' she asked sharply.

Surprised, Juno took her eyes from the road and looked at Lexia. 'I didn't mean *anything* by it. I don't know much about celebrity and the paparazzi, but I assume if you give them what they want, they'll go away. They probably just want photos of Cillian and want to know what you're up to and how you feel about coming back to your hometown after such a long time.'

Lexia's shoulders, beneath the heavy, warm coat, visibly relaxed. 'Suppose,' she said, sounding like the fifteen-year-old Juno remembered so well from her last visit home before Lexia left for London, Aunt Georgina's and instant stardom.

Jean Barlow, the school secretary, was obviously waiting for them. 'Mrs Beresford had another appointment,' she said, smiling at Lexia and then at Cillian. She'll only be ten minutes, but I can show you round, show you our nursery class where Cillian will be if you decide to entrust him to us.' She giggled slightly, obviously in awe of Lexia. 'Actually, Dr Armstrong, if I can just ask you, while you're here…?'

'Hmm?' Juno smiled at the woman who was a patient at the surgery.

'What do you think is the best thing for slight arthritis. We're all getting older, aren't we?' She giggled confidingly at Lexia who seemed not to know what to say. The last memory Lexia had of the school was when she was in Y6 and struggling over her Science SATs, nervously biting her nails and unable to remember all the different parts needed for the reproduction of a flowering plant. 'I just wondered if you had any advice?'

'Me?' Lexia asked anxiously, looking to Juno for help.

'Me, I think, Lexia.' Juno smiled. 'Do you know, Jean, I have a hallux rigidus…'

'Oh?' It was obvious Jean, wide-eyed and listening intently, didn't know whether to be sympathetic or impressed.

'Stiff toe, to the man – woman – in the street. Anyway, I take a Boswellia supplement every day. It was initially seen as a cure for stiffness in horses.'

'Really? And has it worked? Have you noticed a big difference?'

'Well, I'm in fine fettle and down for the 2.45 at Kempton Park this afternoon.' Juno smiled.

'Lovely.' Jean Barlow beamed while Lexia, at Juno's side, started to giggle. 'I'll go onto Amazon and order some right now… Ah here's Mrs Beresford now.'


'So, Mrs Ryan, we're happy to offer Cillian here a place in our nursery. We do have a waiting list at this time of year – any time of year, really – but we've had four children not return to the class after the Christmas break.'

'Any reason for that?' Juno frowned.

Cassandra Beresford smiled. 'Nothing sinister. We had a set of triplets – can you *imagine*? – whose father relocated to Nottingham, and then one little boy whose parents have decided to send him private. There were three on a waiting list and now, Cillian as well.'

'Don't want to come here,' Cillian said mulishly as a couple of the big eleven-year-olds, Tilda's classmates, walked through the hall.

'Yes, you do, darling. It's lovely. Mummy used to come here.'

'Well, I'm *not*.'

'Cillian…' Lexia reached for his hand with hers and he took it, sinking his teeth into the soft flesh beneath his mother's little finger. Lexia gave a little cry of pain while Cillian, red-faced, kicked out at his mother, catching her on the shin before launching himself onto the floor in a paddy.

'Darling…' Lexia seemed unable to move.

'Tell you what, Mrs Ryan, Dr Armstrong,' the headteacher said cheerfully, 'why don't you just leave now, make your way down to my office where Jean will have left some coffee? And I'll bring Cillian down when he's ready. Go on, honestly, leave him.'

'Is he often like this, Lexia?' Juno, shocked by the sudden outburst, steered her sister back towards the head's office.

Lexia nodded miserably, wiping away tears as they walked. 'It's my fault. I'm just a terrible mother. I should never have had him.'

'Don't be daft, Lexia. All kids have paddies,' Juno soothed. The words 'but not as bad as this and at four years old' remained unspoken.

'No, you don't understand. I'm a terrible mother. I shouldn't have had him. I don't *deserve* to have him.'

'What *is* all this beating yourself up about?' Juno spoke

quietly, aware that, even though the head's office door was closed, children and staff were in the near vicinity.

'I thought it was going to be alright up here. That you and Ariadne – and Mum – would be there for me.'

'I am – we are.' Even as she spoke, Juno was aware of the implication of the missing sister from Lexia's list of those from whom she wanted help.

'Hey, listen, I get the impression your relationship with Theo is not the best at the moment?' Juno paused, suddenly feeling the need to air the thoughts she'd been harbouring, but not yet admitted even to herself. 'If it makes you feel any better, I don't think I was in a much better place with Fraser. I think he accepted the post in Boston because he'd really had enough of me. I guess you have to work at these things and perhaps I didn't work hard enough. I'm a bit ashamed really…'

'Really?' Lexia's head came up and she wiped at her face with the tissue Juno found in her coat pocket.

'Hmm. And listen, if you're not happy, then this tension will be transferred to Cillian.'

'See, it *is* my fault he's so badly behaved. I had to go and speak to Cillian's teacher at the end of most days in London. I think he was probably the only four-year-old to be expelled.'

'Expelled? At four?' Juno didn't know whether to laugh or cry.

'Well, no, I'm exaggerating, but they were jolly relieved when we told them we were moving up here. Back home…'

Lexia trailed off as the door opened and Cassandra Beresford walked back into her office, holding Cillian's hand. His face was tear-stained but the anger he'd been feeling had obviously dissipated.

Lexia stood to gather him to her but Mrs Beresford said simply, 'Just leave him. He's fine. He does have something to say though, don't you, Cillian?'

'I'm sorry, Mummy.' Tears started once more.

'So now, I'm going to take him back down to the nursery class for ten minutes to introduce him to the other children, and then we'll have some coffee and a chat. Come on, young man. With me.' She took his hand once more and he followed her meekly through the door.

'You see, *I* can't get him to behave like that.' Lexia looked stricken once more.

'You're his mother,' Juno said. 'He's learned that he's allowed to vent his anger on you. Mrs Beresford, from what I know of her, won't put up with it in school.'

'What about when she asks the prep school in London for a reference?'

'A reference? He's four years old, not applying for a job with KPMG.'

Lexia smiled at that and for a split-second, Juno saw something of the beautiful, quite gentle little girl she'd once been.

'Right, here we are. Where's that coffee? Jean?' The head popped her head back round the door.

'So,' Lexia said, once Mrs Beresford returned. 'You've seen what he's like. Are you still willing to take him? I mean, the school in London won't paint a very good picture of him.'

'No, they didn't. I rang them earlier this morning.'

'Oh.' Lexia was momentarily nonplussed.

'If a child has already been elsewhere, then we need the results of initial assessments; any psychometric testing; is he toilet trained? Is he sociable? Are there any behaviour issues?'

'And there obviously are.' Lexia looked shamefaced.

'Mrs Ryan, Cillian is four years old. He's probably been in the public limelight somewhat with his father being who he is. And of course, your background as well?'

Lexia nodded but said nothing.

'He'll be fine, really, don't worry. We'll work with him, we'll work with you and your husband. Put in place for what to do when he bites and paddies; we obviously can't have him biting the other children.' Mrs Beresford laughed, looking at Juno. 'And I'm sure Matilda will keep him in place, once he's here.'


'So, what do you think?' Juno asked, as she dropped Lexia and Cillian back at home.

'I do feel better, Juno. Really. In fact, this afternoon I'm going to walk down to the village with Cillian. Get some fresh air and find that artisan bakery everyone talks about.'

'What about the paparazzi?'

Lexia smiled. 'Hardly paparazzi, Juno. Just a couple of reporters from the local rag.' She took a deep breath. 'I'll give them what they want. Let them take a couple of photos.'

'Are you sure?'

'Yes, I can do this.'

*

Two hours later, Lexia and Cillian walked back up from the village and towards the house. She'd taken Juno's advice and spoken to the nice girl from the *Midhope Examiner* and the not-so-nice older hack from the national newspaper. She'd said how delighted she was to be back in her hometown, no, there were no plans for any come-back tour and yes, Theo was excited about his new career with Midhope Town. Several photos were taken and, by the time she and Cillian had strolled the ten minutes into the village and back, sharing a warm and fragrant loaf from the bakery as they walked, it was getting dark.

So, she didn't see the figure, all dressed in black and blending into the misty dusk of the February afternoon, until she was almost home, scrabbling in her bag for the card to activate the huge metal gates to the complex of five houses.

'Hello, Lexia, remember me? I think we need to have a chat, don't you?'

# 13

*November 2002*

*Lexia*

'No way, Lexia. There's no way you're going to any audition in London for *TheBest*.'

'It's not in London,' Lexia tutted crossly. 'I told you, it's the local heats in Manchester. You don't *begin* in London, that's just daft.'

'Mum?' Pandora glanced across at Helen Sutherland who was curled, foetus-like, in the brown leather armchair Patrick had always favoured, had always sat in when he was at home and watching TV or reading, peering in some frustration at the print, too vain to admit he needed glasses. Helen ignored Pandora, pressing her nose into the battered leather in an attempt to find Patrick's scent. 'Mum? Come on, *you* need to make the decision; *I'm* not Lexia's mother. She's only fifteen – far too young to be heading off to Manchester by herself.'

'What is it you want to do, Lexi, darling? Sing? Of course you must sing.' Helen's words slurred slightly, a result of the heavy medication she'd been prescribed. 'I was singing in the pubs and nightclubs in London when I was your age. You have a beautiful voice, darling. Just like me. You know, I'd been invited to do several gigs in Cambridge when I wasn't that much older than you. It was where I met...'

'Mum,' Pandora snapped crossly. 'We know the story of how you met Dad. And you were *much* older than fifteen. You were...' Pandora stopped, trying to work out exactly how old her mother must have been when she'd first set eyes on Patrick. 'You must have been at *least* twenty.'

'I don't think I was, Pandora...' Helen trailed off as her full bottom lip began to tremble and the beautiful doe-like eyes filled with unshed tears.

'Mum, just tell Lexia she's too young. She has school. Anyway,' Pandora went on, 'I'm sure you really *are* too young, Lexia. I'm sure you have to be at least sixteen, maybe even eighteen to enter these things. God, I hate these reality shows,' she added for good measure.

'It's on a Saturday, so you don't have to worry about me missing lessons, and *Dad* says I can go. He's in Manchester and he says he'll take me, meet me off the train and go with me.'

'Daddy did? Your daddy said so?' Helen sat up, staring at Lexia.

'Hmm,' Lexia lied, not looking at her mother or Pandora. She had rung her father loads of times, leaving messages on the answer machine in his flat in the up and coming area of Didsbury. He'd not returned any of her calls but, a couple of days ago, the last time she'd attempted to contact him, Anichka had picked up the phone. Having built Anichka up into some sort of illiterate Russian pole dancer that

Patrick had picked up in one of the seedier nightclubs of Manchester, Lexia had been unprepared, shocked even, for the response once the phone was answered. The cultured voice was that of a young woman but with only the slightest of accents and, while Anichka was obviously somewhat nervous at having this initial conversation with Patrick's youngest daughter, she said she was pleased that Lexia had made contact but unfortunately Patrick was away for a couple of weeks, promoting his new book, a biography of the poet Sappho, in the States.

'That's just *typical* of Dad,' Pandora had fumed when Lexia had related the conversation to Pandora in a whisper while their mother, still curled up in the armchair, had suddenly fallen asleep. 'Writing about lesbians and kinky sex, for heaven's sake.'

While Lexia had no idea who or *what* Sappho was, and was totally clueless as to whether the said Sappho – she'd blushed an adolescent pink at Pandora's words – was either a lesbian, kinky or even both, she kept to herself the bit – in truth, the very *big* bit – in the conversation where Anichka added that *she* too would have been in America with Patrick, had it not been so difficult to find an airline willing to insure a six-and-a-half-months' pregnant woman.

Lexia had put the phone down, gone up to the attic and cried buckets at that. Her dad was going to have another child. She wouldn't be the youngest, his favourite, anymore.

'And Dad says he'll meet you at Piccadilly and accompany you to this thing?' Pandora was asking in a whisper, not wanting to wake Helen who'd fallen asleep once more. 'He'll be responsible for you?'

'Hmm, I said.' Lexia outstared Pandora.

'Well, I'm not ringing him to check,' Pandora snapped. 'Not only do I not know his new phone number – or want to know it, mind – I'm not speaking to him.' Just a few weeks pregnant with her first child, Pandora suddenly felt an overwhelming tiredness and need to be at home. In her own home, lying down on her own bed. 'If that decision's been made,' she went on, 'and I tell you now, Lexia, I think it's a totally wrong decision – you're far too young to be entering competitions like this – then it's out of my hands. Nothing to do with me. I wash my hands of the whole ridiculous thing.'

While, in truth, Patrick Sutherland might not be waiting to accompany her from Piccadilly train station down to the *TheBest* regional auditions at the newly opened Lowry theatre in the Salford Quays, Lexia certainly wasn't alone. It had been Damian St Claire's suggestion, after hearing her impromptu debut performance at the Ambassador Club on the Tuesday lunchtime, that she must, she just *had* to, sign up for an audition.

'Babe,' he'd almost crooned, as Lexia, blushing, shaking and yet triumphant, had walked off the stage and back to where Damian was lighting a cigarette with a gold lighter, 'you are going to be one very *big* star.'

'Mr Scascetti'll want first dibs at this one,' the barman said warningly, frowning at Damian. 'You take your life into your own hands, mate, if you keep this one to yourself.'

'Well, he's not here, is he?' Damian said, smiling at Lexia and ordering her another coke. 'Right, babe, let's check when and where the regional auditions for *TheBest* are happening.

Anytime now, I know. If we've missed Manchester, we can always try Nottingham or Leicester.'

Lexia made sure her mum had taken all her medication despite Helen saying she was fine, she didn't need her pills anymore. Once Lexia had announced she'd been in touch with her dad, that he would be meeting her off the train in Manchester and was going with her to the *TheBest* auditions, Helen had perked up, convinced that this was a first step to his coming back to her and the family in Midhope. Patrick, she confided to Lexia over the burned omelette she'd made a big effort to cook for Lexia the previous evening, would soon tire of this, this, *Russian* trollop. He'd soon be back where he belonged.

*Not if the Russian trollop is seven months pregnant,* Lexia thought crossly. She was glad her dad *wasn't* meeting her, that he had absolutely no idea of her dreams to be even better than Holly Valance, that he was away in America somewhere with some lesbian poet. She didn't *need* him. She had Damien, who'd arranged it all for her and was going to be accompanying her as her agent. Her agent. She had an *agent*.

'Get some makeup on, babe,' he'd said on the phone the day after her singing debut at the Ambassador. 'And some sexy clothes. You have to be seventeen to enter and I know you're only sixteen. I've got the forms here and I've filled them in for you. Just need a parental signature to say you're seventeen and have their permission to enter.' Lexia had given Damian her address and he'd called round the next evening when she knew Pandora wouldn't be there to question him and put a spoke in the wheel. That was the problem with Pandora being a solicitor: she *questioned* everything. Mind you, Lexia thought to herself as she recalled Damian's streaked-blonde hair and *devastating* eyes, she bet anything if Pandora met him she'd think he was pretty hot too. Compared to old Tricky Dicky, anyone would be hot.

Damian had come round to their house after supper, explained to her mum that Mr Scascetti at the Ambassador Club had heard Lexia sing and was convinced she'd be a star like Avril Black. Lexia had been a bit confused at this point – wasn't Joe Scascetti away in Jamaica or somewhere? – but, she thought to herself, maybe he was back and he was going to be there in Manchester too? Helen Sutherland had been more than happy to sign the consent forms, taking a pen and, with the same hand she'd practised over and over again in readiness for signing her one contract with that record deal thirty years earlier, had written her signature with a flourish. 'Now, do tell Daddy when you see him on Saturday that I am so much better and I've forgiven him. He can come home now, the poor darling.'

Damian had looked at Lexia in some confusion but, standing behind the brown leather chair, she'd shaken her head at him at the same time as patting her mother's shoulder.

So here she was, on a wet, foggy early November morning waiting at the bus stop for the double-decker to take her down to Midhope train station where she'd arranged to meet Damian. And possibly Joe Scascetti? Pandora had said she'd come over and drive her down to the station, but then she'd rung to say she wasn't feeling well, was being sick, and unfortunately Richard couldn't come over in her stead as he was still away with work in China, as he so very often was, and could Lexia get the bus down instead?

Lexia had been up since six, willing the temperamental boiler to work a bit faster so that she could wash and condition her hair into a shiny semblance of Holly Valance's. She'd gone through everything in her – let's face it, limited – wardrobe, had tried various pieces of underwear and nightwear from her mum's top drawer in an effort to copy the skimpy outfit she'd seen Holly Valance wearing on *Top of The Pops* but had rejected them all, realising she just looked like a little girl in her mum's nightie.

In the end, she'd pulled on pink cargo pants and her favourite pink Juicy Couture top that Juno had posted down from Aberdeen for her fifteenth birthday. She spent ages on her makeup, copying the eyeshadow and blusher Holly was wearing in a photo in *Smash Hits* and then she'd left the house after laying the breakfast table with juice, cereal, bowl and spoon to encourage her mum to eat something alongside the drugs she'd been prescribed. Lexia knew to leave out only the daily allocation of pills, hiding the full bottles and packets in a cupboard that she and Pandora had decided upon, weeks before.

At eight o'clock on a Saturday morning Midhope train station was quiet – just a handful of people, resentful at having to work at the weekend, making the short journey to Leeds, or the slightly longer one across the Pennines to Manchester. There was no sign of Damian on the steps of the station where they'd arranged to meet, and certainly no indication that any of the other passengers, reading newspapers, queuing for tickets or simply standing looking bored, could be Joe Scascetti. Lexia looked at the departure board and saw that there was a train to Liverpool, calling at Manchester Piccadilly, five minutes later.

'Hi, babe, I'm here.' Damian kissed Lexia's cheek briefly before heading for the ticket queue, and she watched as he talked with the ticket master, laughing at some comment he'd made as he glanced over at Lexia herself. He was so lovely; so tall and gorgeous. She was so lucky to have this twenty-three-year-old helping her to become famous.

'You are looking *hot*.' Damian grinned down at her. 'Let me see what you're wearing under your coat.' He frowned slightly. 'You'd probably have been better in a short skirt, but never mind. Too late. Now, have you been practising, *sucking*—' he gave her a wink which she didn't really get '—on those cough sweets I gave you?'

Lexia nodded, too in awe of this gorgeous man to do little else. On the train Damian bought her a coffee, told her all about the band he was in that was just about to hit the big time – a record deal was imminent – and then asked her more about her family.

'Is your mum OK? You know, right in the head? She seemed a bit spaced out the other day when I was round at your place.'

Lexia felt a pang of hurt, somewhere in the region of her tummy, that anyone should think her mother wasn't like other mothers. 'She's fine.' Lexia tried to smile. 'She's just going through a bit of a bad time with my dad away at the moment. He's a Classics professor at Manchester University,' she boasted, 'but away in the States for a while.' No way was she admitting to anyone that her dad had moved out and left them. That he hadn't loved her enough to stay. That he obviously thought it OK to leave her to look after her mum by herself.

Lexia was bitterly disappointed to realise she wouldn't be singing in front of the four judges who habitually sat on the judging panel of *TheBest* on TV. She'd been desperate to sing in front of the curmudgeonly Steve Silverton who had discovered and taken on numerous boybands over the past ten years, as well as Kika Everton, one of her favourite singers, who was also judging this year's competition. Even Damian had thought that would be the case.

''Fraid not,' one of the black T-shirted admin workers frowned, obviously fed up with explaining the reality yet again of the day's initial proceedings. 'You'll be given a couple of minutes to show us what you can do and then, if you're any good, we'll ask you to come back here again to Manchester for the regional rounds in front of the judges.'

'So, the judges aren't actually here?' Lexia whispered, catching hold of Damian's sleeve.

'Bollocks, it doesn't look like it. I need a fag... Just hang on here, don't lose our place in the queue.'

Four hours later, it was Lexia's turn to leave the rain-soaked queue snaking round the outside of the Lowry and actually enter the building itself. She'd spent a lot of that time just standing patiently by herself. Damian had a couple of mates in Manchester to catch up with, he'd said, leaving her to her own devices. She was hungry, having missed breakfast, but far too nervous to leave her place in the queue to find something to eat.

Another two hours and she was called forwards.

'Right, love, you've got all the forms filled out?' The admin guy – a totally different one this time with SAM printed in large black letters on his lanyard – didn't look up as Damian handed them over and Lexia was directed to a mike in the centre of the room. 'Right, go for it.'

The lack of any musical accompaniment didn't worry her at all. Lexia did indeed go for it, closing her eyes and belting out the same Holly Valance number she'd performed at the Ambassador Club earlier in the week.

'OK, OK, stop... that's fine.' Lexia opened her eyes to see the admin guy staring at her. And then smiling. 'Wow. Simply wow. That is some voice.' He continued to stare, scrutinising Lexia's face, taking in every aspect of her. He looked down at the application form and then back up at her.

'You're seventeen?'

'Hmm.' Lexia felt herself redden.

'You do know you have to be seventeen by the end of the current year in order to take part?'

Lexia nodded.

'So, what year were you born?'

Lexia froze, her panicked brain unable to subtract seventeen from 2002. The silence stretched into the distance as she desperately tried the alternative method of adding two years to her correct birth year. '1988,' she finally managed to stutter.

'That makes you just fourteen.' He smiled with a modicum of sympathy at her, but shot a look of distaste at Damian. 'Lexia, you've got one hell of a voice, I really mean that. You'd have been through to the regional auditions here in Manchester like a shot if you were seventeen. I assume you're sixteen? We check all birth certificates of those who we call back, so you'd have been found out then anyhow. Go away, come back next year when you're seventeen.' He turned to his assistant who was looking at the file in front of her, obviously marking off names. 'Tell the next one to come in, Zainab.'

'I need a drink.' Damian slammed out of the glass doors of the Lowry, marching forward at such a pace that Lexia had to actually run along the pavement, her best Nikes splashing through the puddles as she attempted to keep up with him.

'Can you hang on? Damian, wait, I've got stitch.'

He slowed down to a walk and then, scowling, turned to wait for her. 'Mental maths obviously not your best subject at school then?'

'I don't seem to be really good at *anything* at school,' she panted sadly, bending over to stop the stitch. 'Apart from singing.'

'Well, I need a drink. Or a spliff. There's no point in trying to get you into a *pub*, is there?'

Lexia felt the tears well as Damian stood in front of her, glaring down at her. And then he smiled. 'Not your fault, I suppose.' He slung an arm around her shoulder. 'Come on, my mate lives two minutes away. He'll give us a drink.' She cuddled up to him, pleased that he seemed less cross with her and, as she did so, felt his hand reach under her Juicy Couture top, his fingers moving exploratively as they walked.

# 14

'You're looking a bit dolled-up for work, aren't you?' Tilda looked up from poking bits of her toast through Lady Gaga's cage – Juno had strictly curtailed the gerbil's free-range roaming ever since she'd seen, out of the corner of her eye, a little bump tunnelling along the bottom of the duvet cover while she was reading in bed. As she'd explained to Izzy, the morning after that little episode: 'I've been doing a catch up of all the *Luther* series I've missed. I'd watched that murderer in the clown mask crawl on his stomach, unseen, along the floor of the double-decker bus towards his victim, seen another murderer creep out from underneath his victim's bed; even managed to continue watching – admittedly with my hands over my eyes – that murderer pretending to be a cat in the loft before leaping out at the husband and bashing his head through the ceiling to the wife below. But that bloody gerbil, tunnelling away in my bed was the last straw. I was a nervous wreck.'

'Dolled up?' Juno sniffed unconvincingly, wincing against the pain in her toe from the too high heels. Oh, but they were beautiful – black patent L K Bennetts that showed off her legs in the sheer dark tights to perfection – but she knew she'd soon be kicking them off under her desk and reaching for her flatties.

'Well, yes,' Tilda insisted, posting the final crust through the bars of the cage. 'You usually have your thick black tights on and those old flat things you wear on your feet. I'm glad to see you're making a bit of an effort with yourself at last.' She scrutinised Juno's outfit more closely. 'I've not seen that skirt before.'

Probably because I've never been able to get into it before, Juno thought.

'But it's a bit tight isn't it? Can you actually *breathe* in it?'

Tilda had a point there; the two slices of toast and marmalade she'd just eaten were in danger of reappearing around the beautifully cut lines of the Jill Sander pencil skirt she'd optimistically bought in the January sales last year. And never worn.

She was, Juno admitted to herself, probably behaving like a love-sick teenager. But, she also conceded, she wouldn't really know because, as a teenager, she appeared to have missed out on such things. There'd been a few simmering looks over the dissecting of the dead rat she and Michael Roberts had shared in A level biology but, then again, she could have misread the signs, with Michael simply attempting to keep down his lunchtime spam fritters and Manchester Tart as they opened up the poor dead animal.

Juno sighed as she heard Doreen letting herself into the house through the kitchen door, and reached for her warm winter coat. She was, she accepted, a total amateur at the reading of any possible signs because she'd never opened that particular map of the heart before. Her three Science and Maths A-levels had taken every bit of her time and energy when she might have been open to flirting with the boys at Westenbury Comp and then, at Aberdeen, there *had* been more than a couple of flings and fumbles but, really, more a result of copious amounts of cheap cider than from any lingering looks across the university library or over Bunsen burners in the labs.

And then, she sighed once more to herself, there'd been Fraser.

'You're looking… different?' Declan peered over his reading glasses at Juno, momentarily distracted from the paperwork Marian had assaulted him with as he attempted to slide through reception to the safety of his own practice room. Marian glanced up at his words and stared at Juno.

'Bit tight, that skirt, isn't it?' She raised an eyebrow before nudging Declan back to the job in hand.

'You're going to need *me* before lunchtime, if you insist on wearing ridiculous shoes like that.' Anne Ellison, who rented part of the surgery for her podiatry practice Anne Did Those Feet frowned at Juno. 'Mind you, they're pretty gorgeous. Now, why would you be looking so glam? Hmm? On a weekday Wednesday morning? Nothing to do with our new lovely locum? Hmm?'

'New locum?' Juno pretended indifference.

'Oh, of course, you won't have met him yet, with you being part-time. Well, Juno, he is *gorgeous*. He's really tall, has these amazing green eyes…'

'I *have* met our new doctor,' Juno said quickly, determined that Anne shouldn't think she had one up on her. 'In fact,

I spent Friday evening with him as well as him helping me with my new bathroom on Saturday afternoon.'

'Oh?' Anne was momentarily nonplussed. 'Well, you can keep *your* hands off him. You're married.'

'I wasn't *planning* on getting my hands on him.' Juno felt herself flush and wondered if her nose – already the somewhat Roman, Sutherland beak – had lengthened.

'Well, I certainly am.' Anne grinned wolfishly. 'He's already booked in for a foot massage. Now, changing the subject, this singing competition of your sister's?'

'Oh, it's common knowledge already, is it?' Blimey, Pandora certainly didn't hang around once she got the bit between her teeth.

'On the wall, look…' Anne wafted a manicured hand to her left.

'*Thieves want your purse!!*' Juno read the words on the garishly coloured poster and laughed. 'Well, they can bugger off and get their own. They're not having mine.'

'No, you daft thing. Next to it.' Anne turned this time, just as Scott Butler made an appearance in reception from Juno's old practice room, making his way across to speak to Marian. Juno felt her pulse quicken and turned her attention quickly to the new poster up on the wall.

'I'm really up for this,' Anne was saying. 'I just *love Jesus Christ Superstar.*'

'*Jesus Christ Superstar*?' Juno frowned, momentarily forgetting the reason her pulse was racing. 'I don't remember *that* being mooted on Friday. I thought there was going to be a *vote* on which musical we were putting on?'

'I've no idea, I don't know anything about any votes. Pandora and her mate were in yesterday – they're putting up their posters all over the village – and first rehearsal is tomorrow evening.'

'Is it?'

'Morning Anne, Juno.' Scott Butler had appeared at their side and Juno felt her heart actually race. This was ridiculous. She was going to end up with a heart attack or high blood pressure at least.

'Morning Scott.' Juno was trying desperately not to squeak, to show some nonchalance at his presence but, with the rolled-up shirt sleeves of his crisp navy linen shirt making contact with her arm, as well as a faint tang of some aftershave she didn't recognise playing havoc with her olfactory senses, she wasn't having much success.

'So, it's *Jesus Christ Superstar* then?' Scott was saying. 'Brilliant. I love it.'

'You can sing?' Juno looked up at him, meeting his eyes for the first time that morning. Oh, but he was glorious.

'Well, as much as the next man.' He grinned. 'I'm up for it, anyway.'

Juno was definitely going to be up for it too – singing, that was, and anything else that might be on offer – if Scott Butler was going to be at rehearsals. The new year, so far, was definitely beginning to shape up nicely: Lexia back, her new chucks, the new doctor, and now this production.

'I bet there won't be *many* men.' Anne frowned. 'There never are in these choirs. It's always female-heavy. And that mate of Pandora's – what's she called – Jennifer? You know, the consultant woman? For some reason she keeps calling me *hon*. Honey, I can just about cope with, but I *hate* being called *hon*.'

'Something against Germans?' Juno asked idly as Anne

frowned again and Scott laughed out loud. Oh good, she'd made him laugh.

'Could you lot take up your positions?' Marian barked from Bomber Command post behind reception as Izzy hurried in, late as usual. 'I *am* trying to run a surgery here, you know.'

'Have you saved seats for us?' Izzy, along with Clementine Ahern from 'Clementine's' restaurant in the village, and two other women Juno didn't know, was heading her way down the far aisle of Westenbury village hall. Juno indicated the seats she'd bagged, and saved with her own bag, scarf and hat hoping that Scott Butler would, when he turned up, come and sit with them. Ariadne, deeply entrenched in an article in that morning's *Guardian*, was on Juno's other side and the four newcomers quickly filled up the vacant seats. Bugger, that meant Scott wouldn't be sitting with them. Mind you, all those present would soon be split up into their respective singing voices, and she couldn't see Scott being a second soprano like herself and Ariadne.

'Juno, this is Harriet Westmoreland and Grace Stephenson – you've heard me talk about them before – and, of course, you know Clem. This is great, isn't it? It's like a girls' night out. Can we go off to the pub after this?' Izzy beamed at them all.

'I can.' Juno smiled. 'But I've left Mum in charge of my two, so I don't want to be too late. She doesn't do it very often and I'll have to run her home afterwards. Isn't Declan coming too? We're going to need *some* men.'

'He and Scott are doing the late shift, so they won't be

over for a while. Mind you, Declan's tone deaf. He can't sing a note.'

Juno laughed. 'Well, he can practise. Or mime. We can't do a production like this without *some* men…'

Juno broke off as Pandora took to the stage, flanked by Jennifer Danton-Brown and another woman Juno had never seen before.

'Welcome, welcome,' Pandora trilled. 'What a fabulous turnout for our first meeting and rehearsal. Now, I know it's all been a bit rushed, a bit last minute – and I hold my hands up and take the blame for that.' Pandora actually held up her hands but didn't, Juno noticed, add the truth that she'd almost thrown away the entry forms into her kitchen bin the previous summer. 'Now, if you haven't handed in your application form, including all your contact details and singing voice as well as your cheques, please do so at the break. If you're not sure if you're Soprano or Alto, Tenor or Bass—' Pandora gave a little tinkle at the very thought that anyone *could* be unsure '—then do find us at the break and we'll be able to head you in the right direction. I'm sure most of you here know our very own Dr Jennifer Danton-Brown, the county's Chief Guider, who will be in charge of all the admin, but I'd like to introduce Sally Russell. I've spent the last week or so, ever since I knew this production was a possibility, in pursuit of Sally…' Here Pandora gave another little over-dramatic tinkle of laughter before executing several jogging steps on the spot and wiping her brow. What the hell was she doing? Juno stared up at the stage towards her sister. Training for a 5K? 'She's the musical director down at Midhope University and, not only is she very professional and very experienced in musical theatre, this will be the *third* time she's actually put on a production of *Jesus Christ Superstar*. So, you can see why I wanted Sally on board.' Pandora beamed across at her new mate, Sally, a tall, strikingly attractive blonde around Juno's age, and was about to launch once more when she was interrupted by a voice from the back.

'Won't we need a full orchestra for a big do like this?' Everyone craned necks to see who was asking.

'No, that's the beauty of this particular production.' Pandora beamed. 'We need a very skilled and talented solo electric guitarist, particularly for that wonderfully evocative opening to the show…'

'Has she thought about Brian May?' Ariadne whispered across to Juno. 'He went down a storm on the roof of Buckingham Palace at the Queen's Golden Jubilee. I've heard he can hold a note and I bet he's short of a few quid now that Queen have disbanded.'

'Shh,' Juno giggled.

'It's just that me and my mate here were in a group in the Seventies,' the disembodied voice went on. 'You might remember us: Ricky Rover and The Rovers…?'

The assembled choir turned to one another, chatting among themselves.

'Who…?'

'Who did he say…?'

'Something about ravers…?

'Or was it rivers…?

'Never heard of 'em…'

'You know, we were actually professional. Toured with Sweet in 1972…'

'Who is it?' Izzy half stood to get a good luck at the

speaker. 'Oh, it's only Colin Murphy,' she sniffed somewhat disparagingly. 'You know, owns the chippy down North Street. God, he must be seventy if he's a day.'

'Thank you for that, er, Ricky.' Pandora continued to beam. 'Sally here will be talking to the music students at the university with the plan to get some of them on board, but, come and see us at the break and we'll have a chat. Now,' she went on, 'we intend a weekly rehearsal from 7.30 until 10 – after this week it will always be Monday – with a fifteen-minute break somewhere in between and with the actual performances – one of which will be seen by someone from Sir Andrew's Really Useful Group – in July. This is a wonderful opportunity the village has been given to take part in one of Sir Andrew's major productions and I'm sure you can understand why we will need monetary contribution from yourselves for the hiring of the village hall, for our piano accompanist, Geoff, and for the printing of the musical scores. I'm sure I don't need to remind you all to have plenty of liquids with you – and no, Gerald, I don't mean a pint...' More tinkled laughter and a raising of an imaginary glass on Pandora's part. Juno stared up at the stage once more. Was she on something? 'I do have to go over the usual stuff about safety and fire drill.' Here, Pandora raised both arms, as if she were aircrew on Jet2, indicating the fire exits. 'And Sally and myself will be auditioning for the major parts of Judas, Mary Magdalene, Herod and the Disciples later on this week. Again, please come and see us at the break and put your names down. I know many of my – *the* – Westenbury Warbler stalwarts are eager for a part, but we have lots of others here tonight, particularly from the Midhope Melodymakers choir – a very big welcome to them – who are also raring to go to show us what they can do. Now…'

'You've not mentioned Jesus, Pandora.' One of Pandora's usual lackeys, a rather diminutive, bald-headed man on the front row stood, obviously disappointed that the main man's part hadn't been mentioned.

For a split-second Pandora looked decidedly shifty and then, glancing at Sally who gave a slight, imperceptible nod in her direction, beamed around at the gathered crowd trying to get comfortable on the hard, wooden chairs. 'We already *have* Jesus… Jesus, *do* come up and join us and introduce yourself.'

'Blimey,' Izzy said in a stage whisper, craning her neck, 'he must be able to walk on water if he's got the part so quickly.'

'Hey, as long as he can turn water into wine, love…' The woman in the next row turned and held up her bottle of Tesco Still. 'He'll do me.'

'Jesus. I mean, you know, *Jesus*, look at Jesus…' Izzy, for once, was stopped in her tracks as a tall, dark-haired man, probably in his mid-thirties, left the front row where he'd been sitting, before walking up the three steps and joining Pandora and Sally. He was obviously already in character, wearing only, on this cold February night when everyone else in the hall was wrapped to the hilt in polo-necks and fleeces, a white flowing shirt slashed to reveal a bronzed six-pack. His dark, wavy hair came to an end on obviously-gym-toned shoulders.

'Everyone…' Pandora trilled, holding out an arm before kissing Jesus as if she were compering the Oscars. 'Everyone, I want you to give a warm welcome to Brett Bailey. Brett is from Barnsley – he's just finished a run of *Joseph* in Sheffield – but has agreed to travel over every week to be with us.'

'Brett Bailey from Barnsley?' Ariadne, at Juno's side, who up until then had said very little throughout the proceedings, gave a loud bark of laughter and then started giggling, unable to stop.

'Oh, but look at him,' Izzy sighed. 'He can lay his hands on *me* anytime.'

'Who can?' Declan frowned down at Izzy. Scott Butler, at his side, had just arrived.

Juno's pulse raced once more as she stole a look at Scott. He was wrapped up against the cold in a heavy navy overcoat, a navy cashmere scarf tied casually around his neck, a contrast to the white in his hair and across his shoulders.

'Is it snowing?' Juno asked in some panic. She hated driving in the snow.

'Shhh,' Izzy whispered crossly. 'I'm trying to listen to Jesus; I'm about to be converted.'

'Converted?' Harriet Westmoreland looked puzzled. 'I never knew you were Jewish, Izzy?'

'Jewish? No, no, agnostic… or is it atheist…? I'm never sure. Whichever it is, I renounce all other religions from this moment on. Shh, shh, Baldy on the front row obviously has a bee in his bonnet about something.'

The same man who'd stood earlier now got to his feet once more, obviously very pissed off that his chance of being Jesus had just been scuppered with the arrival of Brett Bailey from Barnsley.

'Er, put me right, if I'm wrong here, Pandora, but I thought the whole point about this here production was that it was for amateurs? Jesus, here, appears to be a bit more than that.' He glanced round at the choir where several nodding heads emboldened him to speak further. 'You know, Pandora, if he's a professional...'

'You're absolutely correct, Granville,' Pandora said smoothly. 'This competition is for amateur productions. But the rules state we are allowed one semi-professional member of the cast. And Brett is such; he actually has an Equity Card, I believe, although he does hold down a job like the rest of us during the week.'

Like the rest of us? Juno grinned, her mind skittering from amusement at Pandora's implication that she was in paid employment to stolen covetous glances at the good doctor, tempered by panic that snow was coming down and she wouldn't be able to get the Mini up the lane where she lived. She should have brought Fraser's Volvo.

'Ooh, I wonder what he does for a living?' Izzy was saying to Clementine and Harriet, ignoring Declan who was looking daggers at both his wife and then across at Jesus who was leaving the stage. 'Something out of the ordinary, I bet, with that physique and that hair.'

'I was just wondering, Pandora, now that your *very* talented sister is back here in Midhope...' A woman, probably the same age as Lexia, waved a hand at the stage.

'Sisters. *Sisters*,' Ariadne muttered loudly. 'We're *all* back and all *very* talented.' She grinned at Juno.

'Hmm?' Pandora ran a hand through her blonde bob and frowned. 'I do think we need to get on, time is of the essence...'

The woman was not to be put off. 'As I was saying, Pandora, with Lexia Sutherland back in the area, wouldn't that be a coup to have *her* in the choir as well? Does she know about it? Have you asked her?'

'As I think I've just explained, we are allowed just the *one* semi-pro performer. That would exclude any other professional singer as I'm sure you can see...' Pandora was flustered, her hands continuing to run through her hair.

'But surely she's left the profession? She hasn't had an album out for years. She was my friend at school...'

'Now,' Pandora said, a rictus of a smile on her face as she glanced across at the huge clock on the far wall, 'I think it might be time for a break, sort out some dates and times for those who are wanting to audition for the main parts, and then if we convene in, shall we say fifteen minutes? Sitting in our respective singing voices? *I'm* then going to handle the *male* parts. They're always quite hard as I'm sure you can imagine...' She paused, frowning at a couple of titters from the third row. 'Sally will begin to go through the choir's main chorus numbers with the ladies.'

'*Ladies*,' Ariadne tutted. 'What century does Pandora live in, for heaven's sake? We're *women*, you daft bint, *women*!'

Over an hour later, the more sociable members of Pandora's choir had left the village hall in readiness to reassemble in The Jolly Sailor next door. The snow, which had continued to fall for the duration of the meeting, appeared to have stopped and, in its stead, a clear sky revealed a full moon, brightly sharp against any remaining dark clouds.

'I think we should be getting off, Izzy,' Declan was saying as they crossed the carpark. 'God knows what the boys are up to on their own.' Emily, Izzy and Declan's eldest, was in her second year at St Andrew's studying Medicine and, as a result, Robbie had been promoted to chief babysitter in her stead for Sid, aged eight.

'Robbie's fourteen; I'm *paying* him to babysit. He's absolutely fine. Come on, one quick drink and then we'll go home.'

'Come on, Declan, I'm dying for a beer.' Scott had turned to Juno, smiling. 'You're coming, aren't you?'

Juno looked at her watch, desperate to join the others but frightened that the snow might come down once again. The Mini, she knew, was quite dreadful in snow and Helen would be anxious if she was late back, concerned for Juno's safety on the snowy roads but also worried how she was going to get back home herself. Helen would never sleep away from home, having an almost obsessional need to be in her own bed every night. Juno had always felt terribly guilty that she'd been away at university in Aberdeen when her mother had finally given up the fight and succumbed to what would be the first in a series of breakdowns. As a little girl, she'd loved her mother as all little girls love their mothers, but the increasingly strange and erratic behaviour displayed by Helen Sutherland once Juno was in her teens, meant it was a relief to escape the stultifying atmosphere of home. All kids couldn't wait to leave home and spread their wings, Juno had told her eighteen-year-old self as she took the six-hour train journey north to Aberdeen, but she'd continually felt the burden of guilt, constantly reproached herself for, in effect, abandoning her mother when she could, she knew have studied at nearby Leeds or Sheffield. Now that Juno was back at home, back living very near her mother, she felt it was her duty, felt it almost payback time, to not desert her mother once more.

'Tell you what, Juno, I'm not bothered about a drink,' Ariadne was saying. She was quietly taking in the situation, appraising the unmistakable frisson between Juno and this new locum of hers. 'I'll drive up to your place, stay with Mum until you're back – as long as you're not too late – and then I'll drive her home myself. For all my car's a banger, it's brilliant in snow.'

Ariadne smiled to herself as she put her car into gear and headed for the main road through the village and out onto the lane towards Juno's place. She'd never liked Juno's husband, she now admitted to herself – probably for the first time – as she sped, regardless of the wet slush, along the lane. Humourless, sarcastic, pedantic and not even particularly attractive, Fraser Armstrong was, to her mind, an over-opinionated academic.

Juno deserved a little diversion.

# 15

*Lexia*

'So, babe, are we off in for a cup of a tea and a chat?' Damian St Claire, ruffled Cillian's hair as he indicated, with a nod of his head, the huge, locked wrought-iron railings that separated the five houses in the gated community from the rest of the world. 'Nice-looking kid,' he went on, smirking slightly at Lexia as the colour drained from her face.

'Take your hands off him,' Lexia spat, pulling Cillian roughly towards her. Cillian looked up in surprise at her tone of voice and the unexpected handling of him as his mother pushed him forwards towards the gate. 'Keys,' she muttered to herself. 'Where's the sodding keys?'

'Hey, babe, there's no need to be like this.' Damian put out a restraining hand as Lexia brought out a bunch of keys from her pocket with a trembling hand and held the entry fob against the gate, the remains of the artisan loaf she and Cillian had been enjoying together falling to the ground. 'Come on, just two minutes. I've always wanted to see inside one of these joints. And this little chap here and I can get to know each other better.'

'My husband is at home,' Lexia lied as the gates began to slowly swing open. Cillian skipped through and ran ahead, eager to be reunited with games on his iPad.

'Great stuff. All the better, I've always wanted to meet the great Theo Ryan. Does he know... you know, babe?' Damian gave her an oily smile.

'You know damned well he doesn't. I've paid you enough over the years. That last lot, you *promised* that was it. No more, you said. You *promised*.' Lexia's voice rose and Cillian looked back at her as he waited, impatiently, by the glossy black-painted front door of this new house they'd only just moved into.

'Did I?' Damian smiled again. 'Well, maybe I did, babe. But that was four years ago.'

'Three,' Lexia said tiredly, massaging the thump that had started over her right eye. 'I gave you enough to pay you off for *ever*.'

'Inflation,' Damian smirked. 'Brexit. Call it what you will. Your sister's been pretty good over the years,' he added, giving Lexia a long hard stare to gauge her reaction.

'My sister?'

'Oh, sorry, you've *three* altogether, haven't you? Maybe *they'd* be willing to contribute a little too? Your lovely sister, Dr Armstrong, is my GP. Now, that's a coincidence, isn't it? Great doctor,' he went on conversationally. 'Cured my bad back just like *that*.' He snapped his fingers in Lexia's face and she jumped back in alarm. 'Yes,' he went on, his thin face turning towards the gates where a black Porsche that had just pulled up behind them was waiting for access. 'Pandora, the most *upstanding* member of Westenbury community, has been brilliant at paying her debts. But then she would, wouldn't she? Can't imagine the lovely Pandora ever getting behind with her gas or electricity bill...'

Theo Ryan's Porsche suddenly drove past them at speed, pulling up outside the house in one of the three designated parking bays. Theo jumped out, black leather training bag in one hand, and immediately scooped up Cillian who had run to greet him with the other, while his son squealed in delight at seeing his father.

'Loves that boy, doesn't he?' Damian smiled. 'Look, lovely to see you, Lexia, babe. Been too long. I'll be in touch...' And with that, he pressed her arm, none too gently, his meaning apparent, before drifting away into the shadows and back through the still-ajar gates.

'Who was that?' Theo put Cillian down and unlocked the front door, watching as the huge gates clanged shut behind the visitor.

'Press,' Lexia said shortly.

'Didn't look like your usual press,' Theo frowned. 'Which paper?'

'Oh, the local rag... you know. I said we weren't interested.'

Already losing interest, Theo picked Cillian up once more, throwing him up towards the ceiling until he was giggling helplessly. 'Right, Lexia, get yourself dolled up, we're off to a party.'

'A party?' Lexia looked at Theo in dismay, her pulse still racing from Damian St Claire's unexpected visit. Unexpected? She closed her eyes. That was daft; she'd known he'd turn up sooner rather than later.

'Yep. Matt Rogers is having drinks at some club down in Midhope. You know, to welcome the new players, and wives and partners are expected to be there.' He looked at his watch. 'In an hour's time. Come on, sort yourself.'

WAPS? Lexia pondered the handle, probably for no good reason other than an attempt to shift St. Claire from her brain. Is that what they were called now? Instead of the ubiquitous WAG she'd been branded in the early days of her relationship with Theo? She looked Theo full in the face, wondering, not for the first time, what on earth she'd ever seen in him? Fame? Fortune? The money? She'd had all three in bucket loads herself; hadn't been overly bothered about having his as well. 'No, I'm not going.' She frowned. 'You know I hate parties.'

Theo reached for Lexia's wrist, digging his fingers into the soft flesh. 'I think you *are*, darling.' He turned to Cillian. 'Shall we tell Mummy she *has* to go out, Cillian?'

Torn between wanting to be on the same side as his father, but not wanting to be left at home with a babysitter, Cillian didn't say anything and instead, walked over to the ridiculously large TV taking up almost one wall of the sitting room and turned it on.

'We can't,' Lexia hissed, pulling her hand away from Theo's grip and glaring at him. 'We've no babysitter.'

'Ah, that's where you're wrong, my darling girl.'

'There's no way I'm having one of your *floozies* coming here to look after *my* son.' Lexia lowered her voice, but still manged to convey, in a whispered hiss, her contempt for the local football groupies she assumed had already made an inroad into Theo's new life up here in Midhope. He'd attempted the same before, down in London, and Lexia had always managed to send the young girls arriving at their door – dolled up to the nines in their tiny skirts and ridiculously long eyelashes – away, refusing to leave the house to attend the many social events they'd both been invited to over the years and to which, in the early years, she'd adored.

'Sure, and I don't think you could call this one a floozie.' Theo grinned. 'Now, take that *puss* off your face, d'you take me for a complete eejit? I've arranged for an oul wan to come round tonight?'

'An oul wan?' Lexia stared. 'Have you been in touch with my mum?'

'That's a point. Never thought about her, she'd be a *free* babysitter, wouldn't she? Or one of all those sisters of yours I've never really met. Funny lot, your family.'

'Don't start, Theo,' Lexia said crossly. 'I'm not leaving Cillian with someone he doesn't know. Someone *I* don't know.'

'Well,' he said as the front doorbell chimed some tune Lexia recognised but couldn't name – it changed on a daily basis – 'now's your chance to get to know her.' Theo gave Lexia a triumphant grin and followed Cillian, who'd run to answer the door, down the hallway.

Terrified it might be Damian St Claire back again, Lexia was relieved when Theo returned with an elderly woman in tow, but she still looked with some suspicion at the newcomer. Where had Theo found this one? Ah, another one from the Emerald Isle, Lexia realised as the woman spoke to Cillian, chatting away in a soft Southern Irish burr about what he liked to eat, what were his favourite TV programmes? Well, Theo needn't think she was going to be won over that easily. She couldn't leave a four-year-old with some strange woman she'd only just met.

'Ah, you're worried about leaving the little one, I'll bet?' The woman turned soft, kind eyes on Lexia and, for some reason, some daft reason she couldn't explain, she wanted to sit down with this *granny*, curl up on the sofa next to her and tell her everything. Everything she'd not been able to talk about for all the time since it happened. 'I don't blame you. You don't know me from Adam, God bless that poor man's soul. Would you like me to give you the phone numbers of people I've nannied and babysat for in the area? You can have a chat with them? Put your mind at rest?' The woman pulled out a sheet of paper and handed it to Lexia.

Theo tutted. 'Look, Lexia, Mrs Brennan is well known in the village.'

'So was that witch in Hansel and Gretel,' Lexia interrupted and then, as the woman's surprised face turned to a smile, both of them suddenly started laughing and couldn't stop.

'I've had my supper.' Lilian Brennan wiped at her eyes and indicated the paper she'd just handed Lexia. 'But look, why don't you ring Harriet Westmoreland or Grace Stephenson – I've nannied for all their children – and then you go and get yourself ready and I'll make young Cillian here – that's a *fine* Irish name you've got for yourself, young man – *his* supper.'

'I'm not sure he'll want much.' Lexia smiled. 'He's just eaten half a loaf of bread.'

'I'm starving,' Cillian piped up. 'Come on.' He grabbed Lilian's hand. 'I'll show you how to make French toast.'

'*French* toast?' Lilian winked at Lexia. 'Sure, and I know

how to make Irish toast and even English toast, but you're going to have to show me *French* toast.'

As Lexia showered, really seeing for the first time, and marvelling at, the sumptuous bathroom with its luxurious gold fittings, she knew she was going to have to pay Damian St Claire off once again. It shouldn't have, but it had come as a shock to know Pandora had been doing the same all these years. She conditioned and rinsed, casting her mind back over the years to the number of times she'd actually seen Damian St Claire. That wasn't even his real name: it was plain old Damian Sinclair, nothing fancy at all about his last name. How she'd fallen for him when she was just fifteen, letting him tell her what to do: lose some of that puppy fat, shorten your skirts, pout a little more.

And don't bother going into school.

She'd really missed out on her education she thought sadly as she rubbed her hair dry before searching for the hairdryer she hadn't yet unpacked. How was it she had such clever sisters, *really* clever, and yet *she* hadn't even sat her GCSEs? She supposed Patrick had been there for the others, checking they'd done their homework, helping them with their revision and testing them in readiness for exams. Although, to be honest, she couldn't really recall him doing much of that at all. When he *was* home, he was either shut up in his study or, when he was back again, with his tail between his legs after sniffing after some student like the rampant old dog he was, professing his undying love for her mum, he would be holding Helen, kissing her, stroking her and telling her she was everything he'd ever wanted or needed. Ariadne had obviously left home while she, Lexia, was still a toddler and both Pandora and Juno had just seemed to get their heads down and get on with it.

Lexia frowned, unplugging the hairdryer and reaching for primer before starting with foundation. If you'd inherited the Sutherland brains to start with, and not had the worry of looking after a mentally unstable mother once your dad had finally pushed off and left, then yes, there was no reason for her sisters not to have achieved the academic success they all had. But when she'd been in her final year at school, when she should have been working hard for GCSEs and thinking about doing A levels at the sixth-form college down in Midhope – one of the best in the country apparently – she'd just about given up with it all, only going in when they sent someone round to accompany her there before bunking off again once she'd gone to registration, and maybe a couple of the English lessons she really liked. No one there seemed to care enough to make her carry on with all those lessons, the teachers continually surprised, it seemed, that she was clever Ariadne, Pandora and Juno Sutherland's sister. A Sutherland sister that had broken the mould and was, let's face it, thick. What had she overheard one of the teachers call her? One of the '*TAPS*'. She couldn't work out the acronym for ages until horrible, full of herself, Jodie Stringer had put her right. *Thick As Pig Shit*, Jodie had informed her knowledgably with a little smirk before heading off with her gang of girls to maths. Maths had been the worst of all – totally beyond her, all that integration and differentiation. What was all that about?

So, when school and Pandora thought she was at home,

taking care of Helen – which to be fair, she more often than not *was* – or at school, she was at the Ambassador Club or at Damian's dad's place, a scruffy two-bedroomed council flat down by the town ground. Funny how things turned out, with her now married to one of the football club's brand-new expensive players.

Lexia pulled on a plain black cashmere tight-fitting dress that emphasised her slim figure, adding only a pair of gold ear-rings as adornment, before moving over to the massive walk-in wardrobe to hunt for sheer tights and black heels she'd not worn in forever, it seemed, but which she knew were around somewhere. She looked, she realised, like the old Lexi, and was about to rub off the bright red lipstick that had once been her signature trade-mark, splashed over the front-covers of countless glossy magazines and copied by huge numbers of girls and women eager to get the Lexi look, but then changed her mind. What the hell? She added more in defiance, swallowed an extra Valium to get her through the evening and went back downstairs.

'Mummy, you look lovely. *I* want to come out with you.' Cillian looked up from the garishly-coloured pieces of sticky paper and child-proof scissors Mrs Brennan must have brought with her in that oversized bag of hers. His eyes narrowed – a sure sign a paddy was in the offing. He drew in his lower lip mutinously as Lilian Brennan, sat with him at the kitchen table, calmly handed him a day-glow-orange paper tiger.

'But I want...'

'So, where's your panther?' Lilian raised an eyebrow. 'You'll need to mind yourself – my lion's bold, fierce savage. He'll have your panther for breakfast if you don't add his tail quickly. You see, that's where all the magic is – in the tail.'

Distracted, Cillian went back to the sticky paper and scissors and Theo pulled Lexia out of the room. 'Come on, Lexi, you spoil him. It's no wonder he has so many tantrums when you give in to him so easily.' He glanced across at Lexia as she shrugged herself into the long, cashmere camel coat she'd had for years, helping to pull her long hair free from the coat's collar before stroking the back of her neck. 'You're looking hot, girly.' He grinned, moving his mouth down to where his fingers had been. 'Play your cards right and I'll show you a good time once we get back home.' He twisted a strand of Lexia's long hair around his fingers, pulling none too gently until her mouth was level with his own. He'd been drinking, she realised, smelling the alcohol on his breath. If he carried on throughout the coming evening, he'd get to that stage where he was dangerous; where it felt like she was living with a dangerous animal, ready to pounce... *he's bold, fierce savage and he'll have you for breakfast.* Lilian Brennan's warning words to Cillian skittered through Lexia's head and she closed her eyes momentarily.

The best way was to keep her wits about her by not drinking herself, and let Theo drink enough not to make a fool of himself, but to be distracted from any amorous inclinations he might be harbouring. It was a subtle calculation Lexia had come to master over the years. Ha, the maths teacher at Westenbury Comp would be impressed with her ability to work out *this* particular equation.

'I'll drive,' Lexia said, removing Theo's warm fingers from her neck, 'and then you can have a drink.'

'There's something very *sexy* about a woman handling a

powerful car.' Theo gave what she assumed he thought was an amorous glance in her direction – *lecherous* glance came to mind – threw Lexia the keys and opened the front door for her to pass through in front of him in order to place his hands on her bottom.

Lexia shuddered slightly but concentrated on beeping both the Porsche and the huge black gates' locks before walking in front of her husband down the path towards Theo's car.

The private party was being held in one of the function rooms at Brenton Wood, Midhope's largest golf club, several miles from Heath Green, and Lexia enjoyed controlling the car, driving it slowly through the outlying villages and then, more confident, letting the Porsche have its head once they were on the bypass heading for their destination. She'd once had a little Boxster of her own, a sleek flash of silver with a red roof – to match her lipstick – and had loved the feeling of power she'd had over it. But she'd been young and reckless then, the speed of her little car helping to push away the thoughts that, unbidden, returned most nights, manifesting themselves in the same old nightmare that would have her sitting up in bed, frightened and sweating and needing to talk to someone who would listen and understand.

'Fuck's sake, be careful, Lexia.' Theo sat up in alarm as Lexia drove at some speed towards the one remaining space in the club's carpark, cutting up the driver of a large four-wheel drive who'd obviously spotted the space as well and had had the same intention. Theo glanced at Lexia whose face was a picture of fear and triumph. She seemed different this evening – more like the old Lexia he'd gone after and married – the flame-coloured-lipstick-flaunting icon he'd been determined to have for himself. Until she'd gone all weird on him and become as passionate as a wet dishcloth – even worse once she was pregnant with Cillian, but doubly so after his birth.

Lexia felt her heart pound; that had been close. She wasn't sure why she was suddenly feeling a bit braver unless the visit earlier that afternoon from Damian St Claire had finally sparked something inside her and set off a sort of slow-burning anger. That enough was enough – she needed to sort out her demons before they sorted her.

Feeling shaky, Lexia cut the engine, sitting at the wheel until she felt her breathing come back to normal. She glanced across at Theo who was continuing to stare at her.

'You're a mad bitch, Lexia,' he said, shaking his head at her. 'One minute you're as miserable as sin, refusing to have a shower or leave the house, and then you perk up and drive like a maniac, cutting up poor innocent drivers...' Theo stopped. 'Oh Jaysus, I do hope that's not my boss you've just nearly killed. I sometimes think you need locking up like your—'

'Don't you dare,' Lexia hissed in his face. 'Don't you dare call me *mad*. And *don't* bring my poor mum into this.' Lexia flung open the door of the Porsche, slamming it closed as she begun to walk towards the entrance of the golf club on her black patent heels.

'Excuse *me*!' The driver of the four-wheel drive had jumped out of his vehicle, leaving the car where it had come to its abrupt halt when Lexia had nudged him from the parking slot. He was walking swiftly after her, ignoring Theo a few steps behind.

'Yes?' Lexia turned, her bravado disappearing as the man gained on her.

He stopped suddenly looking from Lexia to Theo. 'Lexia?'

Lexia stared, her heart pounding once more at the realisation of just who it was standing in front of her. 'Richard?' Thirteen years since she'd seen him, thirteen years since she'd heard any word whatsoever from him. A hand flew to her mouth and then came to rest on her chest, as if by doing so her heart might stop its racing. She felt she couldn't breathe. Please don't say she was going to have another panic attack right here in the car park in front of the group of people making their way to the main door and who were looking at her with some curiosity as she stood, unable to move, unable to speak.

'It's OK, lovey, it's OK.' Pandora's husband, Lexia's brother-in-law, moved towards her and took her in his arms, stroking her hair and murmuring in her ear. 'Honestly, it's all alright.'

# 16

*March 2019*

March was obviously working hand in hand with the little ditty *'in like a lion and out like a lamb'*. Into its third week, the month felt positively spring-like. Even Harry Trotter, regardless of his reputation as the local molester of innocent walkers appeared to Juno, as she banged shut her back door and made her way round to the front of the house, a calm and sunny presence. She'd had complaints from both the local council as well as Footpaths UK that Harry Trotter had been jumping out at walkers – like some sort of demented highwayman, Juno assumed – and, as it was a public footpath that went through her paddock, she was responsible for his behaviour and walkers' safety.

'Yes,' she shouted pointedly at the pony as she stooped to pick the last of a tiny bunch of snowdrops carpeting the edge of the garden path. 'Don't you dare look at me as if butter wouldn't melt. You've cost me almost five hundred quid having to fence *you* off from terrified villagers. You're like a bloody troll waiting to pounce.'

She paused, breathing in the almost balmy morning air, a sudden picture of a favourite book from her childhood coming to the fore as she continued to watch Harry graze. *'I'm a troll, fol-de-rol, I'm a troll, fol-de-rol, I'm a troll, fol-de-rol and I'm going to eat you up for my dinner,'* Juno sang operatically at the top of her voice towards Harry, almost shouting the word 'dinner' in his direction. He momentarily lifted his head, gazed balefully at the daft woman singing her heart out, before resuming his grazing once more.

'Thinking of what to have for your dinner already, love?' Doreen, dressed as usual for whatever meteorological conditions she might have to battle, was walking determinedly up the drive in her sturdy winter boots, purple rain-mate atop her reddish hair. 'I've got a nice bit of corned beef for me and our Brian.' She paused as she reached Juno. 'Now, talking of food, you've fed the hens, haven't you? Our Brian said to make sure.'

'Of course.' Juno frowned, insulted that Doreen should think her capable of leaving her girls to starve. 'It's Tilda's job, but I make sure she's done it properly. We must be doing something right – we had four *beautiful* eggs this morning.' Juno raised her eyes in the direction of the hens over in the paddock who, following Mrs Thatcher's lead, were making tentative steps on ballerina legs towards Harry Trotter. Taking their lives in their own hands – wings – Juno thought idly as she breathed in the spring-like air and watched the daffodils bobbing slightly in the breeze.

She loved spring with all its promise of warmth and the summer yet to come; the almost rampant feeling of nature preparing itself to get its rocks off. Was her own sap rising, she wondered as she jumped into the Mini and set off for the surgery? She was feeling decidedly frisky, but whether that was down to hormones, the time of year or, more than likely, the time of a certain man, it was, she thought almost sadly, nothing to do with her absent husband.

Fraser had been gone almost three months now and it felt like he'd been gone forever; that thirteen years of married life were in the past and they'd all moved on. Fraser rang dutifully once a week, usually on a Sunday evening when Juno was in the middle of sorting PE gear that hadn't been washed and Gabe's homework he'd assured her had been done but, when she'd demanded the evidence, wasn't forthcoming. Conversations with husband and father were always a bit stilted and both Juno as well as the kids would, after rather long silences, end up saying, *I'll just put Tilda/ Gabe/Mum back on for a word.* It wasn't a good feeling to know she was failing as a wife, that she was relieved when the call ended and they could all get back to doing whatever they'd been up to before Fraser rang.

Izzy certainly wasn't in any spring-like mood that morning. Her face was set like thunder so that even Marian wasn't about to take her on about the late payment of the electricity bill, having second thoughts about wafting said bill in her boss's direction. Instead, Marian pulled a warning face in Juno's direction as she crossed reception and headed for her stock-cupboard practice room. 'Don't know what's up with *her*.' Marian lowered her voice, nodding towards Izzy who was in the process of pinning up new surgery notices at the far end of the room. 'Argument with Declan,' she added almost gleefully, for once taking Juno onto her side. 'Avoid, avoid, or you'll have your head bitten off.'

Juno went down into the Dungeon, as she'd christened her new practice room, peering into Scott Butler's room as she passed. He'd not yet arrived. Juno did hope he wasn't late because of some woman in his bed he couldn't tear himself away from. She did all the initial tasks necessary for the smooth running of a Wednesday morning surgery and, with a good fifteen minutes to spare, made her way across to the kitchen for coffee and hopefully an eyeful of Dr Butler. Izzy was in there, banging cupboard doors and rattling cups, her face set.

'Whoa, what's up with you? You've even frightened Marian this morning.' Juno put up both hands in mock alarm in Izzy's direction.

'That pillock of a husband of mine, that's what's up.'

'What's he done now?'

'Oh, only arranged the most wonderful weekend away in London next week.'

'And that's a bad thing?' Juno laughed, trying to recall a time when Fraser had ever thought to come up with such a weekend away for the pair of them.

'It is when the daft sod's double-booked it. We can't go – it's his sister's wedding up in Newcastle.'

'Didn't he realise?'

'Oh, for heaven's sake, it's her third attempt at a husband. You'd think she'd have learned by now and just gone off and lived in sin with this one, instead of making us all jump through hoops and having us getting our bloody fascinators out once more. She's even wearing *white*. *Again*. Well, I tell you now, I'm wearing the same outfit as the last one… if I can get into the damned thing.'

'Can't you just not go? You know, send your apologies, but work has come up?'

'It wouldn't actually be a lie – about it being a work thing I mean. It's a conference we've been invited to in London on the problems facing small rural surgeries such as ours.'

Juno frowned. 'I wouldn't say our surgery is that small. You've had to open another practice room for heaven's sake – put *me* in the Dungeon…'

'Alright, alright,' Izzy snapped irritably. 'You've made your point about your room. I agree with you, I think the organisers have got the wrong end of the stick with regards to Westenbury, but I don't care, I wasn't going to put them right. A lovely weekend away in London? And Declan coughing up for a fab hotel? And instead we've got to drive to Newcastle – eat soggy sausage rolls and schmooze with yet another set of new in-laws? Paah.' Izzy gave a snort of disgust at the thought, shooting a stuck staple from the gun onto the floor with some force. 'And it'll be a *battle* to get Robbie there. There's some important football tournament on at his club on the Sunday morning. Apparently, your brother-in-law is going to be there giving out the prizes.'

'So, give your excuses and say it's work and you can't get out of it.'

'It doesn't work like that. If the whole family doesn't troop up there en-masse, Declan's mother will cut him out of her will. Again. We're only just back in it after last time.'

'Last time?' Juno started to laugh again.

'Don't ask,' Izzy snapped shortly. 'It's like playing a continual game of Snakes and Ladders with Declan's mother. One mistake and you're right back at the bottom once more, with his brothers and step-sisters and half-sisters – there are so sodding many of them – surging ahead up the ladder of inheritance.'

'Morning.' Scott Butler, glancing at the clock in reception, hurried past them, a fleeting smile on his face.

'You're *late*, Dr Butler,' Izzy called through the open kitchen door, punching a new poster on the unacceptability of Violence in the Workplace onto the wall with considerable and unnecessary force.

'Guilty as charged.' Scott Butler smiled winningly over his shoulder. 'Coffee?'

Juno felt her pulse quicken as it always did in Scott Butler's presence. 'Already got one,' she replied, holding up her mug.

'Thought you'd like to make *me* one, Juno,' Scott called, disappearing into his room.

'Don't even think about it, Juno,' Izzy snapped. 'He should make sure he's here on time. Leave whichever floozy he's got in his bed and—'

'Floozy? Do you think so?' Juno felt her heart drop more quickly than Izzy's expectations with her mother-in-law's estate.

'Oh, heavens, yes, *floozies*. In the plural.' Izzy lowered her voice. 'Declan said when he was at university with him, women flocked, absolutely *flocked*, to his bed. Mind you, that could have just been Declan being envious. I'm with *you*, Juno, don't see what all the fuss is about. And I'm sorry you've had to give your room up for him.'

'Well, you've changed your tune.' Juno stared. 'He was the best thing out according to you – well worth turfing me out of my lovely little room for.'

'Oh, he's a very good practitioner, I can see that. But… you know, why isn't he married at nearly forty? How has *he* managed to stay single when *we've* all had to succumb to it. Given up our fun and games for a life of servitude.' Izzy snapped her staple gun together and threw it onto the table and Juno giggled. One good thing about Izzy, she was always entertaining.

'Oh, just listen to you, you ridiculous woman. Are you hormonal? Perimenopausal?'

'No, I just want a bit of excitement in my life. I want to… I want to explore the Amazon, hike to Machu Picchu… oh I don't know – go cage swimming with sharks in the ocean.' Izzy tutted and looked sad. 'The nearest I'll get to that is in a supermarket trolley in the Leeds-Liverpool canal.' She paused and then visibly brightened. 'Mind you, now I've found *Jesus*, it's getting me through these winter months. Did you see those tight jeans he was wearing at rehearsal last week? He must have performed a miracle to get those on.' She began to laugh and then just as suddenly stopped, staring at Juno who was making her way to the door. 'Listen, why don't *you* take our place at the conference, Juno? I know it won't be the most riveting of weekends, but the hotel is paid for: we can't get the money back at this late date.'

'Me?' Juno turned, surprised. 'Go to London? For the weekend?'

'Why not? The practice *should* be represented now that we've been invited. The conference is only on Saturday afternoon; you could go down on the Friday like we were going to do and spend the rest of the time shopping, seeing the sights, go to a musical.'

'I'm working this Friday. And who's going to look after my two? *And* they're starting on the new bathroom this weekend.'

'What about that funny couple of yours? You know, the hen-man and his live-in lover?'

'No, no, I don't think so.' Juno realised the waiting room was filling up and set off at a sprint down to the Dungeon. 'No, sorry, Izzy, can't do that. That wouldn't work. Sorry, no way…'

# 17

Three days later, ridiculously early on the Saturday morning, Juno was at Wakefield train station with a good twenty minutes to spare before her train to King's Cross was due.

She'd left the kids in bed, anxiously waiting for Ariadne to arrive and take over before jumping into her Mini, overnight case and laptop in the boot, at 5.30 a.m. It was Ariadne herself who'd said she must go, must take up the offer of a weekend away and she, Ariadne, would move in and be a proper aunt for once in her life.

'You won't know what to do,' Juno had argued, when she'd mentioned, in passing, the weekend conference to her elder sister over the phone, and Ariadne had immediately offered to move in and be at the helm for two days.

'How hard can it be? Your two are not babies anymore. I don't have to mix formula or change nappies or make sure they're in bed at a certain time.'

'Well, yes you do.' Juno had frowned to herself. 'They do have set bedtimes you know.'

'Do they? Well then, that's fine. I'll adhere to that. It'll be fun, I can take them to the cinema on Saturday evening.

We can go out for pizza. You know, we can do what teenagers left with their aunt are supposed to do.'

'Gabe will probably just grunt at you.'

'Great stuff, I'll just grunt back. If it makes you feel any better, I'll get Mum over to help.'

'I'm not sure that makes me feel any better,' Juno had said down the phone. 'And you know you'll have to take her home. She won't stay overnight.'

'Juno, stop it. I'm a grown woman. *You're* a grown woman. Now, for heaven's sake, take up the offer of a fabulous hotel room, take an early train down and have a couple of hours shopping before the conference.'

Juno had wavered as excitement at the possibility of a bit of an adventure began to stir. 'It's very good of you, Ariadne. It's daft really, I was actually *born* in London and yet I've only ever been down there a couple of times since – once with you when we went down to find Lexia – do you remember? Are you sure about this?'

'Listen Juno, you sometimes appear to be sinking into a life of middle-aged suburbia.'

'I'm not...' Juno had protested, stung at Ariadne's outspoken words.

'Look, just hear me out,' Ariadne went on. 'I can say this over the phone when you're not in front of me to thump me one. You were always such a jolly, frivolous little girl, full of life, really funny...' She paused. 'But you seemed to lose it all when you decided to marry Fraser.'

'I decided?' Juno snapped. '*I* didn't decide, it was all sort of decided for me.'

'You were an adult, Juno. Lots of women get pregnant and have their baby without marrying the father.'

'But I loved – I *love* Fraser – I don't know what you're implying, Ariadne.' For some reason Juno felt tears start and she took a deep breath while Ariadne continued.

'If that's the case, then wonderful. I'm sorry I said anything. It was crass of me and I apologise. OK, let's move on. I'll have an early night and be at your place early on Saturday morning. I'll bring my marking and some strong coffee and then by the time the kids are up I'll have breakfast ready for them. What do kids eat these days?'

'Honestly? Are you sure about this, Ari?' Juno had hugged herself at the thought of a little outing by herself. 'I'll leave a long list and timetable for you. Gabe will need dropping at football practice and Tilda's probably got another party or sleepover or something.'

'It will be fine,' Ariadne had said. 'Leave it all to me.'

Leave it all to Ariadne? Juno tutted as she bought herself a coffee and a copy of *The Telegraph* in order to look a bit more grown up than she actually felt. Ariadne had been twenty minutes late, giving Juno no time to explain where everything was, and had, instead, airily shooed Juno down the garden path into the still dark morning and on into the Mini.

Once the train was on its way, Juno settled back, tried to stop worrying about the children – *they* certainly hadn't been concerned about being left – and, instead, concentrated on the novelty of two days of freedom and her own company.

The train journey south was only two hours, giving Juno a good five hours until she had to be at the medical conference in Holborn. Her plan had been to go directly to the Clarion hotel and leave her case and laptop there before heading for the retail delights of Kensington High Street and Knightsbridge as suggested by one of her patients at the surgery. When she realised she would be going miles out of her way to the hotel near St James's Park, Juno made the decision, instead, to leave her little case at left luggage in King's Cross, changed into flat walking shoes and then, unhampered by bag or heels, set off.

After treating herself to a most delicious breakfast in Le Pain Quotidien (porridge with granola and compote and a big mug of Earl Grey) on the concourse of St Pancras, all the while marvelling at the surrounding Victorian architecture, Juno headed for Knightsbridge, walking briskly and enjoying the sights and sounds of a busy Saturday morning in the capital. Harrods and Harvey Nicks were everything she'd imagined and, after sighing over and stroking the exorbitantly expensive dresses in Harrods, she settled on buying Ari and her mum a beautifully presented pack of pastel-coloured macarons apiece and then set off once more. Juno glanced at her Fitbit (15000 steps already) and decided she'd save time – and her feet – by jumping on a bus to Kensington High Street.

Juno reached for her purse and, horrified, realised it wasn't in her bag.

It had to be.

It wasn't.

The bus driver set off, waving her to one side of the bus while she stood, continuing to scrabble through the packs of macarons, her reading glasses, directions to the conference and all the other detritus a woman has in her handbag for a weekend in the big city.

The purse wasn't there. For heaven's sake, she'd been off by herself for just five hours and already here was proof she was the scatter-brained idiot Fraser always said she was:

the woman who wasn't fit to leave the sticks by herself. Juno's heart began to pound. As soon as the bus stopped at the next stop she jumped off, retracing her steps back to Harrods, her nose to the ground in the hope of spotting the brown Ted Baker leather wallet Gabe and Tilda had clubbed together and bought her for her last birthday. Losing her children's present to her was bad enough, but *everything* was in there: cards, money, all she'd brought with her.

The sales assistant in Harrods just looked vague, shrugging unhelpfully when Juno managed to get her attention and ask about her purse. Nothing had been handed in. No one had seen it.

Juno tried to think rationally: what does one do in London without a penny to one's name? She needed to get back to King's Cross and retrieve her luggage and laptop. That would be a start. Taxi? Nope, no money and she'd never set up one of those Uber app thingies.

Bus? No money.

Tube? No money.

Walk? Juno realised she'd just have to walk. There was nothing else for it. She took a deep breath, tapped in *Harrods to King's Cross* on Google Maps and set off holding her phone aloft in the direction indicated by the red arrow on her phone. Past Park Lane on her left and on towards Piccadilly. There was Green Park on her right, and then onwards and up Shaftsbury Avenue. Thank goodness she had her comfortable walking shoes on.

Half an hour into the walk, it started to rain. Not pouring down, but that miserable fine spray stuff that you don't realise is actually coming down until your new hair-do is ruined. Tutting, Juno pulled her brolly from her handbag, endeavouring to balance handbag and phone in one hand while shooting up the multi-coloured spotted umbrella. Obviously with too much force – the cheap brolly she'd bought on the market in her lunch hour the week previously shot up... and carried on shooting up, the top leaving the metal stick with a flourish only to descend like some shot-down tropical bird onto the pavement a second later. Gritting her teeth and trying not to cry, Juno picked it up and left it, abandoned, in the nearest bin.

One hour and twenty-three minutes later she'd covered the four-mile distance and King's Cross was ahead of her. Was someone already using her bankcards? She needed to cancel them all. Oh hell, what else was in there? Her driving licence, library card and gym membership. Admittedly she'd not been for months but that, absolutely, was not the point.

Juno reached left luggage towards the back of the concourse and joined the queue there. Who should she ring? She Googled her bank for the lost card number just as she was called forward, and automatically reached for her purse and the Left Luggage receipt.

In her lost purse.

'Look, I've had my purse stolen, or I've lost it. I've no ticket.' Juno looked the attendant, who must have been quite a few years older than herself, straight in the eye, to show what an honest, upstanding member of the community she was.

'Can you describe the case?'

'Yes, yes I can. It's bright purple with an American Express logo and – very helpful, this – the metal handle has been sawn off, leaving two metal sticky-out bits on which to rip your fingers and ladder your tights.' Juno smiled, willing him on to her side. Surely, no one else *owned* a case like that, never mind depositing it in King's Cross left luggage that very morning. It was pretty embarrassing owning a purple case with a sawn-off shotgun (handle, Juno, *handle*) but Fraser had taken all the best cases and she'd not had time, or to be honest, even thought about going to buy a new one. The man peered at her over his spectacles and went off into the back, reappearing just a few seconds later.

'That's it. Thank you. That's the one.' Juno reached for it gratefully, but the man put up a hand like a traffic officer and she stepped back.

'Can you tell me what's in it?'

'What's in it? Erm, yes, well, there's my laptop, and a white nightie wrapped around a Babyliss hairdryer.'

The man unzipped the case, peeping in, but not allowing Juno to have sight of its contents. 'And?'

'And? Oh, golly, erm, a green spotted bra and two pairs of matching knickers.'

He nodded, sagely, looked Juno up and down before delving into the contents of the case once more. 'Tell me the name of all your makeup?'

'What? Right, well there's an Hourglass mascara… It's new and cost me an arm and a leg. Then the rest is Charlotte Tilbury, although I think there's a Rimmel lipstick. Yes, pink, Pink Glow, if I remember rightly. Look, is this all necessary?'

'Name of toothpaste?'

'You're kidding me?' Juno felt the stirrings of a headache and massaged her forehead. 'OK, it's wrapped in a green spotty – matches my knickers – shower cap and is Sensodyne Total White'

'Correct.'

It was, Juno thought, a bit like playing that game at a

party when you have to remember what's on a tray before it's whisked away. She'd obviously passed her A level in left luggage and – heavens be praised – after finding a tenner lurking in the mirror compartment of her handbag, decided to sit with a coffee and decide what to do. 'Just off for caffeine,' she told the left luggage inspector. 'It's a bit unwieldy this case. I'll leave it here instead of dragging it with me into a café and be back again to pick it up in half an hour once I've decided what to do, if that's OK?'

The large cappuccino was a godsend and, while she slowly sipped, savouring the caffeine reaching her brain, Juno tried to work out the best course of action. She had, she assumed, enough money left from the tenner for a tube ticket to where the conference was being held. Once there, surely, she could throw herself on the mercy of the organisers; they'd all taken the Hippocratic Oath hadn't they, and were meant to help others?

Feeling slightly more confident Juno retraced her steps to reclaim her purple case.

'Hi, me again,' she smiled. 'Could you pass me over my case now?'

'Can I see your ID?' The same man looked at Juno through narrowed eyes and folded his arms.

'What? We've been through all this, ten minutes ago. You've seen my toothpaste and nightie, you've had a good root through my knickers. Just pass my case over, would you? I've really had enough of this.'

'Sorry, I need some ID.'

'A letter in my bag?'

He shook his head. 'Your driving licence will do.'

'It was in my purse. It's been *stolen*.' Juno felt her teeth clench as she spoke.

'Your passport?'

'I've travelled to London not Outer Mongolia… although you're beginning to make me wish I had. Why the hell would I have my *passport* with me? Please, come on, you've identified me once. Just give me the case.'

'Sorry, it's policy never to hand over luggage to someone without any ID.'

'So why didn't you tell me this two hours ago when you were rifling through my makeup and knickers? What are you? Some sort of pervert?'

'Accusations like that won't help your case.' The man obviously had damned *cases* on the brain. He turned to serve the people behind Juno and, furiously, she shook his arm.

'I am a *doctor*. Do I *look* like some sort of criminal? Give me my case.'

The man continued to attend to the German couple at Juno's side but simultaneously pointed to a notice on the counter. 'It's here in black and white,' he said calmly. 'No ID, no case release.'

'I'm getting it.' Juno moved swiftly towards the counter. 'Just try and stop me, you pillock.'

'No, you're not.' He didn't look at Juno but calmly shifted her case away once more into the depths of the room behind.

'So, what do you suggest?'

'It stays here at £12 per day until you come back with

ID. Now, could you just move yourself, people are trying to sort their luggage.'

'Juno?'

Juno swung round. Had she imagined someone calling her name? She narrowed her eyes, searching the small knot of people gathered at the entrance to left luggage.

Now, what on earth was *he* doing here?

# 18

Juno stared. There was really very little else she could do apart from the unacceptable alternative of standing and grinning like some sort of poleaxed-meercat which she had a horrible feeling she was about to do. She couldn't quite work out why Scott Butler was now in front of her, looking down at her in some surprise. Surely, he belonged back in Westenbury, back at the surgery, not down here among the travellers at King's Cross?

'Are you going back?'

'Back where?' Scott Butler looked confused.

'New Zealand?'

'New Zealand? Well, unless there's a train I can catch directly to Auckland from here, I reckon I'm in the wrong place. You know, my flight home to New Zealand goes from *Gatwick.*'

'So, you *are* going back? You're going home?' Juno felt an icy lump of something hard around where her heart had, until then, been lodged.

Scott shook his head, taking Juno's elbow and moving her away from the Lost Luggage queue. 'I don't know what you're talking about, Juno. I was just walking past and spotted you.' He paused, frowning as he continued to stare. 'Are you alright? You look... strange... worried?'

Juno took a deep breath, 'I'm standing in for Izzy and Declan at some conference this afternoon. I came down early, put my luggage in here for the morning, lost my purse and ticket and now this man here—' Juno turned and gave the attendant a filthy stare '—even though he's had a good rifle through my *knickers,* won't give me my case back.'

'OK.' Scott quickly assumed control and, even though Juno hated the idea of appearing like some weak helpless woman, was relieved to have someone on her side. Within the next five minutes, Scott – backed by the concourse station police on whom he'd pounced and ushered to the front of the queue – had flashed both his own passport – *was* he heading back down under? – his driving licence and the necessary fee to release Juno's case.

'Do you not have Apple Pay on your phone?' Scott asked, as they walked together from left luggage. 'Or have any of the banking apps to get your cash out? You know, if you go to a local ATM, they give you a code...'

'No,' Juno interrupted tiredly. 'I'm afraid I *don't* know. I'm not up on *any* of that sort of thing. I was still using my cheque book until recently... and I can't pay you back until we're back in Yorkshire,' Juno continued as they headed towards the underground, embarrassed at her apparent lack of modern-day finance technology.

'I think I can manage without the twelve pounds.' Scott grinned down at her and, veering them both towards the taxi rank, added, 'and I think we can treat ourselves to a taxi, don't you?' He looked at his watch. 'Come on, we're really late. We're going to have to head straight there now.'

'So, did you know I was coming to the conference?' Juno looked across at Scott as they sat in the back seat of the black cab. Dressed in a loose-fitting pink-striped shirt, jeans and long navy Burberry mac, Scott Butler oozed style as well as something else Juno was beginning to recognise every time she saw him. She supposed it was sex appeal. Whatever it was, it was making her squirm somewhat, especially when his knee accidentally touched her own.

'How come every time I see you, you're in the middle of some drama or crisis?' Scott sat back in his seat and then sat up again, as if trying to work something out. 'What have you done to your hair?'

'Mizzle.' Juno put a hand to her blonde hair, touching the curls that had replaced the sleek locks she'd set off with that morning.

'Mizzle?'

'Is it a Yorkshire word? I don't know. Anyway, a sort of drizzle that totally ruins your hair when you've walked 432,607 steps through the streets of London in it without a brolly.'

Scott laughed. 'Suits you – you should always leave it natural, like this.' He smiled at her, reaching a hand to move a curl from in front of her eye.

Jesus what was the matter with her? Why couldn't she just relax and enjoy the taxi ride, take in the sights and sounds of London, instead of feeling as though her stomach was in the process of turning itself inside out. 'So,' she repeated, trying to speak calmly and intelligently, 'this conference? You knew I was going instead of Izzy?'

'Not until last night. Declan said I probably wouldn't want it, that he was sure I had *much* better plans for my weekend than sitting through a boring conference on a Saturday afternoon, but there was his place available if I fancied it and a free room going in a rather upmarket hotel to boot...'

'Oh, oh no...' Juno felt herself going pink. 'No, I'm really sorry, Izzy's already given that room to me.'

'Oh, I think you'll find it's *mine* – and the only reason I agreed to come down.' Scott raised an eyebrow and then, seeing Juno's face, started to laugh. 'Don't panic.' He grinned at Juno's confusion. 'Izzy put me right straight away on that score. Said she'd already given it to you. She got really mad again with Declan who she accused of handing out free hotel rooms willy-nilly without consulting her. Apparently, she was only just speaking to him again after he'd double-booked the wedding they've had to go to instead. Which was a bit much seeing she'd already handed it out to *you* without telling *him.*'

'Right, well, I'm sorry about that. It's supposed to be a very lovely room.'

'Honeymoon suite, I heard.'

'So, where are you staying then? Somewhere near?'

'No, I'll probably head back north later this evening. You know, after the conference is over.'

'Oh, right, OK.' Juno felt a sudden rush of disappointment. She'd already seen in her mind's eye a cosy little dinner for two in some little upmarket bijou London restaurant. Bloody hell, what was the matter with her? She was a married woman with two almost teenaged children. And a head of mizzled-messed-up curly hair.

'Unless you fancy dinner somewhere afterwards?' Scott smiled at her. 'You know, just to discuss what we've learned at the conference and how we're going to cascade the information back to the others next week?'

'Really?' Juno stared. 'Do you reckon it's going to be that riveting?'

'Oh absolutely. We have to take this seriously, Juno. You know, take a professional stance; I do hope you're good at taking notes?'

Juno gave Scott a sidelong glance, taking in the gorgeous green eyes and short dark hair. Was he being serious?

The taxi pulled up outside a Georgian building with a cream-coloured stone façade and Scott paid the driver before helping Juno out with her purple case. 'What's with the sawn-off handle?' he asked, sucking at his thumb where the jagged metal had caught the skin.

'Oh, the handle got bashed on one of Fraser's trips abroad and wouldn't then retract back down. He said he wasn't about to throw away a perfectly good case because the handle was no longer "fit for purpose" so he sawed it off. And left me with it...' Juno was embarrassed. Right come on, we're up here.' Avoiding the offending bits of metal, she grabbed the case by its material handle and headed for the entrance.

For almost four hours Juno sat on an inflexible orange plastic bucket chair, trying hard to take in the line graphs, waterfall and pie charts intent on conveying the statistics for small rural General Practice surgeries she didn't really understand. As she and Scott had arrived late (she really would send in a letter of complaint re the King's Cross knicker-rifler) they'd been unable to sit together and, as she squirmed on the hard plastic, she found her eyes drifting again and again towards Scott seated two rows in front of her. He'd shrugged off his coat in the over-heated hotel conference room, the tanned skin of his neck in his pink-striped shirt revealed as he bent over his laptop. Juno felt an almost overpowering urge to go and press her mouth to that place where his skin merged into the curling black hair, to feel the warmth of his skin beneath her fingers, beneath her lips...

'Did you get that last bit?'

'Sorry?' Juno was brought abruptly back from her little fantasy with Scott's neck by the bloke on her right leaning into her, spreading his oversized thighs over onto her bit of orange plastic as he did so.

'That last statistic on the elderly – I didn't quite catch it. Was it 15 per cent or 85 per cent are over the age of eighty in rural communities?'

'Er, the first I think.' 85 per cent octogenarians? Was the man mad? Juno endeavoured to look intelligent as well as absorbed, wanting to escape back into her little Scott scenario. She gave the fat chap an on/off smile, shifting herself pointedly away from the man's bulk and looking once more in the direction of the course leader who happened to be slightly to the north-east of Scott. Did he have chest hair? Scott, not the course leader. Juno tried to visualise Scott's torso inside the crisp, beautifully ironed shirt. Who'd ironed it for him? She frowned. Did Antipodean men iron for themselves? Weren't they all a bit, you know, *Gooday, Bruce,* wielding alligators like *Crocodile Dundee.* Crocodiles, Juno, otherwise it would be *Alligator Dundee.* Or was that just Australians? Did New Zealanders favour sheep? And was she being terribly sexist as well as stereotypical? She was now drifting into a rather lovely scenario where Scott, in the manner of Farmer Gabriel Oak, was chasing towards the high cliffs ahead of them, his precious New Zealand flock of Merinos (it was the only breed she could recall from Westenbury Comp Geography sessions with the teacher whose name she couldn't) about to tumble to their demise and she, Juno, singlehandedly had managed to stop from leaping to their death over the cliff...

Juno's head rolled onto Fatso and she jumped as she realised she'd fallen asleep and, oh Lordy, was dribbling into the bargain. Her ridiculously early start, long tramp through the streets of London plus the almost overpowering heat in the room was having her eyes closing once more. Bit daft, that saving sheep thing; she was probably as nervous of sheep – nasty devil-eyed creatures – as her mother-in-law's hounds and Harry Trotter.

'Mint?' Her neighbour shoved a tube of extra strong mints under Juno's nose and she took one gratefully, sat up straight and tried to concentrate on the lecture which had moved on to incontinence in elderly men in rural areas. Couldn't they just nip over the wall and pee in a field if they got caught short?

A different speaker rose to the rostrum – a woman this time – but the content of her lecture was no more riveting than the last. Juno reached for her complimentary bottle of water and tried hard to concentrate but, by 5 p.m. she was beginning to give up the will to live. When, at 5.30 p.m., the speakers appeared to be wrapping it up and the majority of the GPs present were looking at their watches and reaching for coats and jackets, a couple of them, who obviously had nothing better to do on a Saturday evening in this, the best city in the world, raised their hands in order to pose questions.

Scott turned and very discreetly pulled an imaginary knife across his throat, crossing his eyes in mock despair as he did so. Juno giggled, relieved that it wasn't just her that had had enough. Ten minutes later he stood and made his way towards her, taking her hand. 'Come on, let's get out while we can.'

They walked quickly out into the street, breathing in the cool spring air. Even London city air smelt wonderful after the cloying, stultifying warmth of the conference room. 'I need a drink,' Scott breathed, still holding Juno's hand. 'Or would you rather get a taxi straight to your hotel?'

'Drink, definitely. And a large one please.' Juno stood and turned towards Scott and then found she couldn't tear her eyes away from his as he smiled down at her. The moment, probably no more than a second or two, seemed to go on for ever as the late Saturday afternoon shoppers and tourists tutted and frowned, impatient at the necessity of walking round the pair of them. Scott put up cool fingers and stroked Juno's face briefly before taking her case in one hand and her hand in his other and leading her into a bar on the corner of the street.

The place was surprisingly quiet and Juno was able to find a seat while Scott went to the bar, returning with a bottle of chilled Marlborough Sauvignon Blanc and a couple of glasses.

'Are you going to stay in London tonight?' Juno was unable to refrain from asking.

Scott said nothing but poured each of them a large glass and handed Juno's to her. 'Be careful with that,' he said finally, 'it's a large glass and I bet you've not eaten since lunchtime?'

'Breakfast time actually; no money to buy lunch.' She smiled ruefully at the memory, the heavenly wine hitting every spot that needed hitting, firing up every one of her senses as Scott smiled back in turn. Emboldened by the alcohol she repeated: 'So, tonight? Are you staying in London or are you going to take the train back north?'

'That depends on you,' he said, replacing his glass and taking Juno's hand.

'On me?'

'Juno, you must know I'd like to spend time with you. Be with you...' Scott broke off, frowning.

Juno felt her pulse race. This, for heaven's sake, was all she'd been dreaming of for weeks. Taking a deep breath, she asked, 'But?'

He took her hand. 'But you're a married woman. I've no idea what the state of your marriage is. I don't want to be the one to mess things up for you...'

'I think they're pretty messed up already,' Juno said sadly. 'I mean, I'd be in Boston with Fraser if they weren't, don't you think?'

'I really don't know. You never talk about him. Are you together? What? The last thing I want to be is the cause of... you know...' Scott trailed off but continued to stroke Juno's hand gently. There was something incredibly erotic about the way in which his thumb moved slowly across the base of her own.

'I'm not very good at this,' Juno said before taking a huge gulp of wine and spilling some of the liquid onto her hand.

'I wouldn't have thought you were,' Scott laughed, mopping at her hand with his scarf. 'You really should have something to eat, you know. That's going to go straight to your head.'

'I'm not hungry.' Juno held his eyes, unable to look away. She didn't think she'd ever before felt such a powerful lust for any man; had never before needed so badly to be kissed.

'Come here,' Scott said softly. He took her hands, kissing the tip of each finger in turn before reaching for her mouth. It was barely a kiss, a mere touching of warm full lips to her own, but it was enough to send a bolt of lust right down to the very place it mattered. 'What do you want to do?' he whispered. 'Where would you like to go?'

'I'd like to find my hotel,' Juno said, all caution thrown to the wind. 'And I'd like you to find it with me.'

'Are you sure?'

Juno nodded.

'Come on then, let's go.' Scott hailed a taxi with a confidence that Juno knew Fraser could never emulate. Cabs would usually sail by him as he fussed and grumbled about the potential cost of a ride when they could have walked the distance. Even in the rain.

They didn't speak in the taxi, no arm, leg or particle of clothing touching, and Juno began to wonder if she'd imagined the sexual charge between them. Had she made it all up after a large glass of wine on an empty stomach? Was Scott about to drop her off at the hotel before continuing on to King's Cross and the train back north?

'We're here.' Scott paid the taxi fare and opened the cab door for her.

'Goodness.' Juno was momentarily lost for words as she

looked up at the display of blatant ostentation that was the Clarion Hotel. Almost immediately a uniformed porter – presumably more accustomed to the usual Louis Vuitton and Bottega Veneta luggage of the hotel guests – took charge of her battered purple case, wincing slightly, whether at the sight of the sawn-off handle or because he'd nicked his finger on the rough metal Juno wasn't quite sure.

Five minutes later she had the key card to the room in her hand but, as she turned to look for Scott, was surprised to see him in conversation at the other end of the long stretch of wood and metal that was reception. She made her way over to him, frowning.

'Just booking in,' he said. 'There's a single room free.'

'Oh.' She'd obviously read the signs wrongly and, embarrassed, she turned away.

'Juno.' Scott took her arm and moved her towards the elevator. 'Are you sure about this...?' The elevator door closed on them and Juno realised she'd never been more sure of anything in her life. His hand reached for the back of her head and, clutching a mass of curls, he brought her face up to his own, kissing the corners of her mouth, gently sucking at her top lip until she was convinced her legs would have to give way beneath her. Scott pressed her gently towards the back of the lift and, as they reached their intended floor, simultaneously pressed the lift button so that Juno suddenly found herself whooshing back downwards instead of up. Crikey, this was like something out of a film. Loving every moment, she instinctively pressed her face into Scott's neck and the combination of the movement of the elevator together with the wine she'd drunk and the heady scent of this gorgeous man's skin was enough – she would at a later date tell Ariadne – to have her almost climax on the spot.

They tumbled out of the elevator onto a long, red-carpeted corridor and, following the signs indicating room numbers, turned quickly left and found Izzy and Declan's room. My *room*, Juno thought to herself. *The room where I'm going to make love to a man who isn't my husband.*

And what a room. It was palatial – everything from the heavy, floor-length damask curtains with their twisted rope tie backs, to the bedcover and pillow shams and on to the huge amount of carefully folded and presented fluffy towels was all in cream. The bathroom would have easily fitted three of Juno's bathroom back at home and the ridiculously over the top basket of fruit, together with a selection of expensive-looking chocolates, had her almost gasping in wonder.

'I just want to stand and stare at it,' Juno finally said. 'You know, not disturb any of it by using the towels or eating a banana.'

'Try a grape.' Scott smiled at her delight and threw one in her direction which she deftly caught and ate. He moved towards her, cupping her face in his large, tanned hands. 'Juno,' he almost sighed, 'if I don't make love to you this very minute, I really think I shall go mad...'

# 19

'So, what did you actually get up to in London, Mum?' Gabe spoke through a huge mouthful of toast, his eyes on the previous day's sports pages.

'Up to?' Juno felt herself grow pink and her nether regions respond deliciously as she recalled in detail exactly what she had been *up to* in the Clarion Hotel with the good doctor. Sipping at a huge mug of tea, her appetite for some reason totally gone, Juno gazed out of the kitchen window at the early morning sunshine playing delicately on the burgeoning leaves of a clump of tulips. Juno had planted what had seemed, back at the start of November, a never- ending pile of spring bulbs and here in front of her was her reward. Another month or so and they would be a riot of colour. If someone had told her then, with Fraser standing grumpily beside her, recruited unwillingly to help with the heavier digging, but obviously desperate to get back to the warmth of his study, that by the time the tulips were making their first foray from the dark earth, she would be in love... with another man. Not Fraser.

'Mum?'

'Sorry, darling, what did you say?' Juno glanced at the kitchen clock. 'You're going to be late for school. Where's Tilda?'

'London? What did you do there?'

*Had the most amazing sex I'd ever imagined possible*, Juno thought dreamily. Was this what it was all about then? Had she got to the age of almost forty before understanding what the songs and poetry were all in aid of? Never once with poor old Fraser had she cried out like she had on Saturday evening with Scott. She turned back once more to the garden, watching a couple of wood pigeons sitting side by side on the post of the new paddock fence. They were flirting, the smaller bird bobbing its head towards the larger – probably male – pigeon before coyly stepping along the fence before being followed by the other. Golly, was the whole world, now that spring was bursting forth everywhere she looked, thinking only of sex? Juno frowned, continuing to gaze out of the window towards the paddock. Was she depriving poor Mrs May, Mrs Thatcher and Moaning Myrtle of a bit of fun? Of their rights? Did she need to do what Tilda kept suggesting and find them a rampant cockerel?

'Mum…?'

'Oh sorry, darling, have you had breakfast?'

'Breakfast? Mum, you made me scrambled eggs half an hour ago.' Tilda narrowed her eyes. 'Are you alright?'

'Alright?' Juno smiled.

'You've been a bit strange ever since you got back yesterday. You didn't even have a fit when we told you Aunty Ariadne lost us.'

'Not exactly *lost*, surely?'

'Well, it seemed a bit like it, you know. I'm not convinced she was taking her responsibilities seriously. She said she was happy to take us to the Trinity Centre in Wakefield so

Gabe could spend his birthday money on new trainers if we didn't mind stopping off at the Hepworth gallery for half an hour to look at the current exhibition...'

Current? Juno frowned. When *she* was Tilda's age, a current meant a little black thing in the Eccles Cakes Patrick, with his sweet tooth, had loved so much. Or being warned to stay out of the sea during a week's holiday in Filey when the current was dangerous, and where Helen had cried for the last few days of that week when the much looked-forward to family holiday was spoiled because Patrick suddenly had to go back to sort some problem at university in Manchester. And she and Pandora were literally left holding the baby on the beach while Helen stayed indoors in the lovely flat on the North shore, refusing to get out of bed and join them.

'... and then Aunty Ariadne got *so* involved with Barbara...'

'Barbara...?'

'Hepworth. Which I can understand because the sculptures really are quite stunning...'

'Right...'

'But even *I* got rather bored in the end, and she said it was OK for Gabe and me to go over to the shopping centre. But then we couldn't find her again for ages. We really were *lost*. We could have been kidnapped, *groomed*...'

'Alright, alright, Tilda. Enough. School. Go!'

Oh goodness, Juno thought, as the kitchen door finally banged behind the children. She really *was* her father's daughter. While she'd been frolicking with her knickers down in a posh hotel in London, her poor children had been in mortal danger. She walked over towards the window to throw the remains of the now-cold tea down the sink. The two wood-pigeons were still there but had been joined by a third: a rather cross-looking male. She hadn't, Juno realised with a sinking feeling as she began attacking the dirty breakfast dishes, given a thought to Fraser, toiling away in Boston, working his socks off in the freezing cold of a North American winter, working for the good of her and the children.

'Mortal danger?' Ariadne scoffed that evening as they sat in Westenbury village hall waiting for the others to arrive for the weekly rehearsal of *Jesus Christ, Superstar*. They were eight weeks in and, although Juno was nowhere near word-perfect with the many numbers the chorus were singing, the tunes were firmly in her head. Gabe had taken to joining in with '*Jesus Christ, Superstar, six-foot-tall and he wears a bra,*' whenever she was practising at home, which, he knew, always made her laugh. Her son really didn't have a bad voice at all.

Desperate to see Scott after leaving him at Wakefield train station the previous afternoon, Juno was experiencing that wonderful feeling of 'waiting to catch sight of the love object'. The palms of her hands, as she clutched her file holding the musical's score, were moist with the anticipation and excitement of seeing Scott again. 'Yes, mortal danger,' Juno now repeated, making a big effort to concentrate on what Ariadne was saying. 'Tilda reckoned she was about to be whisked off from the Trinity Centre by white-slave traffickers.'

'I very much doubt it.' Ariadne raised an eyebrow. 'They'd soon realise their mistake with that one and be handing her back where she came from.' She smiled. 'I do like your kids, Juno. I wish I'd been able to spend more time with them when they were growing up.'

'They still are growing up, you daft thing. Tilda isn't eleven yet.'

'She does appear a lot older. I was trying to work out whether I've missed out on not having children myself,' Ariadne said, frowning slightly. 'I don't think I have, to be honest, but I would love to be more involved with your two.'

'Help yourself.' Juno smiled. 'Any time.'

'The thing is, by the time I came back to Westenbury, Hugo was no longer a little boy and then Pandora and Richard had bundled him off to boarding school; I don't feel I know him at all either. But Tilda reminds me so much of myself when I was her age. It's weird.'

'I've always said she's a mixture of you, Pandora and Fraser's mother. I don't think I've even had a look in.'

'They don't seem to be missing Uncle Quentin, do they?'

'Uncle Quentin?' Juno turned from watching the entrance for Scott's arrival and frowned. 'Who's Uncle Quentin?'

Ariadne began to laugh. 'Sorry, I've always called your Fraser Uncle Quentin.

'Have you? Why?'

'You know, in Enid Blyton's *Famous Five*, Aunt Fanny was married to Uncle Quentin. He was the bad-tempered, irritable scientist who kept himself locked up in his study, only coming out to shout at his wife and kids.'

Juno didn't say anything for a while as she digested Ariadne's analogy. 'Well, as long as you don't refer to me as *Fanny* behind my back. So, is that how he came over? Is that how you saw Fraser?'

'Oh, I'm sure he wasn't like that all the time,' Ariadne said, backtracking as she saw Juno's face.

'Actually, I think he probably was,' Juno said slowly.

'He's never really had much time for the kids. You know, he never remembered their birthdays, only ever once went to see Gabe play football – and that was because it was a cup final and I *insisted* he went. From what I remember, he spent most of it in the car, tussling with some problem from work.'

'I'm sorry.' Ariadne squeezed Juno's hand. 'We Sutherland girls don't seem to have much luck choosing men, do we? Dad ruined Mum's life, Theo Ryan appears to be a narcissistic bully…'

'Hang on,' Juno protested. 'I'd say Mum probably helped ruin her own life. And you don't know that much about Theo and Lexia's marriage. You can't go on what you read in those trashy magazines.'

'I'm not. I called in on Lexia yesterday evening on the way home from your place and Theo was there. I think he drinks, Juno. He seemed hammered to me.'

'Hammered? Professional sportsmen don't get *hammered*, do they? They'd soon be on the transfer list…' Juno paused, realising what she'd just said. 'Anyway, these footballers are all fitness mad and at the gym all the time, aren't they? I know when I was round at Lexia's, the fridge was full of eggs and that bodybuilding powder stuff. The press has always liked to make out Theo Ryan's had other women, but I've never seen anything about him being a boozer.'

'I'm worried about Lexia, Juno. She seems to have that same frailty Mum has always carried round with her. Anyway, I've persuaded Lexia that the four of us should go away somewhere.'

Juno frowned. 'Go away somewhere? Where like?'

'I think we should have a weekend away together. Maybe with Mum, as well. We could rent a cottage in the Dales or

The Lakes or maybe go over to the East Coast like we used to when we were kids? You know, all really get to know one another again; we have become pretty dysfunctional as a family.'

'And did Lexia agree to that?'

Ariadne was prevented from answering by Izzy bustling in and settling down on one of the saved chairs beside them. 'Oh good, you've bagged us all seats. Now, Clementine's invited us all back for a drink and nibbles afterwards. It's Rafe's fortieth birthday. He's been out in Syria again – bloody dangerous place – and Clem's so grateful to have him back she's putting on a bit of a surprise do for him at the restaurant.'

'What's he been doing out there?' Ariadne asked, surprised.

'He's one of the BBC's Middle East correspondents. You know, he's sometimes on the telly? Not as much as he used to be when he was based in London, but he's often away. He's missed loads of rehearsals. Anyway, he's quite famous really. We just need your Lexia to join the choir and we'd be bound to win the competition just on the number of famous faces alone.'

'Who's she invited?'

'Oh, you know Clem, she's so lovely, it'll be open house at the restaurant – she doesn't usually open the place on a Monday but she's been busy making a load of canapes and there's champagne. Now, how was my hotel room in London? No, no, don't tell me, I want to prolong the anticipation. Actually,' Izzy lowered her voice and whispered, 'I've just rebooked it for after Easter. Don't tell Declan though, it's a surprise. Actually, might be more of a shock when he realises he's coughing up that sort of hard cash once more.' She started to laugh when Juno, feeling terribly guilty, protested that she should really pay them for her share of the room. 'Oh, don't worry, Juno, we're well in with his mother again after the weekend – after a couple of glasses of champagne she even wrote Declan a fabulous cheque for his birthday…'

'Are we ready to rock, people?' Pandora had taken to the stage with her baton and was gathering the troops.

'I'm just sorry your weekend was spoiled by Scott Butler suddenly deciding he was going to go too.' Pandora rapped her baton loudly in Izzy's direction and glared down at her from her rostrum, but Izzy carried on in a whisper. 'You didn't actually have to *sit* with him, did you? Well, at least you didn't have to share my lovely *room* with him… Sorry, Pandora, over to you…'

'La la la la la la la la la… Scott Butler was with you in London?' Ariadne hissed in Juno's direction in between Pandora's warm up exercises.

'Well, yes… la la la… he happened to be there… la la la la la la…'

'Just *happened* to… la la la la la la la la… *be there*? And that last note was flat.'

'No wonder when you keep butting in…'

'So, you kept that quiet…'

'Shhh…'

'Ah, the dishy doctor's just arrived.' Juno felt her pulse race at Ariadne's words and, continuing to sing the opening chorus, both of them watched as Declan and Scott made their way down to the tenors.

'Don't think you're getting away without telling me

*everything*,' Ariadne whispered as, on Pandora's instructions, they marked with pencil various changes to their scores.

'Shh, the last thing I want is Izzy thinking there's anything going on.'

'And is there?' Ariadne turned, staring at Juno who felt herself go pink under her big sister's scrutiny. Ariadne glanced across the room towards the tenors and, when Juno refused to answer, added, 'Well, he's really quite gorgeous, Juno, I'll give you that. But be careful…'

She was broken off by Jesus hurrying down the aisle to his place at the front where his disciples were gathered.

'Sorry, Pandora, sorry all, my apologies for being late. Something came up…'

'Yes, your bloody cock, no doubt.' The words reverberated loudly round the village hall as the choir turned en masse, craning necks and whispering:

'What did he just say?'

'Did he just say *cock*?'

'No, don't be silly, it was *clock*. Clock wasn't it? Something about his *clock*? That's why he's late…?'

'No, definitely his *cock*…'

There was a sudden silence in the room, like the proverbial calm before the storm and then, without further warning, Herod, aka Philip Braithwaite (Braithwaite's: Family Butcher Since 1930) launched from his position in the third row, leaping on Jesus and knocking him to the floor. Taken by surprise, the pair rolled across the dusty wooden floor towards, and then actually underneath, the stage, Herod flinging punches as well as insults, and then reappearing, this time Jesus on top as the Almighty gained the upper hand.

Juno had an awful feeling that the disciples were on

the verge of shouting, 'Fight! Fight! Fight!' when Mary Magdalene upped and ran across from the first sopranos and attempted to pull Herod – aka Philip Braithwaite – from Brett Bailey from Barnsley.

'Get off him, Phil, you fool. You're hurting him. Look, he's bleeding.' Rosemary Braithwaite thumped her husband hard on his arm and bent down to help Brett up from the floor.

'For the love of God, get up the pair of you,' Scott shouted as he and Declan raced down the aisle towards the three of them and, while Scott manhandled Brett Bailey to one side of the room, Declan took hold of Philip Braithwaite, pulling him across to the other. Juno watched aghast at the scene unfolding in front of them all, thinking that Fraser would never in a million years have got involved.

'If you go with him now, that's it, that's the *end* of you and me…' A now tearful Philip shouted after his wife as she, in turn, hurried after Brett Bailey, who, after shaking off Scott, had grabbed his jacket and marched towards the entrance.

'I must have been mad joining up with an amateurish bunch like you lot. I've performed at *The Crucible* in *Sheffield*, for heaven's sake. Westenbury Village Hall? God, give me strength! I'm out of here and, without me, this poxy little production is going *nowhere*.' Jesus actually hissed the words, swinging his black coat around his shoulders like the baddy in some amateur panto.

'I was very tempted to shout back, "Oh yes, it is,"' Ariadne giggled as they all trooped out of the village hall, with those invited carrying on up the hill, past the church and on to Clementine's, the much revered fine-dining restaurant run by Clementine Ahern. 'Unfortunately, I reckon we're snookered. Not much poor old Pandora can do when she's one Jesus, one Herod and one Mary Magdalene short of a production.'

'I can't believe Jesus was actually having it off with Mary Magdalene.' Izzy was most put out. What's Rosemary Braithwaite got that I haven't? Well, I'll tell you: haemorrhoids, that's what.'

'Isn't that breaking the Hippocratic oath, Izzy?' Ariadne ventured.

'Yes, sorry, you didn't hear that from me. As far as I'm aware, Mary Magdalene *doesn't* have, and never has had, bum grapes.' She paused. 'Honest.'

'Where's Pandora now? Is she coming to Clem's?' Juno felt terribly sorry for her sister. She might be an absolute pain at times but she was, after all, her sister. She turned and, seeing Pandora head for the carpark instead of following the chosen few up the hill, began to run back towards her. 'Come on, Ariadne, let's grab her. She can't go home like this.'

The two of them broke off from the others and ran the few hundred yards back in the direction they'd just come. 'Pandora, come on, come to Clem's with us. Don't go home.'

'Richard will be waiting for me.' Tears were coursing down her face, her mascara running in rivulets towards her mouth so that she resembled a somewhat pathetic-looking Alice Cooper.

'No, he won't,' Ariadne said, taking Pandora's car keys from her hand while Juno handed her a tissue. 'It's Monday night – you've always gone on about how Richard is *always* at his Rotary thing on a Monday night.' She patted Pandora's arm. 'We'll be able to find another Jesus. Surely Sally Russell, with all the productions she's done, will know where there's a spare one hanging around?'

Juno wanted to laugh at that, as if there were any numbers of the Almighty just hanging around to step into Brett Bailey's shoes, but Pandora shook her head, and started crying once again, huge fat tears that she appeared unable to control and which dripped messily onto the collar of her pristine white shirt. 'There are productions in rehearsal all over the place at the moment,' she sobbed, 'you know, because of this competition. All the good ones have been scooped up. Any left are not worth having.' Pandora's tears disintegrated into huge sobs where she appeared to be finding it difficult to breathe. Juno suddenly realised she'd never seen Pandora cry; never seen her anything but in total charge of any situation. It was a bit like seeing one's headmistress, or Mrs Thatcher (the actual Mrs Thatcher, not one of her chucks) totally out of control.

Juno looked across at Ariadne and pulled a worried face. 'Come on, Pandora, it's not that bad; you'll laugh about this one day.'

'I can't do it any longer,' she sobbed, rubbing at her eyes and reminding Juno of her kids when they were toddlers and too tired to be reasoned with.

'Well, no, you don't have to…'

'*It*,' Pandora snarled before collapsing into huge sobs once again. 'I can't do *it* anymore.'

Ariadne put her arms round Pandora. 'What is it, Pandora? What can't you do anymore?'

'It. It *all*. It's been going on too long. I'm scared, Ariadne, frightened of it *all*.'

# 20

Juno had only once been to Clementine's restaurant before, when Fraser had surprised and delighted her by making a booking for the pair of them to celebrate their wedding anniversary the first year they'd moved down from Aberdeen and into the house in Westenbury. The evening, to which Juno had so looked forward and for which she'd bought a ridiculously expensive dress she couldn't really afford, had gone steadily downhill when her mother-in-law had arrived unannounced from Scotland in pursuit of a rare Cleveland Bay stallion in nearby Dewsbury and descended, horsebox and all, just as the babysitter had arrived, insisting she'd have a quick wash and brush up and join them for their meal. Fraser and his mother had spent the evening complaining about the tiny portions and ridiculous expense of the meal and Juno had wanted to cry.

'Where's Pandora? Is she OK?' Izzy made her way straight over as Juno was directed into the Orangery by one of Clem's helpers. Izzy had a mouthful of canapé, as well as another delicious looking morsel in one hand and a large glass of champagne in the other. 'God, these are fantastic.' Izzy chewed and swallowed, closing her eyes in ecstasy. 'I've been on a diet all day just so I could pig out on these tonight.

And Ariadne? Is she not with you either?' Izzy glanced over Juno's shoulder, raising an eyebrow as well as her glass of champagne as she noticed that Juno wasn't accompanied by either of her sisters.

'I don't think Pandora will make it here now,' Juno said, accepting her own glass of fizz while simultaneously trying to work out where Scott was in the room. 'She's terribly upset that her dream of Westenbury being in all the papers as the winner of the village choir competition has been totally kyboshed. You know what she's like. She sets herself such high standards, such high expectations of everything she attempts, and this has been a real kick in the teeth for her. I've actually never seen Pandora cry before – well I don't think I have, apart from maybe at Hugo's christening – and she wept buckets tonight.'

'It's not such a big deal, is it?' Izzy frowned, obviously trying to put herself in Pandora's shoes.

'It is to Pandora. She feels totally humiliated, let down by us all.'

'Well, that's just daft. It was just a bit of *fun*, not the end of the world.'

'To say you're a doctor, you don't have a great deal of empathy, Izzy.' Juno felt cross on her sister's behalf.

'A bit unfair, that.' Izzy frowned. 'I empathised totally with Mrs Jackson this morning when she told me that now Mr Jackson has discovered Viagra, she doesn't have a minute to herself to listen to the *Archers...*'

'Pandora not come back with you?' Scott was suddenly at Juno's side and she smiled up at him, delighted not only that he was here and had come to find her, but also grateful that he'd interrupted the conversation between herself and Izzy. Much as she loved Izzy, her friend did have a flippant side that, on occasions like now, when Juno was feeling upset at Pandora's obvious, and what had been quite shocking distress, was not only inappropriate, but, frankly, grated.

Izzy, frowning slightly at Scott, moved away in search of more entertaining company and, as she did so, Scott smiled down at Juno. She considered throwing caution to the wind by putting her arm on his – she really wanted to wrap her arms and legs around his waist and feel his warmth and inhale his maleness that, while in London, she'd made her own – but knew to keep her distance. Tongues from the chattering classes in a village like Westenbury would soon be going ten-to-the dozen if it was rumoured that the new dishy locum was having it off with his – married – colleague.

'Ariadne has driven back home with her. She said she'd wait with her until Richard returned from his meeting and then come back down and join us if she can.' Juno shook her head. 'I've never seen Pandora like that before.'

'She's seen her dream in tatters,' Scott said. 'What do you expect?'

Juno finally allowed her eyes to meet his. God, but he was gorgeous. She felt a bolt of lust go through her as he returned the stare and it was all she could do not to reach up and touch his face. 'Oh,' she suddenly realised, 'you're hurt…'

'Jesus had a pretty good right hook,' he grinned. 'One landed as I was trying to get him off Philip Braithwaite.'

'You're going to have a black eye in the morning.'

'Yep, looks like it. Juno, did anyone ever tell you, you have the most wonderful mouth?'

Juno shook her head. 'No, I can't say anyone ever has.'

'Well, I'm telling you now, it's infinitely kissable. Just looking at it makes me—'

'OK, everyone, if I could just have a word?' Clementine Ahern moved to where the drinks were laid out. 'Thank you so much for coming over this evening – and obviously a lot earlier than anticipated.' She looked round the Orangery. 'Is Pandora here? Sally? No? Look, I know Pandora's not here, but I don't see why this has to be the end of the road for the production. I've really enjoyed the rehearsals so far, loved every minute and all that's down to Pandora. I think we all appreciate just how hard she's worked to get this show on the road. Surely, we're not going to let it all go to waste? We just need one new Jesus? Is that too much to ask?'

'Our Granville'll do it!' Janice Winterbottom shouted from the back of the room. 'He's wanted to be Jesus all along.'

'Oh, heaven help us,' Izzy muttered in Juno's ear. 'Granville Winterbum as the Almighty? He's only four-foot-six, and bald as a coot.'

'He can wear a wig,' Juno said, trying not to laugh. Izzy might be flippant but she still knew how to amuse.

'He'd have to borrow Janice's heels,' Izzy said, seriously considering. She linked Juno's arm in her own as they stood listening to Clementine. 'Sorry, if I was a bit, you know, not overly sympathetic,' she whispered. 'Pandora has been an absolute trooper; she doesn't deserve what happened this evening.'

'No, she doesn't. Maybe Clem's right and we *can* carry on...?'

'Lexia. Your Lexia?' Izzy whispered, rather more loudly

now so that those around turned to hear what she was saying.

'As Jesus? Erm? Wrong sex?'

'Hey, times is hard. Beggars can't be choosers. And actually, maybe we could gain points by being gender-fluid?' Izzy laughed and then tutted. 'No, not Jesus, you daft thing. As Mary Magdalene? It's not a huge part. *I don't know how to lo-ove him...*' Izzy sang, so out of tune Juno wondered for a second whether throwing in the towel on the whole production wasn't the best thing after all. 'We need to get Lexia Sutherland,' Izzy now shouted to the room. 'Clem, we need to get Lexia on board as Mary Magdalene. Anyone can camp it up as Herod,' she went on. 'And if Granville will be Jesus – we can always find him a ladder – then we're back in business.'

'Shh,' Juno tutted, torn between wanting to laugh at the image of Granville Winterbottom singing up a ladder and worry that, knowing both Pandora's and Lexia's stance on Lexia taking part in the production, Izzy's putting Lexia forward as a third of the answer to their problems, would never come to fruition.

'Yes, come on, Juno. Lexia's your sister for heaven's sake,' someone yelled.

'And Pandora's,' another shouted. 'If the pair of you want to save the production, Lexia's going to have to help.'

'OK, OK,' Juno protested, when all eyes turned towards her. 'I'll see what I can do. I'm not promising, though; Lexia doesn't sing at all in public these days.'

'Right, shall we move on?' Clementine, seeing Juno was embarrassed, raised a glass. 'I've invited you all here tonight to celebrate Rafe's big birthday. He didn't want any reminder that he was getting any older...'

'The grey hairs are doing that all by themselves,' Rafe Ahern laughed, stroking a newly acquired, slightly grey beard.

'... but I couldn't let the occasion go without a bit of a do.' Clem smiled in the direction of her husband. 'I'm sure most of you know the danger Rafe puts himself in every time he sets off once again to report on the terrible things that are happening in the Middle East and particularly Syria. The minute he's back I can breathe again.' She paused. 'Rafe, I love you. I love everything about you: your humility, your empathy with those who are suffering...' She broke off, unable to go on. 'But most of all I love you because you love me, and have taken on Allegra, loving her as much as our own daughter, Lucinda. Sorry, Rafe, I'm embarrassing you now. Can we all just raise a glass to Rafe? Happy Birthday, darling.'

Would anyone ever look at her in the way Rafe Ahern was looking at – and now kissing – Clem? Juno thought sadly. Certainly, Fraser never had.

'I need some air, Juno,' Scott was saying at her side. 'Come with me?'

With Izzy stuck into the champagne once more and discussing at length with Clem and Harriet Westmoreland how the production could be saved, Juno felt it safe to leave the orangery in Scott's wake. The March night was cold and Juno shivered as the fresh air hit her. Once outside, Scott pulled her into the warmth of his arms and, winding his fingers through her hair, brought her mouth to his own, kissing her gently and then, as she responded, with more urgency.

'I've been thinking about you all day,' Scott breathed into her neck, his hands warm under Juno's best cashmere sweater.

Juno laughed, loving the intimacy, the warmth of his body in contrast to the cold Spring night. 'What? Even when you were examining someone's bunions?'

'Especially then,' Scott laughed. He stroked her face, looking directly into her eyes. 'I don't suppose you can come back home with me after this? I have an almost overwhelming need to remind myself of all your delicious bits and pieces.'

'No, much as I'd like to help you with that, my children are waiting for me at home. Mum's babysitting again, so I can't be too late.'

'It's enough to be with you here, Juno,' Scott said, his voice serious. 'I don't know what you've done to me...' He pulled her closer and kissed her again, his hands moving firmly over her bottom as he teased her tongue and lips with his own.

'This feels so heavenly,' she breathed, kissing him back as he gently pushed her up against the outside wall of the restaurant. 'I don't think I've ever...'

'Juno?' Izzy stared, taking in the situation, for once lost for words. 'Need to get off home,' she said quickly, handing her car keys to Declan who was a few steps behind her, seemingly equally perplexed at the sight of his two colleagues wrapped round each other. 'Robbie's just phoned to say Emily's suddenly arrived back from university for some reason. Well, goodnight. See you both at work.'

'Bugger,' Juno hissed, pulling fingers through her hair and beaming like the village idiot at Izzy and Declan in an attempt to portray nonchalance, and that she and Scott were simply in the process of taking a breath of fresh air while discussing how best to cascade the information gleaned at the weekend's conference rather than anything more defamatory. Izzy and Declan hurried off in the direction of the carpark without a backward glance and Juno closed her eyes, imagining full well their conversation once they were in the car and driving back home.

'I'm sorry.' Scott pulled a face. 'That's the last thing you need.'

'*I* need?' Juno pulled her own face. 'What about *you*?'

'I'm not the one with a husband,' Scott said gently, wiping a smudge of mascara from underneath Juno's lashes. 'But Juno,' he added, as they walked back towards the restaurant, 'I so wish you didn't have.' He allowed Juno to walk into the Orangery alone, as if, to any one observing, she had simply been out to the restroom and, a few minutes later, he headed for the bar, alone.

> Bloody hell, Juno, what do you think you're playing at? Scott Butler is the biggest womaniser out,
>
> Izzy.
>
> Bloody hell, Juno, as soon as you get this message, ring me. Pandora's just told me everything,
>
> Ariadne.

Covered with embarrassment that both Izzy and Declan had caught her snogging the new locum up against the wall in Clementine's garden, Juno had left immediately she received the text from Ariadne, telling Scott something had come up and she had to leave and no, thank you, she didn't need him to leave with her. He'd given her a strange look – probably thinking it was Fraser who'd texted her – and turned back to the bar, ordering another beer while she'd gathered her things and made a dash over to Pandora's.

She'd been met with a sobbing Pandora, a grim-faced Ariadne and Richard who didn't seem to quite know what to do. He'd let her into the kitchen where Ariadne and Pandora were sat over a bottle of gin, suggested she'd probably need a drink too and left the room, returning with one of Pandora's best crystal wedding-present glasses. Then he'd told her to get stuck in, Helen had already agreed to stay another hour with Gabe and Tilda and he'd pay for a taxi to get her home as soon as they told her everything that would, very probably, be soon splashed all over the tabloids.

# 21

*December 2002*

*Lexia*

The disastrous and unproductive *TheBest* audition at the Lowry centre in Manchester didn't put Lexia off from her dream of being the next Holly Valance. The guy who'd listened to her had been so impressed. 'Wow, simply, wow!' Wasn't that what he'd said when he'd heard her sing? Didn't he say that, if she'd only been seventeen, she'd be going straight through to the rounds in front of Steve Silverton and Kika Everton, the judges who could make or break the dreams of those whose only ambition was to win the next series? To be the next new star everyone would be talking about?

So, rather than admit defeat and return her thoughts to school and her GCSEs, the trip to Manchester only made Lexia more determined. She was good – no, she was *really* good – and if it meant exercising a little patience, she would use the time until the following year when she would be seventeen to practise until she was perfect and then, *then* she would take the singing world by storm. Lexia knew she would allow nothing, absolutely nothing, to stand in the way of her fulfilling what she knew was her right, her *destiny* even. She smiled into the darkness of her chilly bedroom while she floated off to sleep, hugging her hot water bottle to her slim body at the very idea that her destiny was already set in stone.

And then there was Damian. He was so lovely, so grown up and knew about *everything*. Nothing like the lads at school with their pink-porridge-acned faces, their cheese-and-onion breath and their constant bra-pinging as they bumped into her along the corridors of Westenbury Comp.

Lexia was starting to spend more and more time down at the Ambassador Club, meeting Damian once she'd legged it out of school and off into town, telling Pandora she'd given up the idea of *TheBest* and was working hard, revising down in the public library for her mock exams coming up in January. Pleased that Lexia appeared to have given up the ridiculous idea of becoming the next superstar, Pandora had bought her a pile of revision guides from WHSmith and even sat down with her to go over her exam timetable, suggesting how to break up her revision time into digestible chunks for each subject. Lexia had gone along with it, had even enjoyed colouring in the timetable with different, vibrant colours, but the minute Pandora left to return home to Richard, she would fling the books to one side and either sit with her Mum and watch *Coronation Street* and *Eastenders* or, more often, brave the cold of the attic, singing and practising, over and over again, with the sole aim of being ready, once she was seventeen, of winning *TheBest*.

Lexia's sixteenth birthday, just before Christmas,

coincided with Pandora's proud declaration that she was twelve weeks' pregnant and, now that any danger of miscarriage was much reduced – Pandora had read every book, magazine and article about early pregnancy – felt able to tell the world of an imminent heir not only for herself and Richard but, just as importantly, for Boothroyd, Boothroyd and Dyson.

On hearing the wonderful news that the Boothroyd line was to be continued – Richard was the only male of four siblings – Richard's father, William Boothroyd, insisted he and Richard's mother take their only son and his wife for a celebratory meal, and of course, Lexia and Helen must join them too, especially as it was Lexia's birthday as well. A double celebration in fact.

'Do I *have* to come with you?' Lexia moaned. 'I really don't want to – it'll be *boring*.' She was hoping Damian would come up with an alternative – maybe take her out for a pizza or something – but so far, despite massive hints that it was her birthday weekend coming up and there was that fabulous new pizza place that all the girls at school had already been to and were constantly talking about, Damian hadn't yet suggested any birthday treat. '*I* don't want to go either,' Helen said, almost crossly, when Pandora issued the invitation one teatime, a couple of days before the proposed event at The Four Fields, Midhope's most expensive and prestigious restaurant. 'Not without your father,' she added, turning back to the early evening quiz show on TV. Helen stared at the screen and then appeared to visibly brighten, swivelling round to face Pandora once again. 'Ring him, Pandora. Ring your daddy and tell him about the new baby and that William insists, absolutely *insists* that, as the other grandfather, he must be there too.'

'Dad's still away, Mum,' Pandora said as gently as she could. 'He's promoting his new book in America.'

'And is the Russian trollop with him?' Helen's eyes had filled with unshed tears as she pitifully searched Pandora's face for the truth.

'No, Mum, I don't believe she is,' Pandora returned soothingly. 'Now, come on, Mum, you and Lexia need to be ready for 6.30 p.m. on Friday evening when Richard and I come and pick you both up. We're going to the Four Fields. You'll like that, won't you? Hmm?'

Pandora frowned slightly as she opened the door to the sitting room on the Friday evening and saw Helen and Lexia ready and waiting for her. 'It's really cold out there, Mum. Do you think you're going to be warm enough?' Dressed in a vibrant yellow, sleeveless satin dress she'd had since her early singing days, Helen would, Pandora knew, be the complete antithesis to Bee-Bee Boothroyd who thought it *de rigueur* not to venture out, even to the dustbin, without being properly dressed in one of her selection of Aberdeen pastel cashmere cardigans and pearls, and with face fully Max-Factored and mouth filled in with her favourite coral lipstick. Actually, Pandora thought as she eyed the stain on the right shoulder of Helen's decidedly grubby dress, she'd take bets that Barbara Boothroyd wouldn't even know where her dustbin was kept, in that huge, manicured garden of theirs.

And what the hell was Lexia wearing too? 'Lexia, we're going to the Four Fields...' Pandora tutted crossly, taking in the low-rise velour boot-cut trousers sporting the lettering 'juicy' on her left buttock. A strange-looking off-the shoulder peasant top completed the, to Pandora's jaundiced eye, unfinished, even primitive, ensemble. 'Where've you got those trousers from?'

Lexia wasn't about to tell Pandora the truth: Damian had given them to her. It was a shame they'd not come with the store's carrier bag or receipt, as she'd have liked to change the colour but, hey-ho, he'd bought them for her and must really love her.

'Could you just pull those trousers up a bit? You're showing all your midriff...' Pandora paused. 'And your pants are on show too, for heaven's sake.'

'They're meant to be.' Lexia raised her eyes to the heavens and, pulling on her black thong, did the same with her underwear. 'Look, do I *have* to come with you?'

'It's your birthday, Lexia. And Richard and I are celebrating... you know, our baby...'

'Can't think of anything worse,' Lexia said, yawning as only a sixteen-year-old can yawn. 'All those sleepless nights you're going to be in for. And dirty nappies.'

'Well, can you at least brush your hair?'

Lexia looked genuinely put out. 'I have.'

'I wish your daddy was here,' Helen said, wrapping her arms round herself. 'Did you ring him, Pandora...?'

'God, give me strength,' Pandora snapped. 'Will the pair of you get your coats and get into the car? William and Bee-Bee will be wondering where on earth we've got to.'

Lexia, beneath the assumed boredom and bravado, was still quite painfully shy in the company of adults, particularly adults like Pandora's mother-in-law who, it seemed, was intent on looking down her – rather long – nose at both Lexia and her mum. William and Bee-Bee (bloody silly made-up name, Lexia thought crossly) were waiting in the bar of The Four Fields but while William was already stuck into his whiskey and cigars and being hail-fellow-well-met with his golf cronies who regularly met up there on a Friday evening, Bee-Bee was looking decidedly sour-faced.

'Ah, at last, you're here,' she said tartly, air-kissing each of them in turn. 'We're going to lose the table if we don't sit down soon.'

'Oh, we're fine,' William laughed, patting Pandora's abdomen. 'Now, how's my grandson? I hope you're looking after him, Pandora? He's going to be running the Boothroyd company one day, you know.' He turned to Helen. 'Helen, how lovely to see you. You're looking as gorgeous as ever. We don't seem to have seen you since last Christmas. Now what will you have to drink? Gin and tonic…?'

'Mum, do you think you should? You know…?' Pandora was smiling, but Lexia knew she was worried, concerned that alcohol didn't mix well with Helen's medication. Actually, alcohol didn't mix well with Helen, period, regardless of any medication.

Bee-Bee raised a knowing eyebrow but William laughed off Pandora's concerns. 'We need a drink,' he boomed, 'to celebrate the new little Boothroyd. And it's your *birthday*, Lexia. Sweet sixteen and never been kissed, hey?' He laughed, planting a wet kiss on Lexia's cheek while simultaneously patting the 'Juicy' on her bum. (Well, she wouldn't say *that*, exactly Lexia thought to herself, thinking of what she'd done with Damian.) 'Champagne, I reckon.' He turned to the barman. 'Bob, can we have a bottle of that champagne we had at Bee-Bee's birthday do? I'm going to be a grandad again, but this one's going to be a *proper* little Boothroyd. He'll have the Boothroyd name. Have you thought about names, Richard?'

'Not yet, Dad. Long way to go yet.'

'Well, you don't want any of these *modern* names – you know, like Damian or Jason or Justin. You want a nice solid Yorkshire name that'll go with Boothroyd.' He paused to draw on his cigar, blowing the smoke in Pandora's direction. 'Benjamin,' he went on, thinking aloud. 'Or George. Or...' He laughed. 'There's always William, after his granddad.'

Pandora smiled, obviously torn between embarrassment at all the attention, and pride that she, Pandora, was the chosen one to carry on Richard's family name started back in the late 1700s when one Josiah Boothroyd had upped from his weaver's cottage in the Pennine hills beyond Colnefirth and, taking advantage of the plentiful supply of moorland grazing for sheep together with the soft water needed to raise a good lather to rid the fleeces of lanolin, began manufacturing the beautiful woollen cloth that had made Boothroyd an internationally recognised name. 'I really like the name Hugo.' Pandora smiled shyly, placing a protective hand to her middle.

'Hugo.' William paused to consider. 'Yes, I like that. Here's to Hugo Boothroyd. Good choice, Pandora.'

Hugo? Lexia stared at Pandora. What a bloody awful old-fashioned name. And wasn't there a car called a Hugo? Yugo? What was wrong with Dylan or Ethan? 'Maybe it'll be a girl?' Lexia spoke for the first time. 'You know, a 50 per cent chance?' She coloured slightly as she tried to work out if she'd got the maths right; she'd never understood percentages. 'And with *us* all being girls, and *Richard* having three sisters,' she went on boldly, 'well, I bet the chances of it being a girl are 70–80 per cent.' There, that would show Pandora she'd been studying those maths revision books.

'Shall we eat?' Bee-Bee looked put out at Lexia's interrupting William and taking over the conversation. 'I think it might be a little cooler in the restaurant,' she added looking pointedly at the bare flesh on show from both Lexia and Helen. 'Have you two brought some little cover-up with you?'

The evening seemed interminable to Lexia, William Boothroyd becoming more red-faced and garrulous in direct proportion to the amount of red wine he was downing. Lexia had been encouraged both by William and Helen – 'you'll need to acquire a taste for it, darling, once you become famous' – to have some of the champagne to celebrate her birthday, and she'd already drunk a couple of rather large glasses, enjoying the bubbles if not the actual taste. She wished she was down at the Ambassador Club with Damian, and wondered if there was any way she could go on there, afterwards. Her mum would probably have let her get a taxi into town if she said she'd arranged to meet some friends from school later to celebrate her birthday, especially as Helen was also getting stuck into the champagne despite Pandora's attempts at keeping the second bottle away from her. But there was no way Pandora would allow it, considering it bad-mannered to leave the meal and saying she was far too young to be wandering the streets of Midhope. Without her coat and with her pants on show.

The champagne was making Lexia feel slightly woozy and, as she placed her knife and fork together correctly after some strange but rather interesting starter she couldn't quite make out the contents of, she realised Bee-Bee was discussing arrangements for Christmas with Helen.

'And will Patrick be around on Christmas day? You know, to see his daughters?'

'A daughter's for life, not just for Christmas,' Lexia said flippantly, as everyone around the table turned to stare.

'Yes, well...' Pandora glared at Lexia and, obviously forgetting she was pregnant, poured herself a glass of wine and took a rather long sip before realising what she'd done and hastily shoving it down the table towards Richard.

The champagne was making Lexia's mouth say things she knew it shouldn't. 'I think Daddy will be far too busy on Christmas day to think about his old family, especially with...' She shouldn't be saying this, Lexia knew. She needed to shut up. She took a huge gulp of champagne. Actually, she was getting to quite like the taste after all. She giggled as the bubbles burst up her nose.

'Especially with...?' Bee-Bee smiled at Lexia and cocked her head encouragingly to one side.

Lexia stared at Pandora's mother-in-law, fascinated by the crimson lipstick that had bled into both corners of her mouth. 'You know, with the new baby and everything...' *Shut* up, *Lexia, stop your mouth talking*!

'Oh, have you been in touch with Daddy, Pandora?' Helen turned a flushed face to her second daughter, her pupils, Lexia noted, huge in her beautiful brown eyes. 'He knows about the baby?'

'Not *that* baby.' Lexia frowned. 'You know, *his* baby.' Lexia reached for her glass, bringing it up to her mouth in order to stop any more of these words she knew she shouldn't be saying, actually spilling out.

'*His* baby?' Bee-Bee Boothroyd was insistent. 'Your *father* has a new baby?'

'Anyone for pudding?' Richard said in some desperation.

'Pudding?' William frowned. 'I've not had my steak and ale pie yet.' He looked at the table in some confusion 'Or have I...?'

'Daddy's got a new baby, Lexia?' Helen was wringing her napkin feverishly between her long, pale fingers so that Lexia, as she watched in fascination, couldn't quite make out where her mum's white skin became the starched white material.

'Well, not yet,' Lexia said, feeling very dizzy. 'And obviously it's not Dad who's going to have it. That would be daft, wouldn't it?'

'So, is it Daddy's *friend*? Is she having a baby?' Bee-Bee's tone was solicitous, but her face, as she moved those bleeding crimson lips once more towards Lexia, was eager, excited.

*The Joker*, that's it, Lexia thought. That's who Pandora's mother-in-law reminded her of. You know, Batman's friend. Or was he his enemy? 'Well, if you can *call* Anichka, the Russian pole dancer, a *friend*. I'd say she's more of an enemy, wouldn't you? Going off with our dad and getting herself pregnant, for heaven's sake.'

Pandora had gone quite white, obviously terrified of meeting Helen's eyes. 'I don't know where you've got this silly story from, Lexia. You can't have spoken to Daddy – he's in America...' She paused, running her fingers through her blonde bob, glaring at Lexia.

'Oh yes, I know that,' Lexia hiccupped, draining her glass

as she did so. 'He's with some lesbians or something.'

'Don't be ridiculous, Lexia,' Pandora hissed.

'I spoke on the phone to the Russian Trollop and she told me… actually, I'm sorry, I need the loo, I feel a bit funny…'

Lexia stood, pushing back her chair and, as a white-faced Helen also stood, holding onto the starched tablecloth and screaming hysterically, 'no, no, no,' she vomited profusely, but very neatly, over Bee-Bee Boothroyd's black patent kitten heels.

That had been the start of Helen Sutherland's descent into the black hole from which, this time, she was unable to pull herself. While William and Bee-Bee had stayed to finish the celebratory dinner, Richard had taken charge, bundling a shocked Pandora, hysterical Helen and weeping Lexia towards the car park. He'd wanted to call a taxi to get them all home but Pandora, practical as ever, had refused.

'I'm fine, I'm fine,' she snapped. 'I'm perfectly OK to drive. There's a Tesco carrier in the boot, Richard. Make sure Lexia has her head in it – I've just had this car valeted.'

'I'm sorry, I didn't mean to say anything,' Lexia wept from the depths of the plastic bag. Pandora had instructed her to take the passenger seat in the front of the car in order that Richard could sit in the back with a shivering Helen, his jacket around her bare arms and shoulders. 'The champagne made me do it.'

'Don't worry, sweetheart.' Richard tried to be jolly while his huge bear-like arms held Helen in an effort to stop her trembling. 'We all threw up with too much alcohol when we were your age.'

'I most certainly didn't,' Pandora snapped. 'How could you have been so *stupid*, Lexia? Just look what you've done to Mum now. And you actually *spoke* to Anichka? On the phone? When? And why didn't you tell *me* she was pregnant?'

As a low guttural moan came from deep inside Helen's throat, Richard snapped, 'Stop it, Pandora. Enough. We'll talk about it once we've got your mum home and into bed.'

Both Pandora and Lexia turned slightly in surprise. This was a first, Richard telling Pandora what to do. Pandora bit back a retort and, grim-faced, concentrated on driving her motley crew of passengers back home.

Back at the house, Pandora took charge once more, bustling round with hot water bottles, glasses of water and a bucket placed strategically by Lexia's bed. Helen was helped out of the yellow satin dress, made to take her medication and put to bed still weeping.

'I can't leave you here like this, with Mum,' Pandora said tiredly to Lexia. All she wanted was her own bed, but Helen's cries of 'I just want to die,' terrified the pair of them.

'I'm sorry, Pandora, but Mum had to know some time that the pole dancer was pregnant,' Lexia wept.

'But did you have to tell her in a posh restaurant, in front of everyone, when William hadn't even been served his steak pie? You should have told *me*, Lexia, and I'd have known what was best to do. Ariadne should be here...' Pandora closed her eyes against the enormity of being in charge of it all. 'She's the eldest. She needs to come back home and sort everything out. Juno too. I don't see why you and I have to bear the brunt of all this. Do you know,

Lexia, I'm never going to speak to Dad again after what he's done to Mum.'

Pandora opened her eyes, saw that her little sister had fallen into a deep, alcohol-induced sleep and, sighing, went to check that her old bed in the small bedroom at the back of the house was made up.

# 22

*March 2019*

*Lexia*

It was exactly a week since Damian St Claire had turned up at the gate of her new home, and exactly a week since Lexia had felt the wonderfully comforting arms of her brother-in-law, Richard Boothroyd, around her in the grounds of Brenton Wood golf club.

With Ariadne and Juno busy working, Lexia had only had minimal contact with the pair of them that week – the former having called round the previous evening on her way home after babysitting Juno's two while Juno was apparently in London at some work conference. But she'd been round to see her mum every single day after dropping Cillian off at Little Acorns. It was so lovely to see and be with her mum; how *could* she have lived all these years without her? She and Helen had shopped at Sainsbury's, or they'd simply sat and chatted for hours, looking at old photographs. And they'd also been out for a daily walk, each one longer and more exploratory than the previous day. While she loved the countryside she'd never in a million years thought of herself as a walker, but she'd even been out walking the country lanes of her childhood by herself and, she laughed at the very idea, had just sent off for her first ever pair of proper walking boots. The walks with her mum were wonderfully good for both of them, but particularly for Helen who was looking so much better than when Lexia had first arrived back home.

The only two occasions she'd felt one of her panic attacks coming on was when Ariadne had appeared unannounced yesterday evening at Lexia's house and it was obvious, to anyone with half a brain – and this was Ariadne, with enough brain power for the whole of Westenbury – that she was having a problem with Theo. He'd been drinking solidly all Sunday and the tension she was feeling as she waited for him to come round from his drunken state on the sofa was only compounded by Ariadne's taking in the whole situation in one knowing glance.

The other had been last Thursday when she and Helen had set off for their daily walk, chatting away about nothing much, happy to be in each other's company. It was Helen's turn to choose their route, and when she suggested they head for Norman's Meadow, the local wildflower beauty spot a couple of miles past Heath Green, Lexia had to fight the rising nausea and racing pulse that heralded a full-blown panic attack. She'd been able to persuade Helen that it probably wasn't a good idea to venture over there because of the new development of rather upmarket houses that was being built at the very edge of the woods right next to Norman's Meadow and, although she'd felt shaky and sick for the rest of the morning, Helen hadn't appeared to notice anything amiss.

Lexia now had Richard's phone number safely in her mobile and she took comfort in the fact that he was there, solid, reliable and at the end of the phone, as they discussed the best way forward with Damian St Claire. She knew it wouldn't be long before he was back with his usual demands.

Well, not this time, Lexia thought determinedly on this Tuesday morning, the beautiful spring-like air, with all its promise of the season to come, filling her lungs and giving her a confidence that was taking her by surprise. She bundled Cillian into his warm coat, popped his bobble hat onto his fair head and set off for Little Acorns. No more. No more, bloody Damian St Claire. What was he but a pathetic little drug addict? Time to have the truth out in the open.

Well, most of it, anyway.

The excitement of having Theo Ryan and Lexia Sutherland living in Heath Green had obviously waned somewhat, she realised, as both she and Cillian waved to the lone reporter leaning against the black gates, crafty fag in one hand, mobile in the other. Mrs Beresford at Little Acorns had suggested Lexia stay with Cillian for the first half an hour or so every morning to ensure he felt settled and she wasn't abandoning him. Cillian had created loudly the first two mornings in Reception class, throwing the chunky wax crayons at her, Mrs Beaumont, his teacher and several of the children, but Mrs Beresford herself had quickly intervened, taking Cillian out and giving him short shrift before returning him to the class and, once he was sitting quietly with a group listening to a story with a nursery nurse, telling Lexia to leave him to it.

This morning, Cillian actually *ran* into Reception, dropping Lexia's hand and heading straight for a little group of children already excitedly handling the musical instruments laid out on a table. Oh heavens, Lexia closed her eyes. Was he going to barge in, grab the drums and tambourines from the other children and shake them loudly in their faces. Or worse, throw them across the classroom in order to hear the crash, bang, tinkle, they would inevitably make?

Lexia watched, hand to her mouth, as Cillian skidded to a halt, eyes wide and bright with excitement and anticipation. There was one tambourine and one metal triangle left on the table and, as Cillian reached a hand for the tambourine, another little pair of hands did the same. Lexia closed her eyes, waiting for the scream of fury she knew would ensue. Nothing. Lexia opened her eyes to see Cillian handing the tambourine to the little bespectacled red-head who'd just missed out to her son. Bloody hell. Cillian picked up the one remaining instrument – the triangle – and walked back towards her, smiling.

'Sing, Mummy.'

'Oh, Cillian, I don't think so...' Lexia glanced round the classroom to where Mrs Beaumont and two of the teaching assistants had stopped what they were doing and were watching with interest.

'*Hush little baby, don't say a word,*' Cillian sang, striking the metal triangle on each alternate beat. 'Come on, Mummy, *sing...*'

Hell, Lexia thought, this is like something out of a sodding film, like that nun singing on the spoof film '*Airplane!*' She hadn't sung in front of an audience for years; she didn't even know if she could anymore, but Cillian was looking at her with such hope in those big brown eyes of his, she sang the first word quietly, clearing her throat when nothing much came out. Cillian stood in front of her, hitting the triangle as she tried again.

And then she was singing, acapella, the beautiful lyrics and tune soaring around the classroom while Cillian accompanied her every now and again on his triangle. As she came to the end of the song there was a silence and then a spontaneous burst of applause from the staff and parents dropping off children who'd gathered to listen to the haunting melody and voice of the once-famous Lexia Sutherland.

Embarrassed, but pleased that she'd managed to sing in front of people once more, Lexia waited until Cillian had re-joined the other children in the classroom and, when he turned and waved her goodbye, sitting attentively at Mrs Beaumont's feet as she called registration, she slipped out of the classroom and crossed the hall towards the heavy Victorian door that led to the playground.

'Mrs Ryan?' Mrs Beresford popped her head round her office door. 'Have you a minute?'

Lexia retraced her steps and headed for the headteacher's office, her heart sinking. Was she going to be told Cillian was unmanageable?

'I just heard you singing.' Cassie Beresford smiled. 'I absolutely loved your albums years ago. Well, I still do, really.'

'Oh, thank you.' Lexia smiled, relieved. 'I thought you were going to tell me something awful about Cillian.'

'Cillian? No, he's settling down, don't you think? I know it's only been a week, but we've seen a marked improvement in his behaviour already. I don't think there's been a paddy for the last couple of days.' She paused. 'You know, he's a *very* bright little boy. Sometimes, when a child has a pretty high IQ for his age, he can become frustrated; frustration can lead to behaviour problems. He needs occupying, needs to play with the other kids.'

'Oh, thank you.' Lexia felt a big smile spread across her face.

'We just wondered, you know, with your being new to the area, whether *you* needed a bit of occupation too?'

'I'm sorry?' Lexia frowned.

'It's just that our Y6 children are looking at future goals and ambitions in their PSHE lessons at the moment. Mr Donnington, their teacher, is hoping to get a few outside speakers in – I think he's going to approach Dr Armstrong – to discuss various careers. You know, how do people get to be doctors, architects and the like? Just a question and answer session really.'

'Yes, but I don't have a career.'

'Of course you do. Or at least you did. The kids would be fascinated to hear your route to success, particularly as you are a past pupil.' Cassie Beresford smiled encouragingly.

'Oh gosh, I don't know, I don't think I'd be any good at talking to children.'

'Think about it. I know your niece is in that class and that might make you feel a bit strange, but we'd love it if you'd think about it.'

'I will. You know, I really will think about it.' Lexia felt a sudden burst of happiness that this was something she might be able to do. That she might be able to encourage kids to follow their dreams, but that the path forwards wasn't always an easy one.

'Well, we'll be in touch,' the head said, smiling as she opened the door for Lexia.

Lexia walked back to her car, a big daft smile on her face.

Cillian was settling well, he was very bright for heaven's sake (his nursery school and previous Reception class had only ever reported what a nuisance he was and that his behavioural issues, unless she sorted them, would only hinder any educational progress he should be making) and she'd just sung again in public (well, if you could call a class of uninterested five-year-olds and a few parents *public*: she giggled to herself at the thought) and, best of all, she was being asked to make herself useful in the school.

Lexia's smile stayed on her face all the way down to the main road, where she positively skipped back towards her car. Her new walking boots might have arrived when she got home: she'd see if her mum fancied a really long walk...

'Lexia! How lovely of you to turn up *here*. What's up? You're looking very pleased with yourself.' Damian St Claire was leaning against the side of the large 4x4 vehicle Theo had insisted she drive up here but, because she was parked right up against the verge, she didn't see him until she'd crossed the main road and was actually at the car.

Lexia ignored him, fumbling with the remote on her key, but Damian crossed in front of the vehicle to stand in front of the car door and make it difficult for her to gain access.

'Fuck off, Damian,' Lexia said hotly. 'You're not having another penny from me.'

'Hey, hey, no need for that sort of language,' he grinned. 'Oh, I think both you and your sister will be coughing up again rather than having your past little history on the front of the papers...' Damian's voice, oily yet conciliatory, was in her ear, one hand on her wrist, the other lifting his T-shirt (oh, he knew exactly how to frighten her) to reveal his naked torso, as she reached for the car's door handle and pulled.

Before she could reply, Lexia's phone rang and, pushing Damian out of the way, she opened the car door, simultaneously pulling her mobile from her coat pocket and slamming the door in his face. Lexia listened to the caller, a look of intense concentration on her face and then, winding down her window, she spat at St Claire, 'Too fucking late, you bastard. It's going to all come out without any help from *you*. And, about time too...'

Lexia put the car into gear and roared off at speed, sending gravel and uprooted grass into the air and Damian St Claire onto the floor.

'What are *you* doing here?' Lexia walked into Pandora and Richard's beautifully decorated hall, too agitated to take in the difference in décor since she'd last been there, over sixteen years previously.

'I've taken the day off school – family crisis, I told the secretary when I rang. The head won't be pleased, but I really don't give a toss. I think this is all a bit more important than a bunch of girls learning Homer, don't you?' Ariadne nodded towards the kitchen. 'Juno's here too; it's her day off.'

'Right.' The new sense of confidence Lexia had been feeling as she'd left Little Acorns had morphed into fury on seeing Damian St Claire waiting for her. Now, with Pandora sitting upright at the kitchen table, her usually immaculately made-up face devoid of any colour, and Juno at her side as they waited for her arrival, she suddenly felt only fear. Had Pandora told her sisters *everything*?

'Where's Richard?' Lexia asked as Juno came towards her, taking her into her arms and giving her a hug. 'He rang me just now. Is he here?' Lexia looked from one to the other of her sisters.

'He was. He rang you from here, but we thought it best he drives up to North Yorkshire to pick Hugo up from school and bring him back here.'

'On a Tuesday morning in the middle of term?' Lexia stared. 'Isn't he going to find that strange?'

'Not as bad as if that little runt, St Claire, does what he's been threatening all week,' Ariadne said grimly. 'Pandora's told us everything, Lexia. We know all about him.'

'I've just seen him.' Lexia frowned. 'He was waiting for me outside the school. You know, when Richard phoned?'

'He was hanging around here earlier too. He must have walked over to find you when Richard put the door in his face.' Pandora spoke for the first time. 'You know, we *can* pay him off again…'

'For another year? Until he's spent up again?' Lexia shook her head vehemently. 'I am *sick* of being frightened, of living in fear that this is *all* going to come out.' She turned to look directly at Pandora as she emphasised the word *all*, the imperceptible shake of Pandora's head, as she held Lexia's eye, telling her what she wanted to know. Lexia relaxed slightly and turned to Ariadne and Juno. 'But it doesn't *matter* anymore. For *me*, anyhow. My big days of fame and stardom are over, thank goodness. I want it all out in the open now. We can hold a press conference…'

'A press conference?' Ariadne snorted with derision. 'You're not the Prime Minister, Lexia.'

'No, but Lexia was a big enough star – don't forget she

was *huge*, and Theo still *is* always in the news – for this to make the front pages of the tabloids. Far better, don't you think, to invite them here and tell them the story yourself rather than that St Claire bastard trying to make himself more money?' Juno smiled at Lexia, seeing she was hurt by Ariadne's cutting remark.

'And of course, once it's out in the open, Damian St Claire loses any bargaining power.' Ariadne paused, a tight little smile on her face, 'And then, of course, you press charges for blackmail.'

'I think,' Pandora said, her large brown eyes stark against her white face, 'the most important thing – the *only* thing – in all this bloody mess is Hugo. How on earth are we – am *I* – going to tell Hugo?'

# 23

*January–March 2003*

Knowing the Russian Trollop was about to give birth to Patrick's baby sent Helen Sutherland on a downward mental spiral that, despite Pandora moving temporarily back home to stay with Lexia and help look after their mother, was relentless and with only one potential outcome.

Christmas was bad enough, with Helen refusing to leave the house to join Pandora and the Boothroyds for the traditional celebratory dinner at *Boothroyd Towers,* as Lexia had dubbed the place. While Lexia herself wasn't overly enamoured at the thought of spending Christmas with the massed band of Boothroyds who, together with Richard's three bombastic sisters and their entourages, were even more unspeakable on home territory, she certainly didn't want to be at home with just her mum, a ready-cooked Co-Op chicken and a Mr Kipling mince pie. She was also quite faint with horror at the thought of seeing Bee-Bee after the totally and utterly mortifying shoe-vomiting episode, although Pandora had tried to pave the way back into the Boothroyd family bosom by standing over Lexia while she wrote a letter of apology, offering to pay for any damage to the black patent Ferragamo kitten heels.

Lexia was saved from both the Boothroyds and a sad dinner-for-two, by both Ariadne and Juno arriving home for a full three weeks' stay over the Christmas break. Although Ariadne, back from her teaching and research post at Berkeley, California, appeared somewhat bad-tempered, even quite miserable most of the time, and Juno spent much of the festive season in her bedroom studying, it was a total relief to hand over the reins of looking after her mum to the older sisters, if only for a few weeks.

Her comparative freedom meant that Lexia managed to escape the confines of home to meet up with Damian more often than before, and was actively encouraged to step up onto the stage at the Ambassador, belting out her own particular upbeat versions of traditional carols which were received with huge cheers and applause.

So when, at the beginning of January, she found herself once more alone with an increasingly morose Helen, as well as the terrifying prospect of mock GCSEs for which she'd done no revision, Lexia's only means of escape was spending even more time down at the Ambassador Club once Helen was safely sedated and asleep in bed.

She knew Pandora would be furious if she guessed what Lexia was up to. Mr Scascetti still hadn't returned from wherever he was wintering in the Caribbean, but Mick behind the bar would give her a fiver from the till and pay her taxi fare home as payment for singing, and she was actually beginning to build up her own little fan base as word got round about the new regular, the talented little girl with the powerful voice.

Pandora was racked with guilt at leaving her mother and her sister more and more to themselves, but was desperately trying to keep down her job as well as her breakfast and it was all that she could do, after a day in the office or in court, to fall into bed and sleep. But the Year 11 tutor at Westenbury Comprehensive seemed to be forever on Pandora's phone informing her that Lexia was bunking off school again or had never arrived and what was Pandora going to do about it?

'I'm looking after Mum,' Lexia snapped one morning in early February when Pandora came knocking on the door at seven-thirty telling her she *had* to get dressed and go to school. 'I'm sixteen, and legally I don't have to go back to school. In fact, you can tell them I've left. I'm not going back, Pandora, it's pointless. I've missed so much and I'm stupid anyway...'

'Don't be stupid, you're not *stupid*. Oh, you know what I mean – you're a Sutherland, we Sutherlands are *not* stupid,' Pandora had said tiredly, sitting down as exhaustion threatened to engulf her once more.

'Well, this one is.' Lexia folded her arms across her pyjamas. 'This is pointless, Pandora. Far better if I stay at home and look after Mum. She shouldn't be by herself, you know that. And once you have the baby, you're not going to have the time or energy to help either. And next year, when I'm seventeen, I'm going to go in for *TheBest* again.'

'Oh, for heaven's sake, Lexia, not that again... I'm going to ring Dad. He'll have to come over and talk to you. Sort you out.'

'No, you're not.' Lexia was adamant. 'You know as well as I do if he comes here and Mum sees him, she'll never let him out of the house alive.'

'Well, I'll tell him he has to come to me and sort you out *there*.'

'Just don't bother, Pandora. I am *not* going to talk to Dad, I am *not* going back to school but I *am* going to be the best singer there's ever been. So, you can just shut up and go home to Richard and have your baby in peace.

How Helen Sutherland found out Anichka had given birth to a son, Lexia would never work out, but two days after her showdown with Pandora, Lexia returned home from a lunchtime session at the Ambassador, followed by an afternoon where she'd trailed after Damian down to his dad's place, unable to find her mum in the house.

Already feeling terribly guilty that she'd been away from the house for more than five hours, Lexia realised it was now after 3 p.m. and getting dark and she didn't know where her mum was. By three o'clock in the afternoon, Helen was usually wrapped up under a blanket on the sofa, TV on and ready to watch *Countdown*. There was a slight covering of snow on the ground outside and as Lexia peered through the kitchen window at the gathering gloom, a movement over to her right had her turning her head in that direction. At first, she thought it must be some sort of large white dog that had found its way into the rose bushes that had once been Helen's pride and joy, and had caught itself there. But then it moved, its huge eyes catching sight of Lexia at the lighted window, and Lexia saw that it was her mum.

Lexia dashed outside, skidding slightly on the settling snow, shouting towards her as she ran.

Helen had hacked off all her beautiful long blonde hair (Lexia and Pandora would find it later in the washstand in Helen's bedroom) and was wearing nothing but a pair of purple pants as, using their bread knife and a pair of scissors, she attempted to cut the last of the rusting yellow roses that had tenaciously hung on to summer. She was shivering as ghostly flakes of snow settled on her ragged scalp, but was triumphantly holding aloft three of the four roses that had survived the autumn frosts.

'For the new baby,' Helen said, stroking the blackened spotted leaves and ignoring the thorns that had pierced the skin of several fingers. 'The baby will need something nice. Babies have to have presents, don't they…?'

'Mum, please, come in.' Lexia was crying, huge tears she didn't seem able to stop falling down her face even though she kept wiping them away with her sleeve. 'Come on, you have to come in. You've no clothes on. You've no shoes on.'

'I just need one more for Daddy's baby.' Helen turned back to the bushes, bending down, catching her pants on the bushes.

Terrified, Lexia ran inside and rang Pandora. When Richard answered, desperately trying to decipher Lexia's garbled words, he took control, rang 999 and within ten minutes had joined Lexia in the freezing cold garden where she was trying to persuade Helen's arms into one of Patrick's old fleeces.

Once the ambulance had left with Helen – who appeared frighteningly calm, smiling and still stroking the roses – Pandora arrived from work, racing breathlessly from her car and up the garden path, and then set to helping Lexia pack a case of overnight essentials before driving off after the ambulance, leaving Richard to lock up the house.

'You're not staying here by yourself,' Pandora had said wearily, before she left to follow Helen to the hospital, her hands alternating from resting on her abdomen to running through her hair. 'You have to come and stay with us until Mum's better.'

'But when will that be?' Lexia found she was crying once more.

'Let's sort this one day at a time,' Richard said kindly. 'It'll be alright. It'll all work out. Don't you worry.'

'It's all my fault,' Lexia sobbed later that evening back at Pandora and Richard's place. 'I went out. I wasn't there. She wouldn't have cut her hair off if I'd been there for her.'

'Nothing is your fault, you daft thing.' Richard had patted her back awkwardly. 'Neither of you... none of us,' he amended glancing over at Pandora's drawn white face, 'could have carried on much longer like this. Really, Lexia, hospital is the best place for your mum. She's very poorly and she'll get some help there.'

Those next few weeks passed in a blur for Lexia. Ariadne and Juno made the journey home again but, for Ariadne, California back to Yorkshire was an impossibly long haul while Juno, in tears, said she was dreadfully sorry but she just couldn't make it down from Scotland every week; she was already finding her coursework frighteningly unmanageable and was having to re-sit the clinical exams she'd failed so badly. Should she quit her course altogether? she asked Ariadne and Pandora.

'Give up your course, Juno?' Ariadne had pulled a face as the three of them sat round Pandora's kitchen table eating Heinz tomato soup and cheese on toast which, after a harrowing visit to the hospital where Helen was sectioned, was both comforting and needing the minimum of effort to make and eat. 'Don't be silly – you've done almost four years; don't give it all up now.'

Juno shook her head doubtfully. 'I'm not sure I'm cut out to be a doctor. And I'm not convinced I'm going to make it anyway.'

'Come on, Juno,' Ariadne snapped crossly, 'you were always good at exams, you sailed through your A levels. Are you seeing someone up in Aberdeen? Are you spending too much time socialising?'

'Not at all,' Juno protested, replacing her last piece of toast back on her plate, uneaten. 'I'm finding the work so hard, I really don't have time for romance, more's the pity.'

'Look, I'm going to have to go.' Ariadne looked at her watch. 'It's a two-hour drive back to the airport with all the weekend road works on the M62. And then a ten-hour flight on top of that,' she added gloomily. 'Where's Lexia?'

'Out as usual,' Pandora sighed. 'I never thought I'd end up being mum to a bolshy adolescent at my age.'

'Hardly an adolescent,' Ariadne frowned. 'She's sixteen, for heaven's sake.'

'Well, she doesn't act like it. Stars in her eyes; convinced she's going to be the next superstar.'

'What does her school say?'

Pandora looked shifty as she stood, stroking her tummy, to clear the plates. 'She's given up.'

'Given up? What are you talking about?' Ariadne stared.

'Don't look at me like that, Ariadne. She started bunking off before Christmas and now she's stopped going all together. She's sixteen, I can't make her go. I've physically taken her there, driven her in, but she just leaves. She's not like the three of *us*. You know that, Ariadne, she's just not academic.'

'Don't think I am either,' Juno said gloomily.

'Of course you are,' Ariadne snapped. 'Look, *I* need to talk to her.'

'You're not her mother, Ariadne,' Juno said, equally crossly. 'Leave the poor kid alone. She's not academic, we've always known that, but no one except Mum would ever accept it. Can you imagine how awful it's been for her? She's always trailed along in the wake of the Sutherland supposed superior brains, and now we've all left home. And then Dad finally does what he's been threatening for years, and ups and buggers off as well. Poor Lexia is left with no one but Mum who, let's face it, is one sandwich short of a picnic.'

'Well, if that's the sort of doctor you're going to become, you damned well *should* give up right now.' Ariadne was furious. 'That's a *nice* thing to say about your own mother.'

'I'm sorry, I'm sorry.' Juno's face crumpled. 'That was awful of me.' She put up her hand to wipe away the tears. 'I just don't know what to do.'

'Mum's in the best place for her,' Pandora said, trying to calm the waters between Ariadne and Juno. 'It's a relief to have her there to be honest… although you can imagine the reaction from my mother-in-law.'

'What? What's any of this got to do with that old boot?' Ariadne paused from pulling on her coat. 'What's bloody BooBoo or whatever she calls herself said now?'

'Oh nothing, nothing.' Pandora started to backtrack; she already knew what Ariadne thought of the Boothroyd entourage.

'Come on, what's she said?' Ariadne wouldn't let it go.

'Oh, something along the lines of there'd never been *any* madness in the Boothroyd family and she did hope this child of Richard's wouldn't be—'

'Don't, don't,' Ariadne snapped, holding up her gloved hands in protest. 'I can imagine the rest.' She suddenly gave a bark of laughter. 'The Boothroyds are *all* bloody mad as hatters, Richard excepted, who, I have to say, has been an absolute trooper the last few days. It goes back to all the inbreeding down the years since the Industrial Revolution. You know, keeping all *that brass*—' Ariadne affected a broad Yorkshire accent '—they've made from trampling over *t'mill peasants*, in their own damned pockets.' Ariadne picked up the hire-car keys. 'I could really do with seeing Lexia before I go. Try and get her back into school, Pandora.'

Getting Lexia back into school was the last thing Pandora knew she was going to be able to do when, turning off her hairdryer one morning several weeks later, she heard the unmistakable sound of vomiting coming from the bathroom next to Lexia's bedroom.

'Lexia? You OK?' Pandora knocked on the bathroom door but, still throwing up, Lexia either hadn't heard or was unable to answer. Had she been out drinking last night?

Was this the result of too much alcohol? Pandora racked her brains as to what they'd had for supper the previous evening. Lasagne. Nothing suspect in her homemade lasagne that she could see. Pandora waited until the lavatory was flushed, tap run on and off and Lexia made an appearance, wiping her mouth on the sleeve of her pyjama top.

'What's the matter, Lexia?' Pandora took in her little sister's white face and knew instantly. 'Oh, Jesus, please don't tell me you're pregnant?'

'I can't be,' Lexia muttered, avoiding Pandora's eye and setting off for her bedroom.

Pandora followed her in, the palms of her hands feeling suddenly sweaty. She wiped them across her skirt and went around Lexia to head her off. 'Have you been *seeing* someone? A boyfriend? Have you got a boyfriend? One of the boys at school?'

'One of the boys at school? No!'

'Right, OK, I'm sorry.' Pandora felt relief flood through her. 'So, is it something you've eaten?' When Lexia didn't answer, wouldn't look at Pandora, Pandora went on, 'Is it Mum? Are you so worried about Mum it's making you ill? It's not your fault, Lexia.'

'It's not one of the boys at school.' Lexia turned to face Pandora, tears rolling down her face.

'What isn't...?' Pandora stared at Lexia, her heart plummeting. 'Lexia, when did you last have your period?'

Lexia shook her head. 'Ages ago.'

'Ages ago? What, a few weeks? A few months?'

'October.'

'October?' Pandora sat down on the bedside chair, feeling sick herself, and tried to do the maths. 'But we're into *March*, Lexia.' Pandora's eyes went to Lexia's stomach, but Patrick's baggy cotton pyjamas Lexia had taken to wearing – Pandora had assumed it was to feel close to her absent daddy – gave up no clues. 'Have you been sick like this before this morning?'

Lexia nodded. 'A couple of times a few months ago, but there'd been a bug going round. And, you know, the time when I threw up over Richard's mum's shoes, I thought that was the champagne. That's why I didn't think I was. I thought you had to be sick every morning. You know, like you've been. And anyway, I only did it the once with him. I didn't think you could get pregnant, you know, the first time.'

'Who is it, Lexia? Oh God, not that Damian chap, the one who said you could win *TheBest*?' When Lexia just looked at her, tears continuing to fall, Pandora snapped, 'Well, we'll have him. You were underage…'

'Yes, I know, they told me I was underage, but I can do it next year when I'm seventeen,' Lexia sobbed.

'Not that, you *ridiculous* girl. Underage for *sex* with an older *man*. It's against the law to have sex with a girl of fifteen. Do they teach you nothing at that school? Well no, of course they don't, you're never effing there!'

Even at the height of her fury, Lexia noted, Pandora couldn't bring herself to swear properly.

'And you can totally *forget* bloody *TheBest* now, Lexia. You're going to be changing nappies and wiping *bums*.'

'I can have a… you know…' Lexia looked at Pandora, eyes pleading.

'Not if you're almost five months' pregnant, you can't,' Pandora said, defeated. 'It's against the law.'

\*

The next day, as the first signs of spring with all its promise of new life and new beginnings began to clothe the hedgerows in acid green, Pandora started to bleed heavily and she knew she was losing her baby.

Richard was away, flogging Boothroyd, Boothroyd and Dyson's finest worsted to the Chinese and, after an interminably long day both in the police cells – where she tried to establish just *why* Billy O'Dwyer was in possession of a six-inch bladed article – and back at her office where she was so tired she'd gone into the stock room and actually laid down for ten minutes, resting her aching head against a pile of unopened boxes of Sellotape and staples, she'd left, late, and gone to see Helen at the hospital.

Pandora had had a pile of files to go through in readiness for her defence of clients in the Magistrates' Courts the following morning, she'd not yet eaten and Lexia, although she was in and Pandora didn't have to worry about where she was, was fast asleep on the sitting room sofa despite the loud belting out of a Holly Valance album at the highest volume possible from her bedroom directly above the kitchen.

Pandora had rung from work to make an appointment for Lexia to see her GP, but had been told there was nothing free until the following week. She knew she had to ring Ariadne; she was the eldest, she'd have to take on some of the responsibility for Lexia.

Pandora closed her eyes, pressing two fingers to her aching temple, but almost immediately moved her hands to her abdomen where the dull ache that always heralded an imminent period was pounding at her tummy. Pandora's eyes snapped open. Imminent period? She was *pregnant*, for heaven's sake. Pandora walked slowly upstairs to her bathroom, praying a mantra on each step, but stopped at the top as the front doorbell sounded and a familiar voice yoo-hooed through the open door.

'Up here, Jennifer,' Pandora called, trying not to cry as she felt a trickle of wetness between her legs.

'I bet you'd forgotten I was coming round,' Dr Jennifer Danton-Brown called gaily, shaking a pile of books in Pandora's direction up the stairs. 'Pregnancy books and leaflets?' She paused and, as she saw Pandora's white face, deposited the books on the bottom step and followed her up. 'Are you alright?'

'I think I'm losing the baby.'

'OK.' Jennifer DB took immediate charge, ushering Pandora into her bedroom and, grabbing a towel from the en-suite, helped her onto the bed.

'We need to get you to hospital,' Jennifer said, after a brief examination.

'No!'

'What do you mean, no? Pandora, you're losing a lot of blood, not just a trickle.' Jennifer frowned as Pandora tried to sit up.

'This is my only chance to have a baby,' Pandora said, dry-eyed.

'Don't be silly,' Jennifer soothed. 'You're not thirty yet – loads of time to try again. Lots of women who miscarry go on to have perfectly healthy babies.'

Pandora shook her head violently. 'It's a miracle I got pregnant at all. We've been trying ever since we got married – two years – and eventually we went to have tests. I've

always had really strange periods, if I had them at all…
and awful acne… as well as constantly piling on weight.'
Pandora stopped talking as a spasm of pain took hold of her.

'Polycystic Ovarian Syndrome? Is that what you were
told?' Jennifer frowned and squeezed Pandora's hand
in sympathy. 'I'm amazed you were able to get pregnant
and get so far with this pregnancy. What are you? About
eighteen weeks?'

Pandora nodded, grabbing hold of Jennifer's hand once
more. 'Jennifer, I need you to help me.'

'I am doing, Pandora, but you need to go to hospital.'

'No, Jen, *really* help me. Help me to do this…'

# 24

*March 2019*

'I'm still totally in shock,' Juno said as the four of them sat down in Pandora's immaculate cream shaker kitchen and she poured a mug of coffee for Lexia. 'After these two—' she nodded towards Ariadne and Pandora '—revealed this little lot to me last night, I went home, put Mum in the taxi and then ended up doing a whole load of housework and ironing: you know, just to get my head round it all. I finally went to bed about three.' Juno sighed. 'I'm absolutely shattered now. I mean, it's like something out of a bloody soap. Are you sure you haven't made it all up?'

'Oh yeah, as if.' Lexia gave Juno a withering look. 'I've lived with "*this little lot*" for the last sixteen years, Juno. You might think, with me banned from coming back home, I should have got over it all by now.'

'I didn't *ban* you,' Pandora said, sobbing once again.

'Of course you did, Pandora,' Lexia said rather more gently. 'But that was the agreement. I desperately didn't want a baby. You desperately did.'

'You never considered a... you know...?' Juno took Lexia's hand across the table.

'Oh, for God's sake, Juno, you're a doctor,' Ariadne tutted. 'Surely you can bring yourself to use the correct terminology?'

'Well, *you* haven't said it,' Juno retorted huffily. 'And yes, you're right,' she relented, 'I'm hopeless at saying *abortion*, probably because I considered it myself when I found myself pregnant with Gabe.'

'I never knew that, Juno. I'm sorry.' Ariadne sat down at the table. 'Why didn't you?'

'Why didn't I what?'

'You know...'

'Have a...?'

'Hmm.'

'Because, although – and I *can* say this now – I knew I didn't love Fraser in that heart-stopping way you *should* love someone who says it would, perhaps, be best, if you married him, I *did* want my baby. I couldn't go through with a... you know...'

'I probably *could* have had a termination,' Lexia sighed. 'There, is *that* a better word? Albeit a very late one. You know, I was pregnant at fifteen to a much older man – been taken advantage of, I suppose. Groomed, I guess you'd call it today. God, I was naïve. The daft thing is, I only ever did it with him once. And I hated the whole messy business so much that, although I really was convinced I was in love with him, that he would be the one to shoot me to stardom and I kept hanging round him, kept on going down to the Ambassador Club and spending afternoons with him down at his dad's place, I made sure I didn't do it with him again. I don't think Damian was that bothered. He said sex with me was like humping a sack of potatoes.' Lexia went quite pink. 'There, bet that's shocked you all, hasn't it? Sexy Lexi, rubbish in the sack.'

'Oh, for heaven's sake, Lexia, you were fifteen,' Ariadne said crossly.

'Yes, well.'

'Can we just talk a bit more about the whole pregnancy thing?' Juno asked. 'You know, before Hugo arrives? Oh Jesus, my stomach churns every time I think about your telling him the truth, Pandora.'

'*Your* stomach? What about mine?' A fresh outburst of tears from Pandora at Juno's words.

'So just go back to the evening when you, you know, lost the baby, Pandora.' Juno handed Pandora the roll of kitchen towel and held her hand, something she'd not done since they were kids.

'Well, Jennifer told me I just *had* to go to hospital and that if I didn't get in the car with her and let her drive me there herself she was going to ring 999 for an ambulance. I had no choice. Jennifer drove me there in her car and Lexia came with us. I lost the baby, ended up having a D&C the next day and then, basically, was told to go home and try to get pregnant again as soon as possible. Which I knew, with the Polycystic Ovarian Syndrome, was never going to happen. I was *never* going to produce a Boothroyd heir to take over the mill.' Pandora paused to wipe her eyes and blow her nose, before reaching into one of the drawers for a pack of Marlboro and a yellow plastic lighter.

'Bloody hell, Pan, what are you doing?' The others stared.

'My guilty secret,' Pandora sniffed, before lighting up and inhaling deeply.

'Well, that's not going to help your singing voice,' Ariadne said crossly.

'It's never done mine any harm.' Lexia smiled, reaching over and helping herself to the pack.

'Or mine.' Juno grinned, taking a cigarette for herself and lighting up as well. 'God, that's heaven.'

The three of them blew smoke towards the kitchen ceiling while Ariadne flapped her hands and went to open the kitchen door.

'Anyway,' Pandora went on, 'I was *so* depressed when I came out of hospital. Richard was in China and knew nothing about either Lexia being pregnant or me losing the baby. Jennifer wanted to try to ring him and get him to come home, but I knew he'd be devastated. He was so excited about being a dad – proud that he'd done something right for once.'

'What do you mean, *something right*?' Juno squinted at Pandora through the smoke from her cigarette.

'William Boothroyd's always bullied Richard. Bullied and belittled him for not being a confident, public-school rugger-bugger like him.'

'Blimey, Pandora, I always thought you really liked your father-in-law,' Ariadne said. 'I mean, *I've* never been able to stand the arrogant, bigoted tosser, but *you've* never said a word against the Boothroyds.'

'No, well, Richard's always tried to please him. Even when he was sent off to boarding school at seven and terribly homesick, he never said anything. He never told his father he cried every night because he was bullied there, too, for being, you know, a bit plump and hopeless at games. So, anyway, when we'd been trying to get pregnant for two years and nothing was happening, we were round at the Boothroyds' at Christmas and, after downing a bottle of claret, and obviously thinking he was being very funny, William suggested perhaps Richard should be sitting on *top* of the Christmas tree, that he must be a bit of a, you know, a bit of a *fairy* not to have me *up the duff,* as he so eloquently put it.'

'You *are* joking?' Ariadne was furious. 'I'd have told him to fuck off,' she exploded, 'and mind his own fucking business.'

'No, you wouldn't, Ariadne, because that would have made things worse. William would have had something else to have a go at Richard over – you know, was he a real man or a mouse to let his wife stand up for him against his father?'

'Well, I don't know how you've put up with the bloody Boothroyds all these years.' Juno shook her head. 'I thought *my* mother-in-law was bad enough but...'

'Oh God, I feel sick,' Pandora muttered, glancing up at the kitchen clock as she spoke. 'How the hell am I going to tell Hugo I'm not his mother?' She rubbed her hands over eyes that were red from crying. 'Anyway,' she went on, sighing hugely as she spoke, 'Richard was so happy he'd got me pregnant and was going to carry on the Boothroyd name at the mill, I didn't want him to be alone, by himself in China, when he found out, and I told Jennifer she absolutely must not phone him.'

'And the whole totally ridiculous idea that Pandora was cooking up, even as she was trying to hold on to her own baby,' Lexia began to contribute to the story, 'would probably never have come to anything if Aunt Georgina hadn't arrived from London to see Mum in hospital.'

'Oh, yes, she came up quite a bit when Mum was first

sectioned, didn't she?' Juno frowned, remembering. 'It made me feel a bit less guilty that she was around, you know, when Ariadne and I couldn't be with Mum as much as we should. Did she stay at Mum's or with you, Pandora?'

'A bit of both, really. She used to come up on the train – she never did learn to drive until much later – and the second time she came up was two days after I'd lost the baby. Because Richard was still away and because I was in a pretty bad state, she stayed with Lexia and me.'

'And I wasn't in a much better place,' Lexia added and then smiled. 'Poor Aunt Georgina. It must have been hell coming north for her, coping with a sectioned sister and finding two sobbing, equally mentally deranged nieces into the bargain. Being pregnant at just sixteen was the absolute end of the world for me; there was no way I could become a superstar if I had a baby to look after. And where was I going to live? Back at home? With Mum once she was out of hospital?' Lexia actually shuddered at the thought. 'You know, I adored Mum, but I was a kid myself for heaven's sake, and a pretty naïve one at that. I wanted to be the next Holly Valance, not trapped at home with a baby and a mad mother to look after as well.'

'Oh, don't call Mum "mad" Lexia.' Juno frowned.

'Hang on a minute. It was OK for *you*, Juno. You were away in Scotland having a great time as a student. And you'd had Dad at home all the time you were growing up. *You* hadn't been left to pick up the pieces and left to look after a mother spiralling out of control. *You* didn't find Mum in the garden in the snow in just her purple pants...' Tears filled Lexia's eyes, but she dashed an angry hand to her face, cleared her throat and went on. 'I even went down to Damian's place to ask if I could live there with him and his dad.' Lexia gave a short bark of laughter. 'God, can you imagine, down on Emerald Street? Where every druggie and street walker in Midhope are doing their daily deals?'

'So, you told Damian? About the baby?'

'Of course I did. I thought he'd let me live with him, we'd have the baby together.'

Juno and Ariadne exchanged glances.

'Don't look at me like that, the pair of you. I was a kid, for heaven's sake.'

'OK, OK, sorry.' Juno patted Lexia's arm but she wasn't to be mollified and shrugged it off crossly before reaching for another cigarette. 'So, what did *he* say?'

Lexia folded her arms as she pulled smoke into her lungs and then sat back in her chair. 'Laughed, basically. Said we'd only done it once, and then not properly. It couldn't be his, and to find some other poor mug to blame it on and not come running to him for money to get rid of it.'

'What a sleazebag.'

'And, Jesus, this is Hugo's real father?' Juno pulled a face. 'You *can't* tell Hugo this, Pandora.'

'If you *remember*, this is what this is all about,' Pandora said angrily. 'If Richard and I don't tell him, Damian St Claire *will* – it's going to be splashed all over the papers any day when we don't come up with the money he's wanting again. We've paid him off thousands, *thousands* of pounds over the years. Enough. I just can't do this anymore.'

'The night before Richard came home…' Lexia went on, glancing at the clock. 'Come on, Richard and Hugo are going to be here soon, let's just tell you properly what happened. The night before Richard came back from China,' she repeated, 'Aunt Georgiana was here in the kitchen making supper for the three of us. She was singing something or other – you know, she and Mum used to sing together all the time when we were kids – and I joined in. And she just stood, and stared and said, "Lexia, I thought your Mum was good, but *you* are superb. You can't let this go to waste." Or something along those lines. Anyway, she called Pandora in from the sitting room where she was all huddled up, weeping on the sofa – do you remember, Pan? – and together we hatched *The Plot*, if that's what you want to call it.'

'So, did Richard know all along then?'

'Well, yes. As soon as he returned home, expecting to find his happy pregnant wife, he found instead a sobbing no-longer pregnant wife, a sobbing now-pregnant teenager and a determined Aunt Georgina. Richard drove the four of us down to London the next evening and Pandora and Richard stayed the weekend and hatched more of The Plot before driving back north. I stayed with Aunt Georgina and Uncle Carl in Wimbledon where Aunt Georgina was on a mission to have me win *TheBest*, not letting up in her coaching and voice control sessions all the time I was pregnant until it was time for the *TheBest* auditions again when I was just seventeen.

'I reckon you have a lot of Aunt Georgina in you.' Ariadne smiled. 'The same steely determination to get what you want.'

Lexia looked sad for the moment. 'Well, that determination's upped and gone over the years. I'm just an empty has-been now with a secret I've had gnawing at me for years.'

'Stop that!' Juno and Ariadne both interrupted Lexia at the same time.

'But, Pandora, you didn't have the... you know, you weren't pregnant any longer...?' Juno frowned.

'You mean I didn't have a bump any longer?' Pandora smiled for the first time that morning and threw the cushion that had been at her back towards Juno. 'Meet baby.'

'You shoved a cushion up your jumper for the next five months?' Juno and Ariadne stared at Pandora.

'Well, you know I've always been rather good at amateur dramatics. I just played the part, carried on working until I would have done had I continued my original pregnancy, and then we told everyone we were going to London for the weekend to see Lexia. And that, while we were there, I'd gone into labour and had the baby in Wimbledon.'

'And no one suspected anything?'

'No, it really was rather easy. I mean, I did become a bit of a hermit, didn't go out of the way to flaunt my cushion...' Pandora smiled again. 'And Jennifer DB was in on it all and helped enormously. She was probably risking everything by colluding with us, but she did it for me. Absolute brick, that girl...'

'Anyway,' Lexia took up the story, 'I had the baby in Wimbledon with Jennifer DB, Pandora and Aunt Georgina in attendance and gratefully handed him over to Pandora and Richard as soon as he was born. Registering the birth once they drove back up to Midhope with him was, apparently, totally straightforward. No one suspected a thing. I mean, there was nothing *to* suspect. End of story really. Pandora has been a much better mother to Hugo than I could ever have been – I had no interest in him at the time – and well, obviously, Richard has been a much better father than scumbag Damian could have ever been.'

'But why has it all had to be such a secret?' Ariadne asked. 'Why couldn't you just admit to having the baby and letting Pandora and Richard adopt him? You know, have it all out in the open?'

Lexia sighed. 'Knowing what we know now, we should have done that, but Aunt Georgina said my having a baby and giving it away at just sixteen would ruin my image for winning *TheBest*. I needed to be squeaky clean. To be honest, I think she loved the drama of it all, you know what she's like.'

'And I wanted Hugo to be *mine*,' Pandora said fiercely, 'really mine. I wanted the Boothroyds to know that Richard had fathered Hugo, that he was a proper Boothroyd, not a cuckoo in the nest.'

'Oh, for heaven's sake, Pandora. What century do you live in? I think you spend most of your time imagining you're in a Catherine Cookson novel. You're a bright, independent woman. What's all this with the sodding Boothroyds and cuckoos…?' Ariadne actually slammed her mug onto the kitchen table, slopping the remains of her cold coffee onto its shiny wooden surface. She suddenly stopped, turning her gaze from Pandora and staring hard at Lexia. 'But how did St Claire know about what you lot had cooked up?'

'I told him.' Lexia was pink with embarrassment.

'You *told* him? What on *earth* for?'

Lexia shrugged. 'Ariadne, I was a kid and stupid. Dad had gone off with Anichka and just had a new baby. *He* certainly didn't want me turning up on his doorstep in Manchester. Mum was locked up for God only knows how long. I had *nobody*. I had no home. I had no education. I felt like I'd been abandoned and didn't know where, or who to turn to. I suppose I just wanted to make sure Damian knew I was leaving. You know, see his reaction when I told him I was off to London. He just laughed when I found him in the Ambassador Club, drinking. Sort of waved cheerio and went back to his lager. I was really upset when he wasn't a bit bothered I was going. I said something like, "You'll be sorry when I'm famous," and he said, "Oh, so it was all a big lie you made up about being pregnant then? I knew you were lying," and I got really cross then and said, "I *am* going to have a baby, and it's your baby, Damian St Claire, but that won't stop me becoming famous because my sister, Pandora, has just lost *her* baby and she and Richard are going to have *my* baby – *your* baby – and pretend it's theirs." And he just laughed in my face and said "Whatever, babe, great story. Have a good life…"'

'But surely, in years to come you could have denied it all, said he'd made it all up; it was all a load of rubbish?' Ariadne shook her head, bewildered.

'She sent him a letter,' Pandora sighed.

'A letter?'

'From London,' Pandora went on.

'I was homesick, I was having a baby, I was living in some suburb of London where I didn't know anyone. I was by myself all day while Aunt Georgina and Uncle Carl were out at work. I wrote to Damian, telling him again what we'd planned.'

'Why in God's name would you do that?'

Lexia shrugged once more. 'I missed him. I wanted him to know Pandora and Richard were going to take the baby – that I wasn't going to make him responsible, you know, have to pay maintenance.'

'And he kept the letter?' Ariadne raised an eyebrow.

'Why on earth would he do that? Someone with his chaotic lifestyle?'

'I really have no idea,' Pandora snapped. 'Unless somewhere in that drug-befuddled brain of his he saw a way of getting money out of us at some point down the line. When Lexia started to get famous, he must have thought his lottery ticket was up. You can just see him, can't you, scrabbling around, trying to remember where he'd put the letter, and the glee once he found it at the back of a drawer or wherever. He wafts it in my face every time he comes round for his money.'

There was a silence in the kitchen as all four digested this somewhat undigestible little nugget of information.

And then Ariadne frowned. 'I still don't get it. Why have you both let this Damian chap have such a hold over you all these years? There's something else, isn't there? Something you're not telling us, the pair of you...?'

'Mum?' The kitchen door banged open and a blonde-haired, very good-looking boy stood on the threshold, brought to a sudden standstill when he saw all three of his aunts staring in an almost frozen tableau from their seats around the table. He glanced at Lexia, not quite grasping this was the famous aunt whom he'd never met, and then walked over to Pandora, staring down at her. 'What's up, Mum? What is it? Dad wouldn't tell me. Have you got something? Cancer?' His voice broke slightly. 'Because, you know, it'll be alright. It's curable these days.'

When a single tear rolled down Pandora's white face, he put his arms round her, hugging her tightly. 'You've been smoking again, haven't you? I can smell it. Is it lung cancer? Honestly, Mum, nobody dies from it these days. Anyway, you're my *mum* – you can't be ill. Honestly, you just *can't*!'

# 25

'Ah, wondered when *you* were going to show your face.' Izzy was waiting in Juno's dungeon, arms folded as she sat, perched on Juno's desk awaiting her arrival.

'Nothing better to do on a Wednesday morning at eight-fifteen than sit on my desk, Izzy?' Juno said, playing for time. 'Were you not told how unhygienic it was to sit on your desk when you were at school? Must be doubly so in a doctor's surgery.' She moved over to the door to hang up her jacket and then, closing it quietly behind her, faced Izzy, her own arms folded in a parody of her boss. 'OK, out with it, what's the problem?'

'What's the problem?' Izzy tutted loudly. 'What are you up to with Scott Butler?'

'I really don't think it's any of your business, Izzy.'

'Of course it's my business. You're married; he's a notorious womaniser. Just think about what you're doing. And it can't be good when two of the surgery's doctors are in a relationship.' Izzy pursed her lips in disapproval and Juno wanted to laugh.

'Hang on, you and Declan are in a relationship.'

'That's different. I'm married.'

'So am I,' Juno said.

'Now you're just being facetious,' Izzy snapped. 'And, exactly, you're *married*. What's going to happen when Fraser finds out? It's not going to put the surgery in a good light when the patients know the pair of you have been at it over the examining couch. They'll be imagining all sorts of things.'

'Like you are, you mean?'

'So, you haven't... you know?' Izzy, obviously desperate to hear any juicy details of the relationship was seemingly torn between taking the moral high ground as well as bound by her moral compass as Juno's boss, and wanting to know more.

When Juno refused to comment, Izzy went on, 'Look, Juno, you're a mate as well as a work colleague and I have to tell you that Scott Butler is not to be taken seriously. He's just a lovely playboy and you're his new playmate; he's playing you along like he has all the others Declan's told me about. And I know you, you're not a "kiss me quick, let's have a bit of a flirtation" type of girl. You'll take it all seriously, get hurt when Scott moves on to his next challenge and, if – when – Fraser finds out, it'll possibly be the end of your marriage too.'

'Look, Izzy, to be honest, I've so much going on in my life with my sisters at the moment, this thing with Scott...'

'Ah, so you admit it, you have a "thing" going with him?' Izzy's eyes narrowed.

'Izzy, I think it pointless denying anything to you when you saw us together on Monday night at Clementine's.'

'Together?' Izzy scoffed. 'Together? Ha! You were going for it. I seriously wondered if a bucket of water might not be appropriate.' She paused. 'So, is he, you know... good...?'

'Out, go on, out, you baggage. I'm not prepared to discuss my personal life with you, and especially when I'm at work.' Juno opened the door and pointedly held it open until Izzy sniffed, just as pointedly in Juno's direction and left, shouting, as she walked through reception, 'OK, let's rock and roll, ladies and gents: form an orderly queue and let's get this show on the road....'

Once Izzy had gone, revving up a limping Mrs Travers and her bunions towards her own room, Juno closed the door and, breathing deeply, tried to collect herself before the morning's onslaught of medical problems.

*When Fraser finds out it'll be the end of your marriage.*

Wasn't that what Izzy had just said?

Juno sat at her desk and, despite Marian buzzing to say her first patient was waiting, Juno simply sat, staring at the opposite wall. How would she feel if Fraser did find out that she'd been – in Yorkshire parlance – *carrying on* with another man? It was a terrible thing to do to one's husband when he was away, working hard to support his wife and kids. It was deceitful and unfair. She was a player. A philanderer. A cheat.

'Come on in,' Juno called out automatically, when a hesitant knock heralded her first patient. 'Ah, Mr...' Juno looked at her computer, '... Bradbury, come on in.' Juno pulled herself into the present, pushed Fraser from her head and switched on her benign doctor smile at the man in his late sixties who sat down heavily in the chair beside her.

When he said nothing but suddenly put his head in his hands, Juno put her own hand on his arm. 'What is it?'

'It's our lass.'

'Our lass?' Juno stared. '*Your* lass?' Juno wasn't quite

sure who he was talking about. His daughter? His dog? His wife? 'Margaret, you mean?' she hazarded a guess. 'What is it? She's not been to see me.'

'Well no, obviously not. She wouldn't have, would she?' Don Bradbury lifted a pitiful face and said dramatically, 'She's *gone*. I thought you'd have known?'

Oh, Jesus, Margaret Bradbury had died and she'd not been made aware of it? She'd have a few things to say to both Marian and Izzy. Just because she was part-time didn't mean she shouldn't be kept informed of the most fundamental issues at the surgery. Like who was still a damned patient; and who was already knocking at St Peter's gate.

'It must have been a shock,' Juno said sympathetically. 'How are you coping?'

'Not very well, as you can see. Me psoriasis has come back something terrible. That's why I'm here. And perhaps something to help me sleep? It's funny having the bed to yourself after forty years together. What's that song, "*The bed's too big without you*?"'

'Hmm.' Juno racked her brains. 'U2?'

Don shook his head. 'No, course not. Can't imagine Bono singing that, can you?' He gazed round at the surgery. 'Roxy Music?'

'I don't think so, Mr Bradbury.' Juno shook her head and glanced discretely at the clock before asking hopefully, 'Genesis?' Jesus, were they going to have to go through the whole of the Eighties' *Top of The Pops*?

'Nah, they were never the same after Peter Gabriel went…' He continued to gaze round the room. '… and Phil Collins took over. Do you reckon he had an affair with Kate Bush – you know after they did that song together.'

'Who? Phil Collins?'

'No, Phil Collins didn't sing anything with Kate Bush,' Don Bradbury tutted irritably.

'Right, OK, I stand corrected.'

'What was it?' He closed one eye and stared up at the ceiling.

'I'm sorry, what are we actually trying to work out now?' Hell, no wonder poor old Margaret Bradbury had copped it, she must have dropped dead with confusion. Or boredom. 'So, er, Don, how about I write you a prescription for your psoriasis? Hmm? And something to get you through the nights?'

'Please, love, that would help.' Don Bradbury sniffed and Juno passed him her emergency box of pink tissues.

'So, when's the funeral? Or have you actually had it?' Juno handed over his prescription.

'Whose funeral?' Don stared at Juno through the pink tissue.

'Er? Margaret's...?'

'Our lass? Our Margaret?' He started to hyperventilate. 'When? Who said? Who said she's died?'

'Well, you did.'

'Me? I did *not*.' Don was most affronted.

'You said she'd gone.'

'She *has*. She's buggered off with Jack Dobson. We were all at school together. He always fancied her...' He stood, giving Juno a funny look as he did so. 'I should get your facts right, love, before you start accusing folk of bumping off their wife. I'll make sure I see that new chap you've got here next time I come.' He gave her another look and walked off.

'The Police,' Juno muttered at his departing back. 'It was Sting.'

'What was?' Scott put his head round her door. 'God, have you just had Mr Bradbury in here? Good on ya, he's as mad as a… Had him last week and he accused me of encouraging his wife to leave him. Never even met the woman, but I can't imagine she'd need much encouragement. Can I borrow your stapler? I think Izzy's got mine.'

'It's over there on the shelf.' Juno didn't look up but concentrated on typing up Don Bradbury's notes.

'You OK?' Scott closed the door behind him and walked over to her. 'I didn't really want the stapler.'

'Oh?'

'I just wanted to see if you were OK… You know, you rushed off so quickly from Clementine's on Monday.'

Juno turned from the computer and looked straight at Scott, taking in his lovely smiling face, his beautiful green eyes, his blue and white striped shirt and, just half an hour into surgery time, his already-loosened dark blue tie. All she wanted to do was loosen that tie even more, reach her hand into his tanned chest and spend the rest of the morning rolling round on her examination couch with him.

'Am I OK? Scott, if you'd asked me that just a couple of days ago I'd have probably said, "totally".'

'But now?'

'Now, I've got my next patient.' She pressed the buzzer to let Marian know she was ready and turned back to her computer.

'Come on, what's up?'

'I've things going on with my sisters. I know this sounds ridiculously melodramatic but I wasn't there for Lexia years ago and she really needs me – well, all of us sisters – now. Something really strange has been going on with Lexia and Pandora – I can't explain yet. But most of all, I feel terribly *guilty*. At the end of the day, the minute my husband goes away, I jump into bed with the first man who looks my way. What if Fraser is, at this very minute, sat in his doctor's surgery in Boston USA, sobbing into a pink tissue and trying to recall the Eighties' hits – no, of course not: it'd be the *Noughty* hits, wouldn't it? – that remind him of me?'

'Naughty hits?' Scott stared. 'Do you mean naughty *bits*? Your husband is sobbing at his GP's in Boston recalling your naughty *bits*? From what I recall of them, there's absolutely nothing to cry about.' He started to laugh, but when he realised Juno was near to tears said, 'Juno, what is it?' He moved over to where she was sitting and stroked her hair.

'I feel like I've been *on* something ever since you first gave me the middle finger and shunted my Mini—'

'Hardly shunted…'

'Whatever.' Juno turned to face him. 'I need to see Fraser. I've only just realised this, and really, Scott, although of course I'm feeling like this because of… you know… because of *you* – this has nothing to *do* with you. It's all to do with me and Fraser and of course, my kids. He's their dad…'

'Oh, sorry, the receptionist said you were free.' A harassed-looking mother carrying a baby, while holding the hand of one of the two toddlers clinging to her skirt, somehow managed to knock and open the door.

Juno blew her nose on a pink tissue and, smiling at one of the toddlers, said, 'Do come in, Suzannah. Dr Butler is just leaving, now he's got my stapler.'

\*

Juno knew she had two things to do once she got home from work: tell Gabe and Tilda about Pandora and Lexia, that, actually kids, your cousin Hugo's mum isn't your Auntie Pandora. No, no, in fact, his mum is your Auntie *Lexia*. Obviously, just a little mistake. Fancy that! And then, she was going to ring Fraser in Boston and tell him she and the kids were coming out for Easter. It was only a couple of weeks off, Gabe and Lexia would have broken up from school and the three of them could all fly off, stay with Fraser and play happy families.

Or not.

And she would *know*. Know the minute she saw him waiting for them at the airport if she still loved him. Had ever really loved him the way you were supposed to love a husband. The father of her children.

'Is everything alright, Doctor?'

'Sorry?' Juno, in the middle of a men's health check-up the surgery had recently offered to the over-fifties, was trying to mentally work out the time difference in Boston as she felt for any irregular bumps and lumps.

'I said, is everything OK?' The newly retired fireman who was not only in incredibly good shape for his age but rather gorgeous into the bargain (Jesus, Juno, you *are* your father's daughter) looked worried. 'You keep *sighing*. You know, as if there's a *problem*?'

'Oh gosh, no, you're as fit as a butcher's dog. Absolutely.' Juno pasted a huge jolly smile onto her face and, as he stepped down from the couch, slapped his backside playfully with her file to reiterate the fact. Oh, for heaven's sake, what was the *matter* with her? If a male doctor had done that to a female patient he'd be hauled up in front of the General Medical Council. Struck off even.

'That wasn't as bad as I thought it was going to be,' the fireman called from behind the screen as he dressed and Juno tapped the results onto her computer. 'In fact,' he grinned, winking at her as he exited the practice room, 'once you got to the *bottom* of it all, very enjoyable all round.'

Could the day get any worse?

Juno decided she'd invite Ariadne over for tea; it would give her some adult back-up once she explained the complicated story of who Hugo's real mother was to Gabe and Tilda but also get an update, if her sister knew, of how Hugo, a day on, was coping with the revelation that his Aunty Lexia was actually his mother. Fuck, what an absolute mess!

Once her shift was finished, she left quickly even though Marian pounced as she went through reception, saying Dr Butler wanted a word before she left.

'Tell him I was in a hurry, would you, Marian? Supermarket, kids' tea…'

'Well, I will, but he said to be sure to catch you.' Marian arched an eyebrow and gave her a knowing look.

Oh bugger, had Izzy been gossiping? She wouldn't put it past her. 'Sorry, things to do, people to see,' she called over her shoulder as she hurried out. She had an awful feeling that if she was alone with Scott, she'd end up flat on her back again – revolting expression, she censured herself as she swept out of the carpark, the Mini behaving itself for once – and Juno knew she had to stop all that and work out just what was happening with her marriage first.

She was an *honourable* woman, she reminded herself as she chucked pasta and mince into her trolley. She wasn't a cheat (well, that blatantly wasn't true, she rebuked herself as she added a bottle – sod it, two – of a really good Merlot).

She was honourable.

*Who has honour?* The words from *Henry IV* part 1, studied for her English Literature GCSE, skittered unbidden into her brain as she leaned over the bakery counter to pick the biggest, most cream-laden and obviously calorific pudding Sainsbury's had to offer.

Who was it, you know, who had it? Honour? Juno closed her eyes momentarily, picturing her sixteen-year-old self, revising up in her chilly bedroom.

*Him who died on Friday.*

That was it. Great stuff. Even Shakespeare was encouraging her to *carry on* with Scott Butler behind Fraser's back – that anyone with any sense of honour actually ended up *dead*. Juno reached for a bottle of Bailey's. She and Ariadne would either be drunk or sick after all this cream, but at least the alcohol would help clear her mind. Or was it the other way round?

Juno threw in a box of Lindt chocolate.

Sod it, she'd never understood Shakespeare anyway.

'I phoned Pandora and Richard last night, and again this morning when I got a chance at breaktime.' Ariadne poured wine into two glasses. 'Apparently Hugo is being incredibly brave about it all.'

Juno frowned as she dangled a sheaf of spaghetti into a pan of boiling water. 'I'm not sure if that's a good sign or not? Surely, he should be ranting and raving and throwing things? Or sobbing, refusing to talk to anyone? Taking it all out on poor old Pandora and Richard for deceiving him?'

'Hmm, and for putting Lexia's showbiz career before the truth. And before him. They went about it all wrong,' Ariadne went on crossly. 'They should have adopted Hugo properly, legally, and told him about his real mother as soon as he was old enough to understand.'

'Yes, but when *is* that age? I can't imagine how parents tell their adopted children that they're not their real children, not their real mummy and daddy.'

'Every day somewhere, wonderful mums and dads are explaining that they aren't their child's birth parents. I guess they're advised how to do it and the younger the child the easier it is. I guess with the deceit Pandora and Richard started – Pandora admitted they actually wrote their own names on the birth certificate – as the years went by, even though it began to not really matter about Lexia's career anymore, you know, as she dropped out of the public eye, it must have been harder to tell Hugo the truth. So they didn't.' Ariadne poured more wine and began to smile. 'Pandora said Hugo was so relieved she wasn't dying of lung cancer – to begin with at least – he just took the truth on board. Anything, after realising he wasn't about to lose his mum, was a bonus. He's incredibly mature for his age, isn't he?'

'Must be what boarding school does for you. Shout the kids in for me, would you? Tilda's out with the hens.'

'And,' Ariadne went on, after sticking her head out of the kitchen door and yelling for Tilda, and Gabe who was knocking a football against the house wall, 'do you know what else Hugo said? He said, if it made Pandora and Richard feel any better, he was relieved he wasn't actually related to William Boothroyd. His grandfather, he said, had always been a racist bigot – kids today are so PC, aren't they? – and he was really sorry if that upset Richard, but he felt he could say it now.'

'Blimey.' Juno stopped grating parmesan and downed half her glass of wine in one. 'Even so, I'm not convinced Hugo won't need counselling. Actually, he *will*. I'll tell Pandora and Richard they really must go down that road with Hugo; there's a great woman we recommend, particularly for teenagers.' Juno smiled and then frowned. 'But what are Pandora and Lexia doing about telling the media the whole story before St Claire gets in there first? Now Hugo knows the truth and St Claire can't get any more money out of them, can't blackmail them anymore, he'll be straight on to the press to sell his story, won't he? God, he'll make an absolute fortune; you can just *see* the headlines can't you, in the tabloids: *Superstar Lexia – The Truth!!* and *Lexi Baby gave away her own baby!!* It'll run for weeks, every magazine and newspaper digging up more and more revelations, more dirt.' Juno's eyes widened at the thought. 'We'll need to protect Mum from it all; she'll find it all so confusing. They'll really go for it too – splash her mental illness all over the front pages. And she's been doing so well at the moment, now that Lexia's back and goes to see her most days. The last thing we need is her having another breakdown... Oh, gosh,' Juno went on. 'I keep thinking of more and more things. You know, Cillian is actually Hugo's *brother*...' She clapped a hand to her forehead before reaching for her glass. 'Fuck, can you just picture Bee-Bee Boothroyd's face when she reads all this in *The Sun*?'

'Can she actually *read*?' Ariadne responded tartly. 'I've never *once* had any intelligent conversation with her that doesn't involve shopping in Harrogate and ladies' lunches.'

'Actually, according to Pandora, she's going...'

'Going where?

'No, actually *going,* going a bit. You know.'

'And since William Boothroyd had his stroke last year,' Ariadne added, 'I'm not convinced *he's* totally with it either.' She sipped at her wine, deep in thought. 'You know, St Claire might not go to the papers.'

''Course he will. He's a little scumbag who's managed to blackmail Lexia and Pandora for years.'

'No, but don't you see, all that will come out and then *he'll* be arrested. You know, for blackmail. And having sex with an underage girl.'

Juno stared at Ariadne. 'Actually, you might be right.' Her eyes gleamed at the thought. 'Do you think we should go and find him, you know, jump on him and threaten *him*, do him over? Turn the tables on him as it were? Hell, I needed that.' Juno drained her glass and poured more. 'I feel like getting totally rat-arsed.'

'Bad day?'

'Well, apart from all this Lexia and Pandora stuff hanging over us and a silly old man saying I'd accused him of bumping off his wife, I realised, today, I've really fallen in love with Scott Butler...'

'Thought so.' Ariadne nodded sympathetically.

'But Izzy assures me – knowing Scott's past history – that he's a player, loves the conquest of the chase and I'm mad to carry on with what I'm doing. And I feel *guilty*. I like to think I am an *honourable* person.'

'None more so, Juno.' Ariadne nodded, tipsily pouring more wine. 'I've always thought that about you. You know, you didn't *have* to have Gabe...'

'Shhh.' Juno frowned, looking towards the open kitchen door. 'That's all I need, for Gabe to think he hadn't been wanted. I can't tell you how much I wanted Gabe. Hello, my darling...' Juno broke off and went to hug her son but he batted her off and reached for the garlic bread. 'I was just saying, I don't know what I'd be without you two.'

'A lot richer?' He grinned. 'I need new trainers. Oh, and I've torn my blazer... and can I have twenty quid for football subs?'

'Right,' Juno said faintly.

'Quite a day,' Ariadne agreed, as Tilda walked into the kitchen.

'Wash your hands, Matilda, and don't even think about getting Lady Gaga out. We're about to eat.' Juno carried plates, cutlery and napkins to the table and then started to giggle. 'Yes, quite a day. Totally finished off by my slapping a rather handsome firefighter's semi-naked backside.'

'You do know,' Tilda said primly, 'you could be hauled up in front of the Medical Council for that?'

Juno, who was still laughing, was saved from any caustic reply by Ariadne's phone ringing, at the same time as the kitchen door opened.

'Dad!' Gabe shouted, his mouth full of another piece of garlic bread. 'What are *you* doing here?'

# 26

Juno couldn't quite take it all in. She felt she was frozen in time – in a sort of framed piece of art in her own kitchen with the others, all staring, like herself, at her husband who for some reason was suddenly newly painted into the same tableau. She knew she'd downed too much red wine, too quickly and on an empty stomach, but why Fraser was standing at the kitchen door, his hands hanging loosely by his side, his face pale as he stared at her, she couldn't think. And even while she *knew*, yes, she knew *immediately* that she no longer loved him, no longer wanted to be married to him, she also knew *he* knew what she'd been up to with Scott Butler. Why else would he be standing there, seemingly unable to say a word, staring at her as if he didn't know her?

And then the still-life picture sprang into life. The second bottle of red wine she'd left to breathe while they drank the first flying from the kitchen top, spilling and splashing a seemingly endless stream of blood over both Fraser and Lady Gaga, while the pan of cooking pasta, not wanting to be excluded from the mayhem, co-ordinated perfectly its decision to boil over, erupting a steaming, spitting tsunami onto the hob and Juno's hand.

But that was nothing compared to what Ariadne was

saying as she stood, mobile in hand, her shocked eyes huge in her pale face.

'Theo's *killed* him. He'd been drinking and was driving, with Cillian in the back, and he's dead…'

'Cillian's dead? Oh Jesus, no.' Juno brought both hands to her face (the burned hand would, later, begin to hurt like hell) and gave a moan of terror.

'No, no, no, no. Not *Cillian*,' Ariadne snapped in some irritation. '*He's* absolutely fine, thank God. Well, as fine as a four-year-old *can* be who's just witnessed his father knocking down and killing someone.'

'Oh, thank goodness for that.' Juno realised she might actually be sick with the shock of it all. She sat down shakily, thrusting her head between her knees as Gabe moved towards her and Tilda grabbed a very affronted Lady Gaga, attempting to wipe her down with a piece of kitchen roll.

'So, *who's* dead? *Who* has Theo killed?' The overwhelming relief that it wasn't Cillian lying broken and mangled in the road had left Juno momentarily forgetting *someone* was dead.

'*Damian St Claire*'s dead,' Ariadne breathed, sitting down at the kitchen table once more and patting Juno somewhat ineffectually on her bent head. 'That was Richard on the phone, Juno. Theo'd been drinking, was bringing Cillian home from school and didn't see St Claire who was skulking down their lane and got in the way. Theo knocked him down… Fraser, how are you…?'

'Where's Lexia? Is *she* alright? Oh heavens, should we go round there? Where is she now?' Juno still felt as though she'd been hit by a ten-tonne truck.

'At the house. Pandora, Richard and Hugo are there.

And that nice Irish woman – you know, the nanny granny Lexia seems to have become so attached to? – she's there too. Look, you and Fraser obviously have a lot to catch up on. I'll get off…'

'No, no, really. Stay, Ari, and eat first.' Juno managed to lift her head long enough to send a silent plea to her big sister not to abandon her to Fraser. Not just yet anyway. She took several deep breaths, concentrating and directing her thoughts back to the other shock of the evening. 'Oh, Fraser, why on earth didn't you tell us you were coming home? Are you back for good?' she asked, her nose firmly entrenched back into her navy work skirt by an over-zealous Gabe. At least this way, she didn't have to meet Fraser's eyes. He didn't appear to have any luggage with him apart from the small valise he'd always taken on short trips away but, she supposed, he could have left all his luggage in the garden. For what reason, Juno couldn't quite think. She raised her head slightly and looked in his direction, but he wouldn't meet her eyes. Hell, he knew. Someone had told him.

Fraser obviously didn't have a clue what was going on, so Juno stood up, ran a hand through her hair, kissed Fraser's cold cheek and took his coat. The best thing for all of them – children excepted – would be to open yet another bottle of wine and try to explain to Gabe, Tilda and Fraser the secrets that had culminated in the shocking event outside Lexia and Theo's house earlier that evening.

'So,' Tilda said through narrowed eyes at the same time as sucking a recalcitrant worm of spaghetti slowly into her mouth.

'Hmm?' Juno found she couldn't look at Fraser, didn't

want to see the hurt in his eyes as he attempted to wind his pasta, like the Italian native he blatantly wasn't, around his fork. It had always irritated her that, before starting a hillock of spaghetti, Fraser's usual *modus operandi* involved taking his knife and fork and cutting the pasta into neat manageable bite-sized bits before popping each one into his mouth and chewing methodically. He'd never shown any *passion* for food: butter running down his chin, eyes closed in ecstasy over a particularly succulent piece of pork crackling.

Maybe she was just a rotten cook?

'So,' Tilda repeated, chewing just as thoughtfully as her father. 'Next time I tell a little fib, you know a little *white lie*, it will all fade into insignificance compared with the whopping great perfidious untruth this family has been telling for years?'

'What?' Gabe glared at Tilda, while Ariadne, apparently forgetting the dreadful news she'd just imparted, gave a little snort of laughter. 'What are you on about? Speak English, you moron.'

'Good God, Matilda Armstrong, you remind me of myself at your age.' Ariadne raised an eyebrow in Matilda's direction, obviously pleased that her own genes had been shared with her only niece.

'What I'm asking,' Tilda said patiently, ignoring her brother, 'is that, next time you ask if Lady Gaga is in bed with me and she *is*, but I say no, she *isn't*...'

'Lady Gaga?' Fraser looked even more out of the loop than ever and Juno felt a frisson of irritation that he'd obviously never been interested enough to know the name of his daughter's gerbil.

'Alright, Matilda, enough.' Juno felt tension run through

every inch of her body as she stood and, rather than meet Fraser's eye, made her way across to the sink, running her burned hand under the cold tap. 'Right, now that we've got that out of the way – and, you two, this is still a *huge* family secret, not to be repeated to *anyone...*'

'Not even Mr Donnington?' Tilda pouted.

'Especially Mr Donnington,' Juno snapped.

'Mr Donnington?' Fraser screwed up his face in that bloody stupid way that had always irritated Juno and she had a sudden urge to slap it. And then felt awful. Oh, the poor man; here he was, all the way back from America to sort out his marriage, in his own kitchen, and she was wanting to commit GBH. Or was it ABH?

'So, now we've got Part One out of the way, can we move onto Part Two and establish just what's happened this evening with Theo and St Claire? Why don't you two go and watch TV? This is adult conversation. Go on, off you go.'

'You're joking.' Gabe and Tilda spoke as one and leaned forward in anticipation.

'Well, I suppose it's going to be all over the papers tomorrow.' Ariadne frowned. 'In fact, I bet it's on the ten o'clock news tonight.'

Gabe whistled. 'What'll happen to Theo Ryan? Will Midhope Town let him carry on playing?'

'Course not.' Tilda was scornful. 'He's killed someone, knocked them down while he was driving under the influence, with a child on board. They'll throw the book at him.'

Juno pulled a despairing face in Ariadne's direction: Tilda had been reading the latest Magistrates' Court Guidelines now, had she? She'd *definitely* know the difference between GBH and ABH.

'What did Richard say on the phone?' Fraser asked, speaking almost for the first time. He really didn't look well at all, Juno thought. He'd lost weight and, yes, in the three months he'd been away, surely more of his hairline as well? Had *she* done this to him? Carrying on with another man? While the cat's away and all that... This was a small village. Someone must have told him. Was it a Dear John letter? A Dear *Fraser* letter maybe from one of her patients with whom she'd not been quite as patient, quite as *sympathetic* towards as perhaps she should? Juno racked her brains. Obviously not that mad coot she'd been forced into the Eighties' pop quiz with that very morning. Izzy? Marian? Bloody Marian, she'd bet any money it was Marian. She obviously fancied Scott herself...

'I'm going round to Lexia's,' Ariadne stated, a good hour after Fraser had first appeared in the kitchen and sat down with them, making his way down his spag bol as if he'd never been away. No, not quite the same, Juno knew. He was different, anxious, on edge.

'Well, you can't *drive*,' Tilda sniffed disparagingly. 'That's *all* we need, another member of the family up for drink driving. It's an automatic driving ban, you know. Mr Donnington—'

'What, Mr Donnington's been banned?' Juno interrupted hopefully. Was there finally a dent in the saintly deputy head's halo?

'No, he told us *that* in PSHE. Mr Donnington says anyone

who drinks and drives is socially and morally bankrupt...'
Tilda broke off at the sudden realisation of the golden
nugget of information she'd be able to offer up to her god
at school in the morning.

Ariadne stood up, laughing at Tilda's words and, reaching
over, patted her niece on the bottom as she and Gabe left for
the sitting room and TV. 'Don't worry, I'll ring for a taxi. It
might be best if I stay with Lexia tonight if she'd like me to.
She can drive me over for my car in the morning.'

*Don't leave me*, Juno's eyes pleaded with Ariadne. *Don't
leave me to face the music by myself.*

'I'll get off then.' Ariadne gave an imperceptible shake of
the head in Juno's direction. 'You and Fraser have obviously
*loads* to talk about, Juno.' She turned to Fraser who was
neatly folding his used paper napkin (yellow bunnies in
celebration of the coming season) into four. 'How *was*
Boston, Fraser? Snowy? And the new job? Demanding?
Enjoying it all?'

'All of those, Ariadne, thank you,' Fraser returned politely.
'Look, it's been a long day. I think I'll just go up and have
a quick shower, Juno.' He kissed Ariadne goodbye, reached
for his valise and headed for the stairs.

'Oh, shoot...!' Juno jumped up.

'What?' Ariadne turned from fastening the buttons on
her jacket.

'The bathroom.' Juno ran to the bottom of the stairs and
shouted after her husband's slowly ascending form. 'The
bathroom, Fraser, er, you'll find it a bit, er, *different*.'

'*He* seems a bit, you know, *different* too,' Ariadne
whispered as Juno returned to the kitchen. 'Not quite as
*Uncle Quentinish*.'

'But did Aunt Fanny ever *screw around*?' Juno said grimly, moving over to fill the dishwasher. 'God,' she berated herself, trying to fit the spaghetti pan into the dishwasher before retrieving it to wash by hand, 'I do hate that revolting expression.'

'Fanny?'

'No, you know, *screw around*.'

'So, what do you reckon to Aunt Fanny then? With a name like that? I bet she was at it hammer and tongs over at Kirrin Island while Uncle Quentin grappled with his scientific inventions and formulae and the kids were all asleep. Mind you,' she went on, seriously, 'they never *did* sleep, did they? Wasn't Enid Blyton always having the Famous Five tucking into sneaky midnight feasts over at Kirrin Island? I bet they never cleaned their teeth after them, and poor old Fanny would have just been going for it when George and Dick and... what were the others...?'

'Anne and Julian,' Juno said, scraping plates into a dish to give later to Myrtle and her mates.

'... Anne and Julian and the dog popped up out of nowhere looking for the hidden treasure and interrupted her session with the gorgeously, rampant dark-haired fisherman. Anne, particularly, wouldn't have been impressed – she was always a bit prudish, a bit grown up, wasn't she? A bit like Pandora really.' Ariadne started laughing and then, when she saw Juno's face, immediately stopped. 'Gosh, I'm sorry, Juno. I'm being a bit flippant here, aren't I? What are you going to do?'

'I don't want to be married to Fraser anymore, Ariadne. I knew it the moment he appeared in the kitchen.'

'The dishy doctor? Is he what's made you feel like this?'

Juno shook her head. 'No, he's just the icing on the cake. Even if Scott Butler hadn't come to work at the surgery, even if I hadn't fallen in love with him, I'd still be feeling the same. It was such a relief when Fraser left for Boston. Now, I just feel tense, miserable that he's back. Like I often used to feel before he went, I now realise.'

'Yes, but he said he's only back for a couple of days. You can stop being miserable once he goes again.'

Juno tutted. 'I'm an honourable woman, as you agreed earlier.'

'I'd had quite a bit of wine...'

'I'm an honourable woman and am, at the moment, living a lie.'

'Which this family seems to be jolly good at.' Ariadne raised an eyebrow.

'Well, I must be the exception. I *can't* live a lie. I don't *want* to live a lie.'

'Seriously, Juno, think of the kids. Think about Gabe and Tilda.'

'You saw Fraser with his children this evening, Ariadne,' Juno said sadly. 'Did he hug them, grab them as if he couldn't bear to ever let them ever go? Did he ask about Gabe's football, ask Tilda about Harry Trotter or Moaning Myrtle? He appeared to have no knowledge of Lady Gaga and yet Tilda had that gerbil long before he left for America.'

'I just feel really sorry for him,' Ariadne said. 'It's the way he was brought up. He can't help it.'

'So do I, but, Ariadne, I can't live another fifty years with him. Another fifty years sitting across from him while he clears his throat – clears his nose by putting his two-fingered-hanky up his nostrils and shaking it about – his hanky, not his nose. While he chops up his spaghetti and folds his dirty napkin. *Screw it up and chuck it in the bloody bin...* that's what I want to yell at him. That's no way to live the next fifty years, is it?'

'Counselling?' Ariadne asked hopefully. 'No? Just giving you all the options, Juno, before you throw in the towel. And...' She paused at the kitchen door as her taxi pulled up 'If it makes you feel any better, I don't think I could live fifty *minutes* with Fraser, never mind the next fifty years.' She hugged Juno fiercely. 'I never let you lot – you know, Pandora and Lexia and all of you lot – I never say just how much I love you all. You're my family. There, I'm embarrassing myself now, being daft old Aunt Ariadne. Look, what I'm trying to say is, I'm here for you, Juno, if the shit hits the proverbial.' She hugged Juno once more and, slightly tipsily, made her way down the garden path to the waiting taxi.

# 27

Once Ariadne had left in her taxi for Lexia's place in Heath Green, Juno zipped herself into her old navy Barbour and walked down the garden to the bottom of the paddock with the dish of left-over pasta for the girls. Matilda, mindful of the marauding fox that had been appearing earlier and earlier these days, regardless of the lighter evenings now that the clocks had just been put forward for British Summer Time, had locked up the chucks for the evening before coming in for supper. Despite the mass of daffodils, and now tulips that were also showing off their incredible array of colours in the fading dusk, the evening in this first week of April was still chilly and Juno gave a little involuntary shiver as she unlocked and opened the hen's coop and scraped the food into their feeding trays.

Harry Trotter was still grazing in his favourite spot towards the top of the paddock, but raised his head and then slowly walked down towards her. Juno's instinct was to quickly lock up the hen coop and climb back over the fence out of his way but, instead, told herself it was about time she got over her fear of the pony and, steeling herself, moved back to sit on the top of the double-barred gate in the fence, waiting until he came and stood beside her, curious as to what was in her hand.

'Nothing for you, matey,' she said, as he pushed his velvety face into the dish. 'And it's your bedtime.' She put up a tentative hand to his nose and he lifted his head as though about to rear back but, instead placed his face back in the empty dish, blowing air through both nostrils. 'You're very beautiful,' Juno whispered as he finally allowed her to touch him. 'Next time, I'll bring you something and we can get to know each other properly? Hmm…?'

'Blimey, you're braver than me, Mum. I wouldn't get in there with him. He's a maniac.' Gabe had come out to find her and stood, shivering, on the other side of the fence. 'What are you doing, anyway?'

'Oh, just gathering a bit of courage.' She smiled as she continued to stroke Harry's nose, delighted that he was allowing it.

'Courage?' Gabe frowned. 'You're not thinking of riding him, are you?'

Juno laughed. 'No, just thought it was about time I got over my fear of horses,' she said, though that wasn't what she'd meant.

'Mum?'

'Hmm?'

'We're not going to go and live in America, are we?'

'You don't want to? You don't want to go and live out there with Dad?'

'No.'

Gabe turned and walked back to the house and then turned again towards Juno. 'Oh, I came out to tell you that new doctor of yours – the Australian – just rang you on your mobile.'

'He's from New Zealand.' Juno felt her pulse immediately rev up. Jesus, between Fraser turning up unannounced, her standing her ground with Harry Trotter and now Gabe speaking to Scott, she'd probably speeded up her whole system so much she'd knocked several years off her allotted lifespan. 'Why didn't you bring my phone out to me, or call me in?'

'I just assumed you were with Dad upstairs.'

'What did you tell him?'

'Oh, just that my dad was back from America and you were upstairs in the bedroom with him.'

'Right.'

'He said it wasn't important and he'd see you at work.' Gabe picked up his football and played Keepie-Uppie all the way back to the house.

'Oh, heavens,' Juno whispered into Harry's neck. The pony gave her and the empty dish a look of utter disdain, before wheeling round and cantering off at speed. 'Well, you can shut up as well,' she sniffed, before climbing down from the gate and going inside to find Fraser.


'Why didn't you ring, Fraser? Why on earth didn't you let me know you were back for a few days?' Juno closed the bedroom door behind her and folded her arms.

'I'm not sure. To be honest, Juno, I didn't *need* to come back for a meeting in Leeds.'

'You didn't?'

Fraser shook his head but didn't say anything, instead neatly folding the clothes he'd travelled in and discarded for a clean shirt and sweater. 'Where are the children?' he eventually asked, sitting down on the edge of the bed and looking, for the first time since he'd arrived back, directly at Juno.

'Downstairs, watching TV. You know, to say you've not seen them for over three months, you've not shown them a great deal of attention.' Or affection, she wanted to add.

'Actually, Juno, there was so much going on down there this evening, I felt somewhat shell-shocked. I have to say, it was like coming back to a different world. All this drama? It all seems a bit over the top? Rather typical of your lot, I suppose, but I still don't totally understand what's been going on with you and all your sisters?'

*Typical of* my *lot?*

'Join the club.' Juno sat down beside him, her stomach churning as she tried to work out exactly where she was going to start with what she had to say to Fraser.

'Juno, we need to talk.'

Oh hell, he knew what she'd been up to.

'I don't think you've been totally honest with me, have you?'

Juno didn't answer. Let him come out with what he knew – surely the best plan of action without implicating herself too much?

'For a start, this bathroom must have cost way more than the estimate you emailed me back in January?'

'Sorry?'

'The bathroom? Not really my cup of tea, you know, and it's obviously gone way over the budget we agreed.'

'Very probably,' Juno murmured. Was Fraser *really* discussing the damned bathroom when there were clearly more important things at stake here?

'And when you said you'd bring the children out to Boston for their summer break, I'm not convinced it was really your intention. Was it?'

'Yes, yes, of course it was,' Juno said hotly. No, no, it probably wasn't, was what was really going through her head. Oh, poor Fraser, what had she done to him? He obviously felt so unloved. But this was no good. She had to tell him the truth.

'Juno...'

'Fraser...' They spoke as one.

'Look, Juno, there's no easy way to say this. I've met someone else. I'm *with* someone else and I'm not coming back.'

'Oh!' Juno stared at Fraser who was finding it very difficult to meet her eyes. 'Oh!' she managed to get out once more.

'I'm so sorrrry, Juno.' Stress was making Fraser's Scottish burr more pronounced. 'You may have not been overrrrly honest with me, but I, blatantly, have been living a lie. I knew I was going to have to be a man, you know, be a man and fly 3000 miles back home—' oh, glory be, had he been listening to The Proclaimers? '—and tell you to your face.'

'Well, yes, thank you for that.'

'And Laura said—'

'Laura?'

'Laura McCaskill. She's a research chemist with me in Boston.'

'Laura McCaskill?' Juno frowned. 'Wasn't she in Leeds with you? Didn't we sit with her at one of your company dinners last year? That really, *really* boring one where everyone on the table was discussing *Recent Advances in Atomic Layer Division*? And I came home and, to get over it all, got stuck into the box set of *Outlander* and a box set of Thorntons...?'

'Deposition.'

'Sorry?'

'*Recent Advances in Atomic Layer Deposition.*'

'Yes, that's the one.' Juno stared at Fraser. 'So, this Laura McCaskill has been out in Boston with you?'

Fraser looked decidedly shifty. 'She was already there when I arrived. She'd taken up a position with the Boston office in the summer.'

'But she wanted *you* out there too?'

'Look, I *am* trying to be honest here, Juno. Laura and I knew we had a lot in common when we met in Leeds. We're both *passionate* about Polymer Bioconjugates.'

'While I was just passionate about...?'

'That Scottish Highlander in a Jacobean kilt.' Fraser frowned. 'But to be fair to you, Juno, you've always been *totally* passionate about the children – I really can't fault you there – and... and sticky toffee pudding. You know, you *were* beginning to put on a bit of weight—' he looked Juno up and down '—which you appear to have lost now. You're looking wonderful, Juno. And your hair suits you like that, you know, curly, more natural. I do hope, Juno, you've not lost weight because of me? Worrying about me? Missing me? That would make me feel really bad.'

Ignoring this, Juno asked, 'So the main reason you went out to Boston when they asked you...?'

'I asked *them*.'

'Right, OK, so the main you reason you asked *them*

for a year in Boston was so you could be with this Laura McCaskill? Is that what you're now telling me?'

Fraser nodded. 'Laura said she was going, that it would make me think about what I wanted.'

'What you wanted?'

'Well, yes, was I prepared to break up my marriage for Laura?'

'And now you realise you are?'

Fraser nodded dumbly and took Juno's hand. 'I'm so sorrrry, but Laura and I want to be together. We have so much in common.'

'You said.'

'And Laura, coming from Scotland, well, she really gets on with my mother.'

'Laura's met your *mother*? Bloody hell. When?'

'We travelled back up to Aberdeen together – that conference last May? My mother joined us for dinner.'

And she actually gets on with her?' Juno snorted. '*Fucking* hell.'

'There really is no need for foul language, Juno. Laura never swears. But yes, they're great pals. Get on like a house on fire.' Fraser sighed. 'And I'll be the first to admit, I've not been the best father to Gabriel and Matilda. I've never really *got* the children like you have. I don't really *understand* them.' He paused and took Juno's hand once more. His was warm, clammy but, after all, he was her husband: she didn't feel it the done thing to pull her hand away, even while he was telling her he was going back to Boston to be with Laura and then, more than likely, they'd be relocating back up to the Aberdeen office together by the following year.

'The thing is, Juno, you and I, we really have nothing in

common, have we, you know, apart from the children? It's really not been right between us for years. And, I have to say, living down here in Yorkshire, you know, in *England*, hasn't really been my cup of tea.' He paused, frowning. 'You're... what's the word...?'

'Frivolous? I think you once described me as *frivolous*. Is that the word you're thinking of?'

He nodded, looking slightly ashamed. 'You know, I want to see the children. There's no reason why they can't come out to Boston this summer. You could put them on the plane at Manchester and I'll be there at the other end to meet them. Or—' the thought had obviously only just come to him '—my mother could bring them out? Be with them there in the apartment when I'm at work?'

'And leave her dogs and horses?' As well as Tilda leaving Harry Trotter? Although Mr Donnington would be out of the equation by then, she mused. 'We'll see. You'll have to put it to the kids. Now, do you think, perhaps, you should go down and talk to your children? See what they've been up to recently? And then – tomorrow I think, it's too late now before their bedtime – we'll have to explain things to them, together.'

'You mean discuss how we're going to share custody of them?' Fraser screwed up his face. 'You're taking all this very well, Juno. I thought you'd be devastated, throwing things at me.' He seemed slightly miffed that she hadn't chucked a few things his way.

'I hope we can be grown up about this, Fraser. As you say, we've not really had much in common over the years.'

And, while a part of Juno was feeling terribly sad – sad for her marriage, (she was picturing it as a living entity that, through no fault of its own, was suddenly being thrown into the recycling bin along with yesterday's newspapers) and awfully, guiltily sad for her children who, through no fault of their own, were about to lose their father to an obviously *unfrivolous* (was there such a word? She must ask Tilda) Laura McCaskill – the main emotion that was whizzing round her brain was one of profound relief that she was no longer going to be living with a man she didn't love, was no longer going to be living a lie.

'I'm going to leave you with the kids,' Juno said, standing up and patting Fraser's shoulder, 'while I pop over to Lexia's and find out a bit more what's happened down there this afternoon.'

'At this time?' Fraser looked at his watch, one, Juno realised, she'd never seen before. 'It's going up to nine. Do you not think it better you stay here and we discuss things – you know, money, what's going to happen to the house, the mortgage...?'

'I don't think there's anything to discuss with the *house*,' Juno said tartly. 'Now I've done the bathroom, I'm staying put. It's the kitchen next. Look, Fraser, I *know* you'll want to maintain the kids...' Juno didn't know anything of the sort – Fraser was looking decidedly nervous at the very notion of maintenance.

'Of course, of course,' Fraser hurriedly interrupted. 'I'm aware of my responsibilities.'

'But, if necessary, I'll go back to work full-time. Now, I really do want to be with Lexia, she's been through so much lately.'

'But you've been drinking.' Fraser frowned.

'Yes, and rather a lot. I'll ring for a taxi.'

'Another taxi?'

'*Another* taxi, Fraser. Now, Tilda is usually in bed by nine, Gabe not much later, although they'll both argue the toss. Alright?'

'Well,' Juno said out loud, as she closed the kitchen door behind her, 'you weren't expecting *that*, Aunt Fanny!' She buttoned up her jacket against the chilly April evening air and walked down to the garden gate to wait for the taxi, her mind reeling.

It was nearer ten by the time Den's Cars, the village taxi firm, had deigned to send up another taxi to take Juno over to Lexia's place. The long winding country lane, off the main road running through the village of Heath Green, had a couple of police accident signs and blue and white tape cordoning off an area near the top of the lane where the modern gated hamlet of five huge blonde-stoned houses stood in all their imperious, upmarket glory.

'Summat's up,' the youngish driver said in excitement. 'Summat's going on. When I brought the other one over – your sister, is she? – there were still a couple of police cars here and they asked me where I was going.' He seemed disappointed that he wasn't going to be asked again, that he wasn't going to be part of the investigation. 'Theo Ryan's place, isn't it? And Lexia Sutherland? God, I loved her when I were fifteen. Had all her posters up on me bedroom wall. Spent more time with Lexia Sutherland – in me bedroom and in me head, of course—' he gave a somewhat dirty laugh and looked pointedly down at his nether regions '— than with me own family when I were a kid.'

'Right. How much do I owe you? I'll need a lift back in an hour or so.'

Juno paid the driver who'd got out of the taxi, eager to accompany her up to the large black gates in order to find out more or, even better, to catch a glimpse of his teenage icon. Ariadne, standing at the door of Theo's and Lexia's house, beckoned her up the drive as the gates slowly swung back and open.

'How is she?' Juno closed the front door behind her and followed Ariadne, who appeared to have sobered up somewhat, along the magnificent cream-carpeted hall towards the kitchen where, several weeks ago, Juno had encouraged Manchester United footballers down Cillian, along with his soft-boiled egg.

'How are *you*?' Ariadne whispered. 'Fraser found out about you and Scott Butler?'

'No, but I've found out about Fraser and Laura McCaskill... long story, I'll tell you later. How's Lexia?'

'Not looking her best.'

'Well, no, I'm not surprised...' As they walked into the kitchen and Juno saw Lexia sitting at the table, she stopped and stared, clapping a hand to her mouth. 'Oh, for heaven's sake, Lexia, what's he done to you?' Lexia's right eye was a purplish black, almost closed, and her right arm, in her white T-shirt was badly bruised. 'Has St Claire done this to you?'

'Shhh,' Lexia and Ariadne spoke as one. 'There's a policewoman still here. She's just nipped to the loo.'

'Can I get you a coffee or a nice cup of tea? Kettle's on.' The rather motherly woman standing by the huge Aga smiled at Juno.

'Sorry, Juno, this is Lilian. You know, the lovely lady who

babysits and does a bit around the house for us – for me.' Lexia smiled fondly at the woman.

'Ah, Mrs Doubtfire?' Juno smiled also. 'I know Harriet Westmoreland always calls you that, doesn't she? You're getting quite a reputation round here for being brilliant with kids.'

'I don't think it's kids who need much looking after round here at the moment,' Lilian Brennan said seriously in her lovely Irish brogue, nodding in Lexia's direction. 'I'll just pop up and make sure the little one's OK, Lexia, darling. I've made a fresh pot of tea.'

'It *wasn't* St Claire,' Ariadne whispered. 'We're trying to keep it quiet that Lexia had anything to do with *him* in the past.'

'It wasn't St Claire that Theo knocked down?' Juno stared. 'Who was it then?'

'No,' Ariadne tutted irritably. 'It *was* St Claire Theo knocked down and killed. It *wasn't* St Claire who gave Lexia the black eye.'

'Who was it then?'

'To say you're an intelligent, professional woman, Juno, you can be incredibly thick at times.' Ariadne tutted once more.

'It was Theo, Juno.' Lexia attempted a little smile, but it was obvious she was near to tears.

'But why? What had you done?' Juno was totally mystified, couldn't quite take it all in (there had been one *hell* of a lot to take in, this very strange evening) but then she saw red. 'Theo's done this? Theo? Where is he? I'll have him. How dare he do this to you…? Where is the bastard…?'

'I told him about Hugo. Told him how I'd had a baby

when I was just sixteen and that my nephew, Hugo, was actually my son and, more than likely it was going to hit the papers any day. You know, once St Claire started telling his story, now that we're refusing to give him any more money. Whether Theo was upset that I'd kept all this from him or whether it was because I'd given a shedload of money to St Claire over the years or, more likely, because all this was not going to make Theo Sutherland, ace footballer, look very good, he lost his temper and went for me. He'd been drinking as usual, how much I don't know, but certainly there was alcohol on his breath.'

Lexia accepted the mug of tea Ariadne poured for her. 'Anyway, Theo said I couldn't possibly pick Cillian up from school looking like I did – terribly worried now, of course, at what he'd done to me – picked up my car keys and took off in my car to get Cillian.'

'But if he'd been drinking,' Juno frowned, 'how could you let him go and pick up Cillian when he wasn't fit to drive?'

'I couldn't stop him. I rang Little Acorns straight away, you know, to tell them *not* to let Theo pick up Cillian. All I got was the answer machine. I rang and rang and then decided to take Theo's Porsche to pick him up myself. But his car wasn't there. He'd been for a lunchtime drink with someone – probably one of his floozies – after training, and obviously left the car somewhere and got a taxi home. By the time I got through to school, Theo had picked him up and was driving home. Apparently, St Claire was skulking down the lane, off his head on something, jumped out at the car as it came back, presumably thinking it was me driving, and that was it.'

'Oh, you poor thing, Lexia.' Juno shook her head.

'Everything's happening at once to you.' She paused. 'Has Theo done anything like this before?'

'He's always been a bit rough with me. I guess he hates that I haven't lived up to the dream he thought he was marrying. You know, the Sexy-Lexi in all the daft magazines. And, I've spent a lot of the past few years, particularly since Cillian was born, being very depressed, very anxious...'

'Anyone would be anxious if they thought they were going to get a black eye like that every time their husband came home from work.' Juno went to sit by Lexia, examining her injuries. 'Anyone looked at this eye, Lexia?'

'Lilian's patched me up a bit. It's fine.' Lexia shrugged away Juno's tentative fingers on her arm, reached for her sweater and pulled it on, covering her arms. 'Anyway, as I was saying, to begin with we were fine, living the high life, enjoying our so-called fame. But then Theo would take it out on me, you know, if the manager had taken it out on *him*, or if he'd missed a penalty or something. Verbally to begin with and then a few bruises here and there. You know...'

'No, we don't know.' The police constable from the Domestic Violence Unit came back into the kitchen, reaching for her jacket slung over a chair. 'No one has to put up with this. Now, I can stay, Lexia or—' she glanced at the kitchen clock '—now that your sisters and Mrs Brennan are here with you, I can push off. We've got the pictures of your injuries and your statement. I'm afraid this isn't going to go away. The press will be swarming like flies once it all gets out. You've agreed that you're happy for us to go to the Magistrates' Court in the morning to take out a Domestic Violence Protection Order...'

'What does that do?' Ariadne asked.

'Stops Mr Ryan having any contact directly or indirectly with Lexia for up to twenty-eight days. He'll get one chance tomorrow, or the day after, to be accompanied back here by one of my colleagues to get as much stuff as he wants. After that he can't. Any further restraining order Lexia wants to put in place after that will have to be passed by the magistrates.'

'But Theo will want to see Cillian. He adores Cillian...' A single tear rolled down Lexia's cheek.

'He'll just have to see him through a third party, Lexia, not you. Through his solicitor, possibly. Once I've been to court tomorrow that'll give you a chance to sort yourself a bit.'

'Sort herself?' Ariadne asked.

'Where she's going to live, what she wants to do.'

'Can't she live here?' Ariadne asked. 'It is her home.'

'Yes, of course, if she wants...'

'Will you all stop talking about me as if I weren't here? As if I were a child?' Lexia said, crossly. 'I know exactly what I'm going to do. I'm going home.'

'Home?' Ariadne and Juno turned back to Lexia.

'Mmm. Cillian and I are going to go home. Back home with Mum.'

# 28

Realising Scott Butler wasn't in his practice room and didn't appear to have actually arrived yet, despite the fact that it was almost eight-fifteen and the waiting room was already starting to fill up with his patients, Juno went to find Marian who seemed to have disappeared from her command position in reception as well.

Where the hell was everyone? Not arriving back from Lexia's place until well after 2 a.m., Juno had slid self-consciously into her side of the bed, while Fraser either was, or was pretending to be, asleep. She'd left the house that morning, leaving a pale-faced Fraser obviously not quite sure what to do with himself, the detritus on the breakfast table, a once-more-escaped-in-the kitchen Lady Gaga, and a bad-tempered Brian Goodall turning vegetable beds at the top of the garden by the paddock fence. Juno felt tired, gritty-eyed and, although she knew she wasn't looking her best, was desperate to know what Scott had wanted when he'd phoned last evening while she was endeavouring to be Harry Trotter's new best friend. And to assure him that being *upstairs in the bedroom with my dad* certainly shouldn't be misconstrued as anything more than her husband fastidiously folding his pants while informing her he was leaving her for the non-frivolous, non-swearing Laura McCaskill.

As Juno left her dungeon once more, heading upstairs to the main reception area and practice rooms, she cast her mind back to the one time she'd met the woman her husband was leaving her for. Obviously, Laura's scientific brain was what he was after; Juno couldn't recall his colleague being a sex-god siren draped in pink satin, luring Fraser to her side over the dried-up inedible chicken and flabby roast potatoes that seemed to be *de rigueur* at these corporate dinners. On the contrary, Laura McCaskill had come over as a somewhat pale little thing, thin of body as well of hair. Had she, Juno, become so upholstered with her love of sticky toffee pudding – wasn't that what Fraser had implied last night – that she was unlovable? Despite the relief she was feeling that she would no longer be sharing her bed and her bank account with Fraser, Juno was also feeling desperately sad and guilty about her children: he was their father after all. Had she been *frivolous* with her relationship with their dad? Should she have tried so much harder? Ignored the irritating throat clearing and two-fingered hanky up the nostril method of cleaning out his nose? Ignored Fraser's parsimony with money and his inability to find *Fleabag* even remotely funny or entertaining?

With all that was going on with Lexia, and now being rejected by her husband for a sandy-haired string bean, Juno was starting to feel thoroughly depressed. *Oh, for heaven's sake*, she chided herself, *get a grip; you no longer wanted to be married to Fraser. You have what you wanted.*

'Juno, there you are. I've been looking for you all over.' Izzy, in the process of marching through reception, peered over her reading spectacles. 'Just heard about Theo Ryan,' she said volubly. 'Bad business. How's your sister coping? Have the police let him go?' Izzy batted the volley of questions in Juno's direction while the patients in reception, as well as Anne from Anne Did Those Feet, searching for a file behind the reception desk, visibly leaned in Juno's direction, ears flapping.

'Have you seen Dr Butler?' Juno asked, ignoring all questions with regard Theo Ryan or Lexia.

Izzy took Juno's arm, heading her into her own practice room where, once in, she closed the door behind them.

'He's taken a day off. Very last minute but, to be honest, Declan and I couldn't really refuse. Scott's not taken one day off in over three months. Even covered when Declan was ill with that dicky stomach, last month.'

'Right. Is he ill?'

'Who? Declan?'

'No,' Juno tutted, tiredness making her irritable. '*Scott*.'

'Didn't sound it. Sounded quite jolly really. Look, Juno...' Izzy hesitated before rubbing Juno's arm in a measure of sympathy. 'I know you've got a bit of a thing for our dishy doctor at the moment, but please don't break up your marriage over him. I said before, he's a bit of a womaniser, a bit of a ladies' man.'

'*A ladies' man*?' Juno snapped. 'Izzy, you sound like my granny'

'Hey, don't shoot the messenger,' Izzy retorted. 'Look, I wasn't going to tell you but Declan and I took Emily over to The Coach and Horses at Upper Clawson last night. She arrived home unexpectedly on Monday evening – oh, of course, you knew that, that's why we left Clem's in a hurry.

You know, while *you* were wrapped round Scott Butler up against the wall.'

'Alright, alright, you've made your point...'

'Poor lamb's finding university a bit stressful. Have to say, when she suddenly arrived back home, mid-term, I had an awful feeling she might be pregnant or something.'

'Kids today have *much* more sense than to get pregnant,' Juno snapped again. 'What is it? What are you trying to tell me?'

'So, we decided to take Emily out somewhere quiet so we could persuade her to carry on with her course... it's her cadaver that's getting to her. Apparently, she's got a real old codger who grins at her lasciviously every time he's brought out of the fridge.'

'And? Come on, Izzy, I've got patients waiting.'

'And Scott was there.'

'Oh?'

'With a very young, very beautiful girl. She was quite gorgeous, Juno.'

'Right.' Juno felt her heart plummet.

'I just thought you should know,' Izzy said, rubbing Juno's arm once more. 'You know, before you did anything daft like thinking Scott was serious and telling Fraser you'd met someone else.'

'Right. And did they appear to be, you know, *together*?'

''Fraid so. When he caught sight of us, you know gawping, he was terribly embarrassed. Didn't wave us over or introduce us. It didn't help that Emily's tongue was virtually hanging out at the sight of him too. He's a menace; got women of all ages falling over him. I remember Declan's *mother* having the hots for him too, years ago. Wouldn't surprise me if she'd included *him* in her damned will.'

'I've got work to do,' Juno said numbly. 'Thank you for telling me, Izzy.'

'Juno, I wasn't being a gossip,' Izzy said seriously. 'I just didn't want you throwing away your marriage, your kids' happiness, you know?'

'I know.' Juno closed Izzy's practice room door quietly behind her and headed down to her dungeon.

'Right,' Ariadne said bossily down the phone at lunchtime, 'we're all going to Filey tomorrow.'

'Who is?'

'*We* are. We *all* are. It's all arranged.'

'Aren't you working? Aren't you at school?'

'Break up for Easter this afternoon. You must know that because your kids do too. I've checked.'

'Yes, but I'm not a teacher or a schoolchild. I have to work tomorrow and Friday.' Juno felt quite weary at the conversation. Ariadne could be so demanding, so *bossy* when she'd had one of her ideas.

'I thought you were part-time. Make sure your part-*time* isn't tomorrow or Friday.'

'Don't be ridiculous, Ari. Those are my days, my shifts. There's no way I can just troll off to the seaside for two days. And who's going to look after the kids? Fraser's leaving for Boston tomorrow and I can't ask Mum.'

Juno could almost hear Ariadne tut. 'No, we're *all* going. One of the blokes at school has got this huge seven-bedroomed place up near Glen Gardens Park and it's free this weekend before Easter.'

'That's because it'll be freezing in Filey at the beginning of April. And there's no way Gabe will want to be going off with his mum, his aunties and his granny to the seaside when he can be at home and playing football with his mates.'

'Just tell him Hugo is going.'

'Hugo is?'

'Hmm. Lexia and I started talking about Filey last night after you'd gone – you know the holidays we used to have there as kids – and I knew Jim Lindley at school has a place there. He says we can have it for tomorrow and Friday night, but he's got people going in late Saturday. It'll be fabulous. Pandora and Hugo have already said they want to go and Lexia's going to ask Lilian – you know, her lovely Irish lady – to come to help with the kids and Mum.'

'I can't have time off work, Ariadne.' Juno felt a headache coming on. A two-day mini break, away from the reality of her dysfunctional relationships with men, would have been wonderful. No, not *wonderful* – she'd still have to shop and cook and wash up – but it would be something different.

'OK, well if you won't try to do a swap, then we'll just take your two with us. It's time the cousins all got to know each other properly.'

'I can't see Gabe wanting to go with you.'

'Don't give him a choice. We'll play football on the beach, and rounders. And—'

'—freeze to death in that wind blowing off the North Sea.'

'And eat fish and chips and fresh crab sandwiches.' When

Juno didn't say anything, Ariadne went on, rather more gently, 'Lexia and Cillian, particularly, need to be away, out of sight of the media, Juno. Lexia's already gone to Mum's, packed a few things and gone over there to escape the press who're hanging around. I just hope they don't follow her; I'm not sure Mum could cope with it all.'

'Declan, Fraser has fallen in love with another woman and is leaving me for her.' Juno had taken her secret cache of cigarettes from the bottom of her filing cabinet and gone to join Declan in the tiny walled garden at the back of the surgery where he was already lighting up, leaning against the garden's one tree – a rather scruffy-looking weeping willow – eyes closed and drawing smoke deep into his lungs.

He opened one eye, squinting at Juno and moving over slightly so she could share the tree. 'Supposed to have given these up for Lent,' Declan said ruefully. 'Don't tell Izzy. Sounds like *you* need one, though. If it makes you feel any better, I never thought you and Fraser were suited. You're far too gorgeous for him.'

'Right, I'll take that as a compliment.'

'It was meant as such,' Declan said comfortably. 'How are you feeling?'

'Shell-shocked really. Look, Declan, there's been a lot going on recently with my sisters and now Theo Ryan.'

'Bad do that. Damian St Claire was a patient of mine.'

'Hmm, I know. I saw him a couple of times when you weren't around.'

'Total heroin addict of course. Never understood where

he got all his money from for the cocaine and heroin he's done over the years. If Theo Ryan hadn't knocked him down and killed him, I honestly don't think he'd have lasted much longer. He was in a bad way.'

'So, Declan, please can I have tomorrow and Friday off? You can tell Marian it's stress, that I need to be there for Lexia, that Fraser's left me; tell her what you like. I'll make it up by working next Monday and Tuesday instead. I'll even ring all my patients today and cancel their appointments and re-schedule them for the start of next week.'

'Fraser leaving you had nothing to do with Scott, had it?'

'Scott?'

'Hmm.' Declan was obviously embarrassed. 'I feel somewhat to blame, bringing in Scott to the surgery, you know, knowing his past history, his reputation. Fraser didn't find out?'

'No, he actually went out to Boston, intentionally, because of this woman.'

Declan whistled. 'Blimey. How do you feel?'

'Well, I *could* say I'm on the verge of a breakdown so you'll give me the next two days off. But I am an honourable woman and I have to tell you that although Fraser's leaving has made me feel a total failure, as well as obviously unlovable, I will get over it. Of course, it's Gabe and Tilda I'm worried about.' Juno glanced across at Declan. 'And actually, I'm a bit upset, if you must know, that Scott Butler has found himself another woman, a younger, prettier woman.'

'Oh, Izzy told you? I told her not to. She can't keep her mouth shut, that wife of mine. I'm sorry, Juno, Scott's always been the same, ever since I've known him. Always loved women, always breaking hearts; even had the landlady in his student digs after him at one point. I'm sorry you fell for it. You take tomorrow and Friday off. I'll square it with Izzy and Marian, and if you can do Monday and Tuesday instead, that would be great, but if you can't don't worry.'

'Thanks, Declan.' Juno reached over and kissed his cheek. 'I owe you one.'

'Wow, look at this place.' Ariadne, who'd never been known for her exuberance, was ecstatic. 'Seven bedrooms, four bathrooms, sleeps thirteen, a playroom with smart TV and Play station.' She was reading from the brochure on the hall table. 'What do you think, Mum? Fabulous isn't it?'

'Lovely, darling.' Helen Sutherland had been somewhat nervous at the thought of the two-hour car journey from Westenbury, as well as actually staying away from home for the first time since her last time in hospital, ten years previously, but Ariadne, who was driving her mother, Lexia and Cillian, had stopped en route for coffee and shortbread at a rather quaint little roadside café once they hit North Yorkshire, and she'd begun to relax and actually enjoy the outing.

'Jim's grandparents used to own and run this place as a small hotel apparently,' Ariadne informed the others as they all trooped en masse to bag their bedrooms and explore the rest of the house. 'It was done up for Airbnb a couple of years ago. Ooh, bags I have a room overlooking the sea.'

'Do I have to share with Matilda?' Gabe, resentful at being forced away to Filey on the first day of his Easter break, was still sulking.

'Well, how about you share with Hugo, and then Matilda

can share with me?' Juno asked, tiredly. She *was* tired – exhausted and wrung out, she realised. She and the children had waved Fraser off back to Manchester airport and Boston, still without them knowing she and Fraser were splitting up. They'd both bottled it, and she knew she was going to have to sit down with them both pretty soon and explain the situation. 'Aunt Lexia and Cillian can share a room, and then everyone else should be able to have a room each. Are you OK with that, Hugo?'

Hugo smiled at her. 'That's fine, Aunt Juno.'

Gosh, he was polite, Juno thought. And, such a lovely boy too. How on earth could he be Damian St Claire's son? Perhaps boarding school was the answer.

Juno had checked her phone constantly for any message from Scott, but he seemed to have gone to ground. Or gone to another woman's bed, she thought ruefully. And let's face it, she, Juno, had only managed that one fabulous, wonderful night with Scott in London, unable, after that, to leave Gabe and Tilda for any repeat performance. A knee-trembler up against Clem's restaurant wall didn't count, she supposed. With a young, free, single woman he could be at it hammer and tongs. Like Aunt Fanny and her rampant fisherman...

'What's so funny?' Pandora was at her side as Juno smiled to herself, recollecting Ariadne's tipsy account of the Famous Five's aunt. *Infamous* now, Juno supposed.

'Oh nothing. How're you doing now, Pandora? It's been an absolutely awful few weeks for you.'

'Quite awful few *years* really,' Pandora sighed. 'I'm actually quite grey under all this blonde.'

'Are you? Really?'

Pandora nodded. 'I'm just so *glad* St Claire is dead. Is that awful of me, to wish another human being dead?'

'Is it bollocks.' Ariadne had joined them in the kitchen where Pandora was beginning to sort through the huge box of groceries, casseroles and home-baking she'd spent the previous day shopping and preparing for. 'For heaven's sake, Pandora, he blackmailed you for years.'

'Not always,' Pandora sniffed, tears in her eyes. 'There were times when he was in prison, you know, when he went quiet. Probably frightened the prison guards would realise what he was up to. I always knew when he was in there for dealing, and dreaded the moment he'd be released. The relief, the utter relief it's now all out in the open, that Hugo knows but that there's no reason why the media should now ever know what really happened...' Pandora suddenly sat down, as if her legs were unable to keep her upright, tears rolling down her face. 'It's like a huge stone's been lifted off my chest,' she sobbed. 'That I can actually *breathe* again properly for the first time in sixteen years.'

Ariadne insisted they all – *no, Gabe, you can't stay here on the PlayStation* – walk along Filey beach, where they ate ice cream cones before returning the same way, taking it in turns to piggy back Cillian, and then all piling in to help with supper.

'There's really not much to do.' Pandora smiled, taking out the huge casserole she'd put into the oven together with enough baked potatoes to feed an army. 'But you could lay the table, Matilda and Hugo, if you would. And you pour some wine, Juno. And you, Mum and Lilian, well, you go and put your feet up in the sitting room.'

'I'm not used to being waited on.' Lilian frowned. 'There must be something I can do?'

'Actually, you could wash this salad, if you would, Lilian, and then, then I think we're just about ready.'

'Have you noticed how Cillian keeps following Hugo around?' Juno asked, once the others had left the kitchen. 'He's become quite infatuated with him, hasn't he?'

'I suppose at some point we're going to have to tell him that Hugo is actually his brother,' Pandora said, pulling a face. 'It's all so damned complicated, isn't it?'

'Well, I shouldn't worry about that at the moment. He's not five yet. Plenty of time for explanations in the years to come when everything's settled down a bit.' Juno sipped at her glass of wine. 'God, I didn't half need this.'

'So, Fraser's gone then?' Pandora gave her a look. 'How are you? You OK?'

'Apart from feeling an absolute failure? You know, that there must be something inherently wrong with me that my husband doesn't want to be with me?' Juno paused and then smiled. 'But I do feel free. It's a wonderful feeling.'

'You don't look as if you're jumping for joy.' Pandora gave Juno a hard stare.

'Oh, you might as well know, I was having a bit of a thing with Scott Butler.'

'Were you? Goodness, I'd never put you down as the sort of person to have an extra-marital affair.' Pandora looked quite shocked.

'Neither would I,' Juno said ruefully. 'I'd always kept any affairs, you know, being rolled in haystacks with Gabriel Oak and Sergeant Troy in *Far From the Madding Crowd*, strictly in my head.'

'Both together? A threesome?' Pandora looked even more shocked at this little revelation than Juno's admitting she'd been *up to no good* with Dr Scott Butler.

Juno laughed. 'Ooh, there's a thought. Anyway,' she went on, downing the remains of her glass of wine in one, 'I appear to have fallen for Scott Butler's charms, stupid naïve woman that I am, and...'

'And he's seeing someone else?'

'Well, yes.'

'He's a very attractive man. Half the women in Rushdale Avenue spend their time peering round curtains at him.'

'You included?'

'I think I've had rather more important things on my mind lately, don't you?' Pandora said tartly, the old Pandora. 'However, I did see a rather gorgeous, very stylish, dark-haired woman going into his house yesterday.'

'Young?'

'I couldn't really tell from behind my curtains,' Pandora said seriously. 'But, put it this way, Juno, it wasn't his *mother*.'


Cillian was fast asleep in bed, worn out by sea air and the excitement of being with so many different people. Hugo, Gabe and Matilda had taken themselves off to the playroom and Helen and Lilian had taken a fresh pot of tea into the sitting room and were catching up with *Strictly* on the smart TV in there.

'This is such an amazing place,' Juno said as she placed the last of the plates into the dishwasher and went to join the others at the kitchen table. 'I'd love to come here in the summer.'

'Well, I don't see why not.' Ariadne smiled, pleased at her success in persuading her sisters to this two-day jaunt. 'It gets pretty booked up in the summer though.' She turned to Pandora, re-filling her glass for her. 'I'm sorry your *Jesus Christ Superstar* production all fell apart, Pan. Is there no way you can revive it?'

'Oh, heavens, Ariadne, don't you think we've enough on our plates at the moment without attempting to get *that* little show back on the road?' Pandora sighed heavily. 'Although, I must admit, I was *so* enjoying it. In fact, I absolutely *loved* it. But it's all too late; Sally's already been poached by another company and, at the end of the day you can't put on *Jesus* without a *fabulous* Jesus. Well, *any* Jesus, really. Or Herod. Or Mary Magdalene. We lost the job lot in one fell swoop if you remember.'

They all nodded and drank their wine. There didn't seem to be any counter argument to what Pandora was saying.

'*You* could be Mary Magdalene, Pan,' Ariadne said eventually. 'You know you've a fabulous voice.'

'I have,' Pandora said seriously, and Juno wanted to laugh. 'And I did consider it, but I can't be *all* things to *all* men. You know, I can't be choir leader *and* conductor – especially now Sally has defected to the damned Halifax Harmonies – and take on a major role like Mary Magdalene as well.'

'I bet you could, Pandora.' Lexia smiled, speaking on the subject for the first time.

'Thank you, Lexia,' Pandora smiled back, 'but no, I couldn't.'

'Right.' Ariadne stood and went to close the kitchen door. 'Now that the four of us are here, are you going to tell us, you two—' she nodded towards Pandora and

Lexia '—just why you've both been so frightened that you actually allowed that little scumbag to blackmail you all these years?'

'You *know* why, Ari, you know why we had to keep St Claire quiet: to keep the truth from breaking and ruining Lexia's career, for Hugo's sake, for Richard's sake with the Boothroyds...' Pandora's voice was brisk, irritable at Ariadne's going over old ground. 'And, and for *my* sake as Hugo's mother.' Tiny spots of colour had appeared in Pandora's cheeks and she refilled her glass and folded her arms.

'Tell them, Pandora.' Lexia put a hand on Pandora's arm and, although she spoke quietly, there was a slight ghost of a laugh in her voice. 'Tell them what we did. He's dead. We *can't* be sent to prison now.'

# 29

*Westenbury, 2007*

'Lexia, we need you back up in Yorkshire, on your home territory for this photo shoot.' Jaz Burnley, the American in charge of all Lexia's PR now that she'd split from Gals and was flying high as Lexi, not only insisted in placing the emphasis on the second syllable so Yorkshire became York*shire,* but was also adamant that Lexia agree to her agenda. 'Your fans want to see where you came from, what your background is. They need to see you with your family. You know the sort of thing: arms round you, been there for you from the beginning, supporting you, cheering you on...'

'But they haven't.' Lexia frowned. 'You *know* that.'

'Well yes, but that doesn't fit in with your image. I know we've revved it up a bit lately, shortened the skirts and added your signature red lipstick that all the kids are now going for, but people still like to think you're just a step away from the bosom of your family; that the folks back home mean everything to you and that you love your mom and all your siblings.'

'It's not their fault,' Lexia said abruptly, 'that they've not been down here in London, I mean. It's all just... well, complicated.'

'Well, how about we just *un*complicate matters, a bit?'

Lexia felt slightly panicky. Before Pandora and Richard had taken the baby, travelling back up to Yorkshire with him just three days after the birth from which Lexia was convinced she was going to die (never, ever, she told herself, would she *ever* again go through the pain and ignominy of any of that again; how her mum had done it four times she couldn't imagine) Pandora had come to her with tears in her eyes and said she needed to be sure, absolutely *sure*, that Lexia wasn't going to regret giving away her baby.

'Regret it?' Lexia had stared. 'No. I don't *want* a baby. You know that. I can't become famous with a baby.'

'Oh, Lexia, will you stop all this about being famous? Just grow up a bit, act your age, will you? You're not giving away one of your *dolls*. This is a baby, Lexia, *your* baby.'

'But, Pandora, I don't *want* a baby. You take him, you look after him.'

'But do you *promise* me that you won't change your mind in six months' time? That two years down the line, when all this singing and becoming better than Holly Valance nonsense has come to nothing, you won't be turning up in Yorkshire wanting him back?'

'Never.'

Pandora, gazing down with absolute love at the tiny baby boy in her arms, had hesitated before taking Lexia's hand in her own. 'Lexia, Richard and I think it best if you don't come back to Westenbury.'

'Well no, obviously, I won't for a while…'

'No, Lexia, we don't think you should come back at all.' Pandora couldn't quite meet Lexia's eye.

'What? Ever?' Lexia had stared at Pandora, trying to work out exactly what her big sister was saying. 'What about Mum?'

'Please, Lexia, just think about the baby. You've given him to us now, you've agreed to this, and he has to believe – has to *know* – that *we* are his real mum and dad.'

'You're never going to tell him?' Lexia looked down at her hands. 'You know, that *I'm* his real mum?'

'Lexia, we've talked and talked about this, you know we have.' Pandora was white-faced apart from two pinpricks of colour in each cheek. 'This is what we agreed. If you want the best for him, then you have to let him go properly. You know, if you'd put him up for adoption, you wouldn't be allowed to see him ever. It's the same thing really; if you want us to take him from you, you have to let us have him *completely*. No turning up in a couple of years telling Juno and Ariadne, telling Mum, *actually he's not Pandora's baby, he's mine*. Will you promise me this?'

'But I don't know what you mean, I can't come home? Why not? I'd never say anything; I'd never tell anybody.' Lexia took hold of her big sister's arm and tried to smile. 'I don't *want* to come home at the moment, you know that, Pan. I'm going to win and be famous. Aunt Georgina says so. But once I've made it, you know, once I'm on the telly like Holly Valance, I can come home then, can't I? Mum'll want to see me. And Juno and Ari? They'll wonder why…'

'Lexi, come on. Think of the baby. Think of me and Richard.'

'But what about *me*? What about me and Mum?'

'Please Lexi. You have to make this decision now. No going back.' Pandora's face was set.

Lexia had stared at Pandora, and when she saw that Pandora was serious, that Lexia must do what she said, that there was no alternative if her sister and Richard were going to take the baby for her, she'd turned her face away and nodded. What would she do with a *baby*? She didn't want one. That was all there was to say about the whole situation.

And she'd kept her promise: cut herself off completely from her family, even from her mum. And, to be honest, she hadn't really missed them. Life was all too exciting to be thinking of home and of her past life. Aunt Georgina had taken her over completely, moulding her, coaching her and even, once she'd won *TheBest* and become the accepted lead singer with the other three girls, leaving her job as music teacher in a large London comprehensive in order to become her agent, full-time. The months went by and the little village of Westenbury, and the unpleasant memories of her last year at home once Patrick had upped and left, seemed a lifetime ago.

It *was* a different time – her past, of which Lexia no longer wanted any part. She'd shrugged it all off, buried it deep inside her and, while Aunt Georgina continued to drive up north to visit Helen, and was able to give Lexia the news that her mum was still in and out of hospital but appeared to be slowly improving, she kept her promise to Pandora and didn't return. Both Ariadne and Juno had constantly phoned, written letters, sent birthday and Christmas cards and both, separately, on a couple of occasions, turned up at Aunt Georgina's but, once she began to make money – lots and lots of money – and the whole Lexia circus that controlled, and manoeuvred her, had moved her into an apartment with the other girls, her two elder sisters had appeared to give up on her, finally accepting that she had cut them out of her life and moved on, and they must do the same.

And now Jaz was saying she must return home for some photoshoot for *Blast*, a new magazine taking off big time in the States. Lexia chewed on her nails and considered, while Jaz frowned. 'Will you stop biting those nails, Lexi? That's not the image we're trying to portray. So, you're going out for dinner with Theo Ryan next week?' She now nodded her approval. 'That's good. We like that. Although,' she frowned once more, 'not overly original, I guess. Well, at least he's an *Irish* soccer player, a *bit* different from Victoria and Cheryl...'

'You can't take photos of my mum; she's not well.' Lexia felt an instinctive urge to protect, but whether it was Helen or herself, she wasn't sure.

'I know that, Lexia, and to be honest, it's probably not the best image – you know, mental illness – we want to portray. So, these sisters of yours? We need to contact them?'

'Ariadne is doing something at Berkeley in California and Juno is up in Aberdeen. They're scattered all over the place, not at home in Yorkshire at all.'

'And the other one? Persephone?'

'Pandora.'

'I knew it was another one of these weird names your

parents landed you all with. So, *Pandora*. Give me her contact details and I'll speak to her.'

'She won't want to have anything to do with any photoshoot. She's very, er…' Lexia searched for the right word. '*Private*.'

'You're making this very difficult, Lexia.' Jaz raised an eyebrow and glared pointedly as Lexia continued to bite her nails as she considered the implications of returning home.

'It's not my fault,' Lexia snapped. 'You're making out my family are intentionally keeping out of my way.'

'I think it's you doing that, yourself, hon. You've *always* given that impression. Look, we're going to take you up to York*shire* next week, take some pictures of that quaint little village of yours, your old home, this club you started out at, any local beauty spots. I'll sort it all out with Persephone.'

It had been Aunt Georgina who had finally persuaded Pandora to take part in the photoshoot, telling her that Lexia was coming up to Westenbury anyway and that she and Richard needed to be there for her in the eyes of Lexia's adoring public. Otherwise, they'd be opening a can of worms, with the media swarming round trying to work out just *why* Pandora refused to see her little sister. Better just to smile and go with the flow, she told her.

The *Blast* team had driven themselves and a wardrobe of outfits up north at the crack of dawn in the middle of a seemingly endless June heatwave – gloriously warm hazy mornings that stretched indefinitely into blazing afternoons before cooling down into mellow, yellow evenings. Jaz Burnley and a couple of her sidekicks followed on behind while Lexia and Aunt Georgina brought up the rear in Georgina's brand-new BMW.

Once up in Midhope, the *Blast* people had stopped for breakfast and a team meeting to discuss the various locations and the sponsored designer labels Lexia was to wear and Aunt Georgina had driven Lexia and herself to the hospital where Helen had recently been readmitted after nearly two years of living back at home. And while it had been wonderful to see her mum, to hug her and tell her all about what she'd been doing – her success, her number one album, the photoshoots – Lexia walked back down the steps of the hospital towards the car with a solid lump of something indiscernible in her heart and in her throat, feeling only terrible guilt that she was leaving Helen alone once more.

And it was so *hot*. Again, and again, the makeup girl dabbed and wiped at her face, adding yet another coat of lip gloss which melted immediately in the unforgiving heat or was swallowed as Lexia nervously licked at her lips. And here was yet another location, another change of clothing, and once again she was poked and prodded and persuaded into a pose which, to Lexia, was not only horribly uncomfortable but ridiculously over the top.

After she'd been photographed in the – somewhat overgrown – back garden at home, cuddling Hercules, the ginger tom, who'd strolled over from old Mrs Taylor's house where he stayed when Helen wasn't around, they were on the move once more.

Lexia had balked at the suggestion of a photoshoot at the Ambassador Club, but Jaz and Euan, the photo-journalist from *Blast* were adamant that's what the American readers wanted to see. 'Where it all started, hon, you know?' Half an hour later the vans and car were parked up on the backstreet and Lexia was leading Aunt Georgina and the crew inside.

'Just a couple of minutes?' Lexia pleaded, impatient to get it over and done with and be back outside in the sunshine. The place was virtually deserted – just a barman she didn't recognise bottling up, and a pink-haired cleaner desultorily sweeping round tables and chairs. Once they'd been given permission from the seemingly uninterested barman, it seemed to take forever for Euan to achieve the effect he desired in the dingy, vague half-light of the club's interior, but eventually he ordered her up onto the stage where she had to take the mike and belt out her latest single. Lexia closed her eyes as directed by Euan, '*show a bit of passion, honeypie*' and so didn't see Damian St Claire until he applauded loudly from where he was standing in the shadows at the back of the club.

'Even better than when I first discovered you, Lexia, babe!' he shouted.

Lexia felt her heart pound, her pulse race, as her eyes shot open and met his. What on earth had she ever seen in him? was her first thought as she took in the prematurely receding hairline and newly acquired paunch straining at his grubby white T-shirt. He looked middle-aged, she realised, seedily unattractive and nothing at all like Duncan James from Blue to whom in her imagination, during the past three years since she'd last seen him, she'd referred.

The *Blast* team turned as one, peering through the gloom to see who'd spoken. Was this someone they could interview and photograph as being part of Lexia's past?

Lexia jumped down from the stage, grabbed her bottle of water and walked quickly to the entrance, ignoring St Claire totally as he reached out a hand to her. 'We need to go,' she ordered the team. 'There is absolutely *nothing* else of interest here…'

Aunt Georgina was at her side, ushering her out onto the pavement and towards the waiting BMW, scanning her makeshift itinerary as she did so. 'Norman's Meadow,' she called back to the others as they started to pack up cameras and lighting. 'Local beauty spot where we've arranged to meet Lexia's sister and family for a picnic,' she added. She pushed Lexia ahead of her. 'That him?' she asked grimly once they got into the car and waited for the others.

Lexia nodded, shaken. 'Do you know, I've hardly thought of him these past few years, but now I've seen him, I feel so angry, so *furious* that he ignored me when I was… you know. I was fifteen when I did it with him. *Fifteen*. A little girl…' Lexia put up a hand to her pounding head. 'I'm due a period. I'm really tense, really hot, really *angry*. Have you any paracetamol?'

Georgina delved through her bag and handed a couple of painkillers to Lexia. 'It's finished, Lexia. It's over.' Georgina opened the window to let out the heat from the stifling parked car. 'The last thing your fans need to know is what happened when you were fifteen. Not good for your image at all, especially as you *gave away* the baby.'

'Oh, thanks very much for *that*,' Lexia snapped. 'That makes me feel a whole lot better…'

'Shh.' Georgina nodded in the direction of Jaz who was making her way towards their car.

'Bit of an unsavoury character, that one,' Jaz sniffed as she poked her head through the open car window while drinking thirstily from her bottle of water. 'Jeeze, it's hot.'

'Rather a hanger on,' Georgina said. 'Thinks he had something to do with discovering Lexia when she was a kid.'

'Yes, he said.' Jaz frowned. 'I know the type; he was trying to get some money out of us.' She laughed. 'I soon sent him on his way.'

'Can we just go?' Lexia pleaded, as the pain over her eye intensified. 'Haven't we enough photos yet?'

'What about your sister?' Jaz frowned once more. 'She's waiting for us at this Norbert's Meadow place.'

'Norman's,' Lexia snapped irritably.

'She'd be really pissed if we didn't turn up. Besides, we have the most *awesome* white Suzy Maclellan dress for you to model.' Jaz gave Georgina and Lexia her most winning smile. 'And, we've the cutest white parasol to finish off the outfit. It'll be *awesome*, quite *sensational*. We'll have you drinking tea and eating cucumber sandwiches in an English meadow with your sibling. The guys back home will just love it.'

'Come on then, let's just do it and get it over and done with and then we can drive back to London.' Lexia closed her eyes, trying to fight the panic she was beginning to feel at the prospect of meeting her baby. But of course, he wouldn't *be* a baby anymore; he'd be having his fourth birthday in August. Surely, Pandora wouldn't bring Hugo – how could she have called her baby that dreadful name – to meet up with her. Surely, she'd leave him with the Boothroyds, or someone else?

It was mid-afternoon by the time the team had packed up and driven the seven or so miles from the town centre, out through Westenbury village itself and, following Lexia's directions, taken the country lanes out to Norman's Meadow. The vans and BMW had bumped over dusty pot-holes, steered around insolent sheep that had obstinately refused to move out of their way, and then been forced to reverse at speed when Lexia gave the wrong turnings. By the time they arrived, even the initial glimpse of bewitchingly beautiful acres of natural wildflower meadow was failing to enchant and Lexia just wanted to throw up. She'd always been carsick – apparently Pandora was the only one of the four of them who wasn't – and it was a total relief when the entourage bumped along to its final resting place and she could get out of her aunt's car and fight the nausea.

Pandora and Richard were already in-situ, sitting in the shade over to the left-hand side of the meadow and, from their straight-backed, unmoving stance, Lexia had the ridiculous notion they were carved out of stone, a permanent part of a natural tableau, about to be surprised and disturbed by the newcomers. Tension was emanating in waves from the pair of them and at first, as she walked slowly over towards them, Lexia thought they were alone. And then a blonde-haired little boy suddenly appeared from behind a particularly large clump of the magenta-coloured Corn cockle, and began to run in ever-increasing circles around his parents, swooping and whooping with arms outstretched while emulating, like every other nearly four-year-old before him, his parody of a flying aeroplane.

Lexia stopped, her heart racing. This was her son, for heaven's sake. The child also stopped when he saw her approach and, obviously bidden by his mother, sat down suddenly at Pandora's side, shy in the presence of someone he didn't know.

'This isn't on, Lexia,' Pandora hissed in her ear as she stood from the white tablecloth spread on the grass and made to put her arms round her little sister. 'You promised...'

'I'm sorry. It would have looked really strange if we'd come up here and there was *no* family willing to be seen with me. Aunt Georgina said, anyway.'

'Aunt Georgina *would* say that.'

'Would she?' Lexia looked at Pandora in surprise. 'Why?'

'Well, you *know*, she's in charge of you now, isn't she? Given up her teaching job... she must be raking it in...'

'Lexia. Hello lovey, how are you?' Richard Boothroyd came between her and Pandora, cutting off his wife's diatribe and hugging Lexia with genuine affection. 'You look fabulous, love. I'm so pleased it's all worked out for you. A very famous sister-in-law. I'm always being asked to get your autograph.'

'You're not going to say anything, are you?' Pandora was fearful 'You know, about Hugo?'

'Of course she isn't, Pandora.' Aunt Georgina was at their side, speaking in a low whisper. 'Don't be ridiculous. We didn't go through all that charade three years ago to out the truth now. Or ever. And don't forget, this is for the American market, I'm not sure it'll even be seen here.' She turned to Hugo. 'And this little chap is Lexia's gorgeous nephew,' she said loudly, smiling for the benefit of the team who'd followed in her wake. 'Now, at Pandora and Richard's request, just one photograph of Hugo please. No more, I mean it. It's not good to have images of small children splashed all over magazines.'

It had been a long day and Euan, obviously at the end of his tether with the journey, the different locations, the heat and, now that he was in the English countryside and surrounded by a mass of flowers, his hay fever, put up his free hand in acquiescence.

'Not a problem,' he sneezed. 'We just want Lexi in the Suzy Maclellan dress and parasol, sitting with her family, and then it's a wrap.'

A wrap? Pandora stared. Did people actually use such clichés?

'Go and get changed, Lexi,' Euan drawled. 'The light here is so fantastic, it won't take long at all...' He sneezed several times. 'Fucking countryside. How do you live in it?'

Pandora, furious at his cavalier swearing in front of her son, glared. 'It's too hot to be here much longer. Can we get on?'

Twenty minutes later, Lexia was in the beautifully cool floaty white dress, white parasol draped artfully over her shoulder as she, Pandora and Richard sat on the grass, pretending to eat the picnic Pandora had brought. Typical Pandora, Lexia thought, she'd really gone to town with an amazing spread of cheeses and pate and, on the instructions of Aunt Georgina, a plate of beautifully cut cucumber sandwiches. There were homemade scones, Pandora's own raspberry jam (even when doing something she obviously didn't want to do, pride hadn't allowed Pandora a jar of Tesco Economy plum and a pack of scones from Aldi) a tiny glass churn of thick yellow cream and a sharp kitchen knife artfully displayed on a snow-white starched napkin atop a traditional wicker picnic basket, filched from Bee-Bee Boothroyd's loft.

'Thank you for this, Pan,' Lexia whispered. 'It really is going to be all OK, you know. Hugo is gorgeous, but he's *yours*. Nothing at all to do with me.' She touched Pandora's hand. 'I miss you all.'

Pandora, as tense as a highly tuned violin string, bristled slightly at the touch. 'But it's just not *on*, you coming back here, Lexia,' she hissed again as Euan turned his camera to the beautiful meadow flowers. 'Don't do it again...' She pasted a rictus of a smile on her face as Euan turned once more to the picnic and called, 'cucumber sandwich anyone?' Euan took one final photograph, pinched a sandwich and began to pack up his cameras. 'Do this for me and Richard, Lexia. And for Hugo. I couldn't cope with you being here, wanting to see Hugo every day.'

'But I miss you all. You're cutting me off from my family, Pandora...' Lexia felt the tears start and she tried desperately to sniff them away with the back of her hand. 'I saw Mum today. I want to be able to come up and see her whenever.'

'You promised, Lexia. If the Boothroyds ever found out that—'

'Fuck the fucking Boothroyds.' Lexia clapped a hand over her mouth. 'I'm sorry, Richard. I don't think of you as one of... you know, one of *them*.'

'OK, Lexia, that's it. Great stuff.' Euan stood in front of them. 'Your little guy's all pooped out.' He indicated with a beringed finger Hugo who had taken himself off to his stroller in the shade and was now fast asleep. 'Are you ready to leave?' He looked at his watch and waved towards the others with a winding up motion of his hand.

'Actually,' Aunt Georgina said, 'I think we'll stay on a bit longer, if that's OK with you, Lexia? We'll hit the teatime traffic and the heat if we leave now. I'm sure she'd like to spend some private time with her family,' she added for the benefit of the others who'd come to say their goodbyes. 'They're so close,' she said artfully.

'I'd like to go back and see Mum again,' Lexia said, grateful to not be heading straight back. 'Just let me take this dress off.'

'It's yours,' Euan said, keys in hand and obviously desperate to get off. 'It's covered in grass stains. And that parasol is dangerous, watch the pointy metal bit at the top, it's incredibly sharp – I've already cut my finger on it. Obviously cheap rubbish,' he grinned.

'Really? I can keep it?' Despite the money accruing in her bank account which meant she was able to buy any amount of designer dresses, Lexia was delighted at the unexpected gift. 'That is so kind. Well then, I'm going to keep it on, it's so beautiful.' She twirled the parasol in Euan's direction and he gave them all a quick salute goodbye before heading off after Jaz, for whom it was pretty obvious he'd got the hots.

With the *Blast* team and Jaz Burnley headed for the M1 and London, Pandora seemed to relax somewhat and began slicing her scones and offering them round to the others who, despite being at a picnic, hadn't actually been encouraged to eat what was on offer. Lexia was tense, upset that Pandora was still telling her she didn't want her to ever come back home. What did Pandora think she was going to do? Race round to the Boothroyds and tell them everything: that their darling grandson wasn't any relation, shouldn't be in line to inherit the family firm and that, in fact his real dad was – judging by his appearance that morning – some sort of layabout drug addict?

Lexia lay down and closed her eyes, breathing in the heady scent of the wild flowers all around her in an attempt to calm her racing pulse and real fury at that bastard turning up and making an actual *claim* on her. She'd always adored being outdoors, loved the wide-open spaces of the countryside; London wasn't really all it was cracked up to be. She found her room in the apartment small and stultifying (she sometimes woke in the dark of the night convinced the ceiling was coming down on her) and had recently given up travelling on the Tube, not so much because she was recognised and mobbed, but because of the tight panicky feeling of claustrophobia she was beginning to suffer whenever she was shut in a small area, unable to get out. Oh, but it was so beautiful up here: her Mum had always loved walking up to Norman's Meadow, but now she was locked up again, unable to leave the ward even if she wanted. Lexia screwed her eyes closed, desperate to rid herself of the image of her mum unable to get out and she, herself, ending up like her Mum, locked up, a prisoner. She was gulping now, trying to take deep breaths, but they were just poor, shallow little things that almost tutted as they tried to send oxygen round her body…

'I do hope you've left a couple of those scones for me?' Damian St Claire was leaned against the Hawthorn hedge – dusty and parched now in the June heatwave – a silly smile on his face and a still-sleeping Hugo in his arms.

'Put him down.' Pandora leapt to her feet, knocking jam and cream flying, and rushed towards her son.

'But why, Pandora? It is Pandora, isn't it? He's much more *mine* than yours. Wouldn't you agree?'

'I don't know what you're talking about. This is *my* son,' Pandora snarled. 'Get your hands off him. Give him to me.'

'Come on, let me have him.' Richard, pale under a summer tan acquired from hours spent on the golf course, spoke calmly but his outstretched hand shook slightly.

'It'll cost you.' St Claire smiled. 'What's the going rate, these days? You know, for me not to shout this all out to the paparazzi. They would *love* it, wouldn't they? They'd lap it up. I reckon I could go and live in the Caribbean or somewhere on what they'd shell out for my story. I bet...' He gave a short cry of pain as something sharp was jabbed into his left side. He looked down in confusion at what appeared to be a white umbrella attached to his less than white T-shirt which was, as he looked down – slowly turning red.

St Claire looked up into the face of the man taking his son from his arms and then turned, confused, looking down, this time to his other side, where something else sharp, smeared with blood – or was it raspberry jam? – was now sticking out of the *right-hand* side of his T-shirt.

Damian St Claire felt the blood drain from his face as it simultaneously seeped through the cheap white T-shirt, before, unable to help himself, he slowly slipped into the gorgeously heady abundance of meadow flowers at his feet.

# 30

*Filey, North Yorkshire, 2019*

'You stabbed him?' Juno stared open-mouthed at Lexia. 'You actually stuck a knife in him?'

Lexia nodded and then immediately shook her head, while a little nervous titter escaped from her lips. '*Parasoled* him actually, Juno. I stuck the really sharp pointy bit of the parasol into him.'

'But then you went for the knife and stabbed that into him as well?' Ariadne had gone quite pale.

'No,' Pandora said, her tone defiant. 'Lexia didn't. *I* did.'

'*You* did, Pandora? *You* stabbed him? Oh, my giddy aunt.' If the saintly Laura McCaskill could manage not to swear, Juno thought, so could *she*. 'So, Damian St Claire is standing there with the scone knife in his right side and a parasol in his other…?'

'Well, not actually standing,' Pandora said, almost brazenly. 'By this stage he'd fallen, well, sort of slid, onto the grass.'

'Oh, it was *terrible*.' Any nervous laughter on Lexia's part had now retreated and she put her hands up to her face, as if to hide from, to escape from, Ariadne and Juno's horrified stares. 'Then his white T-shirt started turning red and that was the worst bit of it all.'

'What did you do? Ring for an ambulance?'

'Well, I have to say, that was my first thought,' Pandora said. 'Actually, no it wasn't. My first thought was, is Hugo alright? I wouldn't have touched him if I hadn't thought Hugo was in danger.'

'And was he OK?' Juno reached for her glass, realised it was empty, and put it down once more. 'Hugo, I mean?'

'Oh, he was fine. He never woke up once. Slept through the whole pantomime...'

'Hardly a pantomime, Pan. Pantomimes are supposed to be *funny*.' Ariadne continued to stare at Pandora and Lexia. 'You could have both been up for attempted murder.'

'Exactly,' Pandora snapped. 'Why the hell do you think we've tried to cover it up for the last thirteen years or so? Allowed effing St Claire to blackmail and control us? If he'd gone to the police at *any* stage in the last thirteen years we'd have been arrested. Knife crime, particularly recently, is hugely frowned upon. You know that.'

'And I was suffering quite badly from claustrophobia at that point – still am to some extent – I knew I'd have *died* if I'd been locked up. Or gone mad, like Mum.'

'Mum's not mad, Lexia,' Juno countered gently. 'She has mental health issues.'

'Juno, I was still only nineteen. Just a kid. I had the world's media clocking every damned thing I did. I was terrified.

Even now, today, whenever anyone mentions Norman's Meadow, all I see is that white T-shirt turning crimson and I have to fight off a panic attack.'

'Are you OK, now?' Juno asked. 'You know, talking about it?'

'I've taken a Valium.'

Juno patted Lexia's arm. 'Don't drink too much of this wine,' she advised.

'I never do.' Lexia smiled, turning back to Pandora who was continuing the story of that hot June afternoon up in Norman's Meadow.

'And *I* had Hugo,' Pandora said angrily. 'I *couldn't* lose him, *couldn't* have it all come out that he was really Lexia's, that he wasn't mine. And that I – a sodding criminal lawyer for heaven's sake – could have ended up in New Hall prison, sharing a cell with women I'd spent the last five years defending.'

'Well, at least you'd already have had some pals in there.'

'Don't be effing flippant, Ari.' Pandora was getting angrier by the second. 'You've always gone on at me, asking why on earth I don't follow my career anymore, why I threw it all up just to stay at home all day. Well, now you know. How could I carry on being a lawyer in the Magistrates' Court knowing that I was as bad as, worse even, than those I was trying to defend? A lot of me did want to go back to work, especially when Hugo went away to school and I was missing him so badly, but there was always Mum to see to and at the end of the day I was guilty of GBH, if not actually attempted murder.' Pandora's face was flushed as she spoke so heatedly and, for once, Ariadne had the grace to look ashamed.

'Sorry,' Ariadne said, squeezing Pandora's arm. 'So, what on earth did you do?'

'Aunt Georgina took complete control,' Pandora said. 'How she and Mum are ever sisters is way beyond me. Anyway, she made Richard – who was almost on the floor himself with shock at this stage – rack his brains to think of any doctor he knew from the golf club who would come and help us, you know sew him up a bit...'

'*Sew him up a bit*?' Juno was horrified. 'You'd stabbed him in two places and you were talking as if you needed a bit of dressmaking doing? A couple of seams running up, a bit of hemming...?'

'Lexia's always made out the wounds to be a lot worse than they actually were,' Pandora tutted.

'There was a hell of a lot of blood,' Lexia protested.

'Yes, there *was*,' Pandora agreed, 'and we all thought, at the time – St Claire included – that we'd nearly killed him, that he was at death's door but, really, the stab wounds were fairly superficial. Anyway,' she went on, 'oh, Tilda, are you alright?'

'Could we have something to eat?' Tilda stood in the doorway, staring at Juno and her aunts, rather taken back at the solemnity of the gathering.

'After that huge supper? There's one of Granny's cakes somewhere.' Pandora frowned.

'That lovely packet of chocolate biscuits will do fine. May we have those?' Tilda affected her most wheedling tone, dimpling at her aunt Pandora.

'Yes, yes, off you go. Take them with you. Close the door behind you. Anyway,' Pandora went on, after Juno had checked the door to make sure Tilda wasn't eavesdropping, 'Richard wasn't much help. So, of course…'

'You rang Jennifer DB?' Juno could see immediately how it had all panned out.

'Did we all have mobiles in those days?' Ariadne looked doubtful. 'I'm not sure *I* did.'

'It was 2007, not the dark ages,' Pandora snapped. 'Of course, we had phones. Anyway, Jennifer was as marvellous as she always is: practical, discreet, totally unflappable.'

'The perfect girl guide.' Juno smiled.

'The perfect *doctor*,' Pandora admonished. 'She was out to Norman's Meadow in ten minutes flat, bag in hand, and soon had St Claire stitched up and full of antibiotics and even more sedatives.'

'But what on earth did you do with him then?' Juno asked. 'You couldn't just leave him there among the buttercups and daisies until he was feeling better.'

'No, of course we didn't just scarper and leave him there,' Pandora tutted crossly. 'We lay him down on Aunt Georgina's back seat. She was furious when she found some blood on her new BMW even though we'd wrapped him in my best – newly starched – tablecloth. And then Jennifer DB accompanied us back to our house.'

'To Rushdale Avenue? You took him back there?'

Pandora nodded. 'I was terrified, you know, with Lexia being in town, that there might be press waiting outside the house, but it was all fine. Damian was able to walk into the house, go upstairs and lay down in the spare bedroom.'

'Blimey. How long did he stay?'

'Well, Aunt Georgina was insistent that she drive Lexia

straight back down to London. I don't think you even went back to see Mum, did you?'

Lexia shook her head. 'I just remember crying all the way back down to London with Aunt Georgina lecturing me about what I could say and what I couldn't. Which was basically nothing. I had to keep my trap shut, she said or my singing days would be over for ever.'

'Hmm, and all the money she was making out of you would have been over for ever too,' Pandora interrupted. 'Anyway, St Claire stayed in the house for two nights. Jennifer was an absolute brick as always – I mean, it certainly wasn't very ethical of her, you know, not reporting a crime – and came back several times to check on him. It was the longest two days of my life. Having to go into my spare bedroom – I'd only just decorated it in the most beautiful Laura Ashley floral pink – and take him food on a tray and, you know, help him to the loo. Anyway, Richard eventually drove him back down to Emerald Street – wearing one of Richard's new T-shirts I'd bought him for our holiday to Tenerife, for heaven's sake – and a sodding great Tesco carrier bag full of twenty-pound notes to pay for his silence.'

'Goodness me. And you never thought able to confide in me or Juno?' Ariadne actually took Pandora's hand in her own.

'No of course not. The fewer people who knew about it all, the better. And anyway, you were still in California, Ari, and Juno hours away in Aberdeen. I told Lexia she had to stay away and never, *ever* speak of either Hugo or what had happened that afternoon, if she didn't want to end up in prison.'

'Bit harsh, that, wasn't it?' Ariadne reached for Lexia's hand this time.

'The only way forward,' Pandora said firmly. 'The only way.'

'And,' Lexia said, 'I *did* stay away and I've never once said a word. To anyone. Whenever St Claire appeared in London, which he has done on quite a few occasions, either Aunt Georgina or I have paid him off. And always in cash.'

'That's terrible.' Juno frowned. 'You must have been a nervous wreck waiting for him to suddenly turn up out of the blue.'

'I was. I am. I'm going to get better now though. He's dead. And I'm glad.'

'But, Lexia, I hate to remind you of this, but it was *Theo* who knocked him down and killed him.' Ariadne was frowning. 'There'll be an inquest, they'll want to know why St Claire was hanging around down your lane. What was he *doing* there? Did you know him? Had you ever seen him before. I mean, was it even *deliberate*? That Theo knocked him down because of what he's done to you over the years. You know, was Theo protecting you?'

'Pandora, Richard and I have talked about this already.' Lexia appeared fairly calm at the prospect of being questioned. 'I shall just say, and I shall stick to my guns – that yes, I knew him when I was fifteen, that he'd actually been my boyfriend, taken me to the Manchester *TheBest* auditions and then that was it. He was a known heroin addict, been in prison, and was hanging about hoping to see me. I've rehearsed this in my head, over and over again, and have even given a statement to that effect to the police already. They can't prove anything else. They won't be able to pin anything on Theo.'

'But there's nothing *to* pin on him, is there?' Juno searched Lexia's face. 'Theo didn't know anything about him, did he?'

'No. In simple terms, Theo was furious that I'd kept the truth about Hugo from him, he'd already been drinking, and St Claire was hanging around hoping to get money from me and fell under Theo's car because Theo had been drinking and was, as always, speeding. I never told him St Claire was Hugo's father. End of story.'

'Well, it's not really the end of the story for you and Theo, is it?' Ariadne stroked Lexia's arm. 'Where do you go from here? Do you want to stay married to him?'

'After what he's done to her eye?' Pandora, after several glasses of wine, was really cross. 'And her arm? Just look at that arm.'

'I don't understand why you put up with this all these years? Why didn't you just leave Theo? It wasn't as if you hadn't enough money to leave and buy your own place.' Ariadne poured more wine.

'I didn't have the confidence to be by myself,' Lexia said sadly. 'And Theo would never have let me take Cillian – and I just couldn't lose *another* child.'

'*Why* would you have lost Cillian? I can't see any family court giving Theo Ryan custody of a child whose mother he's physically abused over the years,' Juno said.

'And who has constantly had other women...'

'And been a bit of a boozer...'

'I've been in a bit of a bad way,' Lexia explained, one

single tear rolling unheeded from her bruised eye down her cheek. 'I've had a lot of anxiety, depression, terrified that St Claire would finally go to the police and show his scars and demand I be arrested. Every time I imagined being locked up, being in a tiny cell with others, I became more anxious, more panicky.'

'But there's no way they'd lock you up, you daft thing. For sticking a parasol in someone who was blackmailing you.' Ariadne almost laughed.

'But I had no one to talk to. I had Aunt Georgina telling me to keep my mouth shut, Pandora telling me I must never return home and all the PR people pulling and pushing me and ordering me around. All I wanted to do was sing and I absolutely adored that, but all the other stuff that went with it just made me anxious. I did the *Graham Norton Show* quite a few years ago – do you remember? – and St Claire was actually sat in the studio audience, on the front row, just sitting there, grinning at me.

'No way! You should have told security,' Juno said, frowning.

'I should.' Lexia blew her nose and dabbed at her swollen eye. 'But I was just twenty-one and wouldn't have known how to do that and, if I *had* have done that, all I needed as he was being thrown out of the studio, was St Claire shouting out he was the father of the baby I'd given away to my sister, as well as lifting up his T-shirt and flashing his scars to millions of TV viewers. More Jeremy Kyle than Graham Norton.'

'Gosh, yes, I wouldn't have put that past him.' Juno, Ariadne and Pandora all nodded in agreement.

'So, when Theo came along, he was like a knight in

shining armour. Someone to look after me, to protect me. He didn't get on with Aunt Georgina – she was incredibly controlling by this point – and he sort of rescued me from her as well. Everything was great for years, and then it all fell apart when I started having real anxiety problems again, as well as every phobia going, but particularly a fear of being in enclosed spaces. Oh, and now a fear of *blood*...' Lexia gave a little laugh. 'Can you *imagine* dreading every period?'

'Oh, I've *always* dreaded mine,' Ariadne interrupted. 'Headaches, bloating, spots, bad temper...'

'Lexia means *real* dread,' Juno said gently. 'I've had patients with just that phobia.'

'So, I've always assumed,' Lexia went on, 'that I was heading the same way as Mum. That if I didn't end up locked up in a prison cell, there was every chance I was on my way to being locked up in a hospital ward. Theo didn't help, constantly telling me I was a mad bitch like my mother and there was no way I'd end up with custody of Cillian. He'd make sure of that.'

'What a dreadful man,' Juno sniffed. 'So, we Sutherland women don't seem to do too well with men, do we?' She paused, looking in turn at her three sisters. 'What about Dad? Has he been in touch with any of you lately? Is he back in the country yet?'

'The usual birthday card and occasional phone call we all get.' Pandora shrugged her disapproval. 'He's still based in Manchester of course, but spends a hell of a lot of the time out of the country, particularly in the States on lecture tours. They love him over there. I've not heard anything from him since we all sat and watched him in that debate on TV last year.'

'For years I've sort of promised Mum I wouldn't have a great deal of contact with him,' Juno admitted. 'I think it's so much better if we still don't meet up with him, you know. Mum would feel terribly betrayed if she thought we three were having anything to do with him, but also with Anichka and Arius. And she really is so much better now, isn't she? She rarely talks about Dad now because she doesn't want to know, it's too painful for her and I think it's better that way...'

'Absolutely,' Ariadne interrupted crossly. 'I've not spoken to him for years and have no intention of doing so. He abandoned us all, just swanned off, and didn't go through any of what *we* went through with Mum, because of how he treated her.'

'It *is* a shame with Arius being the same age as Hugo of course.' Juno frowned. 'Weird, isn't it, that we have a brother we've never seen and who is the same age as Dad's own grandson? God, men, honestly. I reckon you've landed up with the only decent one among us, Pandora.'

'He's my rock.' Pandora gave a somewhat superior smile. 'Don't know what I'd have done without my Dicky Bird...' As Ariadne turned a snort of laughter into a hurried cough and reached for her wine, Pandora patted Ariadne's hand. 'And what about you, Ari?'

'What *about* me, Pandora?'

'Well, you know, do you feel you've missed the boat? You know, not having found a hubby of your own?'

'I was very much in love once, Pandora.' Ariadne gave Pandora a little smile.

'Oh dear. I'm so sorry... it didn't work out?'

'I fell in love with my Senior Fellow when I was at

Berkeley. Had a very passionate affair that went on for several years while I was there. The main reason – apart from Mum – that I came back to the UK once it fell apart.'

'His wife found out?' Pandora patted Ariadne's arm sympathetically.

'No,' Ariadne shook her head, 'her husband.'

'Her *husband*? So...' Pandora stared, as the penny eventually dropped. 'You're...? So, what you're saying is you're a...'

'Yes, Pandora,' Ariadne, obviously enjoying Pandora's discomfiture, spelled out the words slowly and loudly. 'I. Am. A. Lesbian.'

Tilda, who'd quietly opened the kitchen door while the others were lost in Ariadne's Coming Out speech, nodded sagely in her Aunt Ariadne's direction and said, 'Thought so... Right, can we have a bash at Granny's cake now?'


As the Sutherland sisters, all feeling a collective contentment in their newly kindled sorority, started the process of making their way upstairs for the night – turning off lights; running a glass of water; locking doors and hunting for that elusive library book Ariadne was convinced she'd brought with her to Filey – Juno's phone rang. At first, she couldn't quite work out what Izzy was trying to say.

'Speak slowly, Izzy. Have you been drinking?'

'Just a couple,' Izzy slurred. 'We're at Clementine's and I need to talk to you.'

Please, Juno thought, *please* don't say Izzy was ringing her to tell her she'd just spotted Scott Butler up against Clem's wall again, this time with his new woman?

'Been celebrating Declan's birthday with Clem and Harriet and Grace. And their other halves, of course… you know, I didn't want you to think I've dragged Declan out on a girly night. Not on his birthday.'

'Right. OK. Happy Birthday to Declan. Tell him his card's in the post.'

'So, here's the news – and I would have rung Pandora direct but didn't know her number.'

'Right?'

'We've found Jesus.'

'All of you? Good for you. Congratulations. It's a good time, what with Easter next weekend.'

'No, you daft thing.' Juno could hear laughter down the phone. 'Sh, shhh, you lot, I can't hear Juno… No, we've got a new Jesus for Pandora…'

'Has her old one worn out then?'

'He's fabulous. He's rather gorgeous. And wait until you hear his voice. Absolutely superb. Mind you, I'm not sure your Tilda will be overly happy… She guards him very jealously, doesn't she?'

'What, Harry Trotter's agreed to be the new Jesus?' Juno almost looked at the phone, as if she were in a third-rate TV drama.

'Heavens, no, he was a *little hoarse* last time I heard *him* sing.' Izzy started laughing at that, and then coughing, and it was a few seconds before someone obviously passed her a glass of water and she carried on speaking once more. 'We're not going to take no for an answer. We really want to get back into rehearsals, tell Pandora. We absolutely insist. Now, *you're* going to be Mary Magdalene, Juno…'

'Me?'

*Sing Me a Secret*

'Yes, absolutely. You can do it. You have a beautiful voice, Juno, and you just need to take yourself in hand and practise those high notes. We do still need Herod, but that's not a problem. Baldy Wotsisname will probably be able to give it a go, even though he is a midget.'

'Not sure you're allowed to say *midget* anymore, Izzy...'

'What, even before *gems*? Political correctness gone mad. So that's it. Tell Pandora we'll all be in the village hall next Monday evening. I'll put up some notices in the surgery and around the village and in the church. You know, to say we're back in business...'

'So, Jesus?'

'What about him?'

'Who've you found?'

'Oh sorry, of course. The very gorgeous and very talented deputy head of Little Acorns.'

'Mr Donnington?'

'Got it in one.'

375

# 31

'What are you *doing*?' Tilda had come into Juno's bedroom (*her* bedroom, Juno realised, practising the word in her head, not *hers and Fraser's* any longer) and was standing watching as Juno picked Fraser's clothes from the wardrobe.

'What are *you* doing,' Juno snapped, 'standing on the carpet in those filthy riding boots? Go and get them off this minute.'

The Monday morning after their return from the weekend in Filey suddenly felt just that: very Monday morningish. It was raining, and any hint of spring had also been *just that*, with the hopeful new season now retreating back into the grip of a chilly north wind blowing down from the Pennines. The kids were off school, already complaining of being bored; the dirty laundry was Everest demanding she either climb or demolish it and there wasn't a thing in the fridge apart from one half of Helen's banana cake and an out-of-date pot of guava yoghurt that not even Gabriel would eat. On top of that, she felt hungover from the wine she and the others had knocked back over the weekend and, she realised, she was really missing her sisters' company. Not having spent such an extended period of time together with Ariadne, Pandora and Lexia (who Juno was learning to love all over again) she now felt somewhat lonely – bereft even – now they'd all gone their separate ways once more.

And she was now a single mother with a failed marriage. As well as a failed affair.

And it was *that* that was hurting the most. She longed to see Scott, to have him come into her practice room between patients and plant a single kiss on the back of her neck while standing behind her at her desk under the pretext of discussing one of his cases with her; for the pair of them to be standing talking to Marian at reception and feel his hand, very gently, on her bottom…

'So, what *are* you doing?' Tilda asked once more when she'd returned in her stockinged feet. 'Shall we go and do a big food shop?' she went on, not waiting for Juno's answer. 'There's absolutely nothing in the fridge you know. You're being somewhat derelict in your duty as a mother. Anyway, I rather enjoy buying food. And we could have chips in Sainsbury's café. I bet Gabe would come with us if we could have chips.'

When Juno didn't say anything, when suddenly everything seemed just too much and even the prospect of a plate of chips with the kids at Sainsbury's couldn't cheer her up, Tilda asked, 'Why are you doing that with Dad's things?'

'I'm just going to pack them up to send them on to Boston,' Juno said. 'You see, Tilda…'

'He's not coming back again, is he?'

'Again?' Juno asked, stalling for time.

'I think he's happier being in America, isn't he?'

'I'm sorry, Tilda.' Juno sat down heavily on the bed, one

of Fraser's shirts still in her hand. It was a terribly ordinary shirt: one of the white, serviceable M&S shirts that Fraser had always preferred to the more fashionable, youthful shirts with which Juno had tried to tempt him over the years. 'I'm sorry,' she said again, taking Tilda's hand. 'You're right. Dad and I have decided he's probably a lot happier in America.'

'Will we see him…?'

'Yes of *course* you will, you daft thing,' Juno said with forced jollity. 'He might not be living *here* with us but you can go out to Boston in the long holiday. He'd like that. You and Gabe can fly out to see him for the summer. And then, next year, he's more than likely going to be in Aberdeen. That will be nice, won't it? You can go back up to see all your old pals from school.'

'Do I have to *live* there?'

'No, not unless you really want to.' (*Oh, please don't say you want to*, Juno thought.)

Tilda didn't say anything for a while then she looked Juno directly in the face. 'I don't want to, Mum. I love it here in Yorkshire; much more than I did in Scotland. I'm even losing my Scottish accent, don't you think? I can say, "*ger off*" and "*bloomin' heck*" and "*am off 'ome t'our 'ouse for me dinner.*"' She affected a broad Yorkshire accent and patted Juno's hand. 'It'll all be alright, don't worry. I won't need psychological counselling because I'm now the product of a dysfunctional family. So, shall we go for some chips and explain to Gabe what's happening with Dad?'

Although Juno had been really disappointed when the *Jesus Christ Superstar* production had folded, so much else had been going on in her life this past week she hadn't really given it a great deal of thought. Pandora had left a message to confirm rehearsals were back on that very evening and ask if Juno had had chance yet to look at the Mary Magdalene score ready for her introduction to the choir in her new role for which she'd volunteered?

'Volunteered, my backside,' Juno snorted crossly at Margaret Thatcher, Moaning Myrtle and Miranda. (The actual word in mind was *arse* but, mindful of the saintly Laura McCaskill pricking at her brain – as well as the girls pecking at her feet – she'd refrained from the latter.) She carefully rooted for and found four lovely brown warm eggs from the hens' nesting box. Despite the sausage, egg and chips in Sainsbury's café, Gabe was once again 'starving' and already had the omelette pan out ready for action. Explaining to Gabe that she and Fraser were separating didn't seem to have affected her son's appetite one jot. He'd accepted the explanation with a nod of his head and a mouth full of food. She'd have to watch him carefully, Juno thought. Maybe overeating was his way of coping with the news: his comfort blanket. But then, he'd always eaten mountains of food and been, she thought enviously, as skinny as a beanpole.

'He's shooting up daily,' Juno explained to Mrs Thatcher who was looking at her through those beady little eyes of hers, head cocked to one side, looking understandably shocked. 'Oh, *no*, Margaret, it's OK: not *drugs*, his height!' She laughed and then immediately sobered up. What if Gabe did turn to drugs now? His reaction to losing his father? To being the product of a broken home? Juno bit her lip and frowned. Oh hell, what if she had all that to come in the next few years? Just when Gabe needed a role model, another man around to show him the correct way forward in this world of temptation, she'd allowed Fraser to leave; not fought hard enough to keep his father out of the clutches of String Bean McCaskill.

*Get real*, she told herself, *and at least be honest with yourself.* And then, aloud, she admitted to the girls, 'I didn't *want* to fight for Fraser. I was more than happy to give him away. You know, Myrtle, to a good home?' Myrtle appeared to acknowledge and give her blessing to this little admission and Juno smiled down at her. 'Where's Theresa May?' Juno asked the three hens, still clucking and fussing round her wellington-shod feet in the hope of treats.

Out of the corner of her eye, Juno spotted a movement at the new perimeter fence. At first, she thought it was a ginger tom but, even as her brain was processing this possibility, she knew immediately it wasn't.

'Fucking *fox*,' she screamed, any lingering empathy she may have been harbouring re Ms McCaskill's aversion to good old Anglo-Saxon cursing disappearing into the ether as quickly as the errant fox was vanishing into the undergrowth. Juno set off at a gallop, scattering chickens in her wake as she raced across to the gate, leaping up and over it (like something out of the Olympics, she would relate to Ariadne later that evening) in one rather professional (and highly unlikely) move.

'Bastard,' she yelled at the fox's retreating back. 'Cowardly, fucking bastard. Pick on someone your own size next time.' Theresa May's broken, headless form lay at her feet, too late for rescue from the maws of both fox and death and, unfortunately, too late to hide the evidence from Tilda who was already racing across the paddock to join her.

'You've told her what's happening then? With you and Fraser?' Ariadne whispered, as Juno and a red-eyed Tilda sat down on the hard, plastic chairs in Westenbury village hall that evening. 'She looks terribly upset.'

Juno nodded. 'She is. I've had to bring the poor little thing with me this evening. I'm concerned that this outpouring of grief over Theresa May might really be a cover. You know, hiding her *real* feelings for her father leaving.' Juno was speaking to Ariadne while stroking Tilda's arm, but she was simultaneously scanning the hall, trying to work out whether Scott Butler was there; whether he'd decided to continue with rehearsals, or thrown in the towel along with quite a few of the other choir members who either hadn't got the message that all systems were *go* once more, or just couldn't be bothered to turn up. Juno checked the Tenor area where Scott usually sat with Declan but, while Declan was there, engrossed in conversation with Graham Madison, the local vet, there was no sign of Scott. Maybe he was still covering the late shift at the surgery although, with Izzy still not here, it seemed unlikely. More likely, she accepted with a heavy heart, he was off frolicking with his new *young* floozie.

'Grief for Theresa May?' Ariadne stared. 'I didn't hear the news before I came out. Has Boris finally done for her?'

'Boris?' Juno continued to scour the village hall for any sign of those gorgeous green eyes she'd so obviously been taken in by. Was he in the loo? Standing behind her at the

Julie Houston

back of the hall? Talking to Pandora who, with Hugo at her side, was deep in conversation with the vertically-challenged Granville?

'Boris Johnson? Has he finally managed to get Theresa May to stand down then?'

'I've no idea,' Juno said vaguely, finally accepting Scott wasn't going to make rehearsal. She turned to Ariadne. 'What on earth are you going on about Boris Johnson for?'

'You started it,' Ariadne said huffily and rather loudly. 'Going on about Theresa May.'

'Shh.' Juno patted Tilda's arm and then turned back to Ariadne. 'Have a little respect, will you? It's Tilda's chicken – you know, Theresa May – the bloody fox has had her.'

'Oh, I *see*. Little thing.' Ariadne frowned and leaned over Juno. 'Tell you what, Tilda, why don't you come back and stay with me after rehearsal? And then tomorrow, we can drive over to Meadow Hall and have sushi for lunch and I'll buy you a new top or something.'

'Really? Thank you.' Tilda smiled for the first time since her chicken's untimely demise, and sat up in her chair, waiting for a sight of her beloved Mr Donnington as Jesus.

'So, are you all ready, Ju?' Ariadne elbowed Juno. 'Have you been practising your Mary Magdalene this afternoon?'

'For the past couple of hours before we came down here,' Juno nodded gloomily. 'I'm not sure about this at all though, you know.'

'Shh, Jesus is about to sing.' The hall went quiet as Little Acorn's deputy head made his way up to the stage. Izzy was right: Josh Donnington was good, in fact exceptionally good once he'd got over his initial nerves at being thrust into the limelight.

'Thank you so much, Josh, for stepping in at this late date,' Pandora was saying as the rest of the choir clapped and cheered, none louder than Tilda sitting squarely at Juno's side. 'I really do think we're going to be back on track, everyone. Now, we have another surprise: I'm absolutely thrilled that my sister has agreed to take on the part of Mary Magdalene...'

'Here you go, Juno, up you get.' Ariadne elbowed Juno once more.

'... and I'm sure she'll need no introduction. Lexia, would you join us on stage?'

Lexia? Juno had half risen, encouraged with a push by both Ariadne and Tilda, but hurriedly sat down once more as Lexia, who had been sat right at the very front of the hall, almost hidden behind the somewhat moth-eaten navy velvet curtains, now stood nervously as the hall erupted. There was cheering, drumming of feet and even a couple of whistles and, at one point, Juno wondered if Lexia was going to sit back down again, overcome with nerves and panic. But she walked up on to the stage towards Mr Donnington – Juno couldn't quite think of him as Josh (or even Jesus) – and, as the first haunting notes of 'I Don't Know How to Love Him' were played by Geoff, the pianist, there was complete, almost palpable, silence in the village hall.

Juno felt the hairs on the back of her neck stand as Lexia started singing the beautiful lyrics and knew that, while she herself could be said to be a fairly competent vocalist, compared with Lexia there was absolutely no contest.

'Bloody hell,' Ariadne breathed. 'I'd forgotten just how incredibly good our baby sister is. Sorry, Juno, you'll have to take a back seat here, I'm afraid.'

'Mum, she's just amazing.' Tilda was, for once, almost without words. 'And so was Mr Donnington. Wasn't he? He's really good, Mum, isn't he? Don't you think he's good?'

Trying not to feel *too* miffed that she'd been thrown over for a better offer, Juno smiled and nodded in Tilda's direction, pleased that at least her daughter appeared a lot happier than a couple of hours earlier. The choir swung into a full run through of all the numbers but, although Izzy had finally arrived, rustling her scores noisily and shifting everyone along so she could sit with Clem, Harriet and Grace, Scott hadn't put in an appearance. So, that was that then.

Pandora was a hard taskmaster and, because they'd started later than usual and had so much to get through with the new main parts, didn't even allow a short break but insisted they drink their water and carry on.

Towards the end of this particularly arduous rehearsal, as minds were wandering to thoughts of slaking thirsts over at The Jolly Sailor, Pandora signalled Geoff, the pianist to stop playing. 'I know we've already had a couple of fabulous surprises this evening but—' she held up her hand like Dermot O'Leary on *The X Factor* '—as they say in showbiz, *you ain't seen nothing yet...*'

Who does? Juno mused, still smarting a little from being made redundant as MM before she'd even started. *Who* said that?

'... so, take it away, Herod!'

Little Midget Gem Granville (Juno thought the PC army would be OK with her *thinking* the word *midget* as long as she made it a prefix of the lovely jewel-like word, *gem*) appeared to have grown. Was he wearing his wife Janice's high heels? Quite possibly, because the rest of his outfit and whole demeanour was decidedly camp. Wearing a bright yellow baggy suit, with an Elvis-type purple wig to hide the fact that he was follicular-challenged, as well a pair of huge sparkly sunglasses, Granville minced across the stage and launched into Herod's only number from the production.

He'd just got to, *'Prove to me that you're no fool, walk across my swimming pool'* when Izzy leaned over the three choir members separating herself from Juno and hissed in her direction, 'Bloody hell, Juno, did *you* know?'

Juno could only shake her head and watch in bewilderment as realisation finally dawned and Scott Butler, a cross between Julian Clary and Elton John at his wackiest, continued to camp it up across the stage, belting out the song and hitting every note true.

As Scott brought the song to its conclusion with a particularly camp gesture of his hand, the rest of the choir erupted, standing on its feet, clapping, laughing and cheering, none more so, Juno saw, as she turned her head slightly, than the very attractive dark-haired woman standing directly behind her. She was a-whooping and a-hollering and doing that circular hand movement Americans do (and which Juno hated) at ball games.

'That's *her*.' Izzy leaned over towards Juno once more. 'You know, the woman he was with in The Coach and Horses the other evening? She's soon got *her* feet under the table, hasn't she?' she sniffed. 'Whooping along like a demented banshee.' And then, seeing her stricken face, patted Juno's hand sympathetically. 'She's young enough to be his daughter, for heaven's sake. Come on, let's drown your sorrows in the pub.'

As Juno shook her head, just wanting to go home to

distance herself from Scott and his new girlfriend, Izzy patted her hand once more. 'What about the teacher?' she asked hopefully. 'Do you think you could fancy Mr Donnington? Is *he* free, do you think?'

'I just want to get off,' Juno said, trying to smile as the reality of Scott's situation with this new woman finally went home. Like a bolt in a door she thought. What a ridiculous pushover she'd been, falling for the first man to give her the eye in her newly semi-single status. Embarrassing or what? 'Tilda's going to go across to the pub with Ari for a quick lemonade, and then she's staying the night with her,' she told Izzy. 'I'm off. I'll leave you all to it. See you at work on Wednesday.'

As she left the village hall carpark, accelerating quickly to avoid the choir members spilling out from the hall's green-painted double wooden door, Juno saw a flash of yellow and purple as Scott, one hand on her arm, escorted his new woman towards The Jolly Sailor.

# 32

She was obviously getting a bit careless, not looking after things as they deserved to be looked after. Juno contemplated her mug of tea, her solitary kitchen and the events of the last few days as she leaned against the ancient Aga for warmth, unable to stop a tear rolling down her cheek. She sniffed as it was joined by several others, dripping unheeded into the collar of her denim shirt and turning the faded sky-blue almost navy.

First Fraser, leaving her for the String Bean, then poor old Theresa May, victim to the bloody fox and now Scott, cavorting in a yellow suit and purple wig, leaving her for a – let's face it – much younger and exceptionally attractive new model. She'd not worked hard enough at her marriage; not protected Theresa from her murderer and not been attractive enough (sexy enough?) to keep her lover from straying. Even the kids had been more than happy not to spend the first days of their Easter break with her. Juno glanced towards Lady Gaga's cage at the far side of the kitchen: she'd bet anything the gerbil had buggered off too.

A slight scratching, scurrying sound emanated from the cage and Lady Gaga suddenly popped up, ignoring Juno as she tried to force herself though the narrow metal bars, intent on her freedom once more. Juno walked over, opened the cage door and reached in for the gerbil, seeking comfort from the warmth of the tiny creature.

'I messed up here, didn't I?' Juno stroked Lady Gaga's silky head gently as the gerbil looked up at her in surprise.

*Total pushover,* Lady Gaga agreed before giving her a look of utter disdain and setting off at speed along the kitchen work tops and disappearing behind the fridge.

Juno walked over to the sink, rinsing her cup before upending it on the draining board while simultaneously glancing out of the window and into the garden. Her heart began to hammer as she realised someone was out there.

A flash of yellow and purple caught in the one, outside light and then a tentative knocking at the kitchen door.

'You left,' Scott said, unsmiling as she opened the door to him. 'Was my singing that bad?'

'You looked to be otherwise engaged,' Juno responded tartly.

'As have you, the last few days.' Scott shivered. 'Look it's still feels like winter out here and this cotton suit isn't much protection against your perishing English weather. Are you going to let me in?'

Juno peered over Scott's shoulder into the dark of her garden. 'Are you alone?'

'Alone?' Scott shivered once more. 'Apart from that damned pony of yours giving me the evil eye and following me along the other side of the fence as I walked past?'

'Oh hell,' Juno pulled a face, 'I haven't put him away for the night. I promised Tilda I would…'

'Look, Juno, I've really been needing to talk to you. I

rang before you went off for the weekend and your son said you were in bed with your husband.'

'No, he *didn't*,' Juno snapped. 'He said I was in the *bedroom* with my husband…'

'Same thing.' Scott frowned.

'No, it's *not*,' Juno snapped again.

'Please, Juno, I'm freezing my tush off out here.' Scott held up his hands towards her and she saw the tips of his fingers were white.

'Reynaud's disease,' Juno sniffed, still with her foot in the door.

'Yes, I'm a doctor, I'm quite aware of that,' Scott said crossly. 'Had it all my life but much worse when I'm here in your freezing cold country.'

'You'd better come in.'

'Are you alone?'

'Why are you repeating what I just asked *you*?' Juno led Scott into the kitchen as, out of the corner of her eye, she saw Lady Gaga looking down at her from the safe haven of the top of the pine kitchen dresser.

*Pushover*. Juno could have sworn the gerbil was shaking her head sadly.

'Your husband's gone?'

'Well, he doesn't appear to be here, does he?'

'Your sisters told me.'

'My sisters?'

'All three of them were in the pub. With your daughter too. She's great, isn't she?' Scott smiled for the first time since he'd arrived.

Ignoring this, (*sucking up*, Lady Gaga sniffed) Juno

turned to Scott and folded her arms as he pulled off the purple wig and ran still-frozen fingers through his dark hair. 'So, talking of daughters, your new *girlfriend*?' Juno glared. 'She's young enough to be your *daughter*.'

'You're right. She is.' Scott smiled down at Juno, flexing his fingers as the blood began to pump painfully back through them.

'Oh.' Well, that took the wind right out of her sails. The bastard could at least have looked ashamed, contrite, at his admitting that yes, he had a new woman.

'She is,' Scott repeated.

'I know, I *saw* her,' Juno glared at Scott. 'She *is*.'

'No, she *is*.' Scott began to laugh.

'Is what?'

'My daughter.'

'Don't be ridiculous. You can't have a daughter that age.'

'But I can. And have… Look, Juno, do you mind if I get changed out of this yellow suit? I feel at a bit of a disadvantage in it. I'll just get my jeans from the car. Any chance of a coffee?'

Back in his mufti of faded denims and navy sweater, Scott sat at Juno's kitchen table, hands clasped round a steaming mug of coffee. 'Juno, Maya was as big a shock to me as anyone.'

'Maya's the girl? Your daughter?'

Scott nodded. 'I had absolutely no idea I had a daughter… had ever *fathered* one. You know, I've always wanted children.'

'Not really a *child* though, is she?' Juno, sat opposite

and drinking in every aspect of this gorgeous man she'd so fallen in love with, raised an eyebrow.

'No.' Scott was visibly sad. 'She's twenty-two. If I'd only *known*. If she'd have only *told* me.'

'Who? The mother? Maya's mother?'

Scott nodded. 'I was a bit of a lad when I was here at university…'

'I heard.'

'Declan?'

'And Izzy.'

'I think Izzy's interpretation of me as the Lothario she likes to portray, is vastly exaggerated,' Scott sighed crossly. 'Anyway, I was late applying to do medicine at Sheffield. My parents would have preferred me to study in Auckland or Wellington or even Sydney but I really wanted to come to the UK and at the last minute was given a place at Sheffield. By then the halls of residence were all taken so I was offered digs with Mrs Burkinshaw.'

'Mrs Burkinshaw?'

'My landlady.'

'Right?'

'She was really lovely. We got on straight away and well, one thing led to another.'

'You had an affair with your *landlady*? Oh, for heaven's sake.' Juno glared at Scott before crossing to the fridge for the bottle of wine she knew was in there. This needed alcohol.

'It does sound sleazy, but it wasn't.'

'And where was *Mr* Burkinshaw?'

'In the army. And away a lot.'

'That was handy.'

'Juno, I was just eighteen. I was seduced by an older, exceptionally attractive woman: every young boy's dream. She must have been around thirty-five then and rented out two rooms to students to make ends meet. She always said she couldn't have children. I think she knew *she could*, but Mr Burkinshaw *couldn't*. Anyway, after three months I moved out to share a house with a few others and didn't see her again.'

'And?'

'Tony Burkinshaw, Maya's father, died six months ago – pancreatic cancer. For some reason Esme Burkinshaw decided to tell Maya the truth, you know that her dad wasn't her real dad. Tony knew from day one that he couldn't have been her real father, but apparently was happy to go along with it all if it meant he and Esme had a child. Anyway, Esme told Maya what she knew of me and Maya set out to find me. Ended up tracking down my parents in Auckland who told her I was in England. Back in Yorkshire again.'

'So when did you find all this out?' Juno poured wine for them both.

'Just last week. My mother had given her my address here in Westenbury and she wrote to me. I'd been on the late shift, got home and opened the letter and desperately needed someone to talk to. I just needed *you*, Juno.' Scott took Juno's hand, stroking it gently. 'That's when I rang you and Gabe answered. Said his dad was back. I reckoned the last thing you needed was me on the phone messing things up for you.'

'I think they were pretty much messed up before you even arrived on the scene,' Juno sighed. 'I've failed as a wife.'

'Have you ever thought that Fraser might have failed as

a husband?' Scott continued to stroke her hand, and Juno had to cross her legs as waves of pure lust threatened to have her jumping up and ravishing him, right there on the kitchen table. 'Stop beating yourself up, Juno.'

'So, she came to see you?'

Scott nodded. 'We arranged to meet on neutral ground as it were, up at the Coach and Horses at Upper Clawson. Oh Juno, she's lovely. And so *bright*.' Scott's eyes lit up as he spoke and he started to smile. 'She finished at Durham last year with a first in Psychology. Imagine that! Now she's on with a Master's at Sheffield and going to be a Clinical Psychologist. Not many people get accepted for that, you know. I'm just one proud dad... We've met up every day since Thursday.' He laughed. 'There's so much to talk about; you know, little things like she has Reynaud's like me, she hates Marmite like me, loves otters...'

'Otters?' Juno began to laugh.

'Yes. I've always loved them. Beautiful creatures.'

'Right. So how come Maya was at rehearsal this evening? How come *you're* suddenly Herod?'

'I'd been telling Maya about the production, how it had fallen apart because we'd lost Jesus, Mary Magdalene and Herod. When Izzy told me it was being *resurrected*—'

Juno giggled. 'Apt description.'

'... and that you were going to be Mary...'

'... thrown over for a better offer, as you now know...'

'... Maya persuaded me to put myself forward for Herod. We've all been round at Pandora's since this afternoon, rehearsing.'

'All?' Juno frowned.

'Lexia, Maya, Josh Donnington – it's a good job it's

the school holidays – Pandora and myself. Your sister is incredible, amazing…'

'Alright, alright, I suppose you're now going to drool all over Lexia like everyone else does?' Juno knew it wasn't an attractive trait, but she couldn't help herself still feeling a bit miffed, a bit left out.

'I was actually talking about Pandora,' Scott said seriously. 'She's taken all this production on, picked it up again when it had crashed and is quite determined to see us win.'

'Pandora is nothing if not determined,' Juno agreed, relieved that Scott didn't appear to fancy Lexia after all.

'And Ariadne is great too, isn't she? Sparky, a bit feisty?' Juno nodded.

'In fact,' Scott went on, 'I've actually fallen a bit in love with *all* your sisters.'

'Right.'

'But, there's only *one* of you Sutherland sisters I'm so in love with I can't sleep at night just thinking about her.'

'Ariadne?' Juno raised one eyebrow, staring at this heavenly man who was gazing at her with such love in his eyes she thought she might just crumble away into nothing.

'Ariadne, yes, if you say so,' Scott murmured into Juno's neck as he leaned towards her, his mouth moved softly downwards.

'Because,' Juno managed to say as she gave herself up totally to Scott's kiss, to his warm hands on her skin, to the feeling that everything was just as it should be, 'if that's the case, then there's something you should perhaps know about Ari…'

'Juno, do be quiet,' Scott laughed, kissing her some more. 'It's you. It's always been you.'

# 33

*June 2019*

'So, is that Andrew Lloyd Webber chappy out there then? In the audience, I mean?' Despite, or maybe because of, her thirty-a-day Benson and Hedges habit, Doreen Goodall had turned out to have a surprisingly good singing voice: deep and gravelly, a sort of Rod Stewart crossed with Doris Day. Doreen had taken her place in the chorus, stolidly attended all rehearsals, and was now breathing a heady mix of voice-tablet with gin-and-orange-undertones over Juno as they waited in the wings for the final performance to begin. Juno herself was intent on peeking round the velvet curtains of the Lionel Bentley theatre in Midhope town centre, where the Westenbury Warblers were performing Jesus Christ Superstar, watching as the audience began to take their seats.

'No way,' Juno laughed, adjusting her headdress. 'The great Lord Lloyd Webber wouldn't have the time to come to a little back water like Midhope, I wouldn't imagine. It'll be a couple of his minions. In fact, they might have already been last night or the night before. They don't tell us who they are: you know, it's a bit like being a restaurant reviewer, they just troll up and make notes and write if the tart has a soggy bottom or if the wine is corked…'

'Right.' Doreen gave Juno a funny look. 'What wine's that then? The stuff on the table for the Last Supper? And, I'm not sure you should be calling Mary Magdalene a *tart*, Juno. I mean, I know she was a – you know—' Doreen lowered her voice '—a *prossie*, but Jesus wouldn't be too happy with you calling her a *tart*, would he?'

'No, Doreen, I was just trying to make an analogy.'

'That's alright.' Doreen patted Juno's arm kindly. 'There's nothing to make an apology for. You're doing fine; in fact, you and your sisters are the stars of the show.'

Nerves at performing once again, plus Doreen's misinterpretation of what she'd just said as well as her assumption that Andrew Lloyd Webber would be sitting in the audience (perusing the programme to find out what the show was all about in between eating a tub of Dixon's ice cream) was making Juno want to giggle. It was a bit like being at a funeral when, knowing you had to be totally dignified and straight faced, you were in danger of being just the opposite. She recalled how, almost a year earlier, Ariadne had persuaded Juno to accompany her to the funeral of some elderly neighbour of hers and, as they stood at the back of the crematorium, listening to the deceased's niece solo rendition of Sarah Brightman's 'Time to Say Goodbye' but with the added *Aunt Maud* at the end of every chorus, she and Ariadne had almost wet themselves trying to contain the infectious nervous titters that the woman's totally off-key lament was creating. When said niece had presented herself at rehearsals, they'd clutched each other in delighted horror and tittered once more like a couple of schoolgirls in assembly.

'All down to Pandora,' Juno now said to Doreen, pulling a straight face, as well as herself back into the present. She mustn't, mustn't think of that niece's off-key warbling or she'd be a tittering wreck. 'I have to say, she's done absolutely brilliantly. I never thought she'd pull it off, but she's been relentless in her efforts.'

'Tell me about it,' Doreen sniffed. 'I'm exhausted and our Brian's not happy.'

'Oh?'

'Well, I keep having to leave him his tea to warm up himself. He likes his tea, on the table, at half past five and no later. Unless it's Sunday, of course, and then he wants his dinner at half past one, once he's back from the Liberal Club. And then after rehearsals in the evening I'm far too tired for a bit of the old, you know... *how's your father*. With all these extra rehearsals your Pandora's made us come to, he's had to see to himself...'

Perish the thought. Juno closed her eyes momentarily to rid herself of the image.

Doreen broke off as Juno, continuing to peep round the curtain while half listening to Doreen's complaints from behind her, suddenly exclaimed, 'Oh my God, oh my goodness...'

'What is it? Who is it? Is it that Andrew chap?' Doreen attempted a quick squint round the curtains herself, but Juno nudged her backwards and let go of the material she was holding.

'No, I told you *he* wouldn't be here. It's just... just someone I've not seen for a long time.'

'Your Fraser?' Doreen's eyes gleamed. 'Has he come back then? You know, to see you sing?'

'No.' Juno shook her head.

'Ah, an ex then? An ex-boyfriend? You're entitled to see other chaps you know, love, now that your Fraser has gone off with someone else.'

For heaven's sake, Juno thought crossly. Was nothing secret round here? Tilda, obviously gossiping over the tea and custard creams once more. 'No, nothing like that, Doreen,' she snapped. 'Go on, backstage; we're on in twenty minutes.'

Juno hesitated, not quite sure what to do. Should she tell Pandora, Lexia and Ariadne that their father was sitting, three rows from the front, in the audience? She didn't want to put Pandora off from her directing or Lexia off from her solo parts. Thank goodness Helen had been to the performance the previous evening and wouldn't be in any danger of bumping into him.

Juno made a quick decision and went backstage to find Ariadne who was putting the final touches to her makeup.

'Ari, you're not going to believe this, but Dad's in the audience.'

Ariadne, halfway to adding another coat of mascara, paused, the wand momentarily suspended in mid-air. 'Whose dad?'

'What do you mean, *whose* dad? *Our* dad.'

'Oh, has he come?' Juno and Ariadne turned in surprise at Pandora and Lexia who had suddenly appeared at their side. 'Mum said it was OK for us to invite him.' Lexia, beautiful and enigmatic in readiness for her final performance as Mary Magdalene, smiled. 'Look, we didn't say anything to you two in case you were against the idea, or if he didn't actually turn up, but Mum wanted this.'

'Mum did?' Ariadne stared. 'What do you mean?'

'You know how much better she's been in the last few years, and especially since Lexia's been back.' Pandora hesitated slightly and then, in typical Pandora style, was business-like. 'Well, a few weeks ago, when I was round there, Mum suddenly said to us she felt terribly guilty that we were estranged from Dad. That it was her fault we'd lost touch. She didn't want us to be without a father for the rest of our lives – or Hugo, Cillian and your two, Juno, to have never met their grandfather. She said she was happy for us to get in touch with him...' Pandora broke off, looking her sisters up and down to see if they were performance-ready, already somewhat distracted from what she was recounting.

'This isn't just Mum trying to wheedle her way back in with Dad again, is it?' Ariadne snapped. 'We can't have her thinking Dad is coming back to her; we can't go through all *that* again.'

'No, no, not at all,' Lexia said. 'Honestly. She knows that's not going to happen. I actually don't think she *wants* that to happen.'

Pandora was looking at her watch. 'Look, we're about to start. All I'll say is that Lexia and I went to see Dad in Manchester a couple of weeks ago.'

'And you never said anything to us? I can't *believe* this.' Ariadne was furious.

'We had lunch with him,' Lexia explained as Pandora tapped her watch impatiently and frowned at the others. 'He asked if he could come and watch the performance and, well, we agreed. I suppose we should have asked you two first…' Lexia trailed off. 'But I wanted to see him, Ari, I wanted to see my dad.'

'It's OK, Lexia, honestly.' Juno was placating. 'You've every right to want to see Dad. As long as Mum knows about it, and she's fine with it…'

'She's a totally different woman since that terrible time when I was sixteen,' Lexia said. 'She'll probably never stop loving Dad, but she's had a lot of counselling and therapy over the years and accepts their relationship was totally toxic. She certainly doesn't want to go back there, you know.'

'Look, will you lot stop talking about Dad?' Pandora interrupted, irritably. 'He's here, that's good, but can I just remind you that a far more important man – Jesus – is waiting…?' Pandora turned to all the women in the dressing room. 'OK, shake a leg, you lot. Final performance. Good luck, everyone.'


Colin Murphy had been right, Juno smiled to herself as she stood quietly on the risers with the rest of the chorus waiting to sing their first number. Colin's haunting electric guitar solo, introducing the audience to the evening's story, was just that – totally electric – and the usual shivers went down her back as the initial spellbinding chords sounded through the theatre, immediately possessing and thrilling the audience. She felt Izzy, standing on her right, touch her fingers briefly and she squeezed back in acknowledgement before moving her own little finger to touch Ariadne's on her left.

Juno glanced across the stage to where the men were standing. Scott, who would in the second half of the performance leave the chorus to reappear, dressed in his yellow suit and purple wig, to belt out his one number as Herod, caught her eye briefly and smiled before turning his attention back to Pandora.

Oh, but he was gorgeous. Juno mentally hugged herself, distracted momentarily from Colin's dramatic opening solo as she took another brief look across at Scott, just to convince herself he was there, that he was real and just as lovely as when she'd looked a few seconds before. She'd fallen, hadn't she? Fallen in love with Scott Butler and, she daily almost had to pinch herself, he reciprocated those feelings. He was, he'd said, totally in love with her too.

The performance was flawless: Pandora would allow nothing else, Juno knew. Scott had the audience eating out of his hand; had them roaring with laughter as he minced across the stage as Herod, and applauding so loudly that Juno, feeling terribly proud and possessive, wanted to join in and shout, 'And he's mine, you know. All *mine*.'

Lexia, as Mary Magdalene, had the audience actually up on its feet. Many had come from miles around – from Leeds, Sheffield and Bradford – just to see the superstar they'd once adored as Lexi. She didn't disappoint, any initial fears she'd harboured at taking on the role and singing to an audience once more, dissipating at the realisation that she still had it. That she was still Lexi, the girl with the extraordinarily amazing voice capable of stirring hearts and minds. As always, Juno felt the tears threaten as Lexia sang Mary's lament for Jesus and then wanted to laugh as Izzy whispered through clenched teeth, 'Bloody hell, the hairs on my arms have all got erections again.'

And then it was Juno, Ariadne and Pandora's turn.

Pandora had asked the other two if they would take on the role of the Gospel Singers where, towards the very end of the production, they would move to the centre of the stage and lead the rest of the chorus in the huge number, 'Superstar'.

Ariadne had replied, absolutely, as long as Pandora herself join them at that point to make up the required third Gospel Singer.

'Don't be ridiculous,' Pandora had snapped irritably. 'I'm director, producer and conductor now that Sally has defected to the Halifax Harmonies. I can't jump up and down as a gospel singer *as well.*'

'By that stage of the production, everyone will be so revved up they won't need conducting,' Ari had answered firmly. 'Come on, Pan, you love singing, you're a *brilliant* singer and this is your chance to actually sing and take part in your own production.'

When Pandora had continued to shake her head, Ariadne had said, almost crossly, 'You know we'll end up with the funereal niece from hell as a third if you don't do it; she's *desperate* for the part. And Ju and I will end up tittering like we always do whenever she starts singing, and that's your whole production up the swanny.'

That had done the trick. The three of them had spent hours at either Pandora's or Juno's place (Richard, Scott and Lexia providing advice, moral support and alcohol, while Helen and Tilda were on hand with cake), the furniture pushed back as they choreographed dance steps and sang themselves silly.

As she sang and boogied on down with Pandora and Ariadne (who had turned out to be a surprisingly good mover) it went through Juno's mind that she'd couldn't, even if she tried, be any happier than she was at this very moment. It was more than likely the biblical influence, she conceded but, as she held both her sisters' hands, revelling in and loving the audience's cheers and applause, she thought, strike me dead now, God, and I'll die a happy woman.

# Epilogue

*Four months later...*

'Go on, Pandora, it's addressed to you. You open it.'
    'I can't. I daren't. You open it, Juno.'
'Me?'
'You're a doctor, go on.'
'What's being a doctor got anything to do with it? Lexia, go on, you open it. I mean, at the end of the day, we got through to the finals because you were so superb as Mary Magdalene.'
'That's rubbish. We got through to the finals because Pan was so brilliant at directing us there. Anyway, I can't open it, I'm the youngest. You open it, Ari, you're the eldest.'
'Me? I was just in the chorus. Nothing to do with me that we got through. Are you sure it's what we think it is?'
'Well, it does say in stonking great letters on the back of the envelope: *The Really Useful Group*. I mean, I don't think it's your gas bill, Pandora, even though, you know, gas *is* really useful for cooking... and you know... for washing

your hair. Nothing worse than trying to get up a lather when the water's cold...'

'It's just that, once we open it we'll know, won't we? By sitting here, staring at this envelope, we can still believe we've won.'

'But we might have.'

'And even if we haven't, we'll have come second. I mean, that's pretty good, Pan. No, it's not, it's absolutely fantastic.'

'OK, put the kettle on.'

'You're joking, get the champagne out.'

'Champagne only if we've won. Coffee and cake if we're second...'

'Not Mum's. Anything but Mum's...'

'Oh, for heaven's sake, give it here, Pandora...'

Pandora, Juno and Lexia Sutherland joined hands across Pandora's kitchen table, eyes shut tight, pulses racing as Ariadne carefully slit the sealed envelope, took out the single sheet of paper and quickly scanned what was written there.

'OK, sisters of mine, you *can* go for Mum's turmeric and beetroot cake... but... you'll be well within your rights to *crack open the champagne*!'

'Did we win, Ari? Have we won? Did we do it?' Pandora jumped up from the table, knocking her chair to the floor as she did so.

'*You* won, Pandora, it was *your* competition, *your* hard work.'

'I think,' Lexia said, smiling while brushing away a single tear as she moved to the fridge to retrieve the bottle of champagne she'd put there earlier, 'we've *all* won. We're all winners, don't you agree?'

# Acknowledgements

A huge thank you to Robert Berry, Senior Licensing Consultant with The Really Useful Group who not only showed a massive interest in this book, but also gave permission for me to use The Really Useful Group's name, as well as assuring me that Sir Andrew Lloyd Weber wouldn't object to having his name appear in several chapters.

I need to mention Gary Griffiths, choirmaster of both Sing Live and Inspirations in Leeds, the choirs I've sung with for many years. It was he, when we were singing 'Jerusalem', who came up with the one-liner: 'Anne Did Those Feet' and which I blatantly pinched for the name of the podiatrist in Juno's surgery. The idea for Scott Butler taking on the part of Herod, and camping it up wearing the oversized yellow suit and purple wig came directly from Gary doing exactly the same when Sing Live put on its own performance of *Jesus Christ Superstar*. Thanks, Gary.

Thanks, as always, to my lovely agent, Anne Williams at KHLA Literary Agency, and to the fabulous Hannah Smith, my brilliant editor at Aria, Head of Zeus who, together with Vicky and the rest of the team, have helped to make *Sing Me A Secret* the best it can possibly be.

And finally, to all you wonderful readers who read my books and write such lovely things about them, a huge, heartfelt thank you.

# About the Author

JULIE HOUSTON is married, with two teenage children and a mad cockerpoo and, like her heroine, lives in a West Yorkshire village. She is also a teacher and a magistrate.

# Hello from Aria

We hope you enjoyed this book! If you did let us know, we'd love to hear from you.

We are Aria, a dynamic digital-first fiction imprint from award-winning independent publishers Head of Zeus. At heart, we're committed to publishing fantastic commercial fiction – from romance and sagas to crime, thrillers and historical fiction. Visit us online and discover a community of like-minded fiction fans!

We're also on the look out for tomorrow's superstar authors. So, if you're a budding writer looking for a publisher, we'd love to hear from you. You can submit your book online at ariafiction.com/ we-want-read-your-book

You can find us at:
Email: aria@headofzeus.com
Website: www.ariafiction.com
Submissions: www.ariafiction.com/
we-want-read-your-book

f  @ariafiction
y  @Aria_Fiction
o  @ariafiction